*f*6

a publication of F Magazine, Inc.

Volume 6

2005

F Magazine, Inc. is a federal 501-c-3 tax-exempt not-for-profit corporation, incorporated under the laws of the state of Illinois.

Publications of F Magazine have been made possible by grants and gifts from:

The Illinois Arts Council Chairman's and Program Grants
Mirron Alexandroff
Chicago Office of Fine Arts
Columbia College Chicago
Lucy Montgomery
Don Nathanson
Erwin A. Salk
Yale Wexler

And contributions of up to $200 by:

Susan Rue Braden
Betty Brisch
Mary Brophy
Richard Cantrall
Kathryn Devereaux
Dr. and Mrs. David Edelberg
Kathryn E. Jonas
Mary Zoe Keithley
Marie Leadaman
Mitchell and Erin Omori
Richard Riemer
Marian Stern
Richard and Ruth Talaber
Mary Walker

F Magazine invites you to become a patron and supporter of its unique venture in the literary arts.

Board of Directors:
John Schultz, President
Don Gennaro De Grazia, Director
Tom Popp, Secretary
Tim Schultz, Treasurer

Editorial, Business, and Subscription Address:
The Editors
F Magazine
c/o Fiction Writing Department
Columbia College Chicago
600 S. Michigan Ave.
Chicago, IL 60605-1996
f-magazine.org

Corporate Address:
432 Selbourne Rd.
Riverside, IL 60546

Publisher and Editor-in-Chief: John Schultz
Managing Editor: Tom Popp
Associate Editors: Deb R. Lewis, Joe Tower
Assistant Editor: Frank Crist
Director, Distribution and Finance: Deb R. Lewis
Webmaster: Frank Crist

F Magazine primarily concentrates its editorial effort on prose fiction, novel excerpts and short and long stories, with occasional publication of essays, interviews, and poetry. Refer to submission guidelines at f-magazine.org when submitting. No manuscripts will be returned unless accompanied by a stamped, self-addressed envelope. Please visit f-magazine.org.

Cover design, Claudia Laska, zanusi@earthlink.net

Cover image, *Sweets of Sin*, Philip Hartigan, 1997, www.philiphartigan.com
Etching, aquatint, burnishing, drypoint on copper. Plate size 14 inches x 10 inches.
From a suite of ten etchings based on the Circe chapter of James Joyce's *Ulysses*.

She crosses the threshold. He hesitates. She turns and, holding out her hands, draws him over. He hops . . . Kitty Ricketts, a bony pallid whore in navy costume, doeskin gloves rolled back from a coral wristlet, a chain purse in her hand, sits perched on the edge of the table swinging her leg and glancing at herself in the gilt mirror over the mantelpiece. A tag of her corset lace hangs slightly below her jacket.

ISBN 0-932026-73-7

Printed in Canada

This Way Comes A Stranger . . .
by John Schultz

In the first issue of F Magazine, *f1*, I wrote, "Here we begin again with story, image, word, and people." The theater director, Paul Sills, called it an "audacious" statement, concerned as he was about similar issues. I would like to think that this mission statement is as radical and as traditional now as the day it was written and first published.

We seek to promote prose fiction that emphasizes *story*—content, imagery, character, voice, and a rich and dramatic exploration of points of view, style, dimensions of time, and the mixing of the private and the self with the public and social and historical.

F Magazine emphasizes the novel or other longer work in progress, with occasional short stories, non-fiction, interviews, panel discussions, and poetry. There is a particular emphasis in *f6* on the novel in progress. Certain selections innovatively broaden the definition, such as Betty Shiflett's, "Putting Mama in Big Spring," from *Grassfires*, memoir as novel.

F6 begins a new feature in the Rising Voices section, in which appear short, telling excerpts from works in progress. The editors have picked short passages of the sort that the authors might read at a public reading to bring the audience to full attention quickly.

Story is a stranger that enters and re-enters our lives, making the unexpected a familiar and compelling presence.

There is talk now that literary fiction has retreated from *story*, abandoned it and its inherent assumption of a dramatic storyteller, to non-fiction and genre fiction, to use and develop as authors will. Though many literary fiction writers would vigorously disagree, at least about their own writing, this might be a partial explanation for the increasing popularity of non-fiction and genre fiction at the apparent expense of literary fiction.

An F Parable

Directly after the publication of *f1*, there happened a particular situation that came up in which the mission of *f* may have saved me a great deal of trouble. A government investigator came to Columbia College to interview me, in an otherwise empty classroom, about what he thought were protest activities of mine that were of interest to him and his agencies. At one point in his inter-rogation, he looked into his folder and then looked up at me and asked about F Magazine.

"What does the f stand for?" he asked.

"It stands for what you think it stands for and every other word that begins with f, too," I said.

He actually looked slightly entranced as if he were trying out words that began with f: feast, famine, father, flibbertigibbet, fantastic, future, and the one he thought it stood for, too.

"That's what we did," I said. "We needed a name for the magazine and somehow the bunch of us working on what would become *f1* got started on words that begin with f, and every word we came up with was a good sug-gestive word, plus the word everyone thinks of first, too."

We actually talked about *f* for a while, and then he moved into the other subjects that interested him. Then I stood up from my classroom chair, with the fold-down desk, and said that if we were to continue, I wanted a lawyer to be present.

He said, with a touch of sense of humor, "Am I to conclude that the inter-view is over?"

That was on the fifth floor. A half hour later I found him on the first floor by the elevators looking confused and like he was afraid he might be making a fool of himself. Fool. Another f word. "Where can I get a copy of *f*?" he said, a bit embarrassed.

I wondered what he could possibly find in *f1* that would enhance his inves-tigation, but those were strange, contentious, divisive times, in which words said on one side of the divide meant something entirely different on the other side. "Up on the seventh floor in the bookstore," I said, feeling lavish, even if I were somehow contributing to great trouble for myself. If we believed in freedom of speech, shouldn't we act on it? Freedom. f word. I'd be damned if I was going to give him a free copy. Free. You see what I mean? On the sev-enth floor, I saw him at the counter of the bookstore, the bemused student salesperson wondering how on earth this man walked in off the street to buy *f*.

F Magazine continues to explore the storytelling geography of voice, con-tent, attitude and style laid out by all those words that begin with f. As for the investigator, he ended up writing a report (a copy of which I obtained years later) that was more sympathetic than he may, at first, have intended it to be. I can only credit *f* for having crossed the divide, carrying some sense of com-mon humanity with it, to accomplish such a turn around.

Thanks to novelist Don DeGrazia (*American Skin*) for fulfilling in an important way the position of Managing Editor of *f4* and *f5*. We welcome Tom Popp, fiction and non-fiction writer and former columnist and fiction editor of *Velocity* magazine, as Managing Editor. Tom brings his own special energy and liveliness to the project.

Thanks to Columbia College Chicago and to President Warrick L. Carter, Provost and Vice-President, Academic Affairs Steven Kapelke, Dean of School of Fine and Performing Arts, Leonard Lehrer, and the Fiction Writing Department for having provided F Magazine with important support. Thanks to Deborah Roberts, Linda Naslund, Jenny Seay, and Mica Racine for their help. Thanks to the Illinois Arts Council for its support of F Magazine. Thanks to Jerry Clausson for help and guidance.

We think you, our reader, will find much to enjoy in this issue, and much worthy of continuing enjoyment and support.

John Schultz
Publisher and Editor-in-Chief
F Magazine, Inc.

CONTENTS

2005

from *I ❤ the Spirit World*

1.

It's adult entertainment I've been dreaming about ever since I was a kid. It's the blood of Los Angeles. You know how it is. At the age of nine, I found an adult movie in a garbage can at the end of my street, a blank-labeled video-cassette tape, along with two porno mags, *Dirty School Girls Take It* and *Va-Va-Va-Voom,* which were a little too moldy to take home with me. I watched the film that afternoon while the adults and the little sister were gone. I sat in the basement with the air-conditioning on. Outside, through the basement window, it was beginning to get night. The night was saying, *Here I am, a dream.* The night was saying, *Here I am, a mystery.* I sat on the beige couch, holding my breath. The window beaded over with fingerprints of heat. There, all alone, on that strange summer evening, flashing upon the shadowy television screen, were all the mysteries of the world I would ever hope to know before I died, or as I had always planned it, before I would marry the famous actress Tuesday Weld, who was a neighbor of mine, and go off into oblivion, decapitated in a drag-racing accident at the age of twenty-five. Somehow I always dreamt I would die as soon as I turned twenty-five.

The only movie that mattered to me was the one I had found in the trash. It was a LOLA LOVELESSLY feature, all in Spanish, called, "El Hombre Con Los Ojos de Espectulares" about a man with X-Ray Eyes who went around looking at women and who got very sexy with them. As I stared across to where the television was playing, suddenly on the screen, this big senorita appeared, her dark eyes were mammoth, my love, my beauty, a big black-haired pile of a woman lying on her back on a stack of red pillows, in a white robe, with a red rose in her hair, and a purple Mexican tiara, a giant of white curdled softness and flesh and dreams, just lying there, bored stiff, just lounging, and I couldn't look away. I put my fist in my mouth to keep myself quiet because all I could do was stare, even as I heard the adults arriving home now, upstairs. From across the room, MS. LOLA approached and then the man with the X-Ray Eyes appeared and the white robe was gone and she was undone completely. MS. LOLA was a maid, I think, and she was vacuuming, but now completely naked, and it was the most beautiful thing I had ever seen. In that moment, in that single second of stolen time, every clock in the world went quiet, and then I knew it. Before the hairy hand belonging to my father pulled me off the couch and my mother was crying, before the parents were concerned and alarmed and I was escorted up to my room with much shouting, I knew it in my heart, with the tepid conviction of the sweat of my neck and the shaking of my hands, this is more than some kind of nudity, this is more than topless beauty, this is more than some guilt and distress and a feeling of cowardice, this is the very bare, soft, abdominal workings of some secret world and the life I knew was meant for me. At the age of nine, I knew it and said it out loud

Count me in

Count me in for the world of adult entertainment

Count me in for the long strange night

2.

In some essential ways, I was a legend. I had worked at the same adult bookstore for four years and never been promoted. I had a spot where I would stand behind the counter and I would not move from it for the whole eight hours. There was videotape from the store's security camera of me doing this. Months of it. Most of the time, to be honest, I was out of it. Most of the time, I had no idea what was happening. I'd been robbed three times already. I didn't know why someone hadn't killed me.

I sat behind the counter and smiled as an average white man in a black tweed coat brought up his purchases. Two magazines, *BIG JUGS* and *BARELY LEGAL*, excellent reading material, and a videotape. The famous *CHERYL LEE* in *BLOWJOBS ACROSS AMERICA*. I rang them all up. Thirty-two dollars. "Thirty-two," I told him. He handed me two twenties. I noticed that his fingernails were very clean. Very glossy, lacquered like a lady's. I took the money from his hand, put it in the drawer, and then tried ripping him off by just giving him a single back. It's a scam I had. It usually worked, I guess.

"Hey, where's the rest of my change?" the guy mumbled.

"What's that?" I asked him.

"The rest of my change? I gave you two twenties. You owe me another seven bucks." I looked him dead in the eye and then whispered it with a frown.

"Hey, man. I just gave you your change."

"You owe me another seven bucks," he said again.

He moved closer to the register, getting his black eyebrows all in a bunch.

"Listen, man, I might have made a mistake," I smiled. "I can count down the drawer which will take an hour or two and then I can give you a call at work or home or whatever if you give me your number and name. It's just gonna take me awhile is all. If you give me your name, I'll call you where-ever you're gonna be when I'm done."

He stared at me then nodded and put the dollar back in his pocket. "Fuck you." He took his bag and walked away, cursing. I don't know why. They don't argue for some reason. They're too embarrassed to say anything. I pocketed his split, then lit a cigarette.

It was a good cigarette.

Suddenly, I heard some sound coming from one of the back booths. It was a kind of crash. I smashed out the square and then walked around the counter, down the aisle and into the back where the three doors on the three booths were all closed tight.

I knocked on the first door. No one answered. I tried the lock. It was open. I opened the door. No one was in there. There was a tiny TV that kept flashing pictures of naked ladies doing all kinds of things. I went to booth number two, knocked, no answer, tried the lock, it was open, and no one was inside. The rest of the store was completely silent. No one else was there. Chad had already gone home for the day. The third booth.

The third booth.

I went up to it, turned the knob quick without knocking and pulled the door open in a flash. It was dark inside. The light was broke. The TV was off and there were little white tissues lying like folded angels on the floor. I shook my head and smiled and then I felt someone standing behind me and the sound of a .22 cocking snapped into place and some vicious killer pressed the muzzle of his gun against the back of my neck and pushed me face-first down on the floor by kicking in the back of my knees and I started shouting, "The register's open, man! It's open, just take it and get the fuck out!!" and by the way my head was lying, pressed down hard, and from the sounds I was making, I could tell I was crying. I knew it. I knew it. The devil had worked his magic on me. It was over. John Lake, or some other bum I owed shit to, they had me, I knew it, I knew it. The round snapped into the barrel and my blood blew out through the front of my brain. I knew it. I knew it. Without a doubt in my mind. Forget drag-racing. This was exactly how I was going to die.

I got up off the floor and held the back of my neck. No one was there. No one was ever there. But I had those moments, I had very strange moments like that a few times a week. I would hear the round fly through my brain and my whole body would spasm and then I would be lying on the floor by myself shivering. It was a daydream I gave myself to occupy the time, but frequently.

The bell above the door gave a ring and I pulled myself to my feet.

"It's a buck to browse," I said.

3.

Imagine a town: a pink drawing on white paper. There are the hills, the burned-out light bulbs of a liquor store, the white Hollywood sign, a woman's pink high heel left on an empty corner, a gray crowded bus, a tiny white dog with a diamond collar, a young Mexican kid standing on the corner whistling a tune that stays in your ears, this is where I work, this is the air I got to breathe, this is what LA looks like to me.

4.

Phantom people asked me to do them a favor. I agreed. Thankfully. I owed John Lake two hundred bucks and I know I didn't have the cash so I took the chance to square it out myself. I don't know about the Satanic shit. I don't do it and I'm not into it. I've seen weird things go on at John Lake's house the few times I've been by there, mostly black-eyed teenage girls who are chunky and smoking dope and pricking each other with needles and that kind of sleep-over shit and I don't know if they all are really into it or not, but John Lake is a genuine Devil-worshipper and it's real enough to him and I owe him some cash so I don't ask him about it when he fails to mention it.

All I had to do was go to the bus depot on Figueroa and pick up a package from a quarter locker. That was it. Well, hell, of course, I'm not stupid, I knew what was in it. It was going to be cocaine or some goddamn horse tranquilizers or something felonious like that. That's why he asked me. But like I said, I'm not stupid, I knew someone might be watching the locker so I thought I might bring an extra package with me. That way, I could say, "Well, no, officer, this is what I was picking up. My friend left it here, she's in the hospital, she's sick or something," and ditch whatever the hell was in the other package if I had to, I guess. But I forgot the other package when I went and nearly chickened out because of it, I guess.

The idea was to put the key in the little orange lock, grab the package, and get the hell out. If anyone saw me, I would ditch the shit. That was it. I was sweating like hell. My hands were all slick and my cigarette would not light and I started taking all kinds of things as bad signs, all right.

The locker number was 247. It was around midnight when I went. I went after work on a Sunday night. I took the bus so no one could follow me. I took the bus because I didn't have a car. I got there around midnight, like I said. I stood a couple of feet in front of the locker for about five minutes or so. I just stood there. Sunday at the bus depot around midnight was something, I guess. It seemed like everyone was watching with their skinny eyes. There were all kinds of creeps sauntering around. This one guy kept asking me for the time and some chicken-lady was screaming at her kid and this other guy, this other guy who was fat and had a orange baseball hat on that read "Miss America '86," he was just laughing to himself and the bus depot is no place where you ever want to be, because the bus depot is the end of the line for whatever crisis you've gotten yourself into, and all the bad luck has to pile up somewhere right? Well, Christ Jesus. I started thinking about chickening out. I started backing away and then I thought about John Lake. I thought about him sitting in his pool on a shiny green float and drinking a drink and smiling at me and me saying, "I couldn't get it, I couldn't get it," and him just smiling and those teeth, those fucking white teeth and the thin short beard and nicely cut long brown hair and silver sunglasses like a glamorous coked-out movie actor and him saying, "Jay, what am I going to do with you, baby?" and him still smiling like that and I just went up to the locker and slid the key in and pulled the package out and it was a little package wrapped in brown butcher paper and I slipped it into my coat and these two guys stepped forward and I started running and I made it to the bathroom and slid the bolt in the door and I started cussing, "John Lake, John Lake," and I fumbled into the stall and started tearing the box open and the paper cut my finger and these men were pounding on the door and I had the brown wrapping off and I tore open the box and then nothing

nothing

there was nothing inside and there was some white paper, and I tore it out and there was a picture, a color picture of a young boy, who was maybe ten, the kind you get in school, it was a regular class picture and he was smiling right at me, missing two of his front teeth and you could tell he was a good kid and there was his name on back, GARY, and there was a tooth, a little kid's square little tooth in the box there and then the guys started pounding on the door again "Open the door! Open the door!" and oh, shit, I was about to cry and these men were really pounding and I put the picture in my pocket and held the box in my hands and the next thing I knew

the next thing I knew

I was at home, I was at home, standing in front of my parents' house and the goddamn photo was gone and my hands were shaking like crazy. I was standing out in the dark and I had no idea how I had gotten home and my hands would not stop shaking. I tore through all my clothes and the picture and the tooth were gone. They weren't there. I could see them in my mind very clearly. But they were nowhere on me. Christ Jesus, well, just Jesus.

5.

At the porn store, I didn't know I was staring at a picture of two men in love until Chad elbowed me.

"OK, all right, try this," he said, checking in new magazines. He was like two or three years older than me, blonde, with big sideburns, and friendly blue eyes. He made twice as much as me because he gave a shit. It was something I had to deal with, I guess. I looked at him and he leaned over the counter, took a sip from his bottle of soda, and said, "OK, OK, 'Sperms of Endearment.'"

This was a game we played. We'd pass the time in this way.

"'Pocha-hot-ass,'" I said.

"OK, OK. 'Schindler's Fist.'"

"'When Harry Fucked Sally.'"

"'ET, the Extra Testicle.'"

"'Dirty Lancing.'"

"'Shaving Ryan's Privates.'"

"'Flesh Gordon.'"

"'Jurassic Pork.'"

"'The Sperminator.'"

"'On Golden Blonde.'"

"'On Golden Blonde?' That's weak, man," he said, looking up at me. "Finish checking in the gay stuff. I'll be in the back printing up tags," he said and disappeared into the back, just to get high, probably. I looked down at the box of gay mags and sighed, upset by the smiling faces of tanned, inhumanly-proportioned men. I think, *How is any of this supposed to make anybody happy?*

The layout: Aisle One, movies, assorted by type, Straight, Gay, Bondage, creepy foreign avant-garde shit, like GUM ME, BABE, some crazy French flick where this old lady takes out her dentures and goes to town on the Parisian men-folk, giving them all head. There's Aisle Two, mags, same thing for the most part, naked chicks, naked fellahs, and the weird, feces-eating shit. Then there's Aisle Three, where you'll find your accessory-type merchandise, your dildos and blow-up dolls and bondage gear and pony-plugs and the like. There's the front counter where I stand, and finally there's the three back booths where you can pay to watch movies and jerk off if you're in a real hurry. There's a box of Kleenex inside. These two mute Mexican boys come in and mop each booth up a couple of times a day. One of the Mexicans is a nut. He's always singing something in Spanish and dancing with his mop. Like it was a beautiful girl. Singing and dancing and moping up the slop. He doesn't give a damn what he's doing. He's happy. He doesn't waste a second of thought worrying about all the goddamn perverts. Why worry when you're happy, when you're in love or something? But I worry. I think about them, those men. They are the people who really interest me, the booth-fellahs, those customers, I mean. I mean it's weird for me to think that they know I know what they're doing in there. I wouldn't be able to do it. I mean I have, you know, jerked off in the morning before the place is open when no one else is here yet. But I wouldn't be able to get off knowing some creepy dude was standing behind the counter thinking I was thinking about him. That's not sexy at all to me, man. Most of the shit in the store sure isn't. I guess it's like anything. The human heart is a complicated goddamn machine. It ticks and it runs and it's only a rare moment when any two of them find a way to move in time. Most of the other time, you're just fucking lonely.

Shit, I dunno. Maybe I'm just bullshitting. Maybe this has nothing to do with the porn or the customers. Maybe this is all about me and Denise. Denise was this girl I was dating recently. We broke up a few weeks ago. Why? It's personal. OK. We were in bed and she asked me, "What really turns you on?" and I said, "For real?" and she said, "Yeah, tell me," and I said, "I'd like it if you just laid there real still and didn't talk at all for like an hour, so I could just watch you, I'd like that," and then she got upset and started crying. She said it was like I was trying to objectify her. So she wouldn't talk to me after that. So that's the reality of love. You got a certain of dream that you think will save you but you can't ever admit to anybody.

I start to thumb through an issue of VARIATIONS, thinking if I had just lied, I might have a girl to kiss and lay on top of tonight. A thought like that makes you curl your lips back and feel empty inside. The door slips open and a ray of light like the good God's last fond idea shines right in, across the big black counter and along my dry teeth.

A customer walks in.

It is there upon his face right away.

Please.

I am lost. I am doubtful and in need of reprieve.

A reprieve from the snatching jaws of monotony.

Please help me.

"Hey there, chief," I smile. "It's a buck to come in here."

"A buck?"

"Sure, sure," I say. "See?"

There's the big white on black sign that reads, "$1 To Browse."

His lips twitch a little bit. He is a little taller than me, with brown hair that is combed right in place, and perfect white teeth that keep tugging at his bottom lip. He's got a thin little brown mustache and a suit and tie and the sweatiest pair of hands I think I've ever seen.

Look, look at his hands. He rubs them on his pants and stares up at me. Good grief.

"A dollar?" he whispers.

"Sure, chief, a buck." I point to the sign again.

"Do I get it back?"

"Sorry, pal. It's a browsing fee. If you buy something it goes towards your purchase."

"OK, just a moment," he fumbles around inside his back pants pocket and all he has is tens and twenties and a billfold full of credit cards and I look at him and shake my head and think, hell, this guy is just a few years older than me, really. And a pretty-boy, too, I mean, a fellah that puts styling gel in his hair and knows how to use the nose hair clipper and wears his tie tied nice and tight. Like some kind of Joe from a Sears catalog. A real sporty-upper-class type.

"The smallest I've got is a ten," he mumbles, his big broad forehead bubbling with sweat. His fingers keep working themselves up in a panic.

"Shit, man, forget about it. Just buy something, all right?" I say.

"OK," he says and stumbles over to the soft-core rack and wipes his hands on the legs of his pants.

You see that? These guys come in here, all lonely like that, some of them twisting the big gold band on their left ring fingers, like a pack of zombies. It breaks my goddamn heart. I don't know why, but it does. Maybe one person can't satisfy every part of another person. Maybe people are so complex that there's not a part that matches every other part in that other person completely. Or maybe that's not it. Maybe it's because once you're with someone for a while there's nothing left to dream about, to wait for, no more first kisses, no first times, it's all said and done, or what? I dunno. Maybe that's not it either. I mean, sure, sure, he thinks it's good that he's got everything. Everything's safe, everything's secure. He's got the wife, the nice black SAAB parked at a paid meter out front, he's got a few kids maybe, big white house with a chemically-treated lawn in the safe suburbs somewhere, maybe down the street from me, sure, he looks pretty healthy, he still has his health and most of his hair, a job where people call him, "Boss," and say "Yes, sir, there, Mr. Dunderwagon" or whatever the hell his name is, he has money, self-respect, material possessions, let's say this guy even has an appreciation for the Arts and his fellow man, he gives generously to some charity or this or that Art League, maybe he's even traveled, maybe he's seen all the things he's thought there ever was to see, right? Well, my friend, this begs the question, doesn't it? What's he doing in the porn store, huh?

It's all right there, stitched in tiny droplets of blood beneath his sweaty fingertips.

Will you be my priest?

I am a dead man.

I am dying as we speak.

Sure, man, sure his breath is being breathed and his heart is pumping and beating, sure he's got all the signs he's living life, but look at him, he's a ghost, a dead man, a zombie. All his dreams have been made. He's been crushed by the little world he's made, by all that fucking safety. Because he's missing something important. What? What is he missing? The world of make-believe. Somewhere to daydream.

The man steps up to the counter and asks, "I was wondering…"

"Yep?"

"If I was looking for something, you didn't have, would it be possible…"

"What are you looking for? Cause we've got everything legal," I say.

"How long you been working here?" the man asks.

I look this this big guy over and notice some things I didn't notice before: he's got this blue suit coat on with western stitching and brown pants, and brown leather cowboy boots which are really worn and lead me to believe he's from northern California or the San Fernando valley at least.

"I've been working here awhile," I say.

"You know your trade pretty well?" he asks, with a smile.

"Pretty well, I guess," I say.

"You ever see a lady that looked like this?"

He pulls out a blurry color Polaroid and slaps it down on the counter. In the picture is a very beautiful cheetah-woman who is out of focus. She has blue eyes and a soft pleasant round face and this cheetah outfit on, complete with ears that cover most of her head and a tail. She has her one shoulder turned to the camera and is smiling very seductively. "She looks familiar," I nod.

"I took a picture off a motel TV," the guy says. "That's why it's all blurry."

"Huh. What was the name of the movie?" I ask.

"I don't know. You see my problem." He nods and winks at me. "I'd like you to find out her name for me. I mean, I'd give you fifty bucks if you could. Quick cash for a slick fellah like yourself. Easy money."

"Well, I'm sure I can find it out. Just give me a couple of days, all right?"

"Sure thing, partner, sure thing." He leans back and points his finger at me like a gun and then pulls the trigger. "You can keep the picture. I've got plenty." And he does. He must have a dozen of these blurry Polaroids because he fans them out like a deck of cards and then snaps them back into his jacket.

"I'll be seeing you," he nods and steps on out.

Chad ambles from the back room and stares at me, shaking his head.

"What about the queer stuff, damnit? Why don't you ever do what I ask?"

"I'll come in early tomorrow, Chad. I promise."

"Jesus. You are like the laziest human I have ever met. It leaves me in awe. See me? I'm in fucking awe. I mean how fucking old are you?"

"Twenty-four. Almost twenty-five."

"Twenty-five? That's disgusting. Look at you, you're a total wastoid."

"I know."

"Shit, listen, pal, I need to warn you. If you come in late again tomorrow, I'm going to have to fire you. I mean it. I'm very fucking serious about this."

"Fire me? How would you get on without me?"

"I'd find a way. I'm fucking serious about this, OK? I mean it."

"OK, please, listen, if I get shit-canned, I'm out. My fucking parents aren't joking around. They're afraid I'm a bad role model for my little sister. She's like in training for the Math Olympics. They're just looking for a reason to toss me. You'll practically be committing me to a life of sucking dick at the bus station. Is that what you want? Is it?"

"Yeah, well, there's nothing I can do about it, pal. Be here, tomorrow on time, and I promise you won't have to worry about any of that."

"It's not a problem, OK. I've got it planned that I'll be dead before I'm twenty-five. Just keep me around a few more months until then."

"Jesus. Just be here on time, OK."

"You bet. I'll be early. Before you even. I'll be all employee of the month and shit."

"Just be on time, OK. I mean, shit, fucking straighten up or something."

"10-4, boss. Over and out," I say and hurry through the front door.

As you guessed, it is the very shitty part of Los Angeles where I work, a neighborhood called Highland Park, uneven with hills and full of run-down, half-hearted shops, all cheap wigs and used auto parts. I step outside and light a cigarette. I walk down the block towards the bus stop. Every night, on my way over to the bus stop, because, you know, even though I live at home, I still can't fucking afford a car, well, anyways, every night, I always see this dude, dressed up in a white bunny costume, out in front of the Majestic Car Wash on Figueroa Avenue. Every night, no matter what kind of weather it is, raining, hot, whatever, he's standing out in front waving. It's like this beautiful thing you forget to expect, you know. It always gives me a nice feeling. I wave to the bunny and he waves back and I start to think, OK, OK, I do need to get straight maybe. I take the photo of the girl in the cheetah outfit out of my pocket and look at her face and think she might be the most beautiful woman I have ever seen. I get on the bus and look over my shoulder. The sun is setting and it makes it look like LA is on fire. I wonder what in the world is going to save me.

Three chapters from *Hey, Liberal!*

'Tis the Season

Simon felt safest in the mornings. One of many students migrating across an asphalt playground as big as a city block, he paced himself so as not to risk attracting attention. December's cold took a bite out of anything dumb enough to breath, but hey, 'tis the season. Snow, old and already trampled to a bumpy sheet, crunched under his workboots. His rucksack, slung over his back and heavy with homework books, a baseball mitt, and gym shoes, cut into his shoulder blade. Reaching Orchard Street, he stopped short of joining the crowd on the other side in front of Dexter High School. Then he dropped his sack, leaned against a curbside cottonwood tree, and waited for the first period bell to ring. At that early hour, Latino and black gangbangers seldom paid any attention to the sprinkling of white kids. Back in '68, you had to explain to most whites that *gangbanger* means *a person who belongs to a gang*. No joke.

The sun had inched above rooftops and blazed a cheery iridescent light over the Lincoln Park neighborhood. Simon buried his chin into the collar of his Navy pea coat, his fleece-lined gloves and coat pockets losing the battle to keep his fingertips from going numb. On the sidewalk across the street, a black girl huddling with a clutch of friends tilted her head back and cut loose with a laugh that left him wondering, What's so fucking funny?

The bell rang, and after everyone else surged toward the main front doors, Simon brought up the rear. For security reasons the outside door handles to the school's many entrances had been removed, so the crowd waited impatiently until a teacher's aide opened a door from inside. As Simon topped the concrete stairs, something loose and raw tumbled in his chest, but he kept with the flow, the bottleneck of bodies slowly shrinking into the building's dimly lit interior. It was always the same manageable dread—like volunteering to be swallowed alive.

Built over a span of seventy-one years, Dexter High consisted of three connecting buildings, each one a different shade of red brick. At the south end of the block, the "old building" loomed like a misplaced relic out of Rome's Forum, its four iconic columns giving students something to slouch against as they smoked and watched boys pitching pennies on the sidewalk. In the middle of the block, the "new building"—so called despite having been added on just after World War II—doubled the space of its more ornate elder sibling. At the north end, the modern annex—a butt-ugly box—rounded out the drab trio. It was in the annex's auditorium that a white boy named James Jeffrey came to study hall class with a loaded .22-caliber rifle tucked under his trench coat. He whipped out his weapon and calmly proceeded to take random potshots at students. Folks say it was a regular stampede for the exits with people dodging and ducking bullets. Cops hit the scene with a dozen or so paddy wagons and squad cars, and after a little give-up-or-we'll-blow-your-ass-away persuasion, the wacko surrendered without a fuss. Imagine, all those human targets at close range and no one killed or wounded. Classic case of divine intervention.

The next day, Jeffrey was front-page news in all the papers and on TV. To everyone's utter shock, it turned out he was the quiet loner type. Cops with a search warrant found neo-Nazi literature stashed under his bed at home. He confessed to detectives down at the Twelfth Precinct that he flipped out because he was sick and tired of gangbangers shaking him down for chump-change. No one seems to remember exactly how much time he spent in a jail for juvenile offenders, but it's a well-known fact that within a year of the shooting spree, the Jeffrey family cleared out of town—forwarding address unknown.

Nowadays, someone goes postal at a school, and a damn platoon of social workers descends out of nowhere to help students with their post-traumatic stress syndrome, but back then classes weren't even canceled. Hard to believe. The way Dexter's principal, Dr. Jursak, explained it on the Ten O'clock Eyewittness Evening News, he didn't want to "risk further racial violence" by breaking routine. What with the recent riots in black communities across the country that followed the assassination of Martin Luther King Jr., maybe Jursak had a right to fear the worst and sweep the entire incident under the rug. Didn't work for long, though. A month later in May, a rumor that whites had pushed a black man off the Grand subway platform and onto the electrified third rail spread like a wildfire through Dexter. Never mind that the rumor would eventually prove false. In reaction to it, King's murder, James Jeffrey's attack, and the whole slavery ball of wax, black kids had decided by noon that it was Stomp Honky Day. The riot started in the lunchroom. Someone gave the signal, blacks stood up from tables en masse and proceeded to pummel, kick, trounce, fling, and body slam to the floor every white within reach. For those who lived and breathed *street survival*, it wasn't hard to get the upper hand. They gave Hispanics—no slouches in the gang department themselves—a pass. By 12:15, marauding bands of students were going into classrooms and dragging white kids out of their seats. A teacher stupid enough to try and stop an ass-whupping got his jaw broken.

Twenty-seven arrests and a few tense days later, things calmed down. What could Jursak do—suspend half the school? The damage done, kids transferred out of Dexter by the droves, and the student body plummeted from 40 percent white to 12 percent overnight. Next thing you know, the city got serious about its court-ordered desegregation plan and declared a new rule: from that day forward, no more student transfers to public schools outside of the district he or she lived in. Talk about too little, too late for Dexter; the white-flight door was already flung wide open.

In June, Bobby Kennedy bit the dust from an assassin's bullet. Then later that summer, the '68 Democratic Convention lit one hell of a national spotlight on the *City of Big Shoulders*. As "Yippie" Vietnam War demonstrators and police fought pitched battles with rocks and billyclubs along Chicago's lakefront from Lincoln Park to downtown, people started to forget all about the boy with a rifle at Dexter who went off the deep end.

Come fall, Simon turned freshy. He'd moved into the hood with his family only a couple of years earlier. The word *was*, back where he originally lived on the city's all-white, far-northwest side, his Reverend dad had gotten into hot water with his congregation–something to do with the civil rights movement. For Simon, the change of scenery to Lincoln Park was like a switch in planets—heavier gravity, and a long list of alien life forms that included *hillbilly*. Because of classroom overcrowding at Dexter, Simon's schedule called for a fourth-period study hall in the auditorium. His assigned seat, dead center in the fifth row, would have given him a deluxe view of the entire Jeffrey incident had he been there at the time. No one's ever accused the Chicago Board of Education of being *swift* when it comes to repairs, and Simon spotted bullet holes blown through the backs of a couple of wooden chairs near the rear of the auditorium. Chipped into the sky blue plaster ceiling, a scattered handful of other bullet holes looked like stars in a planetarium. Made him feel creepy—hollow all the way down to his toes.

Astronaut Neil Armstrong would set foot on the moon in the summer of '69, a giant leap for mankind that forever buried any chance of James Jeffrey qualifying for an historical footnote. And to think that that kid did his thing thirty-one years before those two boys at Columbine High in Colorado did theirs, shooting thirteen classmates dead and wounding twenty-one more.

Lincoln Park has long since changed from run-down apartments to condos and multi-million-dollar Victorian homes for the rich and famous. Decades ago, the city razed Dexter's baseball backstop and basketball hoops on the crumbling asphalt playground. Then they dumped truckloads of dirt and covered the entire block with a more aesthetically pleasing grassy knoll. In the muggy heat of summer, it provides a place for yuppie sunbathers to bask in a new century, unaware of the bittersweet clouds still lingering from the old one. In an attempt to bury Dexter's stained reputation, the Board of Education changed the school's name to Lincoln Park Academy and turned it into a "magnet school" for Fine, Performing, and Language Arts. The sad truth? History *can* be erased, but not this time.

Whatever the name of that monument to architectural mood swings, the trouble there didn't end with James Jeffrey. On the morning of that brutally cold day so many years ago, as the premature pull of adulthood ripped at the seams of Simon's youth, he had no idea that his trouble would end with another student, Louis Collins.

Tenth Period: Mira, Mira!

In a school where basketball reigned as the supreme sport, most students didn't even know Dexter fielded a baseball team. For just that reason, Mr. Evans, the baseball coach, called for a winter tryout to see how hard a recruiting job he'd have come spring.

Evans had the total of eleven boys line up in a corner of the gym to take some grounders.

"Garcia, catch for me."

A squat built-like-a-bull Puerto Rican boy turned his Cardinals hat backwards on his head and followed the coach until they were over near the pull-up bars, kitty-cornered from the other boys. Evans motioned with a fungo bat for the first player to step away from the line. Then he tossed a rubber-coated league ball up and smacked a hard grounder. The ball skip-bounced across the slick-varnished floor and glanced off the boy's glove.

"Devon, get your ass back to the minors where you belong!" someone yelled. "You field like my grandmama when she tied up in a bag a laundry."

"Shut up!" Devon said, moping to the end of the line.

The boys continued taking turns fielding. The closer Simon got to the front of the line the more his hand sweated inside the pocket of his kangaroo-skin glove. When it was his turn, he stepped away from the line and got into a crouched position. Stay on toes, he coached himself, glove down, set! His eye zeroed in on the ball as it left Evans's hand with a measured toss, then the smack of the bat and a hot grounder coming straight at him. Without any fear that the ball might take a bad hop and hit him in the face, he *looked* the ball straight into his glove, scooped it cleanly, and in one fluid motion came up firing with enough zip on his throw so that the ball *popped* in Garcia's catcher's mitt. Relieved, he hustled to the back of the line. The next boy, a Cuban, yelled to Garcia, "*Mira, mira!*" He fielded a "high chopper."

"*Mira, mira!*" Clyde Porter said. Charging a grounder, he snagged it on the short hop.

The joke took hold, each boy yelling "Look, look!" in Spanish when it was his turn to field.

"*Mira, mira!*" Simon shouted. Being the only white boy trying out for the team, he got the biggest laugh.

A few successful turns later, Simon had gone from nervous to overly confident and bored. On his next fielding chance, he hardly bent his knees, lackadaisically caught the ball, and then flipped a lazy sidearm toss back to Garcia.

"Hold it right there, hotdog!" Evans yelled at him. The pissed-off look on his pale acne-covered face stopped Simon in his tracks.

"Oooooo," someone yelled, "Evans gone teach the white boy a lesson."

Grinning like he knew he'd asked for trouble, but game for any kind of challenge to his baseball skills, Simon crouched low and got set for Evans to bring it on. He heard Clyde yell, "Show him what you got, Simon!"

The coach hit a ball so hard it skip-darted past Simon before he could stab his mitt fast enough to his left. He heard the ball carom in the corner behind him and bang against the end of the bleachers, then saw it dribbling past him out onto the floor again.

Smack!

The next one "handcuffed" him, glancing off the heel of his glove.

"What's a matter, hotdog?" Evans said. "Too *hot* for you?" Simon bounced on his toes in an effort to ready his reflexes.

Smack!

Stretching until he was fully extended, he snagged a smoking grounder, did a complete 180-degree turn and whipped a perfect on-the-mark throw at Garcia.

Smack!

He dove, slid on the floor under the basketball hoop, backhanded a ball, and came up firing another strike at Garcia. The grounders kept coming, each one hit harder than the one before it.

"Evans ain't playing!" someone said.

Simon let his reflexes do his talking, darting, twisting, lunging, scooping, the gymnasium a blur, nothing but the ball, the ball, the ball, his glove like a fully tactile extension of his own flesh. And then that magical moment. He was already moving, reacting to where the ball would go a split second before it even left Evans's bat. The line drive whistled through the air with a *phfffft* and would have taken Simon's head off had he not gotten his mitt in front of his face out of sheer self-defense. He caught it. Fell flat back on his ass, but he caught it.

For a moment the gym was silent. And then Clyde's voice echoed off the beige-tiled walls, "My man, Simon. He *bad*!"

Simon picked himself up off the floor and zinged the ball to Garcia. Evans held the bat by his side and stared at him. Slowly, the stare changed into a grudging smile.

"Not bad, hotdog, not bad. What's your position?"

"Center field."

"More like short stop," Evans said.

"Center field," Simon repeated.

"Forget it, hotdog. L.D.'s got center nailed down. Fastest man on the team last year."

"I can beat him."

"Oooooo, you hear that, L.D.?" someone in line asked. "White boy say he be faster."

"Sheeeeit." This from the boy who looked all legs.

If Simon had been a year or two older, he would have recognized the expression on Evans's face. *No white boy can beat a black boy in a foot race.*

"You ever see L.D. run?" Evans asked Simon.

"No one *see* L.D. run," stated another boy. "That how fast he is."

"I can beat him," Simon said again, heading for the end of the line.

Perhaps intuitively sensing an opportunity to make some cash, Clyde challenged one and all, "Fifty cent say hotdog can beat L.D." Then he strutted over to Simon, leaned in close to him and whispered, "You sure? L.D. faster than a whore in heat."

No problem." From Simon's low-key confidence, no one could have known that the total respect others were showing for L.D.'s speed was beginning to give him the jitters.

"Make it a dollar," someone else returned.

"Hey, hey, cut that gambling out!" Evans warned. He paused, as if intrigued by the cocky freshy's challenge. "All right, hotdog, L.D., get over here."

As the two boys went across the gym to Evans, and the others took spectator seats on the bleachers, Simon heard Clyde's hushed voice, "Make it *two* dollar."

"You covered."

"All right, twice around the gym," Evans told the boys. On the second lap, switch lanes so that it's an even distance."

He pointed to a red line painted on the floor next to the chin-up bars, and the two runners took their places. Simon shook his arms to stay loose.

"On your mark, get set, GO!"

L.D. exploded off the line and took a two-step lead. By the second turn the gap hadn't changed an inch. Arms pumping, legs straining, Simon kicked it up a gear, thinking, Dig! Dig! Dig! They crossed lanes at the end of the first lap and were dead even.

"Go hotdog!" Clyde yelled.

"L.D.! L.D.! L.D.!" another boy screamed.

Feet pounded the floorboards, neither boy able to shake the other. Simon felt his stamina start to give out, as if a claw were raking inside his chest, his calves and hamstrings tightening, on the verge of knotting up. With only half a lap to go, he reached for that something extra deep in his craw that he didn't know he had, sucked it in, and lunged across the finish line. He won by a nose.

"Ahhhh," someone laughed, "white boy beat L.D.!"

Dizzy, not an ounce of effort left in him, Simon stumbled over to the bleachers and collapsed onto the lowest bench. He hung his head between his legs and took long gasping breaths.

"Let's go again!" L.D. said, jumping up and down like a pogo stick, obviously not half as winded as Simon. He must not have wanted it badly enough.

"Boy, you lost!" Clyde yelled. "Hotdog beat your ass." He climbed down the bleachers and lifted Simon's arm as if declaring him champion.

"Two dollar, sucker," Clyde told a boy farther up the bleachers. "Pay up." The moment Clyde let go of Simon's arm, it fell like a wet noodle to the bench.

"*No betting*!" Evans yelled.

"You heard Evans, bets off!" a boy called down at Clyde.

"Aww, scrub," Clyde said, and he headed up the bleachers to go and argue with his friend. Someone passing by Simon patted him on the back, but he didn't bother looking to see who it was. Get up, he thought. Walk it off. He struggled to his feet and clasped his hands behind his head to open up the air passage to his raw lungs. Above the bleachers, outside the tall windows, the sky was darkening into the firm grasp of a winter's early dusk, and ceiling fixtures, caged in wire for protection from balls of all sports, lit the gym in a mellow amber light.

"Lucas! Jackson! " Evans said. "Let's go, two laps around."

At the end of practice, the boys started trailing out of the gym to head down to the locker room. Evans stood in the double doorway leading to the stairs, and as Simon passed by he held his arm out for him to stop. He gave Simon the once over.

"I don't like hotdogs, especially ones like you with mustard to spare."

Simon looked at the floor. "Sorry." He made himself meet Evans's eye. "It won't happen again."

"Better not." Then, "Shouldn't be that fagged out after only two times around the gym. You don't eat your Wheaties or what?"

"I've always been like that. I'm fast but I get tired easy."

"Not when I get through with you," Evans said. "I'm going to work your ass off." He smiled grudgingly again. "Try-outs start in March. Be there."

"Thanks," Simon said, and feeling as if he were floating more than walking down the short hallway toward the stairs, he shook a fist in the air, thinking, Yes!

Money

No more straight-laced parishioners telling him what he can and can't do. Like a great escape, the Reverend Adam Fleming had resigned from Saint James's church on the northwest side of the city and moved his family to Lincoln Park, a neighborhood teeming with Bohemian counterculture. In the spirit of a bold new beginning, he starts the Community Arts Foundation.

First things first. Adam talks a rich donor into footing the down payment for an antiquated bowling alley on Lincoln Avenue. Then he converts the building into an arts complex and gives it the catchy '60s name Mother Earth. Amazing what a few carpenters and a little drywall can do. Before you know it, there are two theaters on the first floor, aptly referred to as Big and Little. On the second floor, bowling gutters are ripped out, the slick varnished maple-wood alleys shoved together, and *voila*! The Upstairs Theater is born. Ring two sides of this third theatrical space with more drywall, and Adam has studios and offices he can rent out to The Peggie Lemond Dance Company, Chicago Muralists' Alliance, Phil's Marionette Workshop, and The Clay Men pottery school. He even rents an office to Rising Up Rage, a radical left-wing political organization. Remember, technically speaking, Adam is still a Presbyterian minister, and Rage's "free people's" health care clinic appeals to his sense of *mission*.

The clergyman-turned-arts-entrepreneur gets a brilliant idea. To keep everyone's rent affordable, yet bring in enough cash to pay him a modest salary, different theater troupes can double up and share Mother Earth's stages. Rainbow has dibs on the Big Theater Monday through Sunday evenings, and the Rock'n'roll Cantata Singers rule the roost on weekend afternoons. The Dingle Beats call the shots in the Small Theater for 7:00 p.m. shows, and then pass the "experimental" thespian baton to the Mime Sweepers at 9:00 p.m. Dream and Flying Onion companies split time in the Upstairs Theater, leaving the Children's Puppet Troupe to work the Saturday and Sunday matinee kiddie crowds. As productions close, new companies rotate in. One happy revolving door of art and political liberation under the same rooftop, right?

Not exactly. The Rising Up Rage folks turn out to be spoiled white kids transplanted from the suburbs and masquerading in a working-class wardrobe of scruffy jeans and threadbare flannel. Their goal? To be deemed as worthy radicals in the eyes of the more famous Black Panther Party. Rage members begin to flex their territorial muscle and love for the proletariat by spray-painting "educational" graffiti all over the Mother Earth building. In the downstairs lobby, a sandblasted brick wall is decorated with SMASH CAPITALISM, and in the center of the room, the front of the ticket-booth island proclaims OFF THE PIGS. On each and every staircase step, the people's power salute of a clenched fist, neatly stenciled in white, makes sure that no paying customers lose their way between the Upstairs Theater and the first-floor bathrooms during intermission.

Adam tries to reason with Rising Up Rage. Can't they take their message to the streets? Not all patrons of the arts believe in their brand of solidarity among the masses. The radicals reward Adam's patience by dubbing him Abraham Lincoln—no intended compliment for the bearded six-and-a-half-foot reverend who could indeed pass for a robust version of the sixteenth president. It is the unanimous belief of Rage members that the emancipator of the slaves was nothing more than a racist given preferential treatment by "sell-out" historians.

Like an infectious case of revolutionary pox, Rage graffiti continues to multiply on walls, threatening to turn the Mother Earth complex into a Marxist-Leninist shrine. One early afternoon, Adam pays a visit to Rage's office and gives the fourteen-strong collective a blistering final warning. Shortly after that, someone sneaks up to the flat, tarred rooftop via the fire escape and takes the liberty to adorn the tethered, ten-foot-tall, fiberglass statue of Mother Earth with a Hitler mustache. Presiding like a naked goddess over heavy traffic on Lincoln Avenue, her arms wrapped around an enormous globe so that her breasts press against the polar icecap to strategically hide her nipples, the new facial growth changes her come-hither grin into a genocidal leer.

By midafternoon, one of the Clay Men—overalls, brawny arms, and pony-tailed hairdo caked and splattered with the slurry of his trade—reluctantly plays messenger and informs Adam of the rooftop desecration. Calling *me* a fascist? Adam thinks. There's nerve, and then there's *real nerve*.

He evicts the merry band of Rising Up Rage, but not before one of them can scrawl on his Community Arts Foundation office door

BAD
VIBES

End of trouble? Nope. Someone drops a dime on Mother Earth. In the aftermath of the Chicago '68 Democratic Convention and its nationally tele-vised riots between anti-war demonstrators and cops, the Honorable Mayor Richard J. and his political-machine cronies don't take kindly to anyone asso-ciating with "agitators," evicted or not. Next thing Adam knows, it seems like every municipal building inspector within the city limits is finding reason to stop by Mother Earth and discover fire code violations. Doesn't matter that the Big Theater has a puny 150 seat capacity, the Upstairs a measly 100, and the Little a laughable 60; same stringent codes apply to them as apply to 3,000 seat venues. Only three exits instead of the required five? That's a $100 fine. Short one fire extinguisher? Ante up another $100. And he can either upgrade the building's electrical from top to bottom or pay $350 each and every month he's not up to code. Sorry, Reverend. The law's the law. Welcome to the city that works.

Several months and $9,000 in fines later, Adam puts two and two togeth-er. In the eyes of city officials, he's in cahoots with people dedicated to over-throwing the government by any means necessary. Don't these same officials realize that Mother Earth is helping to revitalize the inner city by bringing in theater goers with fat wallets from the suburbs? Hell, give him a gun, and he'd personally track down his former tenants and give them a dose of *reverend* rage.

Meanwhile, Maggie Lemond is threatening to break her studio lease because when Phil, the lush marionette maker, gets loaded on gin, he wanders from his workshop over to her dance studio and interrupts rehearsals by invit-ing female dancers back to his studio. His intention? To introduce one, if not several, of his petite limber guests to a new invention called a *waterbed*. The Chicago Muralists' Alliance is complaining that when the Clay Men fire up their gas kiln in the studio adjacent to theirs, they might as well be renting space in the Sahara desert. In the Upstairs Theater, one of the many mismatched chairs bought from the Salvation Army collapses with a customer in it during the Mime Sweepers performance. Despite no broken bones, the "victim" files a $800,000 lawsuit—twice the amount of The Community Arts Foundation's liability insurance coverage. Without giving notice, The Dingle Beats jump ship for a larger space at the Kingston Mines Theater a block south on Lincoln Avenue, leaving Adam scrambling for a new Small Theater tenant. Dream members in the Upstairs Theater are threatening to "crash" the Rock Cantata Singers' show in the downstairs Big Theater and pull the plugs on their electric guitar amplifiers. Dream's objection is not so much that the excessive volume literally shakes their stage from below, as it is that they find themselves prancing and delivering their dialogue in an up tempo entirely counter to the intended multi-layered metaphorical mood of their own show. Rainbow not only doesn't appreciate that the Cantata Singers won't put Rainbow's sets back where they found them after performances, they also conveniently forget to clean up their audiences' spilled popcorn buckets and discarded pop cups in the aisles.

"Come on," Adam says, trying to cajole the three troupes' warring directors during a heated pow-wow in his office to straighten out their differences. "You're telling me that talented guys like yourselves can't figure out a way to get along?"

Ego trumps *talent*, and the Cantata Singers, claiming a lack of artistic freedom as legal grounds for breaking their lease, pull up stakes for the greener non-sharing pastures of the Dayton Street Theater.

Out of charitable concern, Adam lets an elderly street bum, who goes by the single name of *Peace*, to sleep in his office on an air mattress at night. A woman in possession of little more than a few severely crooked teeth, a British accent of dubious authenticity, and wonderfully thick hair usually coifed in a streaming gray ponytail, she keeps her true identity a mystery to one and all. Always dressed in a loose white dress that could pass for a dingy nightie, she seems to float about the Mother Earth complex with an air of ownership and is quick to add her two cents to any conversation within earshot. So, she's a little whacked and subsists off late-night raids on the refreshment stand's leftover popcorn. No real harm done in order to keep her off the streets, right?

Wrong. If any paying customer comes through Mother Earth's front door with a skirt deemed too short by Peace or a halter top cut too revealingly low, the homeless woman will march straight up and tell the offending lady, "What would your Mum say, deary? Dress like a whore, treated like a whore!"

It doesn't take long for the less charitable among the Mother Earth tenants to declare war on Peace.

"Look," Rex Hansen, director of Rainbow, tells Adam. "She's certifiably nuts and scaring off customers. Get rid of her." From behind Rex's wire-frame glasses, his muddy-brown eyes, set so very far apart, give him the look of an all-seeing weasel. "What are you running here, anyway, a damn halfway house?"

"My building, my rules," Adam says flatly. "Peace stays." Sure, he knows the eccentric homeless woman has to eventually take a hike, but he wants to set up some other decent living arrangement for her first. Besides, ever since Rainbow's show *Magnetica Force* got optioned to go off Broadway in New York, Rex and his entry cast have had an acute case of Prima Donna-itis.

"Then I'm withholding my rent."

"Fuck you, Rex." By now Adam has dealt with enough temperamental artist types that he's learned the word "fuck" does indeed come in handy. "Did you forget something? *I* control the box office receipts, not *you*."

A month later, the Magic Aardvark ensemble replaces the departed Rainbow in the Big Theater, but with *Return to Eden*, a show that calls for actors to try and talk the audience into taking off their clothes during the second act, Adam doubts that Aardvark will make its $250 monthly rent anytime soon. One night Peace sticks her head in the Big Theater's main door during a performance and yells up the center aisle, "You're all Sodomites! Burn in hell!" Priding themselves on their improvisational skills, the naked Aardvarks are quick to accept Peace as one of their own by swarming toward her off the stage and up the aisle, probably intent on pulling Peace into the show for God knows what Sodomite purpose. The audience—all twelve members—is none the wiser as Peace shrieks and avoids capture by fleeing into the lobby and slamming the door shut behind her. She never challenges the Aardvarks on their home turf again.

The government's assault on Mother Earth's cash flow continues. Finally, Commonweath Edison pulls the plug on the building's electricity for three months' nonpayment. Before Adam can scrape up the cash to pay the bill, the ice cream in the refreshment stand freezer has melted to vanilla and chocolate glop. All shows are canceled for two nights running—except for the Mime Sweepers. On the second night of the blackout, bravely deciding that the show must go on, they line large candelabras complete with lit candles along the stage's three-sided perimeter, just inches in front of the first rows of Salvation Army chairs. Talk about a *real* fire hazard. Adam isn't in the building at the time, but another impromptu visit by a city building inspector results in him writing out a fine to the lucky person who answers his knock on Community

Arts Foundation's door. Peace.

The next morning, the terrified woman is near tears when Adam arrives at work.

"Pray thee, Reverend! I am a penniless woman. Where shall I ever get $100?"

"There, there, Peace." In the middle of the cluttered office, the walls lined with the eclectic posters of past Mother Earth shows, Adam consoles the woman with a couple of pats on her humped back. Then he follows a natural impulse and hugs her, his great frame all but swallowing her whole. The clergyman's head of unruly wavy hair—significantly longer and hipper than it had been during his clean-cut days in the pulpit—crowns a picture-perfect moment of humanity at its best. "Don't you worry. I'll take care of it. The city's run by a bunch of assholes."

"Reverend!" Peace jolts back a step, her lack of teeth making it appear as if she is constantly munching on her lips. Throwing a chaste hand over her tired breasts, she stares up at her benefactor in utter horror. "Such language! I am a lady, don't forget!"

"Sorry," Adam says. The perseverance in his blue-gray eyes tilting toward surrender, he shrugs and humors Peace by adding, "Just remember, even ladies and reverends have to watch out for assholes."

Two years after opening its doors, "crisis" has become Mother Earth's middle name. The majority of artisans, dancers, and actors in the complex can agree on but one thing: Adam Fleming is making big bucks off of them. On the home front, the Victorian graystone he moved his family into on Kenmore Street has turned out to be a steal as long as he doesn't mind the leaky roof, rusted-out plumbing, occasional attacks of termites, rotten window sashes, and boiler on its last leg. It helps that his wife Helen works as a public school teacher substitute, but it's not like her salary lets a family of four live high on the hog. If his mother and father back home in Houston, Texas—as God-fearing as they were practical—didn't slip Adam a few hundred bucks every now and then, he'd be in deep shit. Then again, gifts from the family patriarch, who proudly toiled thirty-five years in middle management for Standard Oil, don't come without a backhanded price: "Son, first you throw away your career as a minister on that troublemaker Martin Luther King Jr.; now it's this so-called Community Arts Foundation. When are you going to learn that dreams don't pay the bills?"

RANDALL ALBERS

A Good Day for Dying
from *All the World Before Them*

On the morning of the day he would die, his fifty-third birthday, Adam Haskins found himself perched high on the hill that ran like a hog's back along the southern length of his father's farm. Sitting on the damp grass, leaning against the high rear tire of his Massey-Ferguson tractor, he draped sunburned arms across his upraised knees and scanned the sweep of earth extending from the base of the hill across his father's fields toward his own land— the two farms stitched together by a straight fenceline of barbed wire and cement posts a half-mile distant. Beyond lay other farms, the green billow of treetops that snaked through the land following the river's meandering path, and, seven miles distant, the robin's-egg-blue water tower and gleaming tin shaft of the grain elevator rising above the huddled houses of Harris, Minnesota.

It was already the first week of June, and it had been raining nearly every day for the past month. The planting was not yet finished, and water sat in shallow ponds here and there across the broad fields. Where there should have been dark green shoots of new corn in straight rows and undulating seas of new wheat, the glossy sheen on the open fields told anyone passing by on the narrow ribbon of blacktop to the west that even if the weather held, it would be days yet before farmers could venture out on tractors and finish the work that should have been done weeks earlier. By then, Adam realized with an odd sense of relief, he could be gone. Someone else would do the work and the worrying.

He leaned his head against the tire to look up at the sky. Today, at last, the clouds had broken and the bright sun, shocking after weeks of gloom, danced in his eyes, thrilling and mesmerizing him, sent him sailing unwilled, dreamlike, back through the days of his life, the weight of fifty-three years lifting as seasons slid by in reverse, slowly at first, then more rapidly, like fugitives retreating from a shocking present. The soggy, sun-bathed fields of this June day fell away, and he heard instead the sound of his boots crunching through fallen, frosted leaves on the brittle grass of a young farmer's autumn, felt again the exuberance of hurdling fences and racing across open hayfields in a teenager's midsummer, the burning in his chest as he worked his way up this very hill on the bright, slippery shoots of a youth's spring, the sting of frozen fingers curled inside wool mittens as he skated the slough pond during a

young boy's winter. The torrent of memories whirled and leaped, flooding him
with a sudden, heart-wrenching awareness of days and seasons and fifty-three
years gone by with nothing to show for it but a cluster of buildings on a tiny
chunk of earth, nothing to look forward to except more of the same, another
day, another season, another decade or two of work before he at last entered
the earth himself.

Then, as quickly as they had come, the images of his past vanished again,
and he was back on the hill, feeling lightheaded, dizzy, the wetness seeping
through the rear of his jeans from the damp earth, the old familiar fatigue settling into his bones. Wearily, he drew up and leaned forward to rest his chin
on his crossed wrists, his head heavy, oh so heavy, his body weighted with the
futility of locating a pattern in the waste of those fleeing, ungraspable memories. His whole life was a shambles, a lie. No longer the brown-legged youth
leaping fences for the sheer joy of it, no more the young farmer filled with
hopes and plans as he walked the land at his father's side, he was instead, he
saw now, simply a man falling toward old age, marking the years in the deepening lines of his sun-leathered cheeks, the aches in his arthritic knees, the
pains, real and imagined, in his grinding heart.

Nothing had turned out like he'd planned. Or, to put it more plainly, like
his father, Harmon Haskins, had planned when, forty-five years ago if it was
a day, Adam had first ridden to this hilltop on his father's lap, the two of them
lurching on the metal seat of the old hay rake pulled by two monstrous, plod-
ding draft horses, Lucky and Will. He couldn't have been more than six or
seven, his feet not yet reaching the footrests where his father's workshoes
were anchored against the sway and buck of the rake as its steel wheels dipped
into hidden gopher holes and banged against fist-sized rocks. For weeks, he
had been pestering his parents to let him work in the fields, and at last his
father, who had himself begun handling the horses on his own father's farm
practically from the time he could walk (as he never tired of telling his son),
took up the boy's case with Adam's mother, who wouldn't hear of it because
her younger brother had died in an accident involving a skittish, runaway
horse. Finally, after weeks of their onslaught, Irene had relented, on the condition that Adam should begin by only watching Harmon running the team so
he could learn the safe way of doing things without risking his own neck.

Slowly, the two of them, father and son, had made their way up the long
rise to the crest, where the land tabled into a flat field of fifteen or so acres. At
the corner, next to the fence that separated the field from a grove of oak,
maple, ash, and pine, his father yelled "Whoa!" to Lucky and Will alongside
a hulking, rounded boulder fifteen feet across, waiting while his son negotiat-

ed the descent to solid earth. As Adam leaped the last step to the ground, he turned to see his father sitting stock-still high on the seat, the reins resting forgotten in his lap, face speckled with pinpricks of light filtering through the wide, woven brim of his straw hat. He seemed to be surveying the fields spread out at the base of the hill they had just climbed. Adam waited silently until, at last, his father pointed into the distance, saying, "Look, son. You see that?"

He followed his father's gaze, searching for whatever it was that Harmon wanted him to see, a stray cow, a bird, perhaps the telltale signs of a fox or coyote moving through the high grass. But try as he might, he couldn't see anything except the wide, flat fields, some empty, some dotted with grazing cattle.

"You *see* that?" his father asked again. "All that land? That's yours, son. As sure as it's mine. We got to take care of it, you and me. Make something of it. You understand?" Adam squinted up at the looming man and nodded, though at the time he wasn't quite sure just what his father did mean. Harmon lifted his arm higher, still pointing. "And you see that land over there?" His eyes seemed fixed on some distant point beyond their own fenceline. "Someday, things go right, that land over there will be ours, too." He swung his arm to the right. "Or that over there." Swinging farther. "Or that farm over there." He paused, dropping his hand to rest it on the one clutching the reins in his lap, looked down at Adam, the light-speckled face serious. "Or maybe all of it. Maybe, things go right and the Lord willing, we'll own it all. And then you and me, we'll show people what *real* farming is. Haskins and Son. How's that sound?" Not knowing what to say, Adam nodded again solemnly, though his father had gone back to sweeping the horizon, his eyes distant and narrow, as if he were peering through the years into that future when he and his son and his son's son would all be standing shoulder to shoulder, muscling the slings and arrows of fate, and the envy that their toil and their triumphs had engendered.

Finally, his father swung back toward him and punched a thumb in the direction of the boulder, his voice rising, "Now go sit on that rock. While I'm raking, I want you to look at that land out there and think about what I told you." He started to gather the reins and turn to the task, then stopped and stared hard at his son. "And whatever you do," he said, his voice stern now, no longer softened by visions of glory, "don't move off that rock. You wander away and get lost, your mother'll have my hide. And you know whose hide *I'll* have then, right?" He was smiling now, but his tone left no doubt that there would be trouble for sure if Adam strayed.

Now, nearly a half-century later, sitting fifty yards from that same hump-backed rock, Adam saw himself again—a tall-for-his-age, towhead boy in a plaid work shirt and baggy, blue overalls—nod (dutiful to a fault even then!) and climb onto the boulder. By the time he was in high school, he would travel to that spot more times than he could count, whenever he had something to work out for himself, or when he just needed a break from the seemingly endless train of chores. But that day, he had plopped down on the rough granite, his father's words still ringing in his ears, seeing himself at his father's side as they plowed and planted and milked together. And when he raised his eyes to the countryside, seeing cattle feeding in the pastures, cars inching down dusty country roads, farmers and their tiny teams scattered across the prairie cutting hay, clearing timber, cultivating perfect rows of checked corn under a pristine blue sky—all the while hearing his father's voice rising above the whine of metal wheels and squeak of spindly tines as he urged the sweating Lucky and Will around and around the hilltop—Adam felt the stirrings of an unaccountable pride, as if he were God himself studying the earth that he had made.

The flush of pride faded as the morning wore on and the blistering sun rose higher in the sky. Adam scuttled back across the rock's surface bit by bit, trying to stay in the diminishing island of shade from the trees across the fence—until, at last, the island disappeared altogether, and minutes stretched to an eternity in the suffocating heat. At noon, his skin red and prickly, he heard the high, full-throated scream of the creamery whistle wind down from Harris, slicing muffled but insistent through the still air, and jerked out of his reverie to see the horses stop dead in their tracks, ears up. In the split-second pause, his father yanked the lever to raise the tines of the rake before the two lumbering horses abruptly shed their lassitude, lurched around in unison, and cut across the field at a trot heading for home, already tasting the cool water in the shaded cement trough alongside the barn, already chewing hay and oats from the bunk at the corner of the cowyard.

Later, as Adam himself grew and took over the reins to those two horses, he would learn that, obedient as they were at all other times, they would not be coaxed into taking one more step down a windrow, furrow, or fenceline once that noon whistle sounded. But that day, as he sprang up, his bunched calf muscles knotting, then slowly loosening, his rear end prickling from sitting for so long on the hard surface, he expected that his father would yank on the reins and call to Lucky and Will sharply as Adam had heard him do so many times around the yard, then guide the two sweat-drenched draft horses over to where he stood waiting on the rock. Instead, shading his eyes against the noon glare, he saw the horses move not toward him, and not toward the

path that circled down the more gradual grade of the hill, but right over the
edge of the hogback, traveling across the steep hillside at a sharp angle and
making a beeline for the gate as his father clung to the rake's metal frame,
shouting "Easy!" and fought to keep from sliding off during the quick, jostling
trip down the rutted hill. Watching the frenzied retreat, Adam cupped his
hands around his mouth and yelled for all he was worth at his father's swaying back. "Dad!" His voice was swallowed by the clang and clatter of the rake,
and he wondered for a moment if he should hop down, follow on foot—but
then heard again his father's words from three hours earlier, "Whatever you
do, boy, don't move off that rock!", and so stayed put. The horses, clattering
rake, and swaying driver reached bottom, wound through the narrow, open
gate, and disappeared down the lane out of sight behind the trees. Adam stood
for a moment longer, feeling suddenly very alone in that wide expanse, then
plopped down heavily on the rock, hearing only the twitter of songbirds in the
woods at his back and his own whimpering as he fought vainly against tears
he knew he shouldn't be crying.

Sometime later, his crying replaced by leaden loneliness and stomach-
rumbling hunger, he was studying the progress of a fat, green caterpillar laboring across the rock toward the worn toe of his brown shoe when he heard his
father shout his name. "Adam!" The sound came rolling up the hill and
echoed in the grove across the fence, as if ghostly beings were beckoning.
Shading his eyes, he squinted down the steepest length of the hill and saw his
father standing at the gate, shaking his head and crooking an arm at him to
come on down. Rising quickly, he leaped off the rock and raced as fast as his
stiff legs would let him down through the tall grass, keeping a careful watch
for ruts and stones that might send him head over tea kettle. As he neared the
bottom, he ventured a glance toward the gate and saw that the spot where his
father had stood was empty. By the time he passed through the opening into
the lane, the receding figure was already halfway back to the buildings.

His own trip up the lane took another eternity, with the hoof-pocked mud
sucking at his caked shoes the whole way. Tears burned his eyes, rippling the
image of his father's back as it moved steadily away from him in the distance.
When he had finally rounded the windbreak bordering the sheds, climbed over
the wooden fence next to the barn, and scurried across the yard to the house,
he saw that his father was already done scraping his boots on the long, metal
flange sunk into the cement at the edge of the landing and now stood, arms
crossed on his chest, waiting for him on the top step. Adam raced up, puffing
and red-faced, braking to a stop at the bottom of the wide steps as he caught
sight of his father's narrow, steel-gray eyes fixed on him intently from under

the wide-brimmed hat.

"Where you been, boy?" Harmon asked evenly, as if he hadn't just walked the half-mile out to the field and back to retrieve his forgotten son.

Confused, Adam gazed up at the hulking figure, open-mouthed. "On the rock," he said tentatively. "Just like you told me."

His father shook his head, shifted irritably, dropped his hands onto his hips. "It was dinner time. Didn't you hear the whistle blow?"

Feeling sheepish, though he wasn't quite sure why, Adam dropped his eyes and stared at his muddy shoes. "Yes," he said quietly.

"Well, you hear that whistle, you got to *move,* boy, not just sit there like a bump on a log. You got to catch up, see? 'Cause I dasn't try to stop those horses once they hit the slope of that hill. One stops and one doesn't, pretty soon they're tangled or the tongue breaks, and the rake runs up on one of their hindquarters. Next thing you know, horse breaks a leg and we end up shooting him right there where he lays. You get my point?"

Adam toed a mud clod at the edge of the steps, seeing Lucky lying on his side in the field, thrashing wildly, a white, jagged bone jutting out of a bloody gash in his back leg, seeing his father trudge up to the fallen horse, chamber a bullet in his rifle, raise the gun, and sight a spot between the horse's huge, terrified eyes, then pull the trigger—the blast exploding, the great, brown beast jerking once as if slapped, then settling into a horrible stillness in the hay stubble, eyes open but unseeing, a trickle of blood sliding through the wide, white blaze down the center of his face.

A lump formed in his throat, the tears once again pressing behind his eyes. Feeling his father's gaze on him like a weight, he shuffled from one foot to the other, uncertain of what to say.

Suddenly, his mother's voice broke the silence, "You men going to stand out here jawing all day or come in and eat your dinner while it's still hot?" Adam jerked up to see her round face behind the screen door, blond hair swept up in a red bandana. Her broad smile narrowed when Adam's father turned and she caught sight of his grim expression. "Harmon?" she asked.

"Be right in," his father said. She paused, her eyes traveling back and forth between the two of them, then nodded and disappeared. His father turned back and stared down at him. "Well?" he asked simply.

Adam wiped a hand across his sweaty brow, fighting to remember the question.

"I *tried* to call you," he said plaintively.

His father studied him. "Not good enough," he said. "If you couldn't catch up, least you could do was have sense enough to get on back to the buildings.

As it was, you saw I had to come all the way out to get you. Waste of time. Now your mother's had to wait dinner on us when she's busy trying to clean house for the Garden Club tomorrow. And I still got to finish the raking and fix the binder before evening chores. Whole show's been stopped 'cause of you. We got *work* to do around here, boy, you understand?"

"But you *told* me to stay on the rock!" Adam blurted. Then, aware that he was risking a paddling for backtalk, he dropped his eyes again to his mud-spattered shoes. A long silence fell over them.

Finally, Adam ventured to look up, and his father spoke. "You got to learn to think for yourself, boy," he said, shaking his head as if it were something that Adam should have known all along. Adam nodded, and his father turned to grab the handle of the screen door. "Now take them shoes off so's you don't get mud all over your mother's brand-clean floor."

Over the noon meal, sitting in the charged silence of the kitchen, Adam's mother gently remonstrated with his father, pleading their son's case. "But he's just a *boy*, Harmon. No need to be gruff." His father, as usual within Adam's hearing, was not to be moved. "Boy's got to learn, Irene. If he ever hopes to be a man, that is."

Think for yourself. Be a man. The words came back to him now with brow-furrowing irony. Had he *ever* learned that lesson? And how *could* he, with the old man hovering over him every minute of every goddamn day, all fifty-three years of his life, watching his every move, telling him when he should plant, when he should put up his hay, when he should take a goddamn dump, for Christ's sake!

He raised his chin from his wrists and turned to stare at the humped rock over near the fence, seeing himself again, a six-year-old boy in baggy pants, cupping his hands at his mouth and shouting, waving arms frantically and jumping up and down to get his father's attention—and felt the frustration all over again, the futility of that act and so many others. He had carried that feeling of helplessness his whole life, a puppet flailing on his father's strings. Harmon the Great. Self-made man. Pillar of the community. A farmer's farmer, everyone said. Nothing, certainly not his own son, would stand in Harm's way when it came to putting up the crops, getting the hay baled, fixing the fences, painting the buildings—all the things that set the Haskins operation apart from those of wanna-be farmers, who stayed in bed until six instead of getting up in the pitch black of four-thirty to milk, who wasted the better part of rainy days down at the Wide Spot drinking beer instead of using the time to repair machinery or do the books or whitewash the barn, who were content to check yesterday's cattle prices in the *Pioneer Press* instead of calling the stockyards in South St. Paul to get the latest quotes, who never even gave a thought to taking an ag econ class at the "U" or traveling around the state to study the top dairy or hog or turkey operations written up in *Hoard's Dairyman* or *Successful Farming*. No, nothing could delay Harmon Haskins's headlong rush to be the best—least of all a six-year-old boy who didn't have sense enough to come in out of the sun at dinnertime. And not even a grown man heading toward old age who'd never quite figured out what it meant to think for himself.

As the unbidden images of that distant day rose again, as he saw himself, a skinny, sunbrowned boy looking up at his father from the foot of the back stoop, he felt an unaccountable rage surge through him—a rage made all the more intense for being unaccountable. His head pounded with a sudden, exploding pain behind his eyes, but it wasn't the rage and it wasn't just the memory of this one day that made him reel and clutch at the grass along his thighs to steady the earth swaying underneath him. It was that these images, which he had greeted as if meeting figures in a dream, with curiosity and anticipation, were threatening now to unlock other images, other moments, and feelings so long pushed into the dim recesses of being as to seem nearly unrecognizable as part of his own life. And that they signaled the beginning of an end, setting in motion a fateful chain of events, unavoidable, unalterable, irresistible, leading to the decision that had been playing at the corners of his mind for weeks, the decision that waited until today, his birthday of all days, to peek from the shadows.

Of all the lessons his father had tried to teach him, there was one he had learned well: Never let anyone know what you're really thinking. Around these parts, folks said it'd be hard to find a guy more easygoing than Adam Haskins—or so the word had come back to him from his wife. Marie had heard it from the women in the neighborhood (not without some consternation on her own part, reading in it the implied contrast with her own volatility). The wives had heard it from their husbands, who never had a bad word to say about Adam, despite their jealousy over his father's luck. Of course, Adam had gotten the message so often—especially from his mother, who repeated the same words about her son, "Perfect. He's just perfect!" over and over to any-one within hearing, like a mother mantra—that he had embraced the image of the kind man, the beneficent man, the humorous man, the difficult-to-get-a-rise-out-of man, and had made it a part of himself almost without thinking. If, as a boy, he raised his voice to a classmate over some playground battle or, later, heard his irritation surfacing with a neighbor backing out of a hay deal or edged toward snapping at Marie or one of the boys about a job left undone, he capped his anger like an old well and, smiling tightly, simply settled into silence, maybe made a joke at his own expense that defused the moment and left no lingering doubt in the listeners' minds about what a wonderful, utterly likable guy he was—all but Marie, that is, who knew what the sacrifice of his honesty cost him.

With himself, though, in those moments where he was alone in the barn or out on the tractor or up on the hill a half-mile away from any other human, he would find himself playing the event over and over in his mind, unable to rid himself of it. He would carry on elaborate dialogues as he fed the cows, replaying over and over what he should have said to that undependable neighbor, or he'd find himself screaming into the wind above the throaty rumble of the tractor's muffler out in the field, or he'd tumble into tears whose source was a mystery to him and sit there on the hogback, alone, furiously yanking clumps of grass out of the earth, soggy roots and all, flinging them toward the ravine that snaked down the middle of the hill. When the mysterious rage or despair or whatever it was (he hardly knew what to call it) was spent, he would stop, feeling utterly foolish, seeing himself as if caught in some guilty act, and think, *A grown man doing such things!* He would gather himself, force the feelings back down into the darkness, pull the cap over the well, and ship a good face to head home all smiles, Mr. Easygoing, Mr. Joviality again.

But it had taken its toll—all those pleasant, forced smiles, all those retorts left unspoken, all that good-humored shedding of the subtle and not-so-subtle digs about the Haskins name, the Haskins money, the Haskins land, the Haskins luck—and like water freezing and thawing in the crack of a rock year after year, those silent resentments and denials of spirit had widened a fissure in his very soul. Not that he'd ever really noticed the gradual erosion of self-esteem that they entailed, so intent was he upon maintaining, even to himself (*especially* to himself, he saw now), the image of calm solidity that smoothed his way through the world. Yes, never let anyone know what you're really thinking. Never let anyone know what you're really feeling. Not even yourself. God help him, Marie had been right all along.

A flock of swallows, twittering wildly, lifted out of the woods in back of the rock, gathered into a net, and swung over his head, sailing down the hill toward the pasture that ran along the sodden expanse of unplanted cornfield. He watched the net of birds stretching, shifting, gliding smoothly left and right, lifting and dipping without breaking. Studying their air dance, he felt his spirits lift momentarily. A quarter-mile away, the flock settled onto the pasture among the silent, tail-twitching herd of grazing young stock and became a barely perceptible smudge on the deep green alfalfa. Abandoned, feeling the weight return to his body after the brief flight, Adam heard the high, mocking whine of crickets coming to him from the long grass all around, and felt himself clinging to that sound in an effort to halt his retreat from the world that for so many years had been his nurse and solace.

Far below in the distance, one of the young stock sent up a series of long, sawing bellows, her neck stretching and head bobbing out of synch with the sound rolling up the hill to him. But he hardly heard her, thinking now of Marie sitting at her window and staring at the barren, snow-swept fields during those long winters, unable to cook or do the housework, unable some days even to get up the energy to dress, just planted there motionless in her robe hour upon hour after first Jake, their eldest, left to fight in Viet Nam and then Jamie, the youngest, went off to the University of Wisconsin to fight against it. And how that terrible distance had settled between them long before the news came that Jake had died in the jungle for who knew what purpose and long before Jamie shook hands with them on the day after graduation, then simply disappeared without a trace, vanished into thin air for who knew what reason. Losing sons like that was trauma enough for anyone, but looking back at it, as he had done so many times during the last few weeks when death started calling to him from the shadows, he couldn't really say that the trouble between Marie and him had anything to do finally with one or two events, however painful. Other people had faced worse and survived. No, it was the whole thing, the whole arc of lives gone wrong. So much promise. So much hope. All the world before them—and now….

He forced away images of his shattered hopes, struggling at least to channel, if not altogether halt, the memory river now threatening to overwhelm him by evoking moments where he had been truly happy, moments when those hopes had run high in his soul. He saw himself, a gangly young man in a blue suit at the altar with Marie, fighting his eager, nervous hands as he lifted the gauzy veil to kiss his new bride and glimpsed her green eyes brimming happily, the cheers and whoops of friends and relatives exploding from all corners of the drafty Methodist Church. Felt the flush of pride as he stood with his father at the dais during the DHIA Banquet in the winter of '49, the two of them together accepting the award for highest average butterfat for a Holstein herd. Felt it again as he sat in the Williams Arena bleachers alongside Marie during the state wrestling tournament, watching Jake on the top step of the award stand bend to get his first-place medal, then turn and grin a white-toothed grin as he pointed up at them, as if to say, "This is yours, too!" And once more at Jamie's graduation down in Madison as his son accepted his diploma and a $5,000 scholarship to grad school for being the department's best student.

The images wheeled toward him in rapid succession and slid by, and for the first time since he had sat down on top of this wind-swept ridge, he found himself edging toward hope. He saw himself at his father's desk picking up a slip of paper filled with figures, the last of which was circled—102 bushels corn/acre—and handing it to his father, who said, "All right. Good going, son. Let's do it again next year, okay?" then feeling the sting of his father's slap on his shoulder blade as he turned and walked out of the room. Saw himself leaning against the mailbox out by the road, reading his name in an article in the Harris paper about the county's new generation of up-and-coming farmers. Saw himself standing at the kitchen counter holding the phone, his mother calling from the hospital to tell him that while he was out picking corn that afternoon, his wife had given birth to a son and he was a father. And later, handing out cigars to men at the elevator, at the hardware store, in the darkened blacksmith's shop, on the lawn outside of church, and down at the Wide Spot, where Lamar Barnes, his father's neighbor and nemesis, swung around on his stool and accepted the stogie with a jibe, "So I gotta put up with *another* Haskins? Well, the least I can get out of it is a cigar!" surprising Adam by smiling broadly and turning to shout at Muriel washing glasses down the bar, "Draw this fellow a beer on me, will ya, honey? I don't care if his old man *doesn't* know shit from Shinola. Any guy who has a kid the same week as me can't be all bad!"—a moment that marked the beginning of his friendship with this neighbor his father hadn't spoken to for as long as he could remember and whose name couldn't so much as be breathed in the house.

Adam closed his eyes and shook his head, trying to settle the whirl of scenes. The faint glimmer of hope had vanished, and instead of lifting him, these moments mocked him with his own vanity and delusion. Lined up end-to-end, they paraded a happiness to those days that struck him now as ill-won and illusory. With such good fortune, he should have made more of his life.

When he opened his eyes again, Lamar's beer-ruddied face, with its shock of jet-black hair, still hung before him, uncharacteristically silent, the dark eyes studying him as if trying to fathom the depths of his soul. "Whatcha doin' up here, boy?" he heard his neighbor's voice say. The lips didn't move, the broad smile didn't waver, but the words came as distinctly as if they were sitting, as they so often had in the years after that day in the Wide Spot, on Lamar's rickety back porch, drinking beer and watching the occasional car slide by the house on the narrow blacktop road not fifty feet distant.

"Not sure," Adam said aloud.

"Yes, you are." Lamar's lopsided grin going wider.

Adam paused, not shifting his gaze from Lamar's glistening black eyes.

"It's your birthday. You should be down at the Wide Spot celebrating. Come on. We'll go hoist a few."

Adam shook his head no. "Can't," he said. "Not today. Too much to do."

Lamar's smile faded, and he threw his head back, letting out a snort. "Too much to *do*? How the hell can there be too much to do *today*? Been rainin' for a month, for God's sake! Fields are flooded, half of 'em. Be like drivin' through Edna's oatmeal. You'd need a rudder on that Massey to get anywhere in that shit. Like as not, you'd be up to your hubs before you got half a round done."

"Gotta get the planter greased and ready. Dad says we get a window in this weather, we're gonna have to go to beat the band to make up for lost time."

"Listen!" The voice was a rasp now. "I don't give a good God damn what Harmon Haskins thinks. If Gabriel himself showed up at his door, that man'd find a way to manufacture a job for him. Never saw a guy so in love with work. He'd have that angel pitching chicken shit before his wings were folded up."

Adam squeezed his eyes shut again. The voice went silent, Lamar's face spun away, and now he saw himself in the chicken house that butted up to one side of his father's barn, standing in the dimness of a long, narrow room, empty of birds and lit only by four dirty windows strung down one wall. He glanced down and saw that he was ankle-deep in watery chicken shit. Suddenly remembering why he was there—it all had to be cleaned, made like new; tourists from Arabia were coming to visit the farm!—he scanned the room, trying to recall where he had propped the shovel. Spotting it just inside the door, he took a step, and started a wave that rolled down the length of the room, sloshed again the far wall, then slid slowly back toward him. He froze, watching helplessly as the wave cascaded around his rubber boots, the muck edging up over their tops and filling his work shoes. Chicken shit squished between his toes as he turned and made for the door, its smell burning his nose.

Reaching the door at last, he looked up to find that the shovel had disappeared. In its place was a harp, mahogany, with golden strings that gleamed in the dimness, and large, the size of a small man. This will have to do, he thought. Resisting the temptation to pluck the strings, he grasped the polished, dark wood of the harp's frame, cradled it clumsily in his arms, and pushed toward an open window in the middle of the wall. He braced himself as best he could in the slippery muck and plunged the harp, fork-like, into the shit, then lifted and twisted, slinging the goo out the window toward the manure spreader parked alongside the chicken house. Shit trailed up the wall and across the sill, and resting the fat end of the harp down in the stew, he leaned out of the window to find that maybe a half-cup had actually made it into the spreader bed. He straightened, got a new grip, and repeated the process over and over, wrestling the harp faster and faster in spite of the growing fatigue in his forearms.

Finally, blinded by sweat, he stopped to wipe his face with his shirtsleeve. Suddenly, he heard what sounded like a trumpet's blast, high and thin, and turned just in time to see the floor alongside the door lift. The whole room seemed to tilt, and another wave took shape, huge this time, with a high froth of yellow at the crest. Panic leaped in his midsection as the wave bore down on him. He dropped the harp, spattering his face and arms, and grabbed a pillar that appeared from nowhere, clutching it as the wave smashed into him chest-high, lifting him momentarily off his feet and filling his nostrils with its thick stench. As the wave passed and he settled, feeling the floor under his boots again, he caught a movement out of the corner of his eye and jerked around. There in the open top half of the Dutch door stood the shadowy form of a man poised with arms extended and a hand resting on each side of the casing, his dark face haloed by the bright sunlight outside. A voice spoke, "What the hell are you doing, Adam? This is no time to be lollygagging around playing games. Let's get this job *done!* And *now!*" Then, as quickly as it had materialized, the form vanished from the square of light—and he was back on the hillside once more in a bright, sweet-smelling June day, his father gone, Lamar gone, hands clutching at the earth alongside his faded jeans as, dizzy and disoriented, he fought to brace himself on the suddenly bucking hogback.

Finally, after a time, the tractor tire ceased its wild bouncing against his back, and the fields far below rolled out again in shimmering sheets of green. The cattle settled featherlike onto the pasture and resumed their silent grazing among the flock of swallows. Rocks and trees, houses and barns, anchored themselves back in place, and cars began moving again in silent procession down the blacktop a half-mile away. But everything seemed weightless, insubstantial, and Adam had the fleeting sensation that all the world, everything he saw, had been fashioned from gauze, might be lifted in an instant and carried away by the slightest breeze. And instead of saying to himself, as he knew he should, *I have to stop this now. I must get up and go back to the buildings, finish chores and get my mind off of this craziness,* instead of even asking simply, *What is happening to me? Why am I letting myself dwell on such thoughts?*—which would have told him at least that, despite the mistakes and lies, despite the failures of will and the endless self-recriminations, somewhere down in the morass and muck of Adam Haskins was a man who had lived and breathed and worked and loved, and who might live and breathe and work and love again, a realization that would have offered him a handhold to the world of the living again—he gave himself up to the dark, swirling currents tossing him like driftwood on dim, unfathomable reaches, and felt his strength carried away.

Then, another voice, something like his own, came to him from a distance, the words rising as if buoyed on water.

Nothing lasts, the voice said. And then, *You will never be free.*

Terror shot through him, his skin went cold, and then his whole body felt raw, exposed, as if he had been flayed or his coat of flesh had been turned inside out. Afraid that if he looked down, he would find nothing but a bloody, pulsing tangle of veins, muscles, tendons, jutting bones, he focused instead on the horizon—the green pastures rising to meet the blue sky with its rolling, white clouds. But the ground, so solid beneath his feet for all these years, seemed now to rise and ripple once more, plants, animals, and all lifting gently, then settling again, lifting and settling, lifting and settling, as if an unseen hand were shaking a monstrous, patterned carpet.

For one so long anchored in the certainty of earth, with its inevitable progression of seasons and habitual rhythms of work, in the faith engendered by generations of Haskinses who had gone before him, and in all the unquestioning comfort of friends, family, and community, this vision of even the land's impermanence was overwhelming. Frantic, angry at himself for having let things go this far, he gathered his will and began to search through the shift and scatter of events that made up his life—trying, hope against hope, to locate the thread that would draw the disintegrating fabric back together again, give him the shape of his existence or, at the very least, that one unheralded and unseen moment where, in fifty-three years of floating through life, things had begun to go wrong. If he could find that thread, he thought, or even just that one moment, he might yet reconstitute his hope and save himself, redeeming what were otherwise simply the bare remnants of memory.

But the images that came to him, jumbled and tinged in umber, were of a past and future that seemed simply to speak an inescapable fate. His marriage was a sham, a game that would, he saw now, be played out for a dreary chain of years until Marie abandoned him, fled the country life she found so bleak for the lights and excitement of life in the city, or until the two of them sank into a lonely, stupefying old age among the urine-soaked vacancies over at the Riverview Retirement Community in Harris, winding down their days with other pallid specters and, like them, repeating the same, tired stories to one another to their last breath. His oldest son, his heir, his hope, was already gone, blown to kingdom come in a war so hopeless, so senseless, so unlike the one he himself had fought hanging in the belly of the bomber high in the skies above Germany, that attaching any shred of honor or meaning to his death was inconceivable, a gesture as empty and fragmented as the gutted and dismembered body returned to them from Nam in the flag-draped casket. His youngest son gone, too—God knew where or why—simply disappearing, and taking with him not only Marie's belief in the fortress of love that she had so carefully constructed to protect his happy childhood from the world's ills but also the last vestiges of Adam's own sweet vision of a future in which his boys worked side by side under his own easy, genial tutelage—father and sons together, buying more land, expanding the operation into something that would have surprised and pleased even Harmon, the boys carrying the Haskins name forward into new generations. All these hopes, gone to dust. And finally even the land had conspired with the elements to do him in, the crops drowning, the cows standing udder-deep in mud, holding back their milk, succumbing to footrot, dying of disease. Try as he might, Adam Haskins could not summon a single image that would justify his faith.

And so it was that—sitting high on the hogback on his fifty-third birthday, the noon sun swallowing his shadow, unable to fix on any moment that might exorcise the loneliness and regret that seemed now, as he ranged back over his life, to have always been his silent companions, and seeing that he had lied to himself from his earliest days and had gone on lying until he no longer knew where the real Adam Haskins left off and where Adam Haskins the son, the father, the friend, the husband, the nice-as-they-come neighbor picked up and took over—the ghostly figure calling to him from the shadows for all these weeks finally revealed itself, beckoning him to a decision that he could at last call his own.

He had never really lived, he saw now. Life had simply happened to him. Raised by his parents to believe that he was bred for greatness, bound for glory, he had turned himself over time after time to his father, his mother, his wife, his friends, had bought into their vision of his life, hook, line, and sinker. He had become so good at pleasing, pleasing, pleasing, that if a life-saving moment existed at all (which was doubtful), it lay so mired within him as to be unrecoverable.

Cursing, he rose, and, one hand on the tractor tire for balance, he shook each leg in turn to get the blood back in them, no longer noticing the brilliant day, the sheen across the fields, the silently grazing cows, no longer feeling the dizziness or aching sense of failure and loss. A strange calmness spread through him, and he felt clearheaded for the first moment in as long as he could remember.

It's time, he thought. Time to choose, for once in my life.

He could crawl up onto the tractor seat, start her up, and drive back down the lane to the buildings where his father would be standing in the driveway, hands on hips, waiting to ask where he'd been all morning when there was work to be done, and tell him, plausibly enough, that he'd been out checking the fields, that it was still too wet to plant, that they might as well go ahead with spraying weeds along the fenceline like they'd planned. Then, after driving home to eat with Marie, who was coming back on her dinner break from her town job at the realty because it was his birthday, he would hop in the truck to head over here again, he and his father would set to work, and the whole round of his life would pick up where it had left off without a word about the struggle that had raged in him this morning on the hill.

Or he could make this trip to the top of the ridge his last, make a decision that no one could take away from him, one that would make up for all the times he had failed to choose, where he failed even to see that a choice was sitting right there in front of him. At the thought, he felt the calm settle into his very bones, and it was with more relief than despair, and with something approaching promised redemption, a peculiar rising in the heart, that he turned on his heel, moved to the back of the tractor, and reached up to unbuckle the two leather straps holding the padded shotgun case to the inside of the wide, fan-shaped fender. He hefted the canvas case, set it on end at his feet, and unzipped it. Reaching in, he grabbed the barrel of the shotgun and slid it out, letting the case fall to the ground instead of laying it across the seat, as he usually did in order not to lose it in the tall grass when he was about to shoot a predator wandering through one of his fields. Carrying the gun loosely in his left hand, he made his way around the back tire to the toolbox bolted to the frame alongside the engine just behind the front wheel. He flipped open the metal lid and began pulling out tools—a hammer, a monkey wrench, a pliers, a wire cutter, two screwdrivers—tossing them on the ground at his feet, until at last the box of shells buried at the bottom finally came into view.

"Who will mourn for you?" a voice asked, flat and clean, as he was picking up the box of shells. He pushed the voice away, trying not to listen as he nestled the box against his body in the crook of the arm holding the gun and struggled to open the cover with his free hand. It caught, and as he worked a finger under the edge to pry it loose, the box sprang free as if alive, tumbling into the grass. A dozen shells, dull red plastic with brass ends that gleamed in the sun, fanned out among the scattered tools.

"Damn it!" he spat.

"Who will mourn for you?" the voice asked again.

"No one," Adam said aloud. He bent to pick up a shell that lay by the toe of his work boot.

"No one?" came the voice again, incredulous.

Adam straightened and blew on the shell, turning it between his thumb and forefinger as he examined it for bits of dirt or grass. No time to have the gun misfire. Not now.

"No one," he said.

"Friends?"

"No."

"Family?"

He thumbed the catch and cracked the shotgun open, slipping the shell into the chamber, thinking of Marie and Irene, the two people who loved him most on this earth, who vied over him daily like two kids fighting over a stray pup. Just now, Marie would be sitting in the kitchen at the farmhouse a mile away, two plates on the table mounded with salami-and-cheese sandwiches, chips, and peeled carrots, and she would be reading through a contract for her afternoon closing while she waited, eyes flicking over her shoulder at the clock above the refrigerator, muttering, "Where is that man?" Finally, swallowing her pride, she would rise and scurry to the wall phone at the end of the counter and call her mother-in-law, see if he had forgotten their "date" and had eaten at Irene's table instead of hers. Irene never said anything directly, but her tone invariably conveyed that Marie was neglecting Adam, should never have taken the job in town, should have stayed home to clean the relentless accumulation of dust, plan menus, make sure meals were served on time and hot so her husband could get back out in the fields as quickly as possible. For Marie, a call like that was always galling but today above all, because after he finished milking that night, the two of them were supposed to head into town for Chinese, his favorite, to celebrate his birthday for real, and now she would have to make up an excuse—or lie outright—in order to avoid having to invite Harm and Irene along. " I want you to myself just once," she had told Adam that morning as she headed out to the car. She was sick to death of Harmon's crowing about the farm and sicker still of Irene's incessant gassing, the way she'd go on and on with her misty-eyed remembrances of Baby Adam—interrupting herself every two minutes to grab the handkerchief from her cuff and blow loudly, then lean over, lay a hand on her son's arm and say, in a voice all high and whiny and broken, "I can't *believe* it, fifty-three years gone by. Passed in a *flash*. Such a *good* boy!"—or start in on her song-and-dance about how soft women were today, how they couldn't put up with half of what she'd had to put up with when she was young, as if labor pains were a thing of the past, as if Marie wasn't a real woman because she hadn't given birth to her boys in the back of a goddamn buggy, or some fool thing, like a *real* farm wife.

For Marie, his death would be one more loss in a life of losses—Jake, her mother and father, Jamie. This would be the worst yet, but he had to believe that sooner of later even this wound would heal, become just another scar marking her ability to survive in a world of pain and woe. Her friends, all sharing the bond of daily abandonment by husbands for whom the farm always came first, would offer sympathy, gently nudge her back into the world, urge her to put the past behind her, to set about beginning a new life, and eventually introduce her to eligible men they knew. And she would marry again, no doubt about it. She still had her looks, and when she spotted someone who might give her all the things he couldn't—easy affection, long heart-to-hearts, time together (above all, time)—she would flash the bright smile that had won him over so many years before, turn on that lilting, flirtatious voice of hers. Christ, she'd have the guy down the aisle before he ever knew what hit him, long before she revealed those black thoughts that clouded her mind for days, sometimes weeks on end. And this time, she wouldn't marry a farmer—no goddamn way—maybe a banker, a businessman, somebody with enough money and time to enjoy life and be an acolyte to her intensity. She'd end up being happier by a long shot than she'd ever been with him. Yes, Marie would be fine.

His mother, though, might not survive. After this, she would court her own death as a relief, maybe even as a chance to rejoin her son in the Great Beyond. Like Harmon, she would feel the sharp blow of disgrace that his death would bring upon the family. His father's reaction would be fury at his son for his treachery (which he would take as a personal act of defiance), but his mother's path would lead inward, berating herself for his failure of will. Where could she have gone wrong? How could she have been so blind as to miss the signs of his impending doom? On and on. She'd sit for long hours at the dining room table, weeping over picture after picture of him in the family albums—a chubby baby lying naked on a bearskin run in the living room, a smiling boy bundled in winter clothes in front of a six-foot snow drift next to the chicken house, a proud young man in his Air Force uniform with one foot jauntily perched on the running board of a black Ford, a grinning groom next to a radiant Marie in the receiving line after their wedding, and others, on his first tractor, playing softball at the Fourth of July picnic, grooming his prize cow at the county fair, clumsily holding his new son at the hospital, lying asleep in a hammock in the yard, a hundred more. *"Adam, Adam,"* she would moan to herself, gathering the hem of her housedress to wipe tears spotting the pictures, *"Adam. My son. Happy times. Happy, happy times—and now this!"*

He felt a clenching pang of regret and thought of writing her a note saying it was nobody's fault, what he was doing, that nothing, no one event and no single person, had brought him to this point, no one could have done anything to stop it, and then end by telling her he was sorry, he loved her, and he hoped eventually she could forgive him, see that everyone was better off now that he was out of the way. And then he thought, no, neither his mother nor Marie would never truly comprehend the reasons that he had chosen to end his life. There would be no acceptance. And there could be no forgiveness.

He snapped the barrel shut and flicked the safety off, forcing the images of his wife and mother away. But they were replaced by a parade of other relatives, uncles and aunts, nieces and nephews, cousins, spouses, and kids, all of them passing his closed casket at the funeral, shaking their heads sadly, later murmuring speculations softly to each other out of Marie's hearing at the reception in the church basement afterwards.

"They say it was an accident. Out hunting and—"

"That was no accident. What the hell would he be hunting at this time of year?"

"Rabbits, maybe? He was chasing one and tripped in a gopher hole. Fell and the gun went off."

"Rabbits! With a shotgun? I doubt it. Always used a .22 when I went with him. And why the hell would he be chasing it instead of just drawing bead on the thing and firing?"

"Well, a badger or woodchuck then. It's possible. Spotted the thing from the tractor, grabbed the gun, and slipped as he hopped off."

"Listen. Doc told me he shot himself in the head. Said the whole back of his skull was gone. Biggest mess he come across in all his days. It's why they couldn't have an open casket, you know. I'm tellin' ya, it was no accident."

"But—"

"But, nothin'. Adam Haskins shot himself, sure as hell, and that's that. The question is, why?"

"Ya got me. Who knows why anyone would do something like that?"

Yes, there would be plenty of talk. Folks would feel bad for him. But mourn? Really grieve his passing? Not likely. Later, after the reception, some of them might head into town, descend on the Wide Spot, order shots and beers in his honor, tell a few stories about him, but when the glasses were empty and the stories ran out, when the talk turned to their wives' house projects and their sons' softball teams and the rotten weather and the lousy bankers who wouldn't loan them a red cent to replant their drowned crops, and still later, after they'd drifted out the door, crawled into their pickups, and made their way down the graveled back roads toward home, whatever was left of his life with them would be locked in their private memories, surfacing afterwards in their talk only briefly, if at all.

"None to mourn," he said without passion, and felt a sense of release. Family and friends would all get over his passing. Soon, twenty or thirty or fifty years down the road, no one would be left who would remember, let alone care, how he had lived or died. With no children to carry on his name, he would be lost to the world, his memory relegated to a simple notation on the family tree: *Adam Jefferson Haskins, b. 1921 d. 1974; son of Harmon Ernest and Irene Heilberg Haskins; m. Marie Toddhunter 1948; father of Jacob Adam Haskins, b. 1949, d. 1967, and James Ernest Haskins, b. 1950 (whereabouts unknown).* Eventually, he would disappear into the mists of memory. And it would be better that way. Meanwhile, time would go on, and the land would remain, generation after generation, millennium after millennium, persisting through change upon change—sheathed in moving ice, eventually covered in expansive glacial lakes, then rising and burned to waste before settling once again into broad plains of deep, fertile soil. And perhaps through it all, somewhere on this hill, or what remained of this hill after glaciers and floods and sun and wind had done their fickle work, a part of him not recovered from the spot he fell—a small bit of bone, a hardened swatch of tissue, a miniscule pebble of blood left over from the Adam Haskins who had lived, breathed, spoken, made love, walked on and worked this piece of land—would remain, mixing with the soil and decayed plants, compressed into fossilized rock, rising and falling, rising and falling in the endless rhythm of the ages, marking the spot of his death and never wholly vanishing from this tiny patch of earth in the vastness of the spinning globe.

Setting the butt of the gun on the ground, holding it upright by the barrel, he stopped and lifted his eyes, seeing the landscape all the way to Harris, seven miles distant. He stepped to one side and made an awkward bow toward the fields, as if bidding adieu to an old friend. Then, straightening again, he lifted and resettled the shotgun, shifting it until the butt of the stock was firmly planted on the ground between his feet. Anchoring it with the soles of his work boots, satisfied at last that the shotgun would not slide in the damp earth, he stooped slowly, deliberately, and curled his mouth around the barrel.

The heat in the smooth metal flashed through his lips, surprising him, and he flinched, straightening. Then, he bent once more, gripping the barrel with his teeth this time. He waited, trying to hold perfectly still. The taste of oil and burned gunpowder filled his mouth, and he fought the urge to gag, nausea surging though him. A tremor of fear rippled through his body, and he calmed himself by taking a deep breath and exhaling slowly around the barrel. Marie's face and then those of his sons suddenly rose before him, and afraid of losing his resolve, he pushed them away, imagining himself instead floating lightly and easily on one of the rolling, white clouds high above his head.

He slid his hand down the barrel and along the side of the stock until he touched the trigger guard. His arm fully extended and twitching—whether from fear or the strain of reaching as he hunched over the barrel, he couldn't say—he gingerly ran his fingers along the inner edge of the guard until he found the trigger. He paused, his thumb barely resting on the thin, smooth curve of metal. A band of what seemed like fog or smoke seeped in at the edges of his vision and circled his sight, as if he were slowly being drawn backwards down a long, hazy tunnel. In the receding center, he saw a caterpillar making its lighted, silent way through a tangle of grass. Green drained from the leaves, which turned amber and lost their outlines; and he thought he might pass out. In vain, he tried to remember a prayer, any prayer. All he could think of was, *"Father, forgive me,"* which he began to repeat over and over rhythmically in his mind as his thumb tightened on the trigger. *"Father forgive me father forgive me father forgive—"*

He closed his eyes and gathered himself, expecting at any moment the blast of pain before the descent into blackness.

Suddenly, a muffled voice sounded his name from somewhere in the distance, as if coming to him from a dream.

"Adam!"

He froze, listening.

"Aaa-dam," it came again, the name drawn out, calling from off to his left, down the hill. He wobbled, shaken, rushing suddenly forward toward the light, the smoky, black band enlarging, the circle widening until the band disappeared altogether. The grass at his feet turned green again and the leaves came into focus, outlined, though appearing flat, two-dimensional, and without substance. A wind rose, whooshing in his ears and bringing with it a cacophony of birds and crickets.

"Adam!" Once more, sharply this time, his name echoing in the woods at his back, *adamadamadamadam. . . .*

He yanked his hand away from the trigger and straightened slowly, feeling the muscles in his back ease, the taste of gunpowder still in his mouth. Blinking against the raging light, he spotted his father far down the hill, one hand up on the gate for support, the other raised to the bill of his hat, shading his eyes against the brightness. Adam's knees went weak, and he felt a sudden sinking in his stomach, followed by a flush of heat underneath his skin at being discovered—the shame of a young boy caught playing with himself, pants puddled around his ankles in the haymow.

His father waved, beckoning him to come down—then again more urgently, as if impatient. Defeat swept through him. And anger. "Jesus Christ," he murmured. "He can't even let me do this. Can't even let me die in peace."

Again a wave, arcing widely this time. "Adam, come here!" The echo rolled through the trees—*herehereherehereherehere*—as if taunting him. He turned his back on the distant figure, flipped the safety on the gun, and tossed it into the deep grass alongside the tractor. *That son of a bitch,* he thought. *Why the hell can't he just leave me alone? Jeezus!* He paused, glaring down the long hill, and for long moment the two men studied each other.

"Just go away," Adam said aloud. "Leave me be. For once in your life, just leave me be." And when he saw his father at that moment put his hands on his hips, plant his feet wide, and just stand there, jaw out, staring up the hill as if he had heard him, as if he were saying, *No, I'm not going. I'm staying right here until you get over this foolishness and come on down to start work again*—when he saw that, Adam felt simple anger turn hard and hot. *No,* he thought, *you are not going to take this away from me, too.* All the memories, all the careful reasoning, all the thoughts of the morning jumbled, raced, and gave way to a rage that filled every muscle. The figure was still staring up at him, unmoving. He felt a pain and looked down to see that his hands were balled into fists at his sides, so tight that his knuckles were white, and he forced himself to uncurl them, flexed his fingers. *Look what he does to me,* he thought, staring at the two red and ragged rows of nail marks across the palms. *Never be free. Never. What the hell kind of life is that?* He shook his head. *None at all. Something has to happen something needs to change I can't go on not like this,* and with that thought a decision was made, one that rose from somewhere deep within him, and he knew what he had to do.

Later, Harmon would try many times, with many people, to give an account of what happened next. But, of course, he had a vested interest in shaping events to his own purposes, which everyone knew were bound up with putting the best face on things, so his story could not really be trusted. Those who admired him took what he had to tell them at face value, shook their heads, maybe went so far as to lay a hand on Harmon's shoulder, saying, "Awful, Harm. Just awful. What a shame. Sympathies to you and Irene." Those who saw him as distant, arrogant, who maybe even feared him a little because they had heard the stories about how he'd dressed down people like Lamar Barnes when they stood in the way of his plans, were less willing to buy Harmon's version of things, and in the weeks after, when they huddled in the grain elevator or ran into each other in the aisle of the hardware store or sat on stools over coffee down at Dot's Polka Cafe, they immediately went to speculating on how Adam could have done what he did. It made no sense. In the end, people accepted whatever story let them sleep at night, believed what they wanted to believe—which is what happens when a neighbor or a friend or a relative does something you just can't figure.

Aware that if he hesitates, if he thinks another thought, the moment might be lost, Adam jerks around to the tractor, plants a foot on the drawbar, and grabs the fender, pulling himself up onto the seat. *No getting around it*, he thinks, *it's him or me.* He bends forward to twist the key, straightens, yanks the throttle lever halfway down, and jams the flat of his sole against the starter button on the dash. The Massey springs to life with a roar, a thrust of black smoke shooting from the exhaust pipe, lifting and pluming. He punches the clutch and shifts into gear, his neck snapping as the tractor lurches forward, *it's my life my life it's him or me him or me . . .* dropping the clutch, the tires catching in the soft earth . . . *nothing to be done can't go on like this . . .* spinning the wheel right in a tight turn, then popping the clutch and shifting into second, the engine breathing, racing momentarily before dragging down again, heading farther up the hill . . . *just can't do this anymore just not worth it never be free . . .* lifting the throttle, jamming the clutch again and wrestling the beast into third, dropping the clutch and yanking the throttle open again, the smell of exhaust thick in his nostrils as the engine strains, smoking pushing upward from the roaring muffler...*won't do it can't do it him or me . . .* finally shifting one last time, into fourth, road gear, picking up speed, moving fast now over the rough ground, Adam jouncing, flung this way and that in the seat as the tractor's front wheels, small under the engine's bulk, dip into hidden ruts, slip over gopher mounds, buck and leap into the air as they strike rocks nestled in the grass, the tractor heading directly across the top of the hogback, then taking another right and gaining even more speed on the gentle downward slide toward the long, bulging rib running across the verge that signals the final drop down a steep, eighty-yard run ending at the gate to the lane.

Reaching that rib of earth, Adam does not stop to study the path down, for there is no path, no double tracks from tractor tires and wagons, not even the wavering single path usually worn by the hooves of cattle three feet inside fencelines, just a steep fall of grass littered with rocks and scarred by erosion. He does not throttle back and brake to a halt to listen for songbirds in the woods, as he has done on so many other of his thousand visits to this hilltop. He does not pause to gaze one last time at the banded fields stretching out before him in the distance, at the cattle grazing lazily far off in the pasture, at the play of green earth against that blue, blue sky painted with rolling, white clouds. Already released from earth, from sky, from all he has loved for fifty-three years, he does not even feel the breeze against his face, a breeze that washes over him and through him, taking with it all thought, all words, all memory, all awareness of this world save for the thin, wavering figure of a man at the bottom of the hill, small and silent, his father, with a hand raised now as if in greeting, or perhaps realizing finally that the tractor is not stopping, lifted in a last attempt to halt his son's foolish rush down the hill.

No, Adam does not hesitate, does not heed Harmon's shout, "Stop! Slow down! Stop, for God's sake!" does not hear anything at all, the incessant voice clamoring in his ears so clearly all morning silent at last, even the rolling groan of the engine swallowed by that imperturbable silence.

And then he is over the rib of earth.

The jutting edge of the hogback recedes behind him, and the tractor picks up more speed, moving impossibly fast, the engine idling back as the huge rear wheels spin freely now and press the grass flat in two rapidly lengthening tracks behind him, the lurching machine racing down, down, front tires striking rocks and washes that lift the heavy front end free from the ground momentarily, the engine suddenly light, flying, before the wheels descend to earth again, bouncing once, twice, then plunge toward the next rock, the next rut, and Adam, hands gripping the smooth, black steering wheel, yanking it this way and that, finds himself fighting to keep to a line of light that has suddenly appeared in the grass, a line extending straight and true from the tractor's nose directly to a brilliant pool of even brighter light, in the middle of which stands a figure no longer recognizable, unmoving. Blackness rushes in at the edges of his vision again, narrowing to a tractor's width, and he is passing now down the center of a long tunnel framing that pool of light and the dark, faceless figure in the distance.

Then, suddenly, though he still has the sensation of movement, of gliding rapidly forward, the pool of light, the dark figure, and the tunnel itself all vanish for an instant, and in that brief crack in time, the moment blooms silently, his vision refocusing, and he sees Marie, not the worry-worn Marie of the last few years but the young Marie, the beautiful Marie, the laughing, carefree Marie of their first days together as husband and wife, and she is sitting facing him on the long, red hood of the tractor, naked, knees gripping the sides, hands draped outward in mid-air for balance, like a circus trick rider, her long, black hair whipping over her shoulders, her face, her leaping breasts, and she is smiling a strange, enigmatic smile, the almost mischievous smile that he remembers from the old days, the days before all their troubles set in, when they were playful and free and together, the two of them against the world. The tractor bucks and she is nearly launched from her seat, arms pinwheeling over her head as she struggles to right herself, and she regains her balance on the slick, red hood with hands still outstretched, floating gently in the air, and she throws her head back, face to the sky, laughing a high, joyful laugh at her feat of daring, Lady Godiva on Twister the Killer Horse, never ridden, never broke, leaving all other riders heaped in the dust at the chute's mouth, until today when, step right up and see for yourself, Marie Haskins, née Toddhunter, the young Indian half-blood, works her magic on the untamed beast, barebacked and bareassed no less, who woulda believed it?

Suddenly, the tunnel with its line of light reaching to the distant, dark figure appears again, but the far end rising now, lifting slowly, the tunnel leveling so that Adam has the sensation not of silent, violent struggle to keep the tractor straight on his headlong rush downhill but rather of being swept cleanly, swiftly, effortlessly forward on smooth, level ground, Twister tamed again, still moving rapidly but easily now, racing light and free across the land, and Marie, hair still whipping, breasts still jockeying, brings her gaze down from the sky, the clouds, her eyes catching Adam's as if she has just seen him for the first time, and a surprised, puzzled expression comes over her features, then turns to the hurt, abandoned look she wears so often these days, the look of a beaten puppy, and she mouths two words that he hears as if her voice were his own—*"Why, Adam?"*—and, of course, he has no answer, no explanation for why he is doing what he is doing, though he would if he could, wants desperately to tell her, wants her to understand everything, flooded now with helpless love, and would tell her if only he could remember the words, and he would reach out to her, too, lay his rough, callused hand on that smooth, white shoulder once more, one last time, if he could wrench his grip free from the twisting wheel; but he can't, and so he says the only thing he can manage, his voice high and plaintive but clear and unmistakably his own, "Marie! My Marie!"

The sound of his voice breaks the silence, the crack closes, the circle of light gone, the tunnel gone, Marie gone, vanishing just like that, and instead of the tunnel, a world bright and green, incredibly green, unfurls before him, a world wide and dizzying that nearly sends him swooning; and suddenly he is aware of flying down the scarred hill, being thrown violently on the metal seat, shaken this way and that as if gripped in the jaws of some huge, angry beast, and when the leap and lurch eases for just a moment, he blinks and sees that this is no dream, that he is on his tractor and somehow he has made it nearly to the bottom of the sidehill, the long stretch that no one has ever dared take a tractor up or down before—*too steep, way too steep, why is he doing this?*—and that he is headed directly at his father, not fifty feet away now, his father inexplicably moving not to safety but right toward him through the long grass, hobbling forward on his stiff, old-man legs and shouting something Adam can't make out, something inaudible beneath the persistent moan of the exhaust pipe, the aperture between them narrowing rapidly and both of his father's hands stretched out in front of him, downturned palms settling and rising and settling again—*Slow down! Slow down!*—rising and settling, the hobbling man and the rushing tractor both closing on the only blemish in the field's smooth grassy run, a soft depression in the earth right at the bottom where the land starts to ease back level again, a sinkhole created by rainwater flowing down hidden runnels and narrow gullies to this lowest of the low spots and sliding over a two-foot drop to form a ragged circle of mud eight feet across, with a round, dark boulder planted smack in the middle. But Adam does not see the sinkhole or the boulder, what he sees is his father's wide-brimmed straw hat suddenly plucked from his head by the wind, lifting away as if by magic and landing out of sight in the grass as the old man stumbles, catches himself, hitching and hobbling forward, still gesturing, Adam close enough now to see Harmon's flushed face, cheeks working as he struggles for breath and running his limping, old-man run toward the nose of the tractor, and Adam, who has not even been aware of steering but rather of simply being carried along toward whatever awaits him, sees a desperation on that face like none he has ever seen before, a look that he might have mistaken for anger if not for how pitiful and small and halting that figure appears as it moves toward the speeding tractor—*what is he doing? what is happening?*—and in a flash he sees that the grille will strike his father, the front wheels will smash him into the earth, pass over his father's helpless, flailing body; and remorse and terror explode through him, jolting him forward on the seat, the figure limping closer, the gap narrowing, and Adam jams his boot onto the twin brake pedals and muscles the wheel right, trying at the last moment to stop, shouting at the top of his lungs, "Dad! Watch out!", the brakes locking up, setting the high back wheels sliding, scarring the soft earth, the narrow front wheels catching in the grass and the steering wheel yanking, pulling, alive and straining in his hands, the tractor and the hobbling figure separated only by the circle of mud now—when suddenly Adam's boot slips off the left pedal and the right wheel still locked but the left spinning freely sends the tractor's front end squirming hard to the side, Harmon pulling to a stop, standing there, eyes wide, as the Massey looms, still rushing forward and slipstreaming toward him on the soft earth, then at the last second throwing himself off to the side, rolling, rolling, to get out of the way, Adam lifting his foot from the brake, turning the steering wheel into the slide, struggling to get the huge machine straight, the tractor heavy again, no longer the light, flying bronco, the spinning of the big back tires slowing a bit, the front end starting to come around, and Adam, in a flash, thinking he's got it made—*yes, yes, it's coming*—Harmon raising his face from the tall grass in time to see the tractor slide sideways past him over the drop-off into the sinkhole, spraying mud, rocking, but staying upright, and, yes, it looks like he's made it, his son has done it, he's home free—when, suddenly, the side of the big back wheel strikes the boulder, and Adam is torn from the seat, launched into the air, arms extended like a diver as he sails over the mudhole doing a slow somersault, almost gracefully, as if he's planned it all, every move, then plunges to earth again, landing awkwardly and heavily on his back, bouncing and rolling and rolling, finally stopping face-down in the grass. And Harmon watches as the tractor's upside wheel, still spinning, lifts from the ground, the tractor tipping, rolling over the boulder, through the mudhole, back onto the grass—and, upside-down, over Adam, the steering wheel striking him—*but just the steering wheel, nothing else, thank God!*—then the Massey turning and righting itself momentarily before going all the way over again, breaking through the fence along the lane, and finally coming to rest on its side with a great, heaving crash. A momentary, unbearable silence, a brief, violent tremor in the grass where his son lies. Then, hissing as white steam billows from the radiator, a pause, and leaking fuel ignites, hungry flames sucking softly at the air. Another pause, then suddenly the gas tank explodes, booming, shaking the earth, and black smoke shoots upward, mixing with the white steam in the clear, clean sky.

Harmon pulls himself up and rushes around the sinkhole. *Medic! Medic!* Reaching Adam's side—*Get an ambulance! Too far from town! No time!*—his son still now, face half buried in the soft earth—*Too far to the house. Can't make it in time. Too old!*—he goes down on one knee, gently touches fingertips to the warm skin at the side of his son's throat, feeling for the jugular, searching for a pulse—though he already knows from the terrible crease just at the base of the neck, the awkward angle of the head, twisted to the left, and the eyes wide, disbelieving, as if Adam were peering over his shoulder at a fearsome pursuer, that his son is dead. *No use. Lord!* The air goes heavy, and an awful stillness settles all around, broken only by the lapping flames. He lowers his head and lays a hand lightly on his son's back, whispering, "Oh, Adam."

Slowly, the world returns, crickets in the grass, birds singing in the grove, the low bellow of a cow in the pasture, and Harmon feels a sudden and horrible emptiness, unlike anything he has ever felt, even in the war where death was a constant companion. Horror and emptiness and disbelief. This can't have happened. Not to Adam. This is his son, flesh of his flesh, his hope and his pride. The son who's been at his side for fifty-three years, who did every last thing that was asked of him, who just a minute ago was alive, whose skin is still warm to the touch. "Oh, Adam," he says again, and though he has not cried in years, the tears rise. "Adam. Adam." Not dead. Not now. That's not the way it's supposed to be, a son going before his father. And he knows that from this moment, for him and for the Haskins world he has worked all his days to create, nothing will ever be the same, that his own life has just ended with that of his son, lying vacant-eyed and broken in the grass.

After a time, his tears settle into the first depths of the grief he will carry forever after, and he rises, turning toward the lane for the long, agonizing walk back to the house—the house where Irene will be waiting at the kitchen table for the two of them to come in so she can serve the noon meal, then bring out the surprise birthday cake she has spent the morning making. Oh, what will he say to her? How can he possibly tell her what has happened to their son, that Adam will not be coming in for cake, not today or any other day, that he is just now lying face-down out in the field, that one moment he was alive and now he is dead, and oh, Irene, I am sorry, so sorry, and I can't think of any way to tell you except to say it out. No, Irene, no use to call the paramedics. Too late. Sit down, Irene, sit down, yes, it's true, God help us, it's true. Our son is dead.

At last he passes through the cowyard gate, walking quickly now, just wanting the next hour to be over, wanting to get through this part so he can be alone with his own pain and begin to move on, begin to think what to do now. For a moment, he finds himself fighting back tears again. This time, his grief is mixed with anger—at fate, at God, at Adam himself for what he has done. He had raised that boy in his own image, taught him everything he knew, all the lessons that a man had to learn in order to make his way and make his mark. How could a son of his do something so foolish, so utterly incomprehensible? In the end, the boy had become a man, had learned every lesson well—except one, the most important lesson of all, how to live in this world.

By the time Harmon rounds the buildings and crosses the driveway, heading for the house, he has fought off his anger and his tears, and though the incredible weight of sadness, and the dread of walking through the door and telling his wife, is still with him, he struggles through scattered and grief-laden thoughts, his son's vacant eyes swimming before him, toward what must happen now in order to go on with living. Climbing the back steps, he stomps his boots on the cement to rid them of the mud and a moment later hears Irene's voice coming through the screen door, calling, "Harmon? Adam? That you finally?" He sees her shadowy form rise from the table and walk toward the door, but as he grips the handle, he pauses, thinking suddenly of his grandson. And an ember of hope flickers to life.

Irene's face swims toward the screen, smiling. "Are those my hungry, hardworking men come home at last?" she asks. "How's my birthday boy?"—cocking her head right and left behind the door as she searches the yard for their son.

Yes, his grandson. Jamie. He has to find Jamie.

Harmon swings the door open and steps inside. "Sit down, Irene," he says. "I have something to tell you."

LILA S. NAGARAJAN

The Healer
from *Indian Summer*

At 6:40 in the morning Dhanushini realized that she would be alone for the next half hour. Her son, Sanjay and daughter-in-law, Sandra had slipped out of the house without telling anyone where they were going. They left five minutes after her husband, Sivaji, drove away in his car for a morning of golf. The servants were cleaning up after breakfast. The man who sold hot, fresh buns from the wooden box on his bicycle had come and gone, so she decided to walk a little before the nurse from the hospital came to administer her two insulin shots. She took the new silver- plated hand basket she had bought at the Kurinji Missionary Co-op sale, wrapped a maroon shawl around her shoulders, and walked into the crisp morning.

Deeply breathing in the sweet morning air she hummed along with the birds singing from the fruit trees in her garden. Her father-in-law, a planter in every pore of his body, designed the garden, using the ancient technique of terrace farming. Sivaji had explained to her many years ago - when they were still newlyweds, that this type of farming slowed down the process of erosion. "This," he said to her, "is most important when you are farming in the mountains." At the time, the garden was still in its period of formation. Looking at the luxuriant garden that grew in front of her now, Dhanushini knew that her father-in-law had built the place with the vision only a farmer could dream up. There were three long terraces, each supported with walls made from granite slabs. The first step was filled with flowers. Dhanushini noticed raindrops balanced on red and yellow rose petals, and on the leaves of poppies and chrysanthemums. The second level held a lone struggling coffee bush surrounded by luscious plum and peach trees. On the bottom tier, her father-in-law planted pear and crab apple trees, which, thirty years later stood tall and strong. All of it was still slightly hidden behind a thin layer of fog that was bound to get thicker if the rain held back.

She would collect jasmine flowers in her basket for the *pooja* after her bath. It would rain again before the hour was through, and even as she thought this, Dhanushini felt the wind pick up bits of leaves and flower petals around her sandaled feet. She moved faster down the stairs that lead into the garden, not taking her usual care. The two jasmine bushes grew tall and wide at the very bottom of the steps. She planted them there after both of her in-law's had passed away. Her original plan was to make them into an arch, but no matter what she tried the bushes grew to a design of their own. Their beautiful cloak of white petal-flowers smelled wonderful and whenever a breeze blew over them at just the right angle the scent would saturate her house.

One minute everything was as it should be. She was smiling to herself, humming a piece of an old Tamil song. Then, somewhere between the chirp of a bird and the fourth step Dhanushini found herself tipped over and rolling. She reached out with her spare hand, still clutching her new basket to her chest, and struggled, without success to get hold of a step and stop her slow tumble. Eventually, Dhanushini lay flat on her back at the bottom of the steps, her head only inches from the fragrant jasmine bushes. At some point Dhanushini felt something snap and rip in her left leg. The pain shot through her leg and stung the tender spot behind her eye.

She lay there stunned for a moment and then yelled out. She knew no one would hear her, the servants were too far away and no one else was home. She felt herself choking on panic. Tears filled her eyes. She felt completely useless, something she was unaccustomed to. She pressed her palms into the concrete under her hips, and ignoring the gravel biting into her soft skin, pushed herself up. The scream that burst into the air from her throat shocked Dhanushini, her leg felt as though it was being torn from her body. *Someone must have heard that!* she thought, and waited for the sound of footsteps. On her back again, feeling the cold, wet ground under her, Dhanushini counted to fifty before accepting that no one heard her. She took deep, long breaths, the kind that is supposed to hold your hand through childbirth and other traumatic experiences. She watched the sun poke up over the wall that separated their house from the missionaries that lived next door. Then she did the only thing she could think of. She prayed.

Dhanushini prayed that she would not freeze to death and that one of the servants would need something soon and come looking for her. She prayed that her leg was not broken, or her back, or even a finger. She prayed that she would not have to go to a doctor because she hated doctors. She asked God to forgive her hatred of doctors, and to bless the one that she would have to go and see. She prayed for her husband, and her children, and her mother, and for the spirits of her father and grandmother. She prayed that the rains would be good this year and the coffee crop would make them all rich. She was asking God to forgive her greed when she saw the slow, white, uniform-clad body of the nurse pant up the driveway.

"Sister!" Dhanushini yelled with all the voice she had left. She could not see which nurse it was from this distance. "Sister! Please come and help me."

Later the nurse would tell others in the hospital that even under such dire circumstances her patient conducted herself no less than a well-mannered lady. Dhanushini was known everywhere for her grace. A true lady, they said, someone to look up to.

At that moment Dhanushini did not feel at all graceful, only relieved beyond words to see the nurse turn in her direction, and then run, swinging her little black doctor's bag at her side.

"Madam! What has happened? Did you take a fall?" the nurse questioned as she knelt down next to Dhanushini. Not waiting for the obvious reply, she continued, "Where does it pain?"

Dhanushini tried to lift her neck to look at the woman, who she now recognized as Sister Nirmala, but the movement sent new waves of agony through her, so she surrendered to her helplessness and said, "Thank you, Sister. The pain is in my left side hip."

"*Chee*, this is not good for you, Madam. We must get a stretcher. Are you cold?" Sister Nirmala asked, standing again.

"Only a little cold. The earth is still wet." Dhanushini was nervous again. Where would they get a stretcher? How long would she have to wait? She looked at the overcast sky, and realized for the first time that Mother Nature had quieted down in preparation for another storm.

"You wait here five minutes more." The nurse said, "I will get blankets for you, and we will make one stretcher. The boys are here, no?" She meant the servant boys. "You don't worry, Madam. Soon you will be inside." And then she left, carrying her bag full of cotton balls and syringes and small fat bottles of Dhanushini's insulin.

Dhanushini prayed out the next ten minutes as she waited. She thanked God for sending the nurse, and such a smart one at that, and she thanked God that she had not given the servants the day off. She promised God that if her leg was not broken and she would not have to see a doctor, then she would be a better mother and wife and lady of the house than she already was. She would build a small shrine for all the Hindu gods and make the whole family worship.

Eventually Sister Nirmala and two servants came back with a stretcher made with her husband's walking sticks and a pile of blankets. Dhanushini worried as soon as she saw the walking sticks. They had belonged to her father-in-law and were the only things of his left in the house. Sivaji had burned everything else days after his father died.

The walking sticks were taller than she; used to climb steep mountain paths, and beat off wild dogs, wild boar, and once in a while, a wayward servant.

"Be careful with those sticks! Don't let them get scratched." Dhanushini warned, trying to see how they had attached the blanket. She hoped they had not used nails.

"They are already scratched, *Akka,*" one of the servants said as he stood off to the side waiting for instructions from the nurse.

Sister Nirmala wrapped Dhanushini's body within the thick woolen blankets. "You were not honest, Madam. Your body is cold like an ice case."

"It is no bother, Sister." Dhanushini clenched her fists waiting for another rocket of hot pain as the nurse slid an edge of the blanket under her.

There was no pain. Dhanushini wondered whether God had answered her prayers or if the part of her brain that processed pain had simply shut down.

"Ready? I will say 'ready, steady, go'. When I say 'go,' you must stiffen your body, Madam, like a cutting board. You boys, when I say 'go' you must quickly lift Madam and put her on the stretcher. Put it flat on the ground now. Ramu, you will lift Madam by the shoulders, and Pandi, you lift her at the knees. I will hold her hip. You must be one hundred percent careful not to jolt Madam in any direction." The nurse shot out orders like a police commander and the boys unconsciously straightened their shoulders and backs at attention waiting for "GO!"

Dhanushini's heart pounded in her head.

"Ready!" The nurse's voice snapped through the chilly air.

"Steady!" Dhanushini closed her eyes and gritted her teeth. It was going to hurt no matter how stiff a board she made herself.

"GO!" Dhanushini tensed her entire body and screamed out as her muscles tightened. Ramu and Pandi moved into action, lifting and placing her onto their homemade stretcher.

Dhanushini did not hear the nurse say, "You are fine, Madam. You are fine and soon the doctor will be here." She did not feel Ramu and Pandi struggle to lift her off the ground and carry her, without jolts or rolls, up the garden steps and into her room.

She did not regain consciousness until the doctor clapped his hands rudely and loudly in her face and yelled, "Come now, Madam! Rise and shine! This is no time to be sleeping!"

Almost a month after the accident, Dhanushini was still lying flat on her back, and her right leg was wound and packed tightly into a thick plaster cast. Sandra walked into Dhanushini's room, and seated herself on a hard wooden stool next to her mother-in-law's twin-sized bed. Three overstuffed pillows held Dhanushini's leg up, and her whole body stayed warm under the thick *kumbli* blankets that made Sandra's skin crawl. The blankets were made of rough wool dyed black and maroon; Sandra would rather freeze to death than cover herself with one of those things. She did not understand how her mother-in-law could stand it. An old metal heater sat on a desk on the other side of the bed closer to the window. Every hour or so a maid would come to the room to switch the position of the heater so Dhanushini could be warmed on both her right and left sides. The heat buzzed and chattered through red and orange glowing coils.

Even with the blankets and the heater on, Dhanushini was still cold. The bedroom windows shook and it sounded like the wind had picked up pieces of tile between long, bony fingers to drag across the roof. No one even paid attention to the rain or the wind anymore. It was as though it did not even exist. Like Sanjay said, during the monsoon season, you just got used to it.

Dhanushini's foot itched and almost threw her into a fit of crying. She could not ask Sandra to touch her feet, and all the servants had been sent out on errands. It did not occur to her that the American girl probably did not have a problem touching her mother-in-law's feet. Dhanushini tried shifting her weight just enough to move the blanket back and forth over the itch. This provided mild relief, but not nearly enough. She tried moving her leg, but the cast was far too heavy. She felt like a caterpillar trying to grow inside a cocoon, all tight and pressed together. But she knew that when this cast was removed, she would not emerge from it like a butterfly with colorful wings, but with a shriveled leg that may never move right again.

"Sandra," she finally said apologetically. "Please give me a shawl."

Sandra jumped to her feet, thankful to have something to do, a chore to occupy the space of silent air that quivered between them. The silent, thick, hot, air. It surprised her that the small heater could produce so much discomfort. She had to consciously ignore the smells and temperature in the room.

"You're still cold, *Athai*?" She walked across the room to the wall closet and opened it. All three hundred and fifteen of Dhanushini's saris made neat colorful stacks on each of the top shelves. Weeks ago, on a rainy day, Dhanushini had pulled them all out and told Sandra where each one was from, who gave it to her, when, and why. It seemed as though Dhanushini chronicled the length and depth of her life with these saris. On the bottom shelf there were shawls and cardigans. Sandra chose a soft cream shawl with a border of embroidered pastel flowers.

"This one is very nice." She said, making her way over to Dhanushini again.

"Mrs. Sampathi gave it to me. 20th wedding anniversary." Dhanushini said.

Sandra rubbed it against her cheek. Her in-laws had been married for twenty-six years now. Their anniversary parties were always a much-anticipated event in the town, people looked forward to the date all year. Sandra wondered if she and Sanjay would last as long, or if she would die of a gastritis attack first. Twenty-six years seemed like a long time. She draped the shawl over Dhanushini's chest and then leaned over her, smelling the three-day-old coconut oil in her mother-in-law's hair. She held her breath. She knew that Sanjay would pitch a fit if he saw her lifting his mother. He constantly worried about the baby. They had not told anyone the news yet, that they were going to have a baby. Sanjay acted like the baby would pop right out of Sandra if she so much as squatted to tie her shoelaces.

Sandra slid her right arm under Dhanushini's shoulders, the way the nurses had shown her, and lifted her in an embrace. The movement comforted both women. Sandra realized that it had been over a year since she had hugged anyone other than Sanjay. A woman's body was so much softer. Dhanushini could not remember the last time she had been given a hug. Sandra held her mother-in-law a moment longer than necessary, and then gently laid her back on the bed. Both women felt that something had changed for a moment or two, that they had not only crossed the physical space that separated them, but momentarily closed the emotional gap.

The pillow under Dhanushini's head shifted, and a skinny magazine slid out from under it onto the floor. Sandra bent to pick it up. The cover had a picture of a beautiful man surrounded by bright orange flames. Above his head were the words, SPIRITUAL AND PHYSICAL HEALING FOR ALL.

Dhanushini watched Sandra's face, and when she could not read anything on it, said, "You read to me please. Nurse gave it to me. This man make magic with prayer. Maybe he help me."

Sandra was confused, but sat back on her stool and opened the magazine. She read a paragraph and then broke the sentences down so Dhanushini could understand better. Then she read another. This went on until she had read all eighteen pages. The beautiful man was a healer, a traveling healer spreading his magic in Kurinji. Most healers, Sandra knew, worked through a certain faith. There was that one guy who lived in a mansion down the road, who healed through the prayers of St. Francis of Assisi. Then there was that maroon-robed monk whose black beard reached his knees; he whispered blessings from the Bhagavat Gita, and then the woman who always wore a blinding yellow sari and carried a staff with the head of a cobra growing out of it; she called on the powers of Goddess Kali. This healer was different, the magazine said, because he employed the powers of all the gods and goddesses. It all depended on the ailment and the person. Sometimes, he invoked the guiding grace of Lord Brahma, and other times he requested that Jesus Christ step in and lend a helping hand. He believed in the rituals of Rastafarians, and danced religiously to the words and music of Bob Marley. If the patient was dehydrated, The Healer begged Allah to guide the patient to that place where everything is green and lush, where water runs in abundance.

Though this healer intrigued Sandra, she knew he must be a fake. How could a mere human being simply touch a person or sing to them or blow the sacred breath of God from their lips and make everything okay? She glanced at Dhanushini who was smiling for the first time since her fall. Sandra did not have the heart to tell her mother-in-law what she thought. It was obvious that Dhanushini had found a way out of her bedridden state.

"We ask him to come here, Sandra! Maybe he will help me." Dhanushini sounded hopeful.

Sandra shrugged her shoulders and said, "I don't think *Maama* or Sanjay will agree, *Athai*."

Dhanushini made a *psh* sound between her teeth. "We will call him when they play golf."

He was taller than Sivaji by two heads, and taller than the youngest apple tree in the garden by one. He was so tall the top of his white turban skimmed the doorframe as he entered Dhanushini's room closely followed by Sandra and the nurse. He wore a white *kurta* that had silver buttons near the collar, and white rubber *chappals* on his feet. His fingers seemed to float like a stream through the air towards Dhanushini as he said, "*Vanakam, Amma*. Are you ready to be healed today?"

His voice was deep and fluid, like water rumbling over and around rocks at the bottom of a riverbed. All three women shivered at the beauty of The Healer. His skin glowed dark brown like the bark of tamarind trees and his eyes glittered like slices of onyx. His eyelashes blinked like the wings of a butterfly, and when he smiled, the nurse almost fell to her knees and wept.

Emptying the white cotton shoulder bag The Healer got right to work. He pulled out a bottle of rosewater, a rosary of sandalwood beads, and a leather-bound Bible, all of which he slipped under Dhanushini's head. He dragged the wooden stool to the foot of the bed and sat across from his patient's bare feet. He reached out and took hold of them.

When The Healer pressed the soles of Dhanushini's feet to his forehead the two Indian women gasped; this was unheard of, an action saved for the worship of gods alone. Dhanushini tried to jerk her feet out of The Healer's grasp, but he only pressed her feet to his head more firmly. He was using his invisible third eye to locate the source of Dhanushini's pain. He absorbed her pulse and her energy, and then he placed her feet back onto the pillow.

"Your cast is useless," he said without any kind of accent at all.

All three women said, "Pardon?"

"The break," The Healer explained while walking around to the right side of the bed, is in the upper thigh." He slid two long, slender fingers into the top of the cast, noting its thickness. "This cast is causing damage. It must be removed." He tapped the top of the cast with his knuckles and it sounded like he was knocking on a door.

"Bring me a small saw," he finally said.

The women stiffened.

"A saw?" Sandra questioned out loud. "What do you need a saw for?"

Dhanushini had visions of her entire leg being amputated and began to cry quietly to herself. The Healer laughed, hearing Dhanushini's thoughts in his own head. He patted her shoulder and said, "Don't worry yourself with such fears. This is a thick cast. A mere knife will not do the job."

A slow redness crept up Dhanushini's neck, embarrassed that he had heard her fears. But now she also knew that she could trust him, so she waived her hand towards the door and asked the nurse to get a saw from the gardener.

It took The Healer half an hour to free Dhanushini's leg of the plaster. She felt a thousand kilos lighter, like an anchor had been removed from her being, and she was now free to float up to the ceiling like a balloon.

The Healer had a way of knowing which gods were good for each ailment. He also sensed which therapy to use for each individual. In order for Dhanushini to wake up the next morning and walk with no pain or limp, The Healer would pray to Jesus. And as he prayed, he would massage her feet, starting with the center of her soles.

He sat on the stool at the foot of the bed again. Sandra and the nurse stood on either side of Dhanushini, who closed her eyes. The Healer folded the sleeves of his kurta up to the elbows, exposing even more of his dark tamarind skin. Sandra could see his muscles ripple like ribbons every time he flexed his fingers in preparation. He started with Dhanushini's left foot, taking it in both of his hands, and used his thumbs to press into the center. Dhanushini felt the deepest pleasure, ever, move through her leg, hips, chest. It moved right into her head in waves of hot pinks and oranges and red the color of hibiscus blooms. She smiled unconsciously, controlling herself from arching her back and moaning from the sensation. The Healer sang The Lord's Prayer with a deep, strong voice. They did not know it in the room, but the rain had stopped, and the wind held itself still mid-gust. The birds that normally burst into chatter the moment a storm ceased remained quiet. As he sang, he massaged Dhanushini's left foot with the shapes of trees and six-petal flowers, peacock feathers, and the claw of a tiger. Finally, he traced an eighteen-petal lotus at the center point of her sole with his fingertip, blew the breath of God onto it to ensure long-lasting health, and sang "Amen." He did the same for her right foot, though more gently.

The compound of Kavimalar sat under a spell for the duration of the song. Nothing moved except for the hands and lips of The Healer. The servants were frozen, squatting on their haunches in front of cooking fires, birds perched on tree branches like wooden carvings, and ladybugs looked like rubies fastened to blades of grass. Sandra and the nurse stood straight backed in rapture of The Healer's voice.

Dhanushini had not stopped smiling.

It wasn't until The Healer sang his final Amen that things began to move again. Sandra wiped tears from her eyes and hoped that the baby she was carrying had heard the prayer, too.

When the healing was over, The Healer said, "Today you get rest. Tonight have sweetest dreams. In the morning, jump out of bed like a spring chicken and go for a jog around the lake."

The women were speechless as they helped him gather the bottle of rosewater and the rosary, and gave him back his bag. He decided to leave his Bible for Dhanushini. The women pressed their palms together in respect and watched him float out of the room, dipping his head as he passed through the doorway.

Once outside, The Healer pulled out a Goldflake cigarette from his bag, lit it, and inhaled great lung-fulls of the wonderfully bitter smoke. He was only human after all.

All seemed to have returned to normal by the time Sivaji and Sanjay returned from their golf tournament. The saw was back in the garden, and the cast disposed of. Sandra had put the Bible under a blue cardigan in the wall closet, and the servants were working in the kitchen preparing dinner.

But Sivaji knew better. Although he could not put his finger on it, he sensed that something was just a little off-beat. If he had just asked any of the ladies in the house, they could have explained to him that nothing was wrong – everything was perfect. Miraculously perfect. But he did not ask, and they did not tell. Sivaji watched them through slanted eyes all evening as they whispered secrets to one another.

The next morning Dhanushini woke up at four o'clock. She did not jump out of bed like a spring chicken, but continued to lie in bed. When exactly was morning? Any time after midnight, or only once the sun had risen? Would she be able to walk if she tried now, or was it too early?

She heard a soft knock on the door and turned her head to see Sandra enter the room.

The walls and floor glowed red from the heater. The curtains were open; it was still very dark outside, though the wind had settled down sometime during the night. Dhanushini already had her glasses on. She was ready for the day to begin. Sandra was too.

"I couldn't sleep," she told her mother-in-law. "It's technically morning, *Athai*. Should we try?"

Dhanushini was unsure. What if it did not work? What if The Healer was nothing more than a beautiful cow herder out to make an easy eight-hundred Rupees? She pushed herself into a sitting position, determined to ignore those kinds of thoughts. She allowed Sandra to support her by the arm and shoulder while she carefully moved her legs over the side of the bed. Dhanushini expected pain when she moved her right leg, the stabbing pain she had experienced less than twenty-four hours ago. But she did not feel any discomfort.

Slowly, Dhanushini touched her feet to the cold floor and then sat motionless for a minute.

Sandra held on to her mother-in-law's arm for dear life. She was terrified of what was about to happen. Terrified that Dhanushini would not walk but fall to the ground on a useless leg, and even more terrified that Dhanushini *would* walk.

For a second, Dhanushini wanted to lie back down, cover herself with her blankets again, and wait until six, when the sun had risen. However, since she was not one to leave things half done, she sucked up a mouthful of air and leaned forward to stand.

Sandra was about to wrap her other arm around Dhanushini's waist to offer more support, but the older woman waived her away, saying, "I will be okay."

Dhanushini stood there a moment with Sandra close behind and then stepped forward on her right leg. She waited for the weakness, for the bone-shattering pain. Neither came. She brought her left leg forward, taking her first full step in over a month.

"*Athai*, you did it!" Sandra yelled.

Dhanushini's eyes filled with tears as laughter bubbled out of her chest. She walked around the room, slowly at first, like a child learning to walk, and then faster, more sure on her feet. By the time she made her way into the living room it was as though she had never broken her leg, or spent the last month lying in bed with her leg bound and gagged in a heavy cast. She was about to burst out of the front door when both she and Sandra froze at the sound of Sivaji's crisp voice.

"What is the meaning of this?" he demanded.

Dhanushini turned to face him, and through a smile that stretched across her entire face said, "Can't you see? I'm going for a walk!"

DOUG WHIPPO

The Ride
from *Jelly's Last Dance*

"C'mon over here and have a seat, Jelly," Mitch said, patting the pavement with the palm of his hand. "We need to have a talk." We'd traveled for hours on Mitch's new Harley. I had no idea where we were and most likely Mitch didn't either and even though I was only eight I wasn't scared. Hanging around Mitch was like that. When you were with him a shield of hope and invincibility protected you and you could be lost in a desert without water or encircled by wolves and still feel safe, armored and without a care in the world. I walked over from where I stood and sat down, cross-legged like him. The day had been very hot and the pavement was still warm, like fresh baked bread. We were surrounded by fields of corn that smelled sweet and green and free. The road was narrow, empty and stretched for miles in either direction.

Mitch looked up at the sky, his hands resting on the frayed kneecaps of his blue jeans. I waited for him to speak but he was strangely quiet and still, lost somewhere in his own thoughts. This was odd. My older brother always had something to tell me: a story, a joke, advice about school or how to handle myself around the neighborhood.

"Hey, Mitch," I said finally, "what're we doing out here? What do we need to talk about?" But he only gave me a weak smile I'd never seen before and returned his gaze to the million little stars shining so brightly above us.

Mitch had shown up in front of the house that afternoon riding his mysterious new motorcycle. He didn't say how he got it. Mom was still working as a nurse at the hospital and wouldn't be home until dinnertime. And when he waved me over to the curb from where I sat on the stoop reading a book and invited me for a ride, I was aboard faster than you could say jump, my arms wrapped around his waist and the soft summer wind running through my hair. I thought we'd be gone an hour at most, but once Mitch hit the backcountry roads he kept going. Much later, after nightfall, Mitch slowed down, pulled off onto the gravel shoulder of some unnamed road, and shut the engine down.

The Harley now rested in the dark, smelling of burnt oil and ticking like a clock. The moonlight spreading out over the cornfields looked like blue smoke.

"You know what a broken heart is, Jelly?" Mitch swung his head back from the horizon to look at me and I saw something in his eyes I didn't recognize. They looked hurt and scared.

"No," I said, my voice flat and slightly ashamed.

"What? Don't you got any girlfriends?" This was more like Mitch. His voice gentle, teasing. But I still felt a quiver of panic in my belly.

"Me? No way. Girls are gross."

"You won't always think that, Jelly." And because Mitch was older than me by ten years and part of a world I didn't know much about, it had to be true. I knew right then, with the quick clarity that comes easily to children, that I would not always be who I was. Somewhere buried deep in the sky above us were people and places waiting to change me.

"What's a broken heart?" When I tried to imagine it, I saw a wind-up soldier doll, upended on a wooden floor methodically churning its legs, yet getting nowhere. Mitch stared down at his hands for what seemed like a long time.

"Hard to explain," he mumbled.

Then I remembered what he said when we were out on the motorcycle. Earlier, he had guided us away from our house, our neighborhood, past the lazy green lawns and yawning sprinklers, past plastic pink flamingoes and ceramic black-faced yard jockeys, past the houses that looked empty and haunted. We leaned our bodies from side to side, in unison, where the avenues curved as we threaded our way through town, past stoplights and intersections, past strip malls and mini-marts and gas stations, out beyond everything and everyone, away, into the steep winding hills and shaded roads of the country where the sun-shadows on the pavement were blue-gray and spotted with light falling through a green canopy of tree branches. I pressed my ear to Mitch's back and heard his heart thumping, rapid and deep. But when I tightened my arms around him, his body felt stiff, tight, like a coiled spring. Usually he carried himself loose and smooth, like water, always so calm. I perched my head on his shoulder and looked at his reflection in the small round mirror attached to the handlebars. His cheeks were red from windburn. His lips were pressed together as if he were trying to hold something in or keep something out. His eyes hidden behind black sunglasses. Fragments of shuddering blue sky hung behind his head. Above the roar of the engine I'd shouted, "Hey Mitch! What's the matter? Where we gonna go?" He clenched his jaw as we leaned to the left, into a long tight curve, our bodies near even with the soaring gray pavement and it seemed like faith, not gravity or speed, that kept us from toppling over as we held the line until the road straightened. When Mitch shouted above the din of the motorcycle's engine his voice traveled a long empty distance before reaching my ears, like when you see a jet plane race across the sky and disappear then hear it's frightening sonic boom.

"I GOT A BROKEN HEART!" he screamed, leaning into another curve. "MY HEART IS BROKEN!" He sounded raw and frayed. I tightened my grip around him and held on.

Now, stopped on the side of the road in the middle of nowhere, I heard his frantic words echo in my head. *I got a broken heart.*

"Can you tell me what it feels like?" I asked, "What does a broken heart feel like?"

Mitch planted his hands on the pavement and pushed himself up to his feet. He walked away, then stopped and stared out at the cornfields. "That's hard to explain, too," he said, "You have to fall in love first, you know. You have to feel love for someone." He turned his head to peer over his shoulder at me, a sad smile on his face. "I don't suppose you've been in love yet, huh?" I shook my head.

"Nope," I said. It was about the only thing I was sure of at that point. "Why do they call it falling in love?" He turned to face me and slipped his hands into his front pockets.

"Because that's what it feels like," he said, "You feel like you're way up high in the sky. You're floating. You feel free and light. It's the best thing ever."

"That sounds like fun," I said. He considered that for a moment. "Well, it is. It is fun. But it's scary, too. You're falling the whole time and there's nothing holding you up and it happens so fast you kind of forget who you are. You have to be strong to be in love, Jelly"

"Why?"

"It hurts. Love hurts. You can't—"

"Wait a second," I said, pointing a finger at him. "Love *hurts*? You just said it was the best feeling you could have."

Mitch looked at the pavement and kicked it with the toe of his black leather boot. "Well you can't stop thinking about the girl you're in love with. You can't sleep or eat. You want her with you all the time."

"So that's what people call love?"

"Maybe for other people it's different, Jelly, I don't know. All I know is what I feel."

"What does a broken heart feel like then?"

Mitch walked over to the row of cornstalks bordering the shoulder of the road. He snapped off one of the stalks and tossed it into the darkness. Then he came back over and stood in front of me. I looked up into his face. He was looking at me but it seemed like his eyes were seeing something else, like for a moment he was gone, back in time, in another place. He took a deep breath and let it fall out of his body. "I don't know why they call it a broken heart, because it feels like you're whole body is broken. Every bone. And you feel raw. Remember when you skinned you're knees a couple weeks ago?" I nodded. I'd taken a pretty bad fall off my bicycle and the skin on both my knees had been scraped off clean leaving bright red, shiny wounds that shot jolts of pain through my body every time I touched them. "So think of it like that, then. Your heart is skinned and every time you think about the girl you love, it just about kills you. And you just don't feel like yourself anymore. You spend a lot of time trying to get back to who you were before but you're gone. You just can't find him."

"You feel this way right now? Like right this very minute?" I asked, afraid of what he might say.

"Yes."

He sat down next to me and crossed his legs. I stretched out and lay back on the pavement, putting my hands behind my head as a pillow. The sky was beautiful and scary to look at. So cold and unfriendly. All those stars hanging up there made you think anything was possible if you could just reach out and touch them. Mitch's words came from a world I didn't understand and wanted no part of, but the more I thought about what he said made me realize that I didn't really have much of a choice in the matter.

"Does everyone fall in love?" I asked.

"Yes."

"And does everyone get their heart broken? Everyone?"

Mitch turned to look at me. "It's like it has to happen to you, Jelly, or you're not really human. You're not truly alive until then, I guess."

"But why would anyone fall in love if that's what happens." I said this as a statement of how I saw things right then and even though it wasn't a question he had an answer for me.

"You can't help it. You just do. You fall. People are weak, Jelly."

Then I asked him who the girl was. I wanted to know what color hair she had and what her smile was like. Was she funny? What did he want from her? He just shrugged. And then Mitch told me he still loved her even after what she did and this made no sense to me at all.

I asked him what was so special about this girl? And when he spoke I heard the smile in his voice. "One night we stayed up 'til dawn comparing the freckles on our bodies. She smelled liked pinecones. Her hands were soft. She had this bit of blonde hair at the back of her neck that always stuck out. I liked the way she walked on the tips of her toes. She had green eyes. Whenever she said 'okay' she left the first letter off, so it came out 'kay.' 'Kay.' And . . . and . . . There were other things, too, Jelly," he said softly. "But that's for another time I guess."

I asked him if he had ever hurt someone. Had he broken someone's heart? Did he do this, too? And he nodded that he had. And I felt like I didn't know him anymore.

"Who was she?"

"A girl I knew a few years back. You know her. Remember Jessica? She came over for Thanksgiving once? We'd hang out in the basement. Get high. Play monopoly. I broke her heart." I did remember Jessica. She was a tiny thin-legged girl with huge brown eyes and a wide pale face. She had white teeth and a bright smile. She wore thick glasses and always read strange books. She was quiet, too. Shy. I liked her. She and Mitch would always sneak away by themselves to the basement to be alone and I was forbidden to follow them. But one night I did. There was a small den in the basement just off from where the washer and drier were and Mitch had turned it into his private hide-away. There was a stereo, a two-seat couch covered with an old blue bed sheet and stacks of cassettes and CD's. And Mitch had put up posters of his favorite bands on the brown paneled walls. Nirvana. Pearl Jam. Metallica. An antique lamp stood on a scarred table in the corner. The door was missing and in its place hung a thick veil of black beads that served as a curtain. One night when he and Jessica disappeared I waited a few minutes, then snuck down to see what they were up to. I crouched behind the washer and saw the soft glow of the lamp coming through the beads but I couldn't hear any talking. Underneath the sound of hard, jagged music playing on Mitch's stereo I heard a long delicate moan. I tiptoed up closer, hid behind a wall and poked my head around to pull one strand of the beads aside. I saw a pool of clothes gathered at the foot of the couch. And there was Jessica, naked, her smooth skin splashed with yellow lamplight, sitting back on the couch with her legs spread wide, staring at the ceiling like she was seeing something magical. She closed her eyes after a moment but you could tell she still saw some beautiful colors against her eyelids. Her face was sweaty; her cheeks all red. She moaned and arched her back and bucked her hips. Mitch was naked and kneeling between her legs, moving his head up and down slowly, then side to side, like he was drawing a pattern with his tongue. Jessica's thighs trembled. Her white fingers stroked and pulled at Mitch's thick black hair. My heart thumped deep inside my chest and echoed throughout the farthest limbs of my body. I felt dizzy and sick. A sweet musty smell hung in the room. My legs weakened beneath me and I brushed up against the curtain. Jessica's eyes shot open and saw my round head and stunned blue eyes. Or maybe she didn't see me because she stared right at me but didn't say anything. Her eyes were syrupy and dazed. Then she grabbed Mitch by his ears, yanked him up to her lips, and buried him in a long, deep, thankful kiss. I thought they'd never stop but finally Jessica pulled her head back and looked at him with her large brown eyes and whispered: "I want you inside me, Mitch. Put it inside me!"

That's about when I'd had all I could take. I wheeled around and scrambled up the stairs.

After that night, whenever I saw Jessica and Mitch, I could see the special way she looked at him. Her face had this sparkle about it and she was always touching him. Stroking his face or the underside of his arm or just holding some part of him. And although I had no idea what the two of them were up to most of the time, I was happy for her. She knew I liked to read and brought me books every once in a while. They were together maybe four months and then they stopped seeing each other. Mitch never told me why.

I thought of her as we sat together out there in the countryside. A light breeze rustled the leaves of the corn and played across my skin. I pictured Jessica out in the world somewhere, out beyond the dark sky above us, confused or lonely, carrying around those awful feelings Mitch had told me about. And I was sorry for her and scared for myself. I stood up and walked away from him and looked up at the moon.

"Why did you break her heart? What did you do?"

"I guess I got scared. I ran away." And the thought of my brother, with his thick body and blunt nose, his sharp brown eyes and quick smile, and even the sadness that he felt now, running away from anything made me question whether I knew him at all. Or maybe I didn't want to know him anymore. I turned back to look at him. I was suddenly mad at something but I didn't know what. I balled up my fingers and found myself standing before him.

"I hope I didn't break anybody's heart." I said. "How do you know when you have?" Mitch looked up at my fists, then at me. A smile meant to calm me down crossed his face.

"Don't worry yet, Jelly. I don't think you have." Then his smile went away. "But you will someday. It can't be helped. You will break someone's heart." He said it as if he were declaring a fact, like he could read the stars or tell the future.

"Why?" I demanded, angry that he was so sure of himself. I felt like I'd just learned the date of my death and from what sickness I'd die.

"Because you're human. That's why. There are things in life you can't escape, Jelly. You have eyes. You have skin. You have a heart just like the rest of us. Sometimes there's no hope. You are what you are."

"Yeah? Animals have the same things as us," I said, calling upon the animal kingdom to gather for my rescue. "Frogs. Birds. Elephants. Whales. They have the same things as us. Do they love? Do they break each other's hearts?"

Mitch stood up and put his hands on my shoulders as if to console me. I brushed them off and took a step back. Mitch raised his eyebrows, alarmed at the way I was challenging him. Usually everything he said was gospel to me.

"No," he said after a moment's pause. "I don't think they do."

"What makes us so different then? Why us?"

Mitch looked up into the sky and exhaled a long steady breath as if he were trying to let go of something he knew he needed but couldn't bear to hold onto any longer.

He was weary. He seemed to just give up on someone. Or maybe he was giving up on himself. Then he looked at me. "We remember too much in this life, Jelly. And it feels like a curse. When I leave this place I'll be glad."

"What?" What place did he mean?

"Don't you ever want to go? Leave? Get away from all this?" He swept his hand in a wide arc that included me and everything around us.

"No."

"Well, someday you just might, Jelly." Then he turned away from me and walked back to his motorcycle. "C'mon. We should go. You know mom's been worried sick for hours." He started the engine and revved the motor. "C'mon! Let's go!"

And I stood in the middle of the road, surrounded by the fields, under the stars, afraid of joining him in some new and terrifying way. But I felt like I was out of choices. So I did. And before I knew it we were racing through the countryside, which seemed stranger than ever. We followed the bone-white beam of the headlight and I felt something wet running from my eyes and I wasn't sure if it was the wind whipping at my face or what lay further ahead that made it happen as the trees blurred into black unknown shapes.

WILLIAM BURCK

from *The Elbows*

Editor's Note: Anatomy Instructor Beaurigard Dormouse awakens one morning to discover his arms strangely rigid, his elbows gone, vanished, absent without leave. The simplest acts, wiping the nose, twisting a doorknob, become challenges requiring desperate innovation. Worse, he learns that his elbows, yes, his elbows! are cavorting around the city in the guise of Siamese twins, attracting celebrity attention. In this adventure, he stumbles into one of Chicago's finest playing operations.

Air currents had been gathering for days over the North Pole, chilling and massing above the fields of sparkling ice into a great frigid air dome that loomed higher and wider, higher and wider, until the laws of meteorology pointed a frosty finger south and declared "Go!" The huge air dome spilled down across the frozen tundra, whistling through the antlers of caribou, rattling along the Canadian Rockies, rumbling out across the snow-covered stubble of the Great Plains, snapping off tree trunks, snatching up whole cattle and flinging them into neighboring fields, and then barreling straight east down Harrison Street past the Central Post Office of Chicago.

Steam rising from city sewers was knocked horizontal. Garbage cans tipped over and rolled into traffic. Paper bags, stray pages of newspapers, coffee cups, handbills, candy wrappers, lottery tickets, half-eaten hamburgers, receipts, and thousands of other items skidded across the pavement, plastered themselves around light poles, against people's legs, on windshields, or simply shot straight into the air and tumbled up between the skyscrapers, where they caught the eyes of countless office workers, who jumped up from their desks, laughed, pointed, called out to one another, waved to workers in neighboring office towers, and in this way managed to escape several minutes of hopeless drudgery as the paper scraps tumbled up into the stratosphere.

It was at this very moment that Anatomy Instructor Beaurigard Dormouse stepped out of the Central Post Office, started down the stone steps, and caught a wintry blast square against his coatless form.

A strange gargling noise escaped from his lips and he scampered down the remaining steps, swung his arm overhead and screamed "Cabbie!" at the top of his lungs. A great bowling ball of wind buffeted this word to shreds, while a page of newspaper blew up against his uplifted arm and fluttered there like a flag on a flagpole. Two westbound Yellow taxicabs totally ignored him, gliding slowly past with empty backseats, as if instinctively aware that the Anatomy Instructor's wallet was empty. Another wintry gust barreled down Van Buren Street and struck him broadside, ripping the newspaper from his arm and sending it tumbling high into the air. Damn it, he shivered, chilled to the bone. He had to get out of here. He had to get home. Hunching his shoulders against the arctic blasts, he began walking west.

But the Anatomy Instructor's home was over two miles away. Within a block, his nose was running like a faucet. Within two blocks, he could not stop the chattering of his teeth. Within three blocks, millions of fire ants seemed to be crawling inside the veins of his arms.

He broke into a trot, hoping to increase his circulation, but his arms swung like pendulums and he immediately lost his balance.

"Whoa!" he cried and narrowly avoided a nasty spill.

Passersby gave him strange looks. The sight of his slender frame stumbling down the sidewalk in a flimsy brown sweater and light grey slacks was an affront to their very nature. For Chicagoans are connoisseurs of the cold who take great pride in their strategies for preserving warmth. One devises a rubberized tube to protect the sensitive tissues of his neck and face. Another swathes himself in scarf after scarf until he appears more bison than human and requires the assistance of his spouse to find the door. One lines his boots with bread bags. Another lines them with the outer leaves of a cabbage, believing that vegetable matter, when subjected to foot friction, generates an organic sort of radiant heat. Some swear by cashmere. Others argue for goose down. And there are even those who fashion insulated parkas from the cushions of an old couch. One such fellow popped his face out of a couch-cushion parka to advise the Anatomy Instructor that he should dress more warmly.

But his words were snatched away by the wind. The Anatomy Instructor could not have replied to them anyway because his lips were frozen slabs of concrete. The pain tingling through his fingers now seemed distant and foreign, like a telephone ringing in someone else's apartment.

Meanwhile, the sidewalks had grown less congested. Trendy clothes boutiques and tony lunch spots had given way to brick warehouse buildings with crumbling doorways, storefront churches with hand-lettered signs, and battered taverns whose signs swung and creaked precariously over the Anatomy Instructor's head.

He could no longer feel his feet striking the pavement and didn't even notice that he had slipped on a patch of ice until he saw the sidewalk rushing up toward his face. But the sidewalk stopped, and he found himself staring with puzzlement at a cluster of rock salt a foot below. He turned his head and saw a large black-gloved hand gripping his shoulder. Attached to that hand was a long arm and a body so large it seemed to fill the entire doorway slanting up to his right. Then the sidewalk began to recede, the doorway straightened, and the Anatomy Instructor found himself face to face with a pewter belt buckle spelling the name, JED, in large block letters.

"Say, Slim," a deep voice rumbled from a cocoon of scarves and knit caps in the upper recesses of the doorway. "You'd best step in out of this cold."

The Anatomy Instructor chattered his teeth in an up-and-down direction as the huge man turned sideways to pull open a door covered with handbills and graffiti.

"Stand inside here," the deep voice rumbled. "Don't go no further. Don't make no noise. Don't touch nothing. Just knock twice when you're thawed out."

Dormouse squeezed past and tried to thank the bundled giant, but could only stutter, "Th–th–th–th–th–" as the door slammed shut, cutting off the blustery roar of the street. He was in a small dark room—some sort of waiting area. Muddy light leaked through two hopelessly smudged windows down onto green naugahyde chairs lining the walls. He tripped on a low coffee table covered with ragged, dusty magazines, and stumbled over to the wall, where a glass partition allowed him to peer into a small office area crammed with desks, filing cabinets and office equipment, all of it possessing the quaint rounded quality of obsolescence. There were adding machines, not calculators; manual typewriters, not computers; rotary phones, not push button; wooden filing cabinets and desks, not metal. Bulletin boards lined the walls, covered with notes, clipboards, and calendars. "Salamander Tool Works" he read across the top of one calendar, and under it the logo, "Salamander Tools—They're Sharp!" Beneath this logo was a blond woman in a cowboy hat whose breasts were swelling out of a buckskin vest. One of her fingertips was pressed daintily against the point of an ice pick, while her lips formed a ruby pout of pain.

"R–r–r–r–ring!"

The Anatomy Instructor jumped back from the glass partition.

"R–r–r–r–ring!"

A phone was ringing in there. He heard a click and saw the reels of a large tape player start turning.

"You have reached the number you dialed," a recorded voice growled. "If you meant to dial this number, then you know what to do. If you didn't, then get the fuck off the line!" There was a long beep, followed by a burst of dry sharp laughter like beebees striking glass. "Heh–eh–eh–eh. Slits . . . Tony. Fucker bought a trey. Says he'll be weekly. Tell Nuts. Oh, and Johnny T– You remember Johnny T. Fat fuck with a fucked-up face. Yeah, he died. Had a marker for fifteen-five. Brother says he'll cover it. We're having a little meet tomorrow." *Click.*

The Anatomy Instructor swallowed hard. What sort of a phone call was that? Was that tool business? And where was the heat in this place? He looked around for radiators, but saw none and continued shivering until all of a sudden his nose seemed to burst into flames. "Ouch!" he yelped. And then his ears seemed to burst into flames. And then he was dancing about, swearing, "Damn it to hell!!" as every tender extremity of his body seemed to burst into flames. Twin rivulets of snot came coursing down from his nose and he couldn't wipe them. He could only double over and groan "Oooohhh!" lean back against the wall and groan "Aaaargh!" sink down into a naugahyde chair and groan, "Ooowwww!"

The front door opened and the magazines on the coffee table fluttered wildly as the huge man poked his cocoon of scarves and knit caps through the doorway and rumbled, "That you making all that noise?"

"I c–can't help it," Dormouse replied, gritting his teeth. "It hurts!"

"Yeah, well you dressed for pain today," the huge man observed. "Keep it down in here," and he ducked back outside.

The Anatomy Instructor endured an eternity of painful thawing. Why couldn't the ice crystals inside of him simply melt? Instead, they seemed to be raking against the walls of his capillaries. He didn't even notice the voices growing gradually louder from within the building. All of a sudden the door was squeaking open behind him, a hand clapped down on his shoulder, and a shrill voice was screaming, "The fuck you doing here?!" right beside his ear.

"Maybe he's a player," a second, thicker voice offered.

The Anatomy Instructor was too startled, too terrified to even turn.

"A player, my ass!" the first voice replied. "Does he look like a player?!"

"A cop, then?" the thicker voice asked.

"A cop!" the shrill voice dismissed this notion with disgust.

The Anatomy Instructor felt the hand leave his shoulder as a short figure in a suit coat rushed past him to yank open the outer door.

"The fuck is this?!" the short figure yelled up at the huge man outside, hooking his thumb over his shoulder. "The fuck is this?!"

"He was freezing," the huge man rumbled in explanation. "He ain't got no coat."

A gust of wind blew the short man's few remaining strands of hair—which had been asked to cover far too much territory—back off the top of his scalp. They wafted ridiculously out behind his head, while his grey suit jacket flapped at his sides.

"That's *his* problem!" the short man was yelling angrily. "That's not *my* problem! *You're* my problem! And that's *your* problem!"

With that, the short man spun about on his small feet. The long strands of hair now blew forward over his face and he shoved them aside with an angry sweep of his stubby hand.

"I'll deal with you later, Jane Addams!" he spat over his shoulder, slamming the door shut and drilling his eyes, which were as tiny and beady as a bird's, straight into the Anatomy Instructor.

"Won't you please get up?" he asked with cloying sweetness, bowing forward at the waist and plastering a smile of mock politeness on his face. Then he stalked out of the room, snarling to the second man, "Bring him!"

This second man was a solid-looking stooge with a tapioca pudding sort of face filled with thick pearly lumps. He looked down at the Anatomy Instructor with dull eyes and snarled, "C'mon," in a way that clearly meant *now*, because he wasn't catching no flak on account of no pain-in-the-ass fuckup.

Anatomy Instructor Dormouse leaned forward in his naugahyde chair, trying to ease his weight gingerly onto his tender feet. But the stooge had seen this type of insolence too many times from smart alecks like his two punk kids. He administered a playful clout to the Anatomy Instructor's ear and was richly rewarded with a yelp of pain.

In fact, the Anatomy Instructor's frostbitten ear felt as if it had been cloven in two. He groaned, staggered to his feet, and groaned again.

"Whatsamatter? A little too much to drink?" the stooge taunted, his lumpy face twisting sadistically as he grabbed Dormouse by the arm and attempted to hurry him along with a little arm-twisting technique he'd learned from Moose Cholock in his professional wrestling days. But the arm wouldn't twist. The little fuck was resisting!

"HEY! The fuck's the problem back there?!" the short man's voice echoed down the hallway.

The Anatomy Instructor's upper arm promptly became a handle by which he was propelled down the hall, down a flight of stairs, down another hall, and into a long low room where pool balls clicked, cards slid across tables, dice tumbled over green felt, money shifted and rustled from hand to hand, and tiny glints of light played off gold rings, gold chains, and wire-rim glasses.

"My God, I've stumbled into a gambling den," the Anatomy Instructor realized.

A pool shark pulled back his cue one extra time. A craps shooter paused before scooping up his dice. A poker player raised his eyes from his cards. The whole room skipped a beat as "Rotten" Rotenza, the pint-sized bagman for Anthony Storelli, and "Lumps" Lepke, his Cro-Magnon muscleman, hustled the terrified stranger through the doorway.

"There's something stiff about that guy," the pool shark thought.

"He's hiding something," the craps player thought.

"Short arms!" the poker player thought, then tossed a stack of bills into the center of the table and declared, "Bet's five hundred."

The room's collective conversation resumed:

"Pass . . . Take three . . . Reminds me of that fucking dog took three bullets in the head and still wouldn't let go of that phone man's throat . . . Nine ball side pocket, one bank . . . Phone man's eyes was bucked out, man . . . Yeah, that was Pasquale's dog. Man trains his dogs with cattle blood . . . Eight the hard way. Double fours. C'mon eight . . . Had to cut that dog's jaws off of him with gardening shears. Dude's throat looked like—gimme two. Dude's throat looked like—I said two, man . . . All right, all right . . . Dude's throat looked like—Man! . . . All right. Here . . . Skin and blood and veins and tubes hanging out all over like some kind of abortion . . . Stop that shit . . . Rack 'em! Your game, Tector . . . That phone dude kept trying to talk. Fucker's laying there dying and he's trying to talk . . . Stop that shit, now . . . Get this man some new dice. He's wearing 'em out . . . But all he could do was wheeze. A wet wheeze. Like a vacuum cleaner sucking up water, y'know . . . I said stop that shit, now . . . Bets? . . . Two hundred . . . Raise that two hundred . . . The rent's four hundred to you, Fat Freddy."

Yellow cones of light flared from hanging pan fixtures down through thick smoke and splashed onto green felt tables. Large pieces of floor-based machinery huddled in shadows along the room's brick walls. Drill presses and belt grinders and band saws and table mills and engine lathes and unfathomable contraptions with thick metal arms, gleaming spindles, rubber drive belts, and large exhaust hoods poked out of the darkness toward the smoky cluster of tables in the room's center. Here and there on the dusty floorboards dark outlines could be seen where these machines had formerly stood.

But all of this was a blur to the Anatomy Instructor. His numb feet tripped and skipped and barely touched the floor as the lumpy-faced stooge's breath wheezed above his left ear and the little man's voice growled below his right ear, "C'mon, you little prick! C'mon, you little fucken prick!"

They dragged him over to a bar, an honest-to-God bar at one end of the room, where a television set sat amidst a cluster of liquor bottles, flickering blue light across the face of a man who had the look of a prizefighter gone to seed—broad shoulders, thick neck, spare tire swelling over his belt. His skin was pitch black and his shirt was sparkling white. He sat cracking walnuts with his bare fingers and staring glumly at the hairy guy with tattooed arms on the television screen who was snarling, "Are you ready for it?" at a naked blond woman spread-eagled across the hood of a Volkswagen beetle in some kind of dingy auto garage.

The little man on the Anatomy Instructor's right stepped forward and cleared his throat. "Found this fuck upstairs, Nuts!" he spat, and the lumpy-faced stooge gave the Anatomy Instructor a push forward.

CRACK! A fragment of walnut shell shot from between the broad-shouldered man's fingers. He worked the walnut halves apart, still watching the television screen, where the tattooed man's greasy hands were leaving dark smudges upon the blond woman's pale breasts.

"Found this fuck upstairs, Nuts!" repeated Rotten Rotenza, and the lumpy-faced stooge gave the Anatomy Instructor another push forward.

Nuts Benedict popped the walnut meat into his mouth, then turned to study them with lazy, hooded eyes, his powerful jaws chewing methodically.

"Who is he, Rotten?" he asked, his voice rich and sonorous as a bass fiddle against the raucous clarinets of the gamblers.

"How should I know who he is?!" Rotten shot back. "Idiot doorman of yours let him in to warm up. What is it with that guy?! He's a putz!"

"That putz . . ." and Nuts paused to dig a fragment of walnut from between his teeth with the nail of his little finger, "is my brother."

"I know he's your brother! But he's a putz, Nuts! You run a fine establishment here. Good take. No heat. Mr. Storelli appreciates that. But I don't know what he would think about this . . . this . . ." Rotten twisted around sharply. "Who the fuck are you, you little prick?!"

The short man's sour breath engulfed the Anatomy Instructor, and for a moment he could not speak.

"Don't fuck with me!" Rotten warned, grabbing the Anatomy Instructor's turtleneck.

On the television screen, the head of the tattooed man was now wedged between the thighs of the naked blond woman, a technique that Lumps Lepke found so instructional he could feel his admiration swelling up in his pants. Which was when Rotten's shout distracted him. He tore his eyes from the television screen. The pain-in-the-ass fuckup again! He clapped one hand down on the fuckup's left shoulder, grabbed his wrist with the other hand and pulled it back and began twisting. But something was wrong. Sure, the fuckup was screaming, but where was that rubbery give that meant tendons were stretching? A deep frown spread between the pearly lumps on his face, and he twisted the arm in the other direction.

"Yeow! Yeow! All right! Stop!" the Anatomy Instructor was yelling. Several gamblers glanced over, but all anyone said was, "Whew, he's really going at her now," in reference to the couple on the television screen.

"Rotten, that's enough!" Nuts Benedict yelled, straightening up on his stool. "Is that any way to treat my guest?"

"Guest?!" Rotten spat, turning around in disbelief. "What do you mean guest?"

A bewildered look had settled onto the face of Lumps Lepke, who had manhandled hundreds of arms in his wrestling days and broken countless more in the service of Mr. Storelli. But he had never come across an arm like this.

The Anatomy Instructor suddenly felt rough fingers probing at the middle of his arm. Damn it, enough was enough! He tried shaking loose from the grip of the lumpy-faced stooge, but a wicked poke in the kidney made him think better of it.

"Yes, this is my guest," Nuts was explaining as he calmly cracked open another walnut. "I was expecting him. A rich surgeon from Schaumburg. He's here to gamble."

"Oh yeah?" Rotten said uncertainly, looking from the Anatomy Instructor to Nuts and back to the Anatomy Instructor, whose face was growing increasingly red as the lumpy-faced stooge continued probing at the middle of his arm.

"Hey!" Lumps Lepke cried, "This guy ain't got no–"

But no one was listening to him. No one ever listened to him, because listening to Lumps Lepke automatically lowered one's intelligence. The effect was temporary, lasting several hours, sometimes as much as a day. But anyone who survived the experience, never repeated it again. Too many bad investments, too many errors in judgment, too many arrests, too many bad marriages had resulted from listening to even one complete thought of Lumps Lepke. Which was why Lumps Lepke had become so adept at physical communication. It was also why Rotten twisted around and shouted, "SHUT UP!" as Lumps held up the Anatomy Instructor's arm and repeated, "This guy ain't got no . . . ain't got no . . . He ain't got no . . ." unable to finish his sentence because he could not remember what you called those things at the middle of people's arms.

"And would you please let go of our 'guest'?!" Rotten screamed, his lips forming the word "guest" as if it were a shard of broken glass, followed by a pause, and then two more shards, "Thank you!" as Lumps let the arm fall free.

"Yes, Rotten," Nuts Benedict intoned. "I do appreciate your taking the time to escort my guest down here to the game room," and his lips smiled while his eyes remained hooded.

"Yeah, well, it's nothing," Rotten muttered, turning toward the door.

Lumps Lepke remained behind, however, picking up a few more pointers from the couple on the television screen.

"The fuck you waiting for, Lumps?!" Rotten shouted from the doorway.

"Oh, and Rotten," Nuts called out, raising his voice to be heard above the noise of the gamblers, "tell Mr. Storelli the take will be double this month."

"Sure, sure, sure. C'mon, Lumps, you fuck!"

Lumps walked reluctantly toward the door, pausing twice to peer back at the television.

"Oh, and Rotten?" said Nuts.

"Yeah?!" Rotten answered a little too sharply.

"Tell my brother that this is indeed the guest I was expecting and not to let anyone else in."

Rotten muttered something under his breath as he swept out of the room.

CRACK! Nuts pulled two walnut halves apart and popped the meat into his mouth, chewing slowly and staring at the Anatomy Instructor. His hand dropped down to flick a switch on the face of the bar.

"Fuck that spade and his no-good putz of a brother," Rotten's shrill voice crackled from a tiny speaker hidden behind several liquor bottles. "That fucking prick'll be history some day, and then we'll see who–"

"Yeah, but–" the thick voice of Lumps Lepke cut in.

"Don't interrupt me, you goddamned–"

"Yeah, but he didn't have no . . . no . . . thing in the middle of his–"

"SHUT THE FUCK UP!" There was a soft thud of a fist or an elbow striking flesh. "Get the goddamned car, fuckhead!"

Nuts flicked the switch off.

"Slits!" Nuts Benedict called out over the Anatomy Instructor's head.

"Yeah?" answered a voice at the craps table.

"Would you please take a five-dollar bill from the house and place it in my bottle?"

"Sure thing, boss."

A man so thin that his shirt seemed to be hung on a hanger rather than a pair of shoulders glided from the cluster around the craps table.

A roomful of eyes flitted nervously from cards or dice or billiard balls toward a five-gallon water bottle nestled at the base of a hulking, grey drill press. The bottle was nearly full of crumpled greenbacks.

That's a nice piece of change, the Anatomy Instructor thought to himself.

More troubled thoughts than this, however, were passing through the gamblers' heads. Do I owe Nuts money? Did I promise Nuts a favor and forget about it? Have I insulted Nuts recently? Done anything he might interpret as an insult?

It had been nine years since Nuts Benedict began putting a dollar into his bottle anytime he heard the word 'nigger' (five dollars if that word was directed toward him). The gamblers had caught onto this practice quickly, and were soon saying things like, "You no good, nappy-haired dollar bill!" when they meant 'nigger'.

But then Nuts began putting money in his bottle whenever anyone pissed him off. He wouldn't get angry, wouldn't say anything to the culprit. He would simply turn to his assistant and say, "Slits, please put a five-dollar bill in my bottle." And Slits would answer, "Sure thing, Boss." And the faces in the room would turn to one another and wonder, "What the fuck is this money-in-the-bottle shit?"

Eventually, someone got up the balls to ask, "Hey, Nuts, what're you gonna do with that money in your bottle?"

"Spend it," Nuts answered, and sat there cracking walnuts with his fingers as they tried to figure it out, wicked smiles spreading across his face whenever their guesses hit the mark.

Was he saving for a new car? Nothing. Was he saving to buy a bigger gambling operation? Nothing. Was he gonna do something with the money when the bottle was full? Wicked smile.

Was he gonna throw a party? Was he gonna take a vacation? Was he gonna retire? Nothing.

The gamblers took Slits out to dinner, got him drunk, got him laid, but all he could tell them was, "The fuck if I know what his bottle money's for."

Two years passed and the bottle was already half full when someone joked, "Hey, maybe Nuts is gonna use that bottle money to take out a hit." They all laughed until they saw the wicked smile spreading across Nuts' face. The speculation grew quite serious.

Was he gonna hit Storelli? Was he gonna hit his ex-wives? Was he gonna hit the fucker who made him put the most money in his bottle? Nothing, nothing, nothing. Was he gonna hit the first guy who pissed him off when the bottle was full? Wicked smile.

The word 'nigger' and its substitute 'dollar bill' dropped from their vocabulary. Everyone started paying their markers right on time. If anyone bumped into Nuts, there would be a chorus of voices, "Excuse me."—"Watch it!"—"The fuck's your problem!" Nobody told jokes anymore—Nuts might find them offensive. But still the money level crept up. And now, seven years later, it had reached the bottle's neck.

Nuts Benedict leaned back on his stool and slapped his belly the way a man slaps his belly when he is quite content with himself. "Well," he addressed the Anatomy Instructor, "it seems that you're a doctor from Schaumburg and you're here to gamble. Bet you didn't know that!"

The Anatomy Instructor allowed himself a nervous chuckle, so relieved was he to be out of the clutches of the lumpy-faced stooge. "No, I didn't know that," he agreed, and added, "Well, I suppose I'll be getting along now," and shifted his weight backward to signal the goodbye phase of their relations.

But Nuts Benedict did not shift his body into the goodbye phase of their relations. He brushed the walnut crumbs from his fingers and pulled a thick black wallet from his pocket. "We have inconvenienced you here," he apologized, "and so I am going to give you a choice. It's a simple choice, really. Take this hundred dollars and gamble it, or walk out of here and make a liar out of me."

The Anatomy Instructor shifted abruptly out of the goodbye phase of their relations and swung a stiff arm up to take the C-note.

"Gentlemen!" Nuts Benedict called out over his head, "Please suspend your games! We have a new player joining us today!"

Seventeen pairs of cold eyes fixed upon the Anatomy Instructor's disheveled form. He heard several snickers.

A poker player with an embalmed sort of waxy skin and the zipper-like lips of a lizard, leaned forward to croak, "What's your game, Cherry?"

The Anatomy Instructor's mind was reeling. What could he play that wouldn't require the use of his arms? Pool? Good heavens, no. Poker? But how would he hide his cards? Craps? How did one even play craps? "Maybe . . ." he began, "Maybe I could just place a wager on, you know, on the horses or something."

"This is not a betting parlor, Cherry," Nuts Benedict's sonorous voice corrected, "It is a gambling parlor. People do not come here to book wagers. They come here to gamble. They gamble, Cherry, or . . ." and his voice trailed off while his fingers closed around a walnut—CRACK!

"Looks like a craps player to me," croaked the waxy-skinned poker player with disgust.

Chairs scraped and gamblers stepped aside and suddenly the Anatomy Instructor found himself at the end of the long narrow craps table.

"Put the money down and make the world go round," said a voice.

Dormouse dropped the C-note on the table's green felt.

"The man bets it all, fifty says he'll fall," said another voice.

"Throw the dice, seven-eleven's nice," added a third.

But how could he throw the dice? His arms felt as clumsy and conspicuous as neon exclamation points. Should he throw underhand like a softball pitcher? Should he throw overhand like a windmill? Should he swing his arm to the side and forward like a turnstyle? But everyone was staring at him. He had to do something.

"The money's down, send the dice to town," a voice growled.

"You're here to play, not to pray," warned another.

Dormouse grabbed the dice, raised his arm in front of him like a crane, and with a flip of his wrist sent them arcing across the table.

"Nice technique."

"Guy's a natural."

"Never seen that."

"Reminds me of "Nickel and Dimes" Dempster."

The craps players leaned in as the blur of red dice and white spots tumbled down the green velvet lane to a stop. A four and a three.

"Naturals!"

"What's that mean?" Dormouse asked.

"Means you got the makings of a craps player, Cherry."

"Good, can I stop now?" he asked as a crumpled C-note joined the one he'd bet. Silent stares leveled at him as the dice were returned, rolling right up to the bumper so that he had to step backward to grab them.

"Lookit dat."

"Won't bend his arms."

"Man's got a system."

"Keep 'em straight—improve your fate!"

These comments made the Anatomy Instructor quite nervous. He bet it all again and quickly flipped the dice down the table, thinking, "Lose, lose, lose." But how did one lose at craps?

A five and a six.

"Naturals!"

"Guy's on fire!"

"Hundred says he can't do it again."

"Covered!"

But he did do it again. This time a five and a two sat innocently on the stretch of green. Hands clapped and heads shook and shirt sleeves were rolled up and drinks were spilled as more gamblers squeezed forward to get in on the action. This had the makings of a run and runs were what they lived for. If not their own, then to bet on the coattails of someone else's. These were true gamblers. Men whose achievements and dreams had drifted out of focus until they no longer existed. Businesses sold to partners or turned over to sons. Possessions liquidated, acquired, and reliquidated on a continuing basis. Men who believed that the good Lord put dice and cards and pool tables on the world for a reason. It didn't matter if your wife divorced you, your children disowned you, and you were beaten up regularly. Not to men like Tuck "the Fuck" Fredricks, who had described his evening of 25 first-throw winners as "without a doubt the finest half hour of my life. Nothing the fuck like it. Nothing the fuck like it in the world." Of course, there had been nothing quite the fuck like the excruciating half hour Tuck spent lying in an alley when he couldn't pay his gambling debts, holding his guts in with his hands until a dog came along and started lapping up his blood, and its owner saw Tuck slumped against the dumpster and started wailing, "Oh, my gawd! Oh, my gawd! Oh, my gawd!" until Tuck summoned up the strength to gasp, "Shut . . . the fuck . . . up . . . and call . . . ambulance." He had lived. Lived to see more runs. And this was one of them. Greenbacks piling so high that the Anatomy Instructor had to lift his arm higher and flip his wrist harder in order to send the dice out over his winnings. Nuts Benedict had dropped his walnuts and raised up on his stool, his face taut because the double take he had promised Mr. Storelli was now sitting in front of this fucking new guy with the stiff-armed style.

The dice tumbled down the table to a stop. A five and a three. The Anatomy Instructor heard groans. What? Had he lost? But the dice were returned. He needed to match the eight. He no longer cared about his arms, no longer cared about his elbows, no longer cared about getting out of the gambling den. He had won eight straight throws and the lingering pain of frostbite had become the fever of the dice. He let them fly with a flip of his wrist, and the solid-soft sound as they rolled across the felt was soothing and rich, like hoofbeats in the sand.

A five and a two.

"Crapped out!"

"Tough luck, Cherry!"

"Helluva run, Cherry!"

His shoulders slumped. Nuts Benedict sagged back down onto his stool with relief. The dice were passed to the next player. The pile of money disappeared, and suddenly Dormouse was angry. He needed that money, damn it! He could have hired a detective to track down his elbows. At the very least, he could have paid to have his clothes altered.

The other gamblers were consoling him and pulling him from the circle of light around the craps table and into the circle of light at the poker table.

"C'mon, Cherry, have a seat"

"Play a coupla hands"

"Don't let it get you down."

Numbly, he took a seat, plopping down because he couldn't lower himself with his arms. The gamblers assigned this behavior to dejection. "Come, come, come. We'll play a hand or two."

The waxy-skinned cadaverous fellow reached a pale blue hand across the table and croaked, "Name's Ed 'the Dead'."

The Anatomy Instructor lifted his crane of an arm and gave Ed the Dead's cold hand a pump.

"I'm Fat Freddy," said a swarthy fellow who did not even attempt to lean his arm across the table. His thin eyebrows seemed to dance perpetually over his eyes in an attitude of daffy alarm, which made him a consummate bluffer.

"I'm Purdy Jewell," rasped the short, rough-hewn fellow to the Anatomy Instructor's left. He barely looked up as he extended a blunt paw and gave the Anatomy Instructor's stiff arm a perfunctory pump.

"And I'm the Gumper," wheezed the wizened old twig on the Anatomy Instructor's right. His arm waited weakly in the air, trembling as Dormouse swung his stiff arm around, then had to back up in order to fit it between the two of them. "And how might we address you, Cherry?" he asked in a voice as thin and reedy as wind whistling through a loose windowpane.

"My name's Beaurigard Dormouse."

"Bo!"—"Bo!"—"Booooooooooo!" they chorused in every octave of the vocal register.

"OK, what's the game? Stud?"

"No way, Fat Freddy, you bluffing son of a bitch! The game's draw. Five card draw."

"But, but–" Dormouse sputtered.

"No buts, Bo!" they chimed, and the cards began flicking from the deck in Ed the Dead's hands and across the green felt table to each player.

"But . . . but I've no money," the Anatomy Instructor wailed, as much in protest of the day's numerous and catastrophic losses as of this card game.

This brought the poker players to a swift halt. Looks were exchanged. Fingers fidgeted nervously, as if to work their way around this obstacle. Ed the Dead leaned his head forward and the dark bags under his eyes twitched. "We'll use IDs," he croaked. "You do have IDs don't you, Cherry?"

"Yes, but—"

"No buts, Bo!" they cut him off.

"The ante'll be . . ." Ed the Dead paused and spilled a sheaf of identification cards out of his wallet. "The ante'll be a library card," and he slid a green Chicago Public Library card into the center of the table.

"A library card!?" Purdy Jewell growled. "What the hell you doin' with a goddamned library card, Ed?" He began pawing through his own wallet. "I ain't got no . . . What the fuck kind of . . . Here! Take a check cashing card for the Jewel," and he flipped it into the center of the table.

"But I need my IDs," the Anatomy Instructor was still protesting. "I can't . . . What if I were to lose?"

"Oh, knock it off, Bo!"

"We saw you at the craps table!"

"Didn't know how to play, eh? Afraid to lose your IDs, eh?"

"No, but I'm not trying . . . Listen, this is a bad time for me right now. I can't be without identification."

The Anatomy Instructor was not being entirely misleading. His traitorous elbows had managed, in just a few hours' time, to forge his signature and empty his bank accounts. But he was more worried about the fact that his wallet was in his back pocket. The contortions involved in retrieving it would not be easy to explain. And so he remained leaning back in his chair, arms angled down so that his hands rested on his knees.

"Antes in?" Ed the Dead was asking.

"Yep."

"You bet."

"Uh–huh."

"Hey, what about Bo?"

They all looked expectantly at the Anatomy Instructor and saw that he hadn't touched his cards.

"Bo!" Ed the Dead called out, leaning forward a bit. "Yoo–hoo. We're playing a game here."

"C'mon, ante up, Bo!" the Gumper wheezed.

"I tell you, I–"

"Ante up, Bo!" Fat Freddy insisted.

"But . . . but . . ." Damn it, he had to end this charade. "I can't, you see, because . . . because I can't bend my arms." He saw the sudden distrust playing at the gamblers' lips, saw the skepticism narrowing their eyes. "It's the cold," he explained. "The cold's stiffened me up. I've got a . . . a condition, and the cold . . ."

"Wha– wha– what the fuck?! You want a hand there, Bo?! That what you're saying?" Purdy Jewell asked. "Stand up already. I'll get that wallet out. Now don't think I'm getting queer or anything," he rasped gruffly, digging his paw into the Anatomy Instructor's back pocket. There was a burst of uneasy chuckles as their eyes darted over to the television on the bar, where the tattooed man was now fucking the blond woman sprawled atop the Volkswagen hood, ramming into her so forcefully that the entire car was shaking.

"There, and don't mention it. Now, the ante's a goddamned library card, Bo."

The Anatomy Instructor poked through his wallet, peering at the cards an arm's length in front of him at the edge of the table. He spotted the blue access card to the restricted anatomy stacks in the university's library, a card he used at least once or twice a week. It could be replaced, of course, but doing so would involve a visit to that damned winking cameraman in Faculty Services who always asked snidely whether he'd seen any good anatomy lately.

"What on earth am I doing here, gambling my library card into oblivion?" he wondered as he flipped it into the center of the table and scooped together his cards, then leaned back to spread them open just above his knees.

"Hey, hey, hey! Let's keep 'em on the table!" Purdy Jewell warned, turning his own cards to shield them from the Anatomy Instructor's view.

Dormouse raised the cards up to table level, cupping his hands around them. When he saw that the first card was an ace, he looked up. "Aces high?" he asked.

"Don't try that rube shit with us, Bo! It may work at the craps table, but this here's the poker table."

"But I wasn't–"

"Bo, cut the crap!"

The Anatomy Instructor looked back down at his hand and saw that his second card was also an ace. He attempted to remain calm. But when he saw that his third card was an ace as well, he blinked several times, pushed his cards together, and slowly spread them back apart. His eyes had not deceived him. He had three aces. His other cards were a two and a seven, but that didn't matter. He licked his lips and peered slyly about at the other faces. The other faces, too, were slyly peering about.

"Bet's to you, Fat Freddy," said Ed the Dead.

"I bet . . ." Fat Freddy dug through his wallet. "Bet's a phone card."

The Gumper's feeble hands extracted a phone card from his tattered brown wallet. "In," he gasped.

"I'm in, too," added the Anatomy Instructor, leaning forward to deposit a silver Sprint card in the center of the table. He considered raising the bet a cash station card. After all, with empty bank accounts, his was useless. But he decided not to tip his hand.

"In," said Purdy Jewell.

"And so's the dealer," chimed in Ed the Dead. "How many you want, Fat Freddy?"

"Three."

"Three. Fat Freddy takes three," Purdy Jewell muttered, and began drumming his fingers on his cards, which lay face down in a neat pile. "Reminds me of that guy took three swallows of Drano on a dare. Got the first two down no problem. But that third one—Hoowhee!"

The Gumper's arm quavered forward with two cards. "I'll take one," he wheezed.

"One . . . One . . ." Purdy Jewell muttered. "The Gumper takes one. Reminds me of that gal took a bullet in the eye. Remember that one-eyed gal, Deadman?"

Ed the Dead did not acknowledge this question, but instead looked straight at the Anatomy Instructor.

"I'll take two," the Anatomy Instructor said, leaning forward to push his cards across the table.

Purdy Jewell frowned and picked up his own cards, studying them as he muttered, "Two . . . two . . . Bo takes two . . . You know, that reminds me of them two guys at the press conference this morning. Didja see them two guys on the TV, Deadman?"

"Can't say as I did," Ed the Dead responded, answering only because it was now Purdy's turn to draw. "How many you takin', Purdy?"

"How many I takin'? Oh, I think I'm takin' me a pair, too. But I'll tell you what—make 'em a matching pair like them twins on the TV. That was some pair, all right." Purdy still had not passed his two cards across to Ed the Dead as he continued, "Yeah, saw 'em on the TV. They was holding a news conference about our alderman."

The Anatomy Instructor was not listening, because he had just peeked at his two new cards. Both were kings and his heart was fluttering like a hummingbird.

"You mean Shabbini?" Fat Freddy asked, his eyebrows dancing across his forehead. Fat Freddy was an avid supporter of the portly Shabbini, having already made four contributions to Shabbini's campaign for Firmness, Prudence, and Exercise.

The Anatomy Instructor looked up.

"Your cards," Ed the Dead croaked. "Purdy! Gimme your goddamned cards!"

"That's right. Alderman Shabbini," Purdy Jewell answered, still holding his cards in his hand. "Our man down at Shitty Hall. Fat fucker exploded this morning."

"No shit! Exploded?" Fat Freddy asked with disbelief and alarm. In addition to his concern for Alderman Shabbini's welfare, Fat Freddy was extremely sensitive to the dangers of body mass.

"Yeah. Body just . . . you know, burst. Couldn't be contained, they said. Clothes gave way. Skin gave way. Dead on arrival. Goddamned tragedy. Broke Mr. Storelli's heart, I understand. Him and Shabbini . . ." Purdy Jewell held two fingers up side by side for a long moment.

Heads were shaking around the table. But the Anatomy Instructor was simply staring at Purdy Jewell with disbelief, remembering his last glimpse of the alderman that morning—sweat streaming down the great pillows of Shabbini's cheeks, his fat lips mouthing, "Help me," as the last button on his reinforced vest threatened to give way.

"C'mon, Purdy!" Ed the Dead hissed. "Your cards, please?"

"Sure, sure," answered Purdy, pushing the cards across the table. "Gimme two. Like I was saying, these two guys at the press conference . . . Saw 'em on the T.V. down at Looie's when we broke for grub. They was twins, y'know, but connected. Fucken—whaddaya call 'em?"

"Chinese twins?" Fat Freddy offered.

"Siamese!" the Gumper gasped.

"Yeah. Siamese twins. Weirdest thing I ever seen. Like these two heads was sitting atop one body, y'know? Two heads. One body. Fuckers said they was Shabbini's media representatives. Yeah, that's what they said. Nobody'd ever hearda them before. Must be from outta town. Gotta be. 'Cause believe me, these guys you wouldn't forget. A regular friggin' freak show! Looie burnt my goddamned steak'n egger, for Christ's sake!"

The Anatomy Instructor's face had grown beet red and his lips were moving.

Ed the Dead drew three cards and glanced impassively at his own hand. "Bets?" he asked, looking up, and spotted the Anatomy Instructor's contorted face.

"Bo, are you all right? Bo!"

"He's choking!" Purdy Jewell yelled, jumping up and slapping the flat of his hand hard on the Anatomy Instructor's back—THWACK!

Every head in the room turned.

"What's going on over there?" Nuts Benedict rumbled from the bar, always wary of the violent potential in a gambling operation. But when he saw the Anatomy Instructor laid out on the table, his arms extending toward its middle like the spokes of a wheel, he boomed "HEY, GODDAMNIT!" so loud that a safety poster peeled off the brick wall and tumbled to the floor.

"I thought he was choking!" Purdy Jewell explained over his shoulder.

"Jesus, Purdy! Take it easy!" Ed the Dead croaked.

"Lookit dat hand!" Fat Freddy cried. The Anatomy Instructor's cards had flipped face up across the green felt. "Full boat. Ace–kinks."

"Fiddle–dee–dee!" the Gumper chimed in.

"Bo? Bo? Hey, Bo, I'm sorry," Purdy Jewell was apologizing as he helped the Anatomy Instructor straighten up in his seat. "I– I thought I was saving your life there. Got a little carried away is all."

"Somebody get the man a drink," a voice at the pool table suggested.

"Slits, please pour Bo a drink," Nuts Benedict agreed.

"Did you say . . ." The Anatomy Instructor gave his head a little shake. "Did you say you saw a pair of Siamese twins?"

"Yeah, on the television. A pair of friggin' Siamese freaks," Purdy growled.

A tumbler of whiskey appeared in front of the Anatomy Instructor, whose glazed eyes were staring at a vision of his elbows, surrounded by reporters, fielding questions, while cameras flashed and television crews recorded it all for the five o'clock news.

"And were they wearing a suit? A grey, pin-striped suit. But special. With four lapels. Four sets of buttons."

Purdy Jewell gave a long low whistle. The gambling around them had stopped. Everyone was listening carefully to this strange exchange. The groans of the man and woman and the rhythmic squeaking of the Volkswagen's chassis filled the sudden silence.

"Did you hear that, Nuts?" Purdy asked over his shoulder. "Bo knows them Siamese twin guys from the press conference. Isn't that interesting? I mean, don't you just find that very interesting?"

The Anatomy Instructor was shivering as his mind raced through the possibilities. They were still in town. They had put themselves in the public eye. He could find them. He could catch them. And when he did–

"Bo, Bo, Bo!"

Purdy Jewell was yelling his name and snapping fingers in front of his eyes.

Nuts Benedict had walked over behind the Anatomy Instructor's chair. "Are you all right, Beaurigard? Why don't you drink your drink? It'll buck you up."

Purdy Jewell scooted his chair closer and placed a rough hand on the Anatomy Instructor's shoulder. "Nuts is right, Bo. You look like you could use that drink. Besides, it's on the house, y'unnerstand. Oblige the man."

"He sure could use a drink," the Gumper wheezed. "Man just lost an ace–kinks full boat."

"Yeah, Purdy, whatcha gonna do about that?" Fat Freddy bleated.

"No, don't worry, it's all right," the Anatomy Instructor protested, "Really, please, I'm fine."

"Naw, Bo," Purdy Jewell began, half sheepish, but also half annoyed at this reminder of his screwup. "It ain't all right. And I'll tell you what I'm gonna do. I'm gonna make it right."

He swept together the plastic cards in the middle of the table and pulled out his money clip, from which he peeled five crisp one-hundred-dollar bills, wrapping them around the stack of cards. The Anatomy Instructor's wallet was sitting on the table beside the tumbler of whiskey. "This is a down pay-ment, see," Purdy continued, placing the stack of money and cards inside the wallet and holding up a hand to cut short the Anatomy Instructor's protests. "Man draws an ace–kinks full boat maybe once in a lifetime. Twice tops. I ain't seen it myself since Doodles Duffy back in . . . Christ! it was back when Shabbini was a ward heeler. And now the fucker's exploded?! Can you believe that? Shabbini explodes and a guy loses an ace–kinks full boat on the same day. I'd like to see some odds on that shit. That shit's scarce. Speaking of scarce," and he leaned closer to the Anatomy Instructor. "Just how well do you know them Siamese freaks, Bo?"

The Anatomy Instructor stared down at his wallet and considered this question. But the more he considered it, the less he wanted to answer it. Especially since he didn't have an answer. How could he define his strange relationship to the Siamese twin elbows? Moreover, he didn't want to define it. He wanted to get home, turn on the news, and begin collecting clues to his elbows' whereabouts. But Nuts Benedict's hands settled onto his shoulders and the many faces around him were staring, lips tight, fingers rubbing unshaven chins.

"Yesterday, everything was different," he answered, "They were . . .

they were my own flesh and blood. But today . . ."

He lifted his stiff arms up from the table with a shrug.

"Wha– wha– whaddaya sayin' there, Bo? You related to them friggin' freaks?" Purdy asked and added, "No offense," under a sharp look from Nuts Benedict.

"I guess you could say we're related," Dormouse reluctantly agreed.

"I know how it is!" Purdy Jewell slapped his hand so hard on the poker table that the playing cards gave a little hop and liquid sloshed out of glasses.

"I was married once," he continued, "I had in-laws. Had this brother-in-law, right? Fucker's lucky to be alive! I mean, I came this close . . ."

The Anatomy Instructor stared at the tiny pinch of space between Purdy Jewell's thumb and forefinger. He could see that the indirect approach was not quite working. "That's not quite it," he explained. "They are—or rather were—my elbows."

"No shit, your elbows?" someone sympathized.

"Jeez, I didn't know they was your elbows," Purdy mused and furrowed his brow.

A moment of silence passed as everyone in the room digested this fact. Elbows. They were his elbows. But what the fuck were elbows again? Were those the guys that twisted arms for protection money? The ones who bent the rules for a price? Didn't Mr. Storelli call his right- and left-hand men his elbows?

Even Nuts Benedict was considering the possibilities. Just who was this guy? He shows up. Makes like a rube. Nobody seems to know him. And yet he claims he had a pair of elbows working for him. It didn't add up. Had he just gotten out of the joint? Or dropped out of sight for a while, had plastic surgery, and now come back to—Shit, was he Mickey "the Hammer" Hammond!? Jesus, had the Hammer come back to reclaim his gambling operation? Nuts glanced at his five-gallon bottle. But the Hammer'd been a big burly guy. Six-foot-two at least. He looked down at the slight figure in the chair. This guy was no Hammer. So who was he?

"Beaurigard," Nuts asked, "What do you do for a living?"

"That's just the thing," the Anatomy Instructor answered in a rush. "I dissect bodies. How am I supposed to do that without elbows?"

A gasp went up around the room. They'd been gambling with a hit man!

"Honest!" Fat Freddy sputtered. "Honest, I wasn't in on that marked-card swindle!"

Nuts Benedict filed away this little tidbit.

"Jesus, Bo!" Purdy was saying, "So these elbows held your victims down?"

"What are you talking about, held them down?!" the Anatomy Instructor reacted with horror. "Nobody had to hold them down! They weren't victims. They were cadavers."

"Jesus, Mary and Joseph!" a voice spat.

"Guy's a sicko!"

Gamblers were crossing themselves.

"That's the problem," the Anatomy Instructor complained. "No wonder my profession gets no respect. I'm an anatomy instructor, damn it! not a grave robber. The whole program's voluntary. People donate their bodies and the university gets them straight from the funeral homes. Every cadaver is registered. I sign the receipts. It's a perfectly legal arrangement. There's nothing–"

The Anatomy Instructor paused, startled by the smiles of relief breaking out around him.

"I'm sorry I got so carried away, but . . . Damn it, what's so funny?"

The gamblers' smiles had degenerated into laughter and now they were joking about hitmen and elbows holding down victims and how it was all a perfectly legal arrangement. At first, the Anatomy Instructor was patient. But when one of them began passing a hat around, saying he was taking up a body collection for science, he felt it necessary to assure them all that the university's cadaver program set the standards for the industry. It was science, he reminded them. It was research. It was passing the torch of knowledge onto future anatomic specialists.

"But suppose I knew someone who wanted to donate his body to science," Nuts was saying.

Well, that person should contact the Anatomy Department at the university, he told them.

"But suppose he died before he had the chance to draw up all of the arrangements."

Well, that would be unfortunate.

"But wouldn't there be a way to–"

The Anatomy Instructor informed Nuts Benedict that his was an ethical profession.

"Yes, I'm sure it is, Beaurigard. So is mine, you see. And when debts are not paid, well . . . as a professional, I need to dispose of my non-performing loans, so to speak." Nuts paused. He did not need to look around the room to detect the sudden deepening of interest.

The Anatomy Instructor did not see how this could involve his profession.

"Oh, but I'm talking about a cooperative venture Beaurigard. My debtors donate their bodies to science. Your profession makes use of them."

But his profession could not accept murdered corpses. The bullet holes, the strangle marks, the marks of violence. There were bound to be questions.

"Slits are you getting this down?" Nuts called across to the bar.

"Sure, boss," Slits answered, grabbing a pad and pencil.

"No marks of violence," Nuts dictated. "Plausible aliases. Tags . . . forms. Talk to your people down at the morgue."

The Anatomy Instructor could see that things were going too far. "Damn it, perhaps some early practitioners *did* acquire their cadavers through dubious channels, but only for the advancement of humankind!"

"But that's what I'm interested in," Nuts assured him, "The advancement of humankind. And perhaps we could help you with your elbows."

The gamblers were edging back in their seats and glancing uncomfortably at one another. They grew even more uncomfortable when the Anatomy Instructor shouted, "This is not right! You are mocking the ideals upon which I have based my career!" This was getting awfully close to water bottle territory.

"I'm only speaking hypothetically, Beaurigard," Nuts apologized.

"I won't stand for such insults to my profession!"

"OK, OK." Nuts Benedict relented, raising his fists and then opening his fingers to indicate he was dropping the matter. "But please keep an open mind. In my experience, there is always room for . . . shall we say . . . innovation."

The Anatomy Instructor clambered to his feet and stood trembling before the huge ex-boxer.

"I'd . . . I'd . . . better be going," he sputtered.

There was a general exhale of relief.

"Can you use a ride home, Bo?" Purdy Jewell offered. "It's dick-freezing cold out there."

"No!" the Anatomy Instructor spat, flinching at the thought.

"Wherever you're going, Slits can give you a lift," Nuts suggested.

"Sure thing, Bo. I'll get my coat," Slits said from the bar.

The Anatomy Instructor paused, remembering the freezing walk he had just endured. But they would know where he lived. "No, I'm not going straight home," he lied, and immediately began threading his way through the tables. His shoulder blades twitched as he felt the stares of the gamblers. He did not even respond when Nuts Benedict's voice rumbled, "Suit yourself, Beaurigard. But please remember that we are very concerned and will do anything. You understand? *Anything*." Nor did he stop when Purdy Jewell yelled,

"Hey, Bo! You're forgettin' your wallet!"

Purdy caught up with him in the hallway and whispered, "Jeez, Bo, be careful," as he shoved the wallet into the Anatomy Instructor's back pocket. Then he raised his voice and added, "Remember, that's just a down payment!"

The Anatomy Instructor did not respond. His anger was fading into a reserved sort of numbness. He simply wanted to get home. He simply wanted to wake up from this nightmare, which continued to torment him with every stiff swing of his arms. He reached the street and walked straight past the huge doorman. Beebee-sized snowflakes stung his cheeks as he leaned into the wind. A block later, a copper-colored sedan cruised past, slowed down, then turned right at the next corner. The Anatomy Instructor quickened his pace. A minute later, the sedan pulled even with him again at a stoplight. He stole a look. Two men in caps and sunglasses stared straight ahead. The light changed and the sedan sped off, once again turning right at the next corner. The Anatomy Instructor ducked into Looie's hotdog stand.

A kid in a blue peacoat was shoving a fistful of fries into his mouth as he shouted into a payphone, "You know it ain't like that, baby. Don't be tellin' those lies."

Looie stood behind the counter in a grease-smeared apron, three patties sizzling on the grill behind him, a smoking cigarette clamped between his lips. He looked expectantly at the Anatomy Instructor, who made a show of squinting up at the menu sign. Looie shrugged and turned round to flip the burgers. The Anatomy Instructor swung his arm up to wipe an arc of condensation from the window so he could peer outside. Snow slashed down thickly, but there was no sign of the copper-colored sedan. All of a sudden, his sinuses cleared and the smell of French fries and grilled onions hit him like a wave. His mouth watered, his stomach growled.

"You know ah'm gonna get a job just as soon as ah fix my car, baby," the kid in the pea coat continued, pausing to swallow another lump of French fries.

"Yeah, so what'll it be?" Looie growled, turning from the grill. He grunted, leaned over the counter, and peered in both directions. "Now, where'd he go?" Looie wondered. "Hunh!"

"Fucken bitch!" the kid in the peacoat screamed, slamming the phone back onto its cradle.

"Hey, take it easy!" Looie warned, pointing his spatula at the kid in the peacoat. "You want cheese?"

"Yeah, gimme the fucken cheese."

*f*₆

Rising Voices

CHRIS MAUL RICE

Guilty as Sin
from *Flint*

Whenever she thought of Fatima, she thought of lavender. Not the color, although the dusty silver of her skin and the pale hue of her eyes were there, too, but the smell and, eventually, of course, her smoky taste on the tongue.

Over the years, she prayed for the memories to dull, for some diversion to shield her from her irresistible daydreams. But they were as fresh and bracing as her mother's slap when she learned of the affair. "Leila, you! You!," covering her mouth with the palm of her hand, the other gripping the brooch just above her heart, the words laser sharp, illuminating the dusky storeroom. Mama didn't have the word to describe what she found so offensive. As if the saying of it, *lesbian*, would make it more real than finding her daughter entwined with Fatima — their legs, a writhing braid, poking from behind the crates of oranges – on the produce-littered floor of the neighborhood grocery's store room.

Since her father's death, just that spring, her mother had asked Leila to postpone college to help in the store. So, instead of going to college like all of her cousins and friends, Leila found herself stocking shelves and waiting on customers. Her only respite from the store's aching boredom was Fatima.

At noon, when Leila took lunch and a book to the storeroom, Fatima would burst out of her pre-med class at the University, run down Court Street, break off a lavender twig out of Widow Gracey's garden and poke the piny bough into her thick black curls. Still running, she would reach the store's back door at exactly ten past noon (just after the sun reached its apex in the cloudless summer sky). Once there, she would put her hands on her knobby knees, breathing heavily, and wait for the big, silver door to open. Once inside, Leila would push Fatima's corkscrew curls off the edges of her almond eyes, palm her round flushed cheeks, and laugh at how her skirt's zipper had twisted to the front during her sprint to the store.

As Mama waited on customers in the front of the store, they would fall against each other, kneading the other's face with kisses until Fatima was able to untie the bows on Leila's smock, pull it over her head and work her hands up Leila's torso to her breasts. They would undress each other quickly, urgently, until Leila grabbed Fatima's hands and pulled her into the tiny apartment of boxes, the width and length of two caskets. And, although their love-making was loud, the swinging doors and stacked cardboard boxes kept their secret. Afterward, wrung out and entwined, Fatima would curl into Leila's arms, back to chest, their shoulders resting on flattered cardboard. Leila would drink in Fatima's smell, of lavender and sweat while stroking the smooth curve made by her pelvis and hipbone. She could still feel it now in her memory: like stroking the iridescent underside of a seashell.

This went on all summer, into Fall, until that day her mother found them and the bracing innocence evaporated. Leila's mother met privately with Fatima's parents who promptly transferred their daughter and her pre-med credits to a school in California.

And now, after 20 years, the death of her mother, a number of brief, stormy affairs, and the constant promise to shutter the Food Fair, this day, like all the others, she found herself in the exact place she didn't want to be: behind the counter. She was thirty eight. Thirty-eight. And that meant, with a gaggle of Lebanese Aunties as constant reminders, that she was ancient. Ancient and, as everyone liked to remind her: unmarried and without children. The Aunties, of course, knew (but were the only ones) of her 'mistake' (as they referred to it) with Fatima and the reason for her unending sadness. But, even so, that was in the past and now was now and because of that, it felt like everything in her life had come down to one thing: numbers. Numbers dictated her life. And she found no softness or roundness or warmth in them.

Years later, when she looked back at this time, she was convinced that it was something in the numbers that drove her to do it. The numbers, goddamnit. Numbers!. Everything in that store had one: a price tag, a serial number, a weight in pounds, grams, pints, liters or gallons. Everything. Everything. And she couldn't bear their mocking preciseness; their intimate smugness. Everything had its place. The ketchup next to the salad dressing. The butter next to the eggs. She wanted something unpredictable, soft and yielding. Everything stocked, stacked, shelved and sold. Mrs. Abraham needed capers. Mrs. Eid needed onions and lentils. Everything was right where they had found it for the last 50 years. She was the only thing in the store without a reason to be there.

She needed a diversion.

She had just opened the store and the eastern light tumbled through the store's front glass windows and onto the speckled counter that ran the length of the front store. The aisles spoked away from this counter so that, by walking the length of the counter, she could see the entire store. It had been so quiet that morning and she had been so lost in her thoughts that she didn't hear him walk through the open door while she knelt, stocking the cigarette slots below the counter.

"Miss Hamady? The deep, unfamiliar voice snapped at her consciousness. As she stood, she saw a young man's torso, his t-shirt snug against his waist. As she straightened, she worked her eyes up from his thick, caramel-colored hands palming the counter; his thick fingers splayed like two fans, the taut muscles of his arms straining the skin, his shoulders wide but delicate. He fingered the edge of an envelope with lottery numbers scrawled sloppily across the back. She felt his gaze resting on her chest just before he snatched the envelope up and waved it in front of his face. His face was familiar and, at first, she didn't recognize him until she imagined how his sharp features had emerged from that soft baby flesh of just a few summers before.

She recognized him only after snatching the envelope out of his hand and announcing, "Mr. Joseph, you're all grown up."

He puckered his mouth to one side and nodded, "You look good, too." She stepped back at his realization of her compliment. Long, black curls fell in front of his eyes. He swiped at them self-consciously with the back of his hand and leaned over the counter. She started punching in the lottery numbers, which, she knew, were for his grandfather. He had brought his Papa's numbers in every week when he was in high school, before he graduated and joined the Peace Corps.

Leila didn't realize it at the time, didn't realize it until much later, really, but this boy's heart-shaped face, the almond eyes, his black curls, the ropiness of his arms and length of his torso – all — smacked of Fatima. But there was something more: a softness in his eyes drinking her in. She hadn't seen that – hadn't wanted to see that — in a long, long time.

"Bobby Joseph. When did you get back from—?"

"Africa. Just last week."

"Africa?" even she could hear the envy in her voice as she handed him the lottery ticket and he paid.

"Uganda, actually." He pronounced it like a news reporter.

"U-GAN-DA," she mocked, rolling her eyes and bringing her hands around to her back to tie her smock strings. Again his eyes followed the swoop of her hips as she tied the smock tight in the back and something about his innocent boldness made her want to slap him.

"I was wondering if you need some help around here this summer."

"I don't *need* help."

"Man, Pops said you'd give me a hard time."

"He did, did he?"

He straightened and brought his hands to his chest, "I was wondering,

Miss Hamady, if I might have a job, just for the summer, Miss Hamady, because, clearly, you don't need help but nothing would give me greater joy than bagging groceries."

She laughed. "I *don't* need it," she said. But I want it, she thought, as she nodded and sent him to the store room for a smock.

She needed a diversion. And here he was.

from *The Enchanters vs. Sprawlburg Springs*

In the front yard, under a moth-infested amber streetlight, the skinheads were circled around Scott, who was on the ground curled up with his arms covering his frizzy head, blubbering for mercy. Three of them were kicking him in the chest and back as the others walked around shouting encouragements. Partygoers just stood around nervously watching through the front windows.

Mickey and I followed Donald down the three steps from the front porch, Donald with the bass hoisted over his head like a sword. He swung it on the back of one of the skin's heads. I'll never forget the sound the bass made, a wooden thwack with just the slightest low ring of the strings. The skinhead fell forward and collapsed onto all fours. Donald kept swinging, and I had to side-step to avoid the backend of the bashings, running to the other side of the rapidly disintegrating circle, no thoughts except swinging my cymbal stand until these thugs left Scott alone. While the sounds of my cymbal stand hitting skulls wasn't as, uh, melodic, as the bass Donald was wielding, it was just as satisfying nonetheless.

But we were outnumbered 15-3, and I'm not much of a fighter. Despite disabling about 1/2 of their numbers, the skinhead's counterattack would have been overpowering if other partygoers hadn't finally joined in. I was punched in the stomach and tackled, causing me to drop my cymbal stand, with three skinheads ready to punch and kick me until my drumming, if not my living, days were over. Mickey was way too big for these skinheads, most of whom were just dumbass kids who didn't know any better, and he could take them out two at a time, and then you had all the fat, scrawny, lanky, geeky male members of The Enchanter contingent, these freaky kids, jumping in like they were soldiers in hand-to-hand combat with the enemy, and I almost wanted to laugh except I could barely breathe from one-too-many kicks to the stomach, and it all happened so fast, the next thing I know Mickey's pulling me up, all like, "Are you okay, Little Buddy?" and I nodded, feeling just a little bit light-headed, but not enough to faint as I watched the few skinheads not incapacitated limp or run away down the street, all of them leaving except for one kid, sprawled out there on the front yard, curled into the fetal position.

"GET UP, YOU FUCKING NAZI MOTHERFUCK!" Donald screamed over him as the rest of us had backed up now that we thought the fight was over.

The skinhead kid laid there in a pool of his own blood pouring out both his nostrils and lips. Donald kicked him in the ribs and yelled, "GET UP, ADOLPH! WHERE'S YOUR WHITE POWER NOW YOU FUCKING COCKSMACK!" He spat in his face. The kid was crying, blubbering something about "stop . . . please . . ."

I walked over to Donald. "Leave him alone. It's over." I said, trying to stand between this kid, because, when I looked at him, I could tell, that's all he was, just a dumb kid looking for something to belong to, no matter how wrong it was, which made him not too far off from the rest of us, but far enough to deserve our contempt, but not this.

"WHAT, YOU'RE NOT GONNA GET UP AND FIGHT NOW THAT YOU CAN'T BEAT PEOPLE UP 15 TO 1 YOU GODDAMN WORTHLESS PIECE OF FUCKING BULLSHIT!?!" Donald yelled, spanking him in the ass with the bass. He didn't even look at me when I told him to stop. His face was all red, eyes bugged out, tall beanpole body bent over the kid at the waist and focused on nothing else like some kind of rabid attack dog.

The kid was really crying now, whimpering through his swollen and blackened face. Renee had come out to us now, watching from the front porch, also in tears. "Donald," she said, "please stop this. They've left, and we have a show to do." She reached out with her left hand and squeezed his right shoulder.

Donald stepped back, catching his breath, still looking like he had more fight in him, more punches and kicks he wanted to throw, but instead, he kneeled down and got right in front of the kid's face and said between gasps for air, "You're gonna tell all your faggot friends who left you here to die that if they EVER think to start any shit with us or our friends, it's gonna be ten times worse, and you'll never read 'Mein Kampf' again, do you understand me, you Nazi shitstain?" To emphasize his point, Donald spat in his face, then walked back into the party, which wasn't really a party anymore, but a bunch of random people standing there in shock.

Renee followed him inside the house, yelling after him, "You didn't have to take it that far, Donald!" I stood there over the kid, and Scott joined me. His left eye was bruised shut, and he kept a white hand towel filled with ice across that half of his head. Me, the wind was still knocked out, but I was slowly getting it back, even though it hurt to inhale.

"How do you feel?" I asked Scott.

"I'll be all right," he said. "Thanks for coming out here and jumping in."

I nodded. It all happened so fast, like everything with The Enchanters. I couldn't process anything more about it. A couple party dudes came up to the kid and picked him up, one on each end, all like, "We gotta get this kid outta here and to the hospital so the cops don't come." They carried him a 1/2 block down to a green pickup truck, where they dropped him in the back, got in the front, and drove away.

Scott and I walked back to the house. Mickey was sitting there on the front porch steps, fat red face curled downward, sad.

"We coulda killed that kid," he said. "We really hurt those guys."

"Fuck 'em," I said, feeling the pains in my chest from those kicks. "That kid's gonna live, and besides, they started it, and he was in there with the other fourteen of 'em wanting to kill Scott here." I sat down next to Mickey and patted him on the back. "They started it, remember? We're just trying to play music and have fun, and we had to defend ourselves. From thugs. Remember?"

"Yeah, I know," Mickey said. "It still doesn't seem right, though."

But I didn't give a shit. The skinheads in our town sucked ass, and they deserved any beatdowns they got. And I'm not a violent person. At all. But those kids . . . it was worth it to see them run away and cry. The concert went on as scheduled, and it wasn't our best, due to frazzled and exhausted nerves and a nearly cleared-out living room from people not all that eager to use party as a verb after the fight, but we got through it. Sometimes, all you could do with these concerts was to somehow survive it, all the unpredictable and myriad insanities thrown at us, most amusing, some not so, but, like I said, never boring.

STEPHANIE KUEHNERT

Nadia
from *The Black Notebooks*

The sight of Louisa and Colette, barefoot and disheveled, dashing around the side of the building for the gated-in pool caught the attention of the night manager. He stumbled up into action, shouting, "Hey, the pool is for guests only!" And then realizing that they might be some of the shady guests that the low prices of the Bay Motel attracted, he added, "The pool is closed after ten!" as he pursued them to the back of the building.

Propelling up and over the short, chain link fence—her heels hitting the cement hard, but she wouldn't feel them throb until much later—Louisa saw them at the side of the deeper end of the kidney-shaped pool—six kids squatted in a tight circle, shoulder to shoulder, heads bowed like they were doing some kind of ritual, maybe a séance. They were just outside of the circle of sodium light cast by one of the lamps that lined the perimeter of the pool area, and as Louisa and Colette got closer the yellowish light revealed the back of the enormous blue jeans that Kyle wore, the ties of Carla's silver halter top, Jessamine's long purple and blue dreds, on the other side, Mike's eyebrow ring and shaved head, the dark roots in Brenda's platinum hair, and another boy that Louisa didn't recognize with waxy, spiked black hair. She couldn't see Nadia at the center of the circle. She was what they were bending over. Louisa convinced herself that it was innocent, that the kids were chanting, "Light as feather, stiff as board, light as feather, stiff as board," in a collective murmur and Nadia would rise up. Maybe the game had scared Brenda, she had thought Nadia was possessed, decided to call Nadia's mother in terror.

Colette's ragged wail shattered Louisa's illusion. "NADIA!" And the circle parted, scattered to the back and side fences. The folded chairs that overbaked guests used to sun themselves during the day clattered against the concrete as the kids knocked them from their resting places against the fence in their stumbled escape. No, Louisa knew threats from the spirit world wouldn't faze these kids, so if something had driven Brenda to call, it was very, very real.

As the circle broke, Nadia was revealed, lying on her back, limbs flung out at her sides haphazardly like she had fallen from the sky when the clouds cracked open for a sudden downpour. Water puddled around her body, fanning outwards and darkening the cement. Wet footprints staggered away from her and formed in front of Brenda as she slowly backed away. Louisa ran for her, clamping her hand around Brenda's right wrist as Colette collapsed on her knees at Nadia's side moaning, "No, no, NO!"

Colette's ringed fingers prodded at Nadia's neck, digging for a pulse, believing that the purple tone glistening through Nadia's translucent skin had to be the sign of blood trying to push forward to somewhere. Colette's hands slid over the straps of Nadia's soaked, glittery black tank top down her clammy arms. She rubbed, waxing her daughter's skin like Nadia was a tarnished treasure chest that had been submerged deep beneath the barely rippling waters of the Bay Motel pool, like if she kept rubbing words would be revealed that Colette would just have to say to unlock Nadia, make her heart pound undeniably, cause her to sit up straight, spewing the water in her lungs freely like a fountain.

Colette quickly moved her hands from her daughter's arms to her chest, pounding on it. Then her fingers flew up, pinching Nadia's nose as she forced her breath in through Nadia's wilted lips. Lifting her mouth from her daughter's, Colette screeched, "Call someone! Someone fucking call someone! I don't know how to do this! Help me!" The word "help" was breathless, Colette giving all her air to Nadia.

The sallow-faced night manager had come to halt at the gate, mouth hanging open, chin dangling like an undercooked dumpling. He had watched the coven of teenagers take flight and the dark-haired woman throw herself on the girl sprawled out unconscious at the side of the pool. Colette's short, black hair was plastered against her neck with sweat and some strands clung to her tear-soaked cheeks as she lifted her head to scream for help, causing the night manager to suddenly spring into action, his sausage-like legs propelling him back toward the office.

Louisa wrenched Brenda out of the shadows at the back of the pool area toward Colette, toward where Nadia lay on the ground. Nadia's bright crimson hair, which Louisa had helped her dye just days ago, was tangled, plastered flat against the concrete beneath her, sticking out all around her head like a flaming crown extinguished by the scummy pool water. Louisa got close enough to see Nadia's face in glimpses in the intervals when Colette lifted her head away from Nadia's during her attempted as-seen-on-TV CPR. Nadia's red lipstick had smudged outwards, giving her cheeks the illusion of pinkness until Louisa saw it staining Colette's face as well. The mascara, black eyeliner, and dark shadow Nadia had artfully smeared before going out that night spread down her face like mud. Louisa caught a glimpse of Nadia's hazel eyes, open, making her face look posed to ask her mother a question or deny a wrong-doing. Louisa was waiting for Nadia to sit up, wrap her arms around her chest, and pull away from her mother, wrinkling her nose and rolling her eyes. "MOM!" she would huff with an over-exaggerated sigh, responding to what she perceived as Colette's melodrama with her own. They would glare at each other for a moment or two, but eventually dissolve into giggles, the way their fights always ended. Louisa believed she could see it happening, but then she felt Brenda stumble.

As they got closer to Nadia, Brenda's long, thin limbs suddenly went limp; she tripped over herself, embodying the awkwardness of her age. At the sight of Nadia's face, Brenda stopped pulling away from Louisa and coiled inward, like a ballerina spinning toward her partner.

"Where did you call from?" Louisa demanded as she caught Brenda, and stared into her brown eyes, which were just as makeup-stained and water-logged as Nadia's.

Brenda's bony face shook like her voice. "Frr-from the p-payphone," she choked, weakly waving her finger to the corner of the pool area directly across from the entrance.

The manager could have run straight to it instead of backtracking to his office, saved time. Brenda could have… "Why didn't you call the police first?" Louisa shook Brenda by the shoulders. It wasn't a very rough shake, but Brenda's body was so weak she wobbled, her wet hair falling in blond clumps across her face.

"We didn't want to get in trouble. We didn't want Nn-nadia to get in trou-ble."

We didn't want to get in trouble, the empty eulogy for Nadia, for Louisa's time in California. Every time she had tried to leave, Colette always said, "You know we'll get into trouble without you."

A Most Memorable Day of Your Life
from *Gig*

"What type of music are we going to hear tonight?"

Fuck this question. I hate it every time it's asked. The guy across from me is holding his wife's hand, waiting for an answer. "All kinds," I say.

He raises his head a bit, closes his eyes and breathes in like there's fuckin' cotton candy air. Sinatra is still in the CD drawer; *Summer Wind* is just ending. "Are we going to hear some more Frankie when dancing starts?" The man moves his hand down to his wife's thigh and pats it.

"Yeah, maybe." A lie.

"Good," the man and his wife smile like Santa's bringing them presents tonight, "Good."

Soon the cake is replaced with bodies on the dancefloor, all of them swaying in unison to *Unchained Melody*, by the Righteous Brothers. The mood is all lovey-dovey because of the wedding and the alcohol, yet it's not enough to keep them out there when *Get Down Tonight* kicks in. The bridesmaids are the only ones left, jiggling and clapping.

I run through the routine of it all, making sure that all the single ladies are out there for the bouquet toss, and the bachelors for the garter throw. Then it's back into dance, hitting the crowd with some group participation songs. Before they even know what's happening, their hands and arms are up in the air forming the letters YMCA. And yeah, I'm here flailing my arms too, to get everyone going, but my mind is a million miles away. There's so much I'm missing because of this gig. I could be out with Katie, or sharing a beer with my friends at the Kerry Piper Pub. But here I am, alone in a room filled with dozens of beautiful women, and drunken guys telling stories.

Jack Peathong makes a move on the maid of honor. He uses a finger to spell out the letters of the song on her back, the area where the dress dips down and shows off skin. His pace is much slower and seductive than the beat of the song. Finally he swings his head around and lands one on her neck. She giggles and shivers like Jack's tongue is making her whole body tickle. I wanna do that.

Each week it gets worse, like you realize more and more that it's a fucking Saturday night and you're fucking working. I'm dating Katie now, but that's fucked 'cause I'm here every Saturday night. Well, not always the

Château Bouche, but here as in behind this equipment. Sometimes I'd like to just chuck it all. Except the CD's.

Jack leads the maid of honor out of the room. She resists a little, holding her ground and waving a no-no finger, but still she is laughing. He tugs a little harder and she goes with in tow. They stumble over a group of vacant chairs. The groomsmen standing around the bar look over, see the exiting, drunken couple giggling, and start cheering for Jack.

Six months. I give myself six months to get out of this business. I do the math; six months equals roughly eighteen more gigs and one hundred, eight hours. I'll tell Katie tomorrow and everything will be fine. Maybe she's my perfect woman. Tiny packages of cake wrapped in wax paper come out of the kitchen on silver trays. Everything will be fine.

I don't give much thought to the next song. It just sorta comes out of the speakers without me realizing it. I'm on autopilot, sticking to the playlist. The sound waves act as a magnet for all the women. They come onto the dancefloor chanting the words to Gloria Gaynor's, *I Will Survive*. Amber is leading the pack, but she comes all the way over to me before joining the group on the floor. I paste my smile back on. It's been off since the lights went dim. Amber reaches her arms around my body and hugs tight. The grip is seamless, her breasts dipping into my chest, my belly protruding into her abs. I can feel her thighs as the rough beading on her dress crushes against my wool pants.

My hand instinctively reaches to the upper tip of her spine and my palm spreads out, catching a few hanging strands of hair. She releases, pushes herself away, and kisses me on the cheek. Her lips are warm and moist and I can visualize the perfect ring of cherry red they'll leave behind. This is no joke, like when John leaned over and kissed his best man. The best part isn't the lips though, it's the tip of her nose, which dips down and presses cold against my face then gingerly lifts back up. Maybe this is *my* perfect woman.

"This is wonderful," she says. "You're doing a wonderful job. Thank you Scott."

Two bridesmaids pull Amber onto the dancefloor before I can respond. They're all singing, "I will survive, hey, hey!"

Amber looks back, just once. My heart cracks when I see her warm smile. She can't hear me, but I whisper to her anyway, "It's not Scott. It's Trent." But there she is, back out on the dancefloor, perfectly content with the misconception that I am Scott. Only six more months.

Three Deaths
from *Murderess X*

We didn't have a gun, so I couldn't shoot my momma. But that's the one that I most fantasized about. Walking up to her when she was doing dishes, asking her to turn around, and unloading all of my bullets into her chest as she did so, her blond-haired head flying backwards, her large body absorbing all the bullets and shooting blood out in return. The bullets would burst through her back and crash into the dishes sitting in our sink, sending shards of cheap, plastic plates everywhere. I would feel the shock in my hands from the gun blasts, hear the ringing in my ears, smell the cordite in the air, and be awash in momma's blood staining my skirt. I always saw myself smiling and grinning in those shooting fantasies, laughing gleefully, as momma crossed over into death. I never knew why I felt that way, only that I did. It was unquestioned.

One night, a couple of months into my short-lived high school experience, I was sitting downstairs, doodling instead of doing my math homework. Momma came in wearing her flannel robe and announced that she was going upstairs to take a bath. She'd been working all day, and, she said, sometimes cleaning the dirt from other people's homes made her feel disgusting, so she would go soak the dirty off. She walked upstairs, to the bathroom with the bathtub in it.

I sat up straight in my chair when I heard the water start upstairs, as though a bolt of lightning directly from God had hit me in the head. I blinked a few times, probably even twitched a little, realizing the simplicity of what I had to do. I smiled, and giggled a bit, and when I heard the water turn off, I got up from the table and walked up the stairs. I went to the bathroom door and, without hesitating, pushed it open and walked in.

Momma sat in the tub with a shower cap on her head full of her dyed-blonde hair. She had a mud pack on her face to get rid of her worry wrinkles. A thick layer of bubbles sat on top of the water, giving off a little steam. Her knees poked through the bubbles because the tub was too short for her to fully lay down in.

I walked over and got the hair dryer, which was always plugged in to the outlet above the sink, next to the tub.

"Hi baby," momma said. "What's up?"

As calm as could be, I turned on the hair dryer and dropped it into the bathtub.

I hadn't really thought about what would happen, so I was surprised. Three sharp pops sounded in a row, each one sending a thick arc of electricity up out of momma's bubble bath, which practically carried momma's big body out of the tub. Three times she jumped and seized, sending water and bubbles all over me, and the shock was so powerful that it knocked me backwards on the third one. I landed on my butt, then all the lights went out. I sat there, a ringing in my ears from the loudness of the shocks, and a peculiar warmth stretching across my belly. I was all wet, and my skirt was sopping with soapy water. The room was dark, almost pitch black, until I adjusted to the darkness.

I sat there for I don't know how long before I decided to go see momma. She hadn't moved the whole time so I figured she was dead. I crawled over to the tub, my stomach throbbing dully, and knelt by the side of the tub to look at momma. I didn't think about being electrocuted myself, but, as the sheriff told me later, the hair dryer had knocked out the power in the house, so I guess I was lucky.

Momma's head lolled towards the wall, away from me. One arm and one leg were draped over the edge of the tub, still dripping sudsy water. Her fingers were balled up into a claw and, interestingly, so were her toes—splayed out wide-wise, but curled in, like little talons.

In order to see her face, I would have to move her head.

I had a little trepidation to do this, as I was a little squeamish to touch a dead body for some reason. I frowned with worry as I gently took her head in one hand and attempted to move it towards me so I could see her.

It wouldn't turn, but when I pulled harder, it sort of just fell straight over at a most unnatural angle. She had broken her neck while jumping around. Her head fell over towards me and I'd been leaning in so close that her nose bumped mine.

Her eyes were bugged out of her head like ping-pong balls. Her tongue had shot out of her mouth almost six inches. I hadn't know there was that much tongue in a person's mouth. Around the tongue, her crooked teeth were firmly clamped, nearly biting all the way through, and covered in blood. Her lips were pulled up into a snarl, exposing most of her gums. Her nose was bunched up like a feral animal's.

But the biggest thing, the thing I remember the most, and won't forget until my dying day, and maybe not even then, was momma's last breath. When her head flopped over, I guess I pushed the last of the air out of her lungs, so when her nose, all pulled up and demonic, bumped into mine, I inhaled her last breath. It was sweet, almost pungent, and as she stared at me with those dead, buggy eyes, I knew that I'd inhaled her soul.

from *The Chapter of Faults*

I laughed in a way you should never laugh at a superior. "Don't you know what postulants are? Postulants are the lowest of low. We have no volition of our own. We do what we're told, when we're told. We do not speak, we do not think. We have no rights to anything, not even our own bodies. Do you know what happened when we first got here? They herded us downstairs to the boiler room and one by one took us behind a screen and shaved our heads like sheep. We *are* sheep. Twice a week we have to go to Chapter of Faults. That's where we line up and kneel for an hour and confess our sins in front of everyone. Our mail is sorted, we can't make phone calls, we can't see our family or friends, we never see a clock. Do you know we're not allowed to say *my* or *mine*? It's in the Rule Book. We're supposed to say *ours*, if we're allowed to speak at all, which we're not. You make fun of our little notepads and pencils, but how else can we ask permission to go to the bathroom? And have you *seen* our bathroom? It's in the dregs of the castle, where postulants belong. A postulant is a sheep who cannot think for herself, and this is our offering for world peace? This is a joke!"

My chest was heaving. I couldn't believe what had just come out of my mouth, and I blamed him for riling me up. I yelled, "Why do I always end up yelling in your office?"

He sat totally still on his desk edge, beaming at me. "Because the anger of the revolutionary beats in your chest."

I looked away, annoyed by his vagueness, and excited. "What does that mean?"

"Margaret, do you think you're the only one who feels this way?"

"No one else seems to mind."

"But they do. Right now there are people all over the world who are asking just what you're asking. How can we serve God's people if we know nothing about the way they live? His Holiness is listening, the church is listening. Change is coming. It's a part of life, like you said. We've been waiting a long time to embrace it. The walls dividing the clergy and the lay people are crumbling. Very soon we will be united, working together for Christ's mission on earth." He came toward me and took both my hands in his. "Margaret, you embody these changes, you embody this spirit of openness. God sent you here for a reason, the same reason he sent me. Christ has given us a call to arms—

we will do all that He has done and more. It is our choice whether or not we answer the call."

What could I say? What could I say when the man I adored told me I had a purpose, and that purpose was his purpose, and that together we would usher in a new era? I stood there, staring at him dumbly, aching at the tautness of his proximity. This was so much better than any kiss—this was his passion, this was real. He saw in me the anger of a revolutionary, which was his anger. He recognized me as his own. He claimed me right then and there.

So I went back. Again and again. Nobody asked me where I went, and I didn't care if they saw me going down the hill each day, though I always entered through the church doors, crept quietly through the back hall to his office, where the newest *Nonpareil* would be waiting for me, along with *Life, National Geographic*, and anything else he thought I might find interesting. Over the long spring and into the summer, as the trees outside his window burst into a green curtain of privacy, I read daily death tolls in Vietnam, studied photos of rows of soldiers, rows of caskets draped with American flags. I read about the civil rights events, the space race, the comings and goings of the Rat Pack. I read about cook-offs and picnics, school referendums and crop quotes, and scrutinized photos of students my own age, in clothes I'd never wear. None of it really *meant* anything to me—I didn't know anyone who looked like that or lived that way. But I took my place on the couch with the afghan and scoured the journals front to back, because I knew it impressed him; I knew it was what he wanted of me, to be strong, to be revolutionary. He saw in me qualities no one else had ever seen—and I wanted to live up to his vision of who I could be, the who God intended me to be.

Some afternoons we would spend the entire hour discussing what was happening in the world, and I would learn more from his knowledge and insight than a whole issue of *Life* magazine. Sometimes he turned on the radio and we listened to the ball game together. Some days he would greet me warmly and get me settled with tea and newspapers, leaving me to read for the whole hour while he worked at his desk. I adored these afternoons because we were silent together, like a husband and wife who have been married a long time. I would watch him under the painting of the angry boy and wonder if it really had been him who had painted it, since I never saw the streaks of anger that would compel him to paint that portrait of Christ.

Everyday I would leave him and climb the hill to the castle and wonder what I was doing. I knew what I was doing: I was falling in love with him. But was he falling in love with me? No—he liked me and cared for me because, as he said, God had brought us there for the same reason—to usher in the new era. I would mull over every nuance of our interaction until I had convinced myself that he had no feelings for me beyond the respect and admiration shared by fellow revolutionaries—the same respect and admiration he felt for Mother Elizabeth. He had taken me under his wing as his protégé, and the warmth and kindness in his eyes were only that of a mentor for his most talented mentee. The kiss that night—it was nothing more than high emotion, as he said, because in all the afternoons I'd seen him since, he never crossed that line again. He kept his office door ajar, stayed behind his desk, and held the conversation to news of the world and Maternity. I would stay up the whole night, playing and replaying every interaction between us, convincing myself this was nothing more than a teacher and his pupil. But as soon as I arrived at his door the following afternoon, and he looked up at me with the joy of someone who has been waiting a long time to receive his prize, I knew. I just knew.

It's Only Flirtin'
from *The Curse*

Iwas at my cousin Ace's house and it seemed my pregnancy made me horny as ever. I was always wanting it. I had forgotten all about Cee's dream and was enjoying the attention that Ace's friend Jimmy had been giving me. Then we were in my big cousin Redderick's van and had been kicking it all day, me and Jimmy. I got sleepy and fell asleep right there in the van. I awoke moaning in pleasure as I felt Jimmy kissing me on my neck and rubbing my nipples like no other. It felt so good I didn't want him to stop. I began to think about how I was pregnant with Cee's baby, which meant I would be with him for life. How he had slept with plenty of girls before and I had only been with him. Before I knew it, Jimmy entered me and I felt like I was in heaven. We'd done it.

The next day Cee called from Gateway Rehab and I just couldn't talk to him. If he could tell I acted differently, he didn't let on. I felt so guilty and angry at myself. All I could think about was, he dreamt this.

May thirteenth, Cee came home clean and his skin looked clearer. He had gained his weight back and was looking good. He promised me that he was ready to be a real man and take care of me and his unborn child. He even got a job. It was never hard for him to get a job, with us both going to Jones Commercial Business high school, he knew all about resumes and interviews. He seemed to be really trying to make things work for us. He told me that with his first check he would split it between us.

But the guilt I felt was weighing me down. I tried to practice truth and didn't like being deceitful. Whenever I tried to work up the nerve to tell him about Jimmy, I couldn't. I replayed different ways of telling him over and over and discarded them. Then the day before he was to get his check, my guilty conscience began kicking in.

We had spent the night over Ace's house. That morning, Jimmy, Ace and Cee decided they wanted to go to the park and play basketball. Ace's girl Apple and I followed. As we walked to Marquette Park, I could feel Jimmy staring at me. I would meet his eyes and see the look of desire and quickly look away. On the way back from the game, I walked with Cee, behind everyone else. Jimmy and Ace decided to go to Jimmy's house, so they cut off from us. "Cee, we need to talk."

"About what?"

"Um, we'll talk once we get to grandma's." We walked a block away from Jimmy's house and walked up the concrete steps into grandma's. We walked down into the basement.

"What you got to tell me?" he asked, once we were on the couch. I was so nervous that I blurted out the first thing that came to mind.

"Jimmy keeps flirtin' with me." I stood there awkwardly, feeling stupid. Cee looked at me.

"What?"

"He keeps flirtin' with me. But don't say anything to him about it. I don't want any trouble. While you were gone, he flirted with me the whole time." I tried to make myself shut up, but Cee was waiting patiently. I continued telling him half the truth.

"You promise you won't say anything?" I asked him.

He nodded. "I won't say anything. I'll be back," he stood walking up the stairs.

"Cee! You promise?" I asked again.

"I ain't gone say nothing, flirtin' ain't nothing to trip over." When he said that, I trusted him, but I paced the basement. I kept looking out the window, wishing he would hurry up and return.

Twenty minutes later, Cee came back down the stairs with a hard look in his eyes.

"What's wrong?" I asked, my heart beating fast.

"He was flirtin' with you. But you fucked him!" he yelled.

"What?" I asked, my mouth in a frown.

"You heard me, please say you didn't. That's all I wanna hear, Jay. Just tell me right now and tell me the truth. But it really ain't no need for you to say shit. Your cousin told me it happened too."

"You bogus! I told you not to tell him, you lied to me."

"Naw, I didn't lie. I told Ace and Ace told Jimmy that you claim he been bothering you. And then Ace and Jimmy told me together."

This shocked me that my cousin had vouched for the issue, but I said nothing. I held my head down.

"I'm sorry, baby," I muttered. I looked up at Cee, with tears in my eyes. "I'm so sorry." He only shook his head, he wouldn't even look at me.

"Hell naw. And you got my baby in yo stomach? That's fucked up."

"I don't know. I didn't have any intentions of doing it. It just happened. I was lonely and you kept accusing me of sleeping with him. Dreaming—"

"Yeah, I even dreamt the shit. I should have known. I should have followed my first mind." I walked to Cee and reached my hand out to touch his cheek. He pushed my hand away. "Don't touch me." I felt stunned.

"Baby, I'm sorry. You know things weren't right for us. You know that I didn't trust you. How you show me no attention." I cried so hard, snot ran out my nose. I begged for at least thirty minutes before Cee would let me touch him. We began to kiss passionately. I followed him into a small room and he laid on his back. I began to kiss him on his neck and touch him. He wouldn't respond. Frustrated, he pushed me off of him.

"I can't do this. Get off me," he said, getting up. "I can't even get hard with you." He walked out of the house leaving me standing staring after him.

The next day, the plan had been set that we were to go and pick up his check together. Actually, the plan had been set for weeks. Just as I knew, I should have kept my big mouth shut, I would never learn.

Cee awoke early and told me that Ace and his friend would be dropping him off at work. I had believed him.

"Cee, you know I need to put up money for the baby. Do you promise that you'll bring the money straight here?"

"I told you yeah. Don't ask me anymore."

I sighed. "I love you, baby. Please believe me. I wish this would never have happened. "

"Whatever." A horn honked outside and Cee ran out. I stood on the porch as he got inside a smoke filled car with the music up at full blast. Ace passed him the blunt and Cee took it as they rode off.

Cee was supposed to have been home by four p.m. No such luck. I kept calling his job. I discovered that he hadn't come in, only to pick up his check. My blood began to boil. I walked down to Ace's house. Just as I thought, Cee was trying to hop back in the car. Ace pulled off, even though they heard me calling.

I had caught up with him an hour later, coming out of the liquor store. When I called him, he looked back at me, a smirk on his face.

"Cee!" I yelled as they took off again.

Finally, I caught him back at Ace's house. "Uh, uh!" I yelled. "Slow down!" I walked toward him, this time they couldn't pull away fast enough.

"Cee, you on some bullshit. You told me you would give me half your check, what's the deal?"

"Man, my check was short," he stated, his breath smelled like hard liquor, his eyes were blood shot red. Ace and everyone in the car had smiles on their faces and red eyes.

I knew then that Cee had been splurging on everyone in the car and dodging me. I sat there stupidly, angrily wishing that I hadn't told him shit.

f₆

Novels-in-Progress and more

ANDREW ALLEGRETTI

Robert Snow's Rules of Order
from *A Fool's Game*

Memories are becoming clearer and distinct from one another. I feel
what has been left in my nets, and realize it is more than I expected.
-Rainer Maria Rilke

I

And then with all the unexpectedness of a dream, the lights of Chicago
were below him, a shimmering sprawl ending abruptly at the shoreline,
where, above the trackless black water of the lake, the sky holds a faint brightening which he knows is morning. Robert Snow leaned closer to the plane
window, his reflection filling the murky glass, and with nothing to impede his
view, he saw the vastness below him and understood for the first time how
impossible it is to comprehend a place so big—that the only way a man can
know something so enormous is through the parts that once belonged to him.
Suddenly, he had the illusion that the floor of the plane had vanished and that
he floated above the shimmer, a disembodied being suspended in the coolness
of this June morning. And without the confinement of the plane, he grasped
the boundaries of the place, saw the darkness beyond the farthest reaches of
the suburbs where the lights scatter and vanish on the old, obscured prairie. He
knew then that the city is contained, finite and transient; but just as he settled
back into his seat, a man's drink-slurred voice rose in the silence of the cabin,
coming from three rows ahead opposite Robbie.

"I'd divorce her if I could keep the dog. She can have every dime. She can
have the god damned house and the god damned cars. All I want is the damned
dog!"

For a moment a woman's voice murmured and soothed, and then the
man's voice rose again, vehement and aggressive.

"The fucking dog is the only one who gives a damn whether I come home
or not! Her kid just looks at me like I'm some fucking cash machine, and all
the bitch does is turn over in bed and slam her pussy shut! I want my own kid
and she slams her pussy shut! Fucking *cunt*!"

Cunt. The utter fury with which the word was spoken jarred Robbie. Now
the first-class cabin is completely silent, a close, almost polite silence of intent
listening. Again came the cajoling murmur of a woman's voice, and Robbie
saw a beefy fist thrust a glass into the air above the seat back—a refill signal

to the stewardess that Robbie had seen countless times on the flight.

"No, you've had enough." The woman's voice spoke clearly this time.

Abruptly the glass vanished, and again the man's voice rose in the padded silence of the cabin.

"All right! For Christ's sake, *all right!*"

Suddenly the woman stood from the window seat, her torso hunched forward beneath the overhead bins, a hand clasping the seat back. But the deep voice made a plea which Robbie could not hear, and as suddenly as she had stood, the woman sat down. Robert Snow sat very still. He waited for the man to speak again, but there was only silence now. *I have no stake in this*, Robbie thinks.

Now he feels the heaviness of his body, the light slow bones, the exhaustion. He has eaten little; has slept less; has pushed and thrashed for two years at the labor case his law firm has won, the victory coming only when he stopped thrashing—achieved a pause in which the game came to him and he grasped it. He turned again to the cabin window. The plane was lower now and the grid pattern of the streets absorbed him. But now his seeing was conscious as he attempted to pick out the streets he knows in the lighted grids below him, a futile exercise, for he can be sure of nothing. Yet, as his eyes swept over the city, he was acutely aware of having belonged to Chicago for a long time, for his mother's people, the Muirheads, had come to those streets below him in the decade before the Civil War; had lived and died there; the inventiveness of their minds and the luck of the draw still providing for his comforts, his perquisites—first-class air travel and the great luxury of a law practice which is pure advocacy on behalf of people who do not often find legal remedy. ("The People's Law Office," his bronze shingle read. "The PLO," the Philadelphia wags said.)

His ghosts are down there. They will not seek him out. But over the next twelve or fourteen hours, he may blunder upon them. Disturbed in their ghost-lives, they will turn pale faces to him as if to say, "Oh. It's you. What do you want?" And he will answer, "Thank you for your treasure. What I have achieved was because of it. And if I have not pleased you, remember that I loved those of you I knew and the idea of those I didn't." And lately he thinks that he has not so much reached the limits of his abilities as the limits of his ambitions. He drew back from the window and glanced down at the settlement papers before him, the distillation of the good fight. There is no reason for him to be here in an airplane at five in the morning. No reason to come to this city he has not seen in almost a decade. Faxes and messengers could have handled it—a courier if necessary—for these papers require only signatures. He knows that his coming to Chicago is like picking at the edges of a scab in order to lift it intact—an act painful for a moment, then not, for the point is to provide the air necessary to the final closing of a wound.

Abruptly, he lifted the bound sheaf of papers, folded the tray table, leaned to the worn leather case beside his seat, brought it to his lap and opened it. And immediately he felt that old grief he thought himself twenty-five years over, for a faint odor associated with his father rose from the case: the blended smells of dry leather, Bay Rum, and overall, a hint of the acrid pipe tobacco his father had smoked. And suddenly there were those winter twilights of his childhood that had evoked an inexplicable melancholy as he waited at the dining room window of the house on Constance Street for his father to come home. And when he came in, there was this case set down on the black and white tiles of the vestibule, and there was the chill of winter in the overcoat when Robbie ran to him, and tears Robbie could not explain deriving from the lonely, winter smell of roasting meat from Peck's kitchen and the prospect of a long succession of winter twilights—an early vanishing of light in a house too large and dark, empty of a dead woman who had been a man's wife and a mother of two boys. One, two—the crisp snaps of the catches are closed—never broken, having lasted his father's professional lifetime and a good part of his own. One, two—they are snapped open again and Robbie sets the papers inside, gazes a moment at the momentous, official look of them. There is no need to read them again. They have been endlessly scrutinized. These papers have invaded his dreams, made them crazy and jangled. Yet he had not blinked. His finger on the trigger had not flinched. And in a few hours on this Monday morning in June a labor strike will end. Dead factories in five states engaged in the trivial business of the manufacture of lawn mowers will groan and snuffle and belch, and the people he has represented will return to that ugly, ruinous labor he despises. The men will guffaw and grab-ass, while the women, their faces flaring with cheap makeup, will gossip and attach wheels the colors of children's toys to thin chaises that will crack and rust in a season.

Again he closed the case, swiped the scarred leather with a hand, the long fingers showing ill-kept nails and his father's ring, a malachite oval held by a fine braiding of gold. And he thinks that a man's things are really talismans and mojo to keep about you for connection and protection, a way to give you something of a man's spirit. He slipped the case beneath the seat in front of him, and his father's quiet manner comes back, an affect perfectly suited to estate planning and probate. A benevolent Tulkinghorn his father had been with the simple manners of a prince; a man so effaced and well-bred that you could put your hand through him, but shadowed by so many things that

Robbie had never completely understood: a wife his father had worshiped while she lived and forever-mourned when she was dead; a highly successful, overbearing, and long-lived father (Judge Alexander Snow, he of the 7th U.S. Court of Appeals) in whose presence Robbie had often seen his father defer, cowed by too many rankling concessions made to the old tyrant; and the war perhaps, for his father had survived the awful siege of Bastogne in the Battle of the Bulge. (Robbie and his brother Chip had fought that battle countless times as teenagers, representing its terrain, forces, and *materiel* with cutlery and glasses moved about the cloth in the candlelight after dinner, sons recounting the battle stories of their fathers as sons have since the first rock was hurled.)

Idly Robbie lay the flank of his palm on the cold plastic of the cabin wall, looked at his watch, registered the hour—5:05 a.m.—and knew that for a moment he had forgotten time, had not spent all his breath in trying to conquer it. The play of light in the gold rectangle of the watch case absorbed him. He knows the engraved words on the back in that place against his wrist which takes the oil of his skin: Robert Muirhead, his maternal grandfather's name; and below it, FROM EMPLOYEES N.C.f., every letter save the "f" in upper case, that mistake resulting from a moment when the engraver himself had perhaps forgotten time. National Car & Foundry, the remains of it down there somewhere below him at Cermak and Paulina, where, during the First World War, armored flat cars mounted with siege cannon had been built—the plant going twenty-four hours a day for years on end, while summer afternoons on the lawn of the place at Greenlake, or in the mauve winter twilight of that glass room at one end of the house in LaGrange, his mother's father, holding the newspapers before him, must have read the appalling casualty figures of Verdun and Passchendale and the Somme and the Marne, and even as the black ink flooded the company ledgers, would have realized the awful uses of the infernal things he had built, would have taken that knowledge to the body of the woman he loved. For without that timeless spasm, a man would disintegrate in the awfulness of so many unspeakable things. . . .

Robbie chilled. He could feel how the skin of his face is drawn, his shoulders rigid with tension, all of him straining for the rest of a body that he has not known in almost a decade and which is impossible for him now.

"Tom," he whispered, addressing him, that man whose body gave him rest for twenty years. And the old loss rose from his diaphragm up into his lungs. "Thomas McCloud," he said, naming him, that man he loves more than any man on earth and who is down there somewhere at the edge of those scattered lights, even now taking his morning run. And suddenly Robbie felt that desolate sense of coming to a place where you once belonged but which no longer belongs to you. And he knew that by coming here again he risked the deadly blue coldness of Thomas McCloud's eyes. And Robbie knows what he will have to remember now.

"So what's this breach, Tom?" he had asked nearly a decade ago of a summer's night on the brick terrace of Thomas McCloud's house far out to the west of Chicago in the gentle roll of the Fox River Valley beneath a sky as clear and star-scattered as the one this jet plane rides.

"Breach?" Thomas had said mildly. "There's no breach, Robbie, but I have a son, a little man almost twelve years old, and I must set an example for him." And Thomas's words were projected from a superb body, healthy with a good life the man had wrested from the air itself. But Robbie had answered quietly, "I measure a man by his courage and his loyalty. I measure a man, Tom, by his strength and his dignity and by his capacity for an informed and selective tenderness. I learned that with you, Tom—not *from* you, but *with* you—and don't you think that might be a wonderful legacy for your son?"

Thomas was silent, then he spoke. "Ah Robbie," he said. "Robbie, it's just too much. Really—it's too much."

And Robert Snow knew that Thomas's words were a sentence of exile. But Robbie had settled back on the cushions of the terrace chaise, and he had smelled a faint odor of rain and sun in the faded cushions. In the darkness he had watched the stars, feeling those still-points that sometimes exist between men, thinking that a sentence of exile is incomprehensible in the face of those still-points.

"We are something," he had insisted, striking the chaise arm with the side of his fist. "We are." And it was a powerful insistence, but Thomas McCloud was silent.

And now the airplane chime sounds. The seat belt sign blinks on, the plane stirring to life as the captain's voice announces the local time and temperature. From all over the cabin there came the muffled sounds of tray tables folded, the soundless glide of seat backs straightened, the sharp clicks of safety belts engaged. And the pretty stewardess with whom Robbie had not flirted moved down the aisle gathering up glasses and coffee cups and crumpled napkins. And there were murmurs of voices all around him, subdued here in the nearly empty first-class section, louder in the crowd beyond the limp aisle curtains. Now he feels the plane begin to slow and drop by degrees. His body quickens, for a night flight is ending—the suspended quality, the intent watching of the lights of nearly half a continent's cities passing below him; the old American movement from east to west, this smooth-slipping along the worn, hard grain of a nation.

And then the stewardess was there.

"Finish your drink, please," she commanded.

When the stewardess leaned to fold the tray table, he smelled her fresh odor—surely a promise of liquid flesh and rest. But when he handed her his glass, there was no electric jolt as their fingers brushed, no recognition as their eyes met, only a deadness between a man and a woman.

And the stewardess knew it.

Half an hour out of Philadelphia, she had used a snifter of cognac as an excuse to talk to him. He had looked up at her from his reading, his clear, brown eyes politely inquiring. She had colored faintly at those courteous, mild eyes and said, perhaps too quickly, "I thought you might like a glass of cognac—I do when I'm flying alone at night." And she had set the snifter down, the liquid suddenly gold as it caught the reflection of the cabin lights. She propped herself against the seat back across the aisle, for he had interested her then. His air of self-possession; the exquisite, gold-filigreed fountain pen with which he wrote; the long, strong legs in faded Levis, the lankiness, the picket-fence straightness of the wide shoulders. All this had attracted her. But as they spoke, there had been no hint of flirtation in his eyes, only an attentive mildness. And presently she sensed that he was more than a disinterested male.

"Good luck today," she said, for earlier he had told her what was bringing him to Chicago.

"Thank you," he answered, but already she had dismissed him. And Robert Snow felt it—the abrupt way a woman can dismiss a man—and on the heels of it, the regret of women; the knowledge that he can offer a woman only kindness, attentiveness, humor, and that extravagant gallantry which is really only a social skill understood as such. Yes, sometimes he felt that old disappointment in himself—the regret of women. "A bachelor without issue," is how the law will describe him when he is dead. But it is more than the regret of women. Thomas McCloud is down there somewhere in that vast city. And *that* is another old regret. But I am lightening the load, Robert Snow thought. At forty-eight, you have to.

Now the plane dipped to the port side, and Robbie's vision tilted up from the city to the brightening sky, and he turned his head, caught a glimpse of the city down the slope of the cabin through the opposite windows. Then, coming out of the wide turn, the plane began to descend rapidly, and, as the wheels thumped into position and the wing flaps dropped, Robert Snow knew that though he had won a substantial settlement at law, his accomplishment would never be known to Thomas McCloud. And Robert Snow regretted that he could not take that victory to Thomas; could not say to him, "This is what I have done. This is what I have made." And he did not want to be a boy again with another boy, tentative and frightened; and he did not want to be a young man again with another young man, joyful and lusty and heedless of time. He had been both with Thomas McCloud. There was no nostalgia in it. There was only a clarity of vision. It was as if you could pluck from the air the prismatic flash of a flawless gem and open your hand and say to him, "This is it, Tom. This is what we are."

The tires jar earth with a rattle from the overhead bins. There is a pause, a breathless tension, and then the nose falls smoothly, and there comes a mad, backward grasp of the engines. His body strains forward against the seat belt, and he feels a tremendous sense of speed and time as the ground lights whip by faint in the brightening air. Then the scream of the engines cease, and there is only the lumbering roll of a grounded bird making a turn off the runway.

A man in the row ahead of Robbie who has been, for most of the flight, only a reflective pate above the seat back, leaps up to snatch his bag from the overhead bin, then dashes to be first at the exit door. And now the curtains separating the compartments are flung back and the aisles of the first-class cabin are packed. Robbie stands, cuts into the press of the crowd, moves forward, glances at the drunken man and that lovely woman still in their seats waiting for the plane to empty before they disembark. The man sits with his head turned away from the aisle, tie loosened, breathing miserably. The woman leans against him, her head on his shoulder, a hand twined around his upper arm. And Robbie is struck by how young they are, early thirties at most, and remembering the man's angry words, he thinks that the fellow is at that age when a man's confused emotions can rule him, as if he is feeling them for the first time. But Robert Snow does not know the secrets of their generation, the commonality of experience that binds them. His brother Chip's daughters, and Robbie's clerks and associates at People's Law, seem to want little of what he knows, and he is acutely aware that he has no absolutes to offer in the way his father's and grandfathers' generations offered absolutes. No, the young must find their own anchors in the great drift of this age which belongs to them absolutely, this time in which they are young.

And he thinks of that time his generation owned absolutely. Thomas saying once after lovemaking, "This is rebellious, Robbie. What we do is rebellious." And Robert jolts now with a sudden recollection of the smooth, liquid skin of Thomas's chest, and it rattles him, the specificity with which Thomas returns. But now the line slows, stops as people lift garment bags from the lockers at the door, and so much comes back. . . .

A sleekly dressed woman, a cousin seven years his senior, declaring at a family dinner that Robbie's mind was "much too fine to be used as cannon fodder." Oh, and doing a chorus-line kick with his buddies, all of them vastly drunk at a nightclub on Ibiza in Spain, to Country Joe & the Fish blasting "The Vietnam Rag" from the jukebox, and when the song ended, collapsing in a heap on the dance floor and pretending they were being machined-gunned; then getting up, doing it again and again until it was all out of them—the fear, guilt, fury and rebellion, all of it bound up with the many contradictions inherent to their privilege. And then, as veterans began to appear on campus, he can remember leaning against a counter in the crowded kitchen at a party in that house he and Thomas shared, laughing and joking and drinking a beer, when a slender man with sharp black eyes, a former infantry officer, suddenly turned to him and apropos of nothing, started to describe in a low voice how he and the men under his command, stoned beyond belief, had fragged a village to have the entertainment of watching the flames; and Robbie had said not a word, only listened, and when the story was done, the man said, "It was like a movie, man. You should have been there." And he had given Robbie a peculiar smile, where, above the perfect white teeth, a flicker of cold light flared a moment in the blank, black eyes, before the man turned to a woman standing next to him and began to chat her up. Robbie had stood a moment there at the kitchen counter unable to move, and then he had gone in search of Thomas because Robbie did not know what else to do. And Robbie found him, stoned and mild and happy sharing an easy chair with Caroline, and Robbie had cupped Thomas's skull, leaned close to breathe a suggestion in his ear. Thomas's eyes stayed fixed and mild as if he hadn't heard, but a few minutes later, they'd gone out behind the garage and Robbie had dry-humped Thomas with a grim and noisy determination standing up against the clapboards damp with April rain; and Thomas saying, "Shit, I came in my pants," and Robbie answering, "Me too." And then the hilarious business of getting rid of their ruined underwear to the accompaniment of much hooting laughter and one-legged, boot-grasping hops and spins and Levi-tangled falls, until Robbie fell for the last time—into a bed of mint and lay there a moment, and, as the fragrance rose all around him, he had breathed the word. "Mint," he had said in reverential tones as though he was saying, "The Dharma-Body of Christ," or had found the sacred Buddha in the hedge at the foot of the lawn. And they had grabbed handfuls of the stuff and raced loose-balled inside to find a recipe for juleps and had begun one of their coordinated operations—Tom reading the recipe aloud, Robbie measuring, and two hippie chicks set to the vicious business of crushing ice in a towel with a ball-peen hammer. Presently,

Caroline came in to stand there in that crazy, jangled, nerve-racked conver-
gence of the public and private realms of those years, excluded in a way neither one of the men had intended, hurt and bewildered by what she didn't
know. But the men knew, which had made everything worse somehow. And
again Robbie hears Thomas say, "This is rebellious, Robbie. What we do is
rebellious." And how stricken Thomas's eyes had been when he looked at
Robbie, and Robbie freezes them there in his mind, those young men of light,
quick bones.

Robbie leans into the airplane locker for his garment bag and when he
turns again to the aisle, he meets the stewardess's cool smile with a cool smile
of his own. For he has sat a summer's evening in the thick hush of a golf
course on a bench among men and women half his age (a middle-aged bachelor who does not know the secrets of the generation that surrounds him; an
officer of the court who ignores the smell of marijuana), and watched a young
woman in a full-skirted white dress made transparent by the moon, climb
higher and higher into the branches of a tree whose rustling leaves seemed to
chuckle at her intrusion; watched with a combination of that baited breath you
hold for the young, and a profound regret that he has, after nearly thirty years
of one kind of love, perhaps missed another. And now he feels that young man
he had been at twenty walking beside him, and there is a whiff of the patchouli
the kid used to wear and shoulder-length, auburn hair shot with gold from the
sun itself, and the young man Robbie had been says, *"You're a fuck up, old
guy."*

"Where did you come from?" a voice retorts in Robbie's mind.

"Shit," the young man Robbie used to be answers. *"I'm always with you.
I'm the gatekeeper under that thinning hair."*

But now Robbie is on the slope of the boarding ramp, and when he
emerges into the terminal he sees the eager faces that do not see him, but
search the ramp behind him for other faces. And there was a time even at this
god-awful hour when Thomas McCloud would have been here. Robert Snow
would seen him there at the edge of the crowd, would have registered
Thomas's solid stance upon the earth, and there would have been the cool signal of Thomas's hand, the faint smile, the meeting of Thomas's eyes, and
Robbie would have seen a question in those eyes that have regarded him in
many ways, but never indifferently. "What have you brought me to?"
Thomas's eyes have always seemed to ask.

"And what does he see in my eyes?" Robert Snow asks himself.

"What you'd see in my eyes now if you'd look at me," the young man he
used to be says.

The passengers from the plane fan out around Robbie and there are greetings and laughter and hugs. Lanky and pale, he moves through them, enters the nearly empty concourse, and suddenly his body is starved for the embrace that would be his if Thomas was here—a touching of bodies brief in time, but seismic in the register of so much that is familiar: the bulk of Thomas's solid shoulders and chest, the heat of his body rising with the laundered, fresh smell from the open collar of the shirt. And Robbie's hand would find that place at the sinewy, solid base of the spine where the power of Thomas's strong back flows down to the rise of the buttocks; and with his hand at rest in that hard place where the long muscles divide, Robert Snow will allow his body to make that final cleaving adjustment and he will think, *I am home and now I can rest.*

And there on the bright, nearly empty concourse, he has a moment of barely controlled panic in which he is certain that he should get the first flight back to Philadelphia. And again he feels that young man he used to be fall into pace beside him, sees the gleaming Russell jungle-boots the kid used to affect, custom-made with canvas inserts at the ankles. He is there again in his light, quick bones, accusatory and sullen, but terrified more than anything, and Robbie thinks that he is committed now to this course of action. And so he telephones the car service to say he's landed, and then he does not know how much later—days perhaps, or years—the terminal doors slide open and there is the low, morning sun and he knows that he has stepped from some hiatus into the real time in which life is lived.

II

And now his eyes snap, all of him alert to the present. "Snow," reads the scrawl on a rectangle of white cardboard, cupped in a lean, brown hand, and held casually by a skinny black guy, his charcoal gray baseball cap worn resolutely forward proclaiming no affinity with things hip-hop, its deep red bill worked expertly into a high, sharp arch that Robbie recognizes of a springtime afternoon and the deep emerald of right field where he poised, glove ready, watching the white, leisurely drop of a baseball from the blueness, and then, as he whipped it to second base, a blur of movement, and the smell of the raked, moist brown earth of the infield. . . .

"Long flight?" the driver asks. The register of his voice is deep. The sound settles in that hungry place at the center of Robert Snow's chest.

"Oh, yes," he answers, "very long."

And he sees the lesson his older brother Chip taught him of a May morning at the start of the Little League season—Robbie's boyhood room, the two

of them seated on the lower bunk, Chip's wide, sun-browned hand demon-
strating the trick of forming that curve of the visor which reappears now
almost forty years later in the shape of the bill of a driver's cap. Two small
boys in the quiet sun-lapped house—the striped uniforms and red caps; the
cool waft of wind up the stairs down which they pelt, spikes punishing the run-
ner; not seeing (because they have trained themselves not to) the open door to
that pretty blue and white room above the first landing where their mother
died and where their father never goes; remembering their mother, if they do,
as light and laughing, hair in a pony tail, freckled nose, scuffed saddle shoes.
Then Peck is there, their father's former orderly, who arrived one morning in
1950 without warning—a forlorn man with no place left to go, come from a
war that had, at age nineteen and within the span of a few months, taken him
forever out of his game. Peck—who'd drawn himself up parade-ground
straight early one November morning on the front stoop of the house on
Constance Street in Jackson Park Highlands in Chicago five years after the
war's end, and shot Robbie's dumfounded father "a salute so crisp I could hear
the wrist bones snap," Chip always said, who'd witnessed it. And was taken
in; given a fly-speckled room above the garage—that musky lair shared a few
nights a month by a succession of hillbilly women with skin the color of old
putty. Yes, Peck is there in Robbie's mind—Lucky Strike at the corner of his
mouth, crew cut, old khakis, armpit-yellowed T-shirt—cursing the May afternoon ruckus on the stairs that has brought him from the slovenly kitchen
where he cooks the bland bachelor food which nourishes them.

Ghosts. Already Robert Snow has found a few, blundered upon them in the
unexpected sight of the visor of a baseball cap.

The driver divests this tall, exhausted man of his garment bag, lifts it easily from the thin shoulder which dips gratefully to receive the courtesy.

And Robbie feels a sudden lightness, the weight of the bag apparent now
that it's gone.

"You know," he says, "I'm so dog tired that I can't remember the walk
from the plane."

The driver smiles, and when Robbie hands him the briefcase and the
leather jacket, he startles at the brush of the driver's hand, for Robbie is so seldom touched that his body has lost the tactile memory of such human contact.
Perhaps it is skin-hunger that has brought him here.

"Nice jacket," the driver says of that soft leather, the shadowed green of
forest moss.

"Thank you," Robbie answers. "Take a look at the lining."

And there it is—changeable silk-satin, the fabric sloughing from dark green to black.

"That's real sharp, man," the driver says, his voice rising with excitement.

And Robbie recognizes this connoisseurship of clothes. It is in Henry Holton, the black guy in Philadelphia who is Robbie's sometime lover— "sometime" when Henry is between women or in the dark times that beset his life; a man whose voice and inflection Robbie sometimes assumes in the long night-talks with ample scotch, cigarettes, and jazz, that end with Henry going or with Henry staying. And Robbie knows that Henry is a manifestation of an unsatisfactory, decade-long compromise with Thomas McCloud, who does not even know that the compromise has been struck. But Robbie knows it. Henry knows it, too.

"Fuck up," the voice of the young man he used to be speaks in Robbie's mind.

"Free yourself from hope and doubt and desire," Robbie answers.

"Right," the withering voice in Robbie's mind answers. *"Ya, right. That's all you've ever had and now you want to be free of it."*

But the morning sky is flawless. Robbie will have this God's-gift-of-a-day. In the midst of the activity in front of the terminal, he stands smoking the first postflight cigarette. A cool north wind touches his neck and he knows the city will sparkle today, the muck of its sky carried away to the south. At the curb the black town-car stands, back door open, the slim driver loading the bags. But Robbie feels that he is fixed in place by the paralyzing fear that having come to this city which no longer belongs to him, he will seek out Thomas and blunder.

"All set?" the young driver asks cheerfully.

Robbie looks at the man, registers in a glance the air of cool and elan. Robbie envies what he imagines the kid's life to be—a girlfriend or wife, perhaps a child, the neatness of his appearance extending to every corner of his life. And Robert Snow regrets the messy complexity of his own existence, sealed as he often is in the exhausting life of his mind. He crushes the cigarette on the pavement, settles into the back seat, feels his body grow heavy with luxurious weariness, and the muffled concussion of the rear door slammed seems to come from far away. He sees the couple from the plane just coming out the terminal doors. They stand a moment in the morning, handsome faces dazed and drained of color, but the driver starts the engine and you want to say, "Tom, I just don't know what to do with everything lately because so much bewilders and boggles." You want to say, "Tom, a few days ago I was remembering the screen of lilac bushes in full bloom outside the dining room windows on Constance Street, and how, when the windows were open, the wind would puff this fragrance all through the downstairs." You want to say, "Tom, it was a wonderful house. It was my mother's wedding present tied up in bows from my Grandfather Muirhead where my parents had twelve years of something so profound that my father never got over whatever it was they had. But Christ, Tom, it was a lonely house! All it offered was room and board. By the time I was seventeen I knew I had to get out of there and my father knew it, too, and I think he was relieved. Isn't that odd, Tom, that my father was relieved to see me go?" You want to say, "Tom, my father once told me not long before he died that you can make all the excuses you want in life, you can blame all you want, but finally it comes down to character. And then he said, 'Robbie, remember this: the only way anyone can take your dignity is if you hand it to them on a platter.'" And you want to say, "Tom, I'm letting go. I have to and it hurts, but I'm letting go."

And the driver does a hotshot slip of the car away from the curb, dives it expertly into a blare of pissed-off horns, then speaks to the mirror.

"What brings you to Chicago?" he asks cheerfully.

"Love," Robbie answers immediately, checking his seat belt. "I'm drawn here by the long chains of love." And he laughs.

"How's that for balls?" he says to the kid he'd been.

"It's a start," the kid answers. *"But I'd have said, 'I've flown a thousand miles to get laid.'"*

"Vacation?" the driver asks.

"No!" Robbie explodes.

"Okay," the driver says, taking up the challenge. "A man drawn by love, but not on vacation."

Robbie laughs again. "No, I'm kidding you. It was long ago and in another country, and besides, the son of a bitch is dead." He laughs again. "Actually, I'm here on business. I'm here to kick some ass and I'm gonna do it."

"A man drawn by the chains of love whose gonna kick some ass," the driver says, laughing, lowering his window to ring a handful of coins into the toll basket.

This is a live one, Robbie thinks. From where he sits in the backseat, Robbie can see the driver's composed profile, the long hands lightly holding the wheel. And Robbie knows exactly what the feel of such a body would be—the hard-slender, wiry waist against the inside of his forearm. But, Robbie thinks, at age forty-eight there is less casual desire. No, he does not desire this young man, for desire has become a capability never exercised casually, but held in reserve, given only when there is a possibility of return. It is not that his body is waning. The morning hard-ons, praise the Lord, still make their appearances, though they no longer cling tight against his belly. The angle no longer defies gravity, and any weight heavier than a sock attached there to show off would fall off and break a toe. He'd done that once for Thomas—attached a leather Dopp kit full of toiletries and turned sideways, throwing a bodybuilder's pose.

"I remember that," the kid he'd been says, *"that was crazy fun."*

"Yes," Robbie says, *"but you were careful enough to hang it low on the shaft. That was no trick."*

The kid he'd been laughs. *"You remember things the way you want to because you're getting old. But I'm not a memory. I'm what really happened to you."*

Robbie lets that one stand.

No, the body is not waning, but lately Robert cannot imagine baring it to anyone who has not already seen it, yet sometimes he feels a rebellious stir that breaks through the caution. And now, for just a moment, he permits himself to take out something stored in his mind, a fragile thing he does not often take out. He unwraps it, looks at it. . . .

For there is in Philadelphia, a man just past thirty and a fine lawyer, better by far than Robbie had been at his age, who, for the four years Tripp worked at People's Law, placed himself in Robert Snow's range of vision where that young man was constant and noticed, and then one day, having accepted a fine offer from a gilded firm, Tripp presented himself to Robert Snow, who looked up startled but not alarmed.

This is too new, Robbie thinks. I cannot think about it now because it is too new. And he feels the young man he used to be sitting sullen and resolute beside him on the backseat of the town car.

But Robbie ignores the hostile bristle of the boy he used to be and instead rolls with the wave of a heart which is opening after being closed for so long. *"You're the best of us all, Robbie,"* that young man Tripp had declared. *Hyperbole, yes, born of too many Guinnesses and the giddy excitement of that student bar near Penn where the entire firm was celebrating the labor case just won. And that man in Philadelphia had spoken with a young man's conviction and direct, guileless eyes and with the posture of his body so proud that Robbie knew in the act of presenting himself, Tripp had drawn upon a man's limited reserve of courage.*

"This is too new. Stop it now," Robbie tells himself and he closes his eyes against the low sun filling the car, for he is frightened of the fragility of people and the responsibility of living every day correctly. And perhaps along with so much else, he wants to say, "Tom, there's a young man in Philadelphia who came up to me and my heart opened." But there are the heavy springs of the car, a suspension that makes you feel like you're riding down the express-way sprawled on a king-sized bed and some days too much oppressive com-fort.

"Are you forsaking me?" asks the kid he'd been, who'd loved Thomas McCloud. Robbie turns his head, remembers the direct, courageous eyes, not yet saddened with time, not yet his father's eyes.

"I don't love like you did. I love differently now," Robbie says. *"At my age, I can't possibly love like you do. It's impossible to love like that again."*

"Shit," the kid says softly and turns to look out the car window.

And Robbie knows how light he'd once been in his bones—the snap and crackle, the sap of him; the kid's impatience with Thomas's hesitation and hedging; the uninformed, headlong recklessness that demanded only faith in the moment; how he could not conceive the cause and effect of his actions, a lifelong falling of the domino chain, a clicking until the end. And he knows, too, that it is not good to go to people when you're damaged. But there he is again, that young man in Philadelphia, quickly shucking his tux and saying easily, "Robbie, let's swim. Come on, let's swim." And Robbie did not know what to do, for he recognized the moment, knew its source in the past and in the present of his senses, and he turned to the lighted clubhouse up the sand and across the wide lawn where Tripp's girlfriend is and where people are, dancing to a small orchestra in a high-ceilinged room with huge, arched win-dows open to the night and the warm, electric air. He turned back to face the man Tripp is, and Robbie's breath caught because at age thirty-two Tripp has just entered the flowering and long season of his manhood.

"No," Robbie said quietly. "You go ahead, Tripp. I'll spot you."

And already Tripp is turning, wading into the Atlantic surf because he can and wants to, and there is the constant, brisk shore wind, and his walk becomes a run, a joyful, forward-falling, whooping charge into the high-curl-ing surf. Robert Snow crosses his arms on his chest, sets one glossy shoe for-ward on the sand, and assumes his role in the exuberant air, which is to keep a sharp eye on the man as he swims alone under the moon, Robbie anxious with desire, but conscious of acting responsibly, pouring all his concentration onto the night-black water in order not to lose sight of Tripp whose white shoulders blend with the caps of the waves.

And suddenly Robbie knew what Tripp would see from the water—the lights of the long, low clubhouse like a land-bound ship, the ballroom its glowing stern, and perhaps Tripp would turn seaward again into the long, rolling blackness of the Atlantic, thinking . . . What? Robbie can only guess.

(But Tripp was not thinking. Tripp was delighting in his senses. He was lost in his senses and in the heave and roll of the waves which lift and toss him and in the noise of the waves which talk to him—the indifferent old ocean which could drown him—in the odd warmth of the water tonight, in the black and in the silver, in the soft, giving sand on which his feet cannot find purchase.)

The dangers are clear, Robbie thinks now in the car heading into town. Vigor and youth are formidable weapons that a young man can turn on you because you are not what he is; that is, you are not young. If Thomas knew, he would be mild and ironic. He would ask in that surgeon's dry voice, "How old did you say?" And Robbie would answer sharply, "He's thirty-two." And Thomas would say, "I see." And Robert would reply, "You don't see. He's different from you. He's generous and affectionate. He's courageous and loving. He's nothing like you at all, Tom." And he would see Thomas's eyes shadow with pain, and there would be all the silence in the world.

And then he'd come back, leaping the waves, that young man in Philadelphia, and he'd stood before Robbie, wearing only cotton briefs which cling, stood pushing back his wet hair, excitement in his voice as he spoke of the warmth of the water, and then because the exuberance of it all was simply too much, he'd turned and dashed at top speed down the beach, and returned at a speed that defied time, and Robbie had been afraid because his heart had opened and he had learned too late to leave well enough alone.

But here is the driver with his capable hands, and here is Tripp with his direct eyes and proud posture. They are here.

"Shit," says the young man he'd been. "We'd have humped on the sand if I'd been there. Shit, man, you missed your moment and you won't soon get another one, believe me."

"No," Robbie answers. "You're right, but it was so much more."

And in Robbie's mind Tripp starts to pull on his tux trousers over the soaked jockey shorts. "Take off your underwear," Robbie says impulsively in a low voice. "You'll be more comfortable." And he blushes furiously in the darkness. Tripp pauses, then says quietly, "Good idea." And Robbie turns away because he is frightened, looks to the lighted clubhouse, then half-turns back to glimpse the white thighs and the darkness there at the joining place. And then all at once it seems—for Tripp moves decisively when he has decided—he stands before Robbie, and Tripp tilts his head back as Robbie's hands saw the ends of the black bow tie up into the fold of the stiff collar of the pleated shirt. As Robbie fumble-loops the ends, Tripp laughs again, and Robbie answers with his own laugh as he concludes a passable knot tied almost by feel in the near darkness. That moment not a year ago was so many things at once: Robbie was his father tying a son's tie; and that moment was of no age; and that moment was both playful and intimate, but above all, that moment was tender. And Robbie rested his hands for a moment on Tripp's shoulders, the white cloth luminous in the darkness, feeling the warmth and shape of the shoulders beneath the fine cotton of the shirt. And the men turned as one, Tripp carrying socks, tux jacket, patent leathers, and balled underwear, but no cummerbund, for, like Robbie, he scorns the thing as useless, and they started across the beach to where the sand meets the grass, returning to all the complications that waited there at the clubhouse and which belong to Tripp and his generation. And they sat for a moment on a sea-facing bench while Tripp raked sand from between his toes, dusting the low arch of his nearly flat feet before he pulled on his socks. Then, as Tripp bent to tie his shoes, Robbie said, "I didn't swim with you because I was afraid of what people would say. I'm afraid of feeding any more talk about us because there's been plenty since you danced with me."

Robbie heard himself. They had danced—a victory dance at that student bar near Penn. Tripp's doing, Tripp's decisiveness.

"Bummer," Tripp said, firmly tying the last lace and straightening to face Robbie. "You missed a great swim. What a bummer." Then, snapping the sand out of his tux jacket, he added firmly, "What goes on between you and me, or between you and me and my girlfriend is not anyone's business but our own."

They stood up from the bench, and, as Tripp struggled into his tux coat and began anchoring the shirt studs sewn on the white tape, the orchestra in the clubhouse ballroom shifted on the downbeat to a Stones' song and the mass of people behind the tall, open windows seemed to move as one body, and Robbie felt Tripp quicken away from him, Tripp's attention turned to Helene, who he had forgotten when he swam and who is there somewhere in that crowd. And though Robbie's own heart had opened, he had no idea of the condition of Tripp's.

"There's a term for this, Tripp, for what this evening's been. *Dolce far niente*, which means a moment of equipoise when emotions are suspended and there is only the sweet moment of life."

"Cool," Tripp says, once again giving his full attention to Robbie. "That's very cool, Robbie. *Dolce far niente*. I'll remember that." But he turns to look eagerly, a little anxiously at the clubhouse. "Let's go."

And then they are walking quickly and Robbie says, "Tripp, I'm flat running out of time."

Tripp does not respond, but as they hurry up the broad steps of the terrace, he rests a hand on Robbie's shoulder. *"Dolce far niente,"* Tripp says smiling brightly, his face fully visible in the light from the ballroom. "I'll remember that." And he bounds lightly, eagerly, up the remaining steps and vanishes into that crowded room where the slender woman he loves is, wearing a pretty gown. In a moment, Robbie follows. At the bar he buys drinks for any face he recognizes and for a quiet, beautiful girl just because she's there.

And the driver registers the silence from the back seat, can see in the mirror the thoughtful look on the drawn face. He does not mind. The guy is cool. The morning is bright, full of promise. Traffic is light. And there is the easy slip of the heavy car into town.

"Welcome back," says the kid he'd been. *"I've got some more for you. I'm not letting you off yet, Old Guy."*

And then without warning, out of the June morning itself, Robbie is drunk and stoned at Caroline's engagement party at Bethlehem in Pennsylvania and it is that late hour when only their generation lingers in the tall old room, and he takes Caroline into that little telephone closet under the front stairs of her grandfather's house, and makes the astonished young woman swear that she will never hurt Thomas. And then out of that moment another moment blooms in Robbie's mind, a time perhaps a year after Thomas married, of going out with him for firewood and holding him in the hushed cold of the winter night. Robbie felt at his ankles the wind across the snow as they leaned together with heavy coats opened, and he found the buttons of Thomas's Levis, fumbled there at that packed, warm place wanting the prize of Thomas's sigh more than anything he had ever wanted until that moment, but with all the senses of Robbie's body extraordinarily alive, he had stopped, stepped away, for this was not a little casual adultery, but something more basic: to burst laughing and bright-faced through the kitchen door and meet Caroline's smile would have been more that Robbie could bear at age twenty-four or twenty-five. And then another time folds over that winter night and Robbie is in a crowded restaurant, the small tables cheek-by-jowl, Thomas drunk and desperate after his brother's death, opening and prolonging a discussion of all that had been between Robbie and himself from the very beginning—talk so frank and fraught, that a man and woman enjoying themselves at the next table had fallen by degrees to silence as they listened to Thomas's headlong monologue which Robbie could not and did not want to stop. Robbie saw the couple's strained faces, saw their troubled eyes when they dared look at each other, and he wondered if they shared a similar history, if there was a man or a woman who loved one of them like Thomas loved him, and for the first time Robbie thought that what he and Thomas had might be very old under the sun. And then, at the end of it, Thomas had said, "You're my brother now," and heedless of his professional license—and Robbie's—had lighted a joint. So many moments. So many, Robbie thinks. But always something quiet, something still. The cool blue touch of autumn over Thomas's house—or his house in other seasons—but Robbie there through twenty years. At peace in those moments, he had always tried to make himself fit unobtrusively into the rhythms of that household, because Caroline and Jim and the house filled with that cool, blue touch, belonged to Thomas. Outside the marriage and woven into its fiber was an intensely private realm which he and Thomas occupied. "You have the power to take me from my son," Thomas had said once. And though Robbie had answered sharply, "Why on earth would I want to do that, Tom?" he had known that if Thomas really believed himself capable of such a folly, then the private realm was doomed, and if the loss of a son through the exercise of reckless desire was what Thomas feared most, then the game had been the most foolish that two people can play. "But this is a sterile pain, a pointless sacrifice that doesn't even draw blood," Robbie tells himself now in the backseat of this car taking him to a city where Thomas is. And some days he wants the finality, that useless finality when you say quietly enough, "Fuck you, Tom. Fuck you." Because Robbie knows that Jimmy may already have begun to look at his father and wonder what the man was meant to be, must already know that his father is haunted by something Jim can't name and Robbie after thirty years of trying cannot name, either.

"I had no idea how much happened after you left me," the kid he'd been says.

"Christ!" Robbie whispers.

And the driver's eyes shift to the rear view mirror. He has heard Robbie's whisper. There have been greater human dramas enacted in that back seat than the whisper conveys. His eyes return to the road as he directs the car into the left lane, slipping past an eighteen-wheeler which passes in a silver blur before Robbie's fixed eyes. Suppressed emotion stirs but there is an odd detachment of his mind. Too much of the last few hours has been spent in sealed places— a dark apartment at two in the morning, a taxi cab in Philadelphia, an airplane, a glass terminal, then this town car.

"It just occurs to me," Robbie says to the driver, "that I don't know your name."

Again the driver glances in the mirror which frames Robbie's drawn face, a mask of exhaustion in which warm, frightened eyes live.

"Steve," the driver says.

"Steve it is," Robbie says. And then he adds in order to free himself from the old pain, "Have you been driving long?"

"Five years," the driver answers.

"You drive very well," Robert says, complimenting this man young enough to be his son. "Very smoothly. You have a steady foot."

And he thinks how easy it would be to have a spree with this kid, to say, "Look, Steve, I grew up here. When I'm finished kicking ass, put the car on the clock and I'll show you all the places where I wasted my youth." But Robbie knows how pointless such a bender would be, because benders waste precious time, and, when they are done, fix nothing.

"Thanks," the driver says.

Robbie half-hears, then he speaks.

"You know," he says, reaching a hand to finger the door lock plunger, "you could take a tablet and make a list of all the times you can remember about a person you've loved. All you'd have to do is write, 'There was the time when we . . .' and fill in the blank and pretty soon you'd have it all, though I don't know if you'd know what it all means when you're done, but you'd have it—the sweep of things." And he thinks immediately, *I should not be speaking like this.*

"That's an idea," says the driver, tilting his chin to the mirror. "You'd have a lot of pictures, right?"

And the driver plays chess in Washington Park with the old men and the ex-cons and he is always very quiet when they speak, when he is allowed to listen, and those games have at their centers an abstraction of expenditure—things held and lost, but always a calculated sacrifice. It is a cold game where old men and hardened men speak across the symmetry of the squares and allow him to listen.

"Yes," Robbie says.

For often when they made love there was a great buffeting force coming from Thomas, something wonderful to Robbie; at other times disconcerting, because the force of the passion seemed to have no connection to him— Thomas thrusting wildly against Robbie, coming quickly, crying out as he does, "I'm sorry, Robbie, I'm sorry," and Robbie would lie beneath him, very baffled, for it was as though Thomas's need in those moments was so hungry as to be undifferentiated. But sometimes there was a peacefulness to it all. Once, as Thomas's hands moved lightly over Robbie's shoulders and back, Thomas had whispered, "Man, I've forgotten how you feel!" But always there was a cry and groan, and a heavy, wet spill on Robbie's belly, and Thomas's ragged voice urging Robbie to his own spill, and then the strong, laboring body slackened heavy against Robbie's, and the tearing breath, and the thick beat of the heart, and the slow pulse of an artery in the neck, and the sweat-slickness of the hard, strong body brought a bright wonder to Robbie, for Thomas's body had always been profound, never trivial, never salacious. To love buoyantly and easily—Robert Snow knew he had missed all that.

"Shit," the driver says, speaking to the mirror. "That must hurt a lot, seeing all those pictures."

"Yes," Robbie answers mildly, "but the body is less urgent."

Shifting uncomfortably in his seat, the driver cannot imagine his body ever lacking urgency, and he stirs in his young man's skin, shifts his body again, and sees a profile in silhouette on the pillow next to him, sharp against the penetration of the street light, and smells her toasty, ripe odor and the fragrance of her room, the light, sweet fragrances of the dressing table blending with the oil soap of the freshly mopped floors. The baby is sleeping—his son is sleeping in his crib next to the bed. City night. The windows thrown open. City night. A June night of velvet air, love—and pictures.

"Right," the driver says. "So you grow up here?"

"Yes," Robbie says.

For always, it seemed, he had tried to give meaning to the acts. But could find nothing of what they meant except that they had somehow closed distance and stopped time. And on the night before Thomas married, Robbie had not known what the act meant that time, either. In that bedroom they shared on the third floor of Caroline's grandfather's house at Fountain Hill in Bethlehem, with the groomsmen asleep stoned and drunk in rooms on either side, they had enacted again at nearly the hour of Thomas's marriage, the expression of that confounding bond they had made. Afterwards, Robbie had lain awake all night watching the deep shadows of the ceiling, and he had listened to the tap of January ice flung against the loose windows and to Thomas draw sleeping breath and expel, and it had seemed to Robbie that Thomas's breathing crowded the room with warm life, and, as Robbie lay shivering in the ruined bed beneath a thin blanket, he had thought, *Something has happened. Something is different now.*

"In the city?" the driver asks of Robbie's growing place.

"Yes. 69th and Constance," Robbie answers.

But the next morning, as he and Thomas dressed for the wedding, pale with exhaustion in that cluttered, bright room in and out of which the grooms-men had burst laughing, joking, swilling warm champagne straight from the bottles, and blowing smoke from their dubies out the windows or up fireplace flues, Robert Snow had been dazed. *I should not be here*, was all he could think as he stood before the dresser mirror fumbling awkwardly at the black satin ribbon that held his pony tail. And he had drifted stunned and exhausted through his duties as usher. Details of the day were vague in his memory. To this hour, he can remember little of the day, except from time to time, across all the public clamor, Thomas would regard him calmly enough as if he were saying, "Be of good cheer, Robbie, this is what I want." But Caroline seemed unsettled as if she could not grasp something playing in her mind that she would need to grasp in order to go on with this man Thomas McCloud. At other times, she was radiant with that certainty come from her belief that she had before her now, a lifetime with this man Thomas McCloud whom she loved. Yet something vibrated in the air, an odd disruption of equilibrium born of what Robbie had articulated one afternoon, months before, when Thomas had told Robbie of his intention to marry. "Don't cut me out, Tom. We don't have to operate that way—like everyone else. God knows, after all we've been through, we don't have to behave conventionally." And then he'd said, "You have to take it on, Tom. You have to take on the world and go ten rounds. What's the point if you don't?" But Thomas had answered quietly. "It's your fight, Robbie, not mine." "No," Robbie said, "it's yours, too. You showed me the enemy, my friend. You took me by the shoulders and turned me around and said, 'There's the enemy, Robbie, right over there,' and now you want me to meet it alone. What's that noise, Tom? You're leaving me to fight this alone?"

And the heavy car moves seamlessly through the light traffic of the early morning expressway, which increases as they near the Loop. All around is low sunlight as if the car is moving through a rose-colored ether, and Robbie feels the urgency of a day beginning; knows that when the car pulls up in front of the hotel, the city will have entered full morning-gear, and he will be spilled into it—the urgency of present time. But now, as a man sometimes frightened of time, he understands that the lovemaking occurring when it did on the night before Thomas wed was many things, but finally, it was the kind of act young men perform when life is spacious enough to contain anything and time is forever.

For twenty years they had gone on, first young men, then older, and still the thing between them was there. And then ten years ago, as Thomas's son Jim approached adolescence, Thomas had ended it. Not abruptly, but in a series of reductive steps—letters not answered, telephone calls not taken, until, reduced to silence and with his exile absolute, Robert Snow no longer knew anything of Thomas's daily life. And because he didn't, Thomas's life became an abstraction, and, as each year of silence passed, Robbie had only a flat stew to stir as he is stirring it now.

"69th and Constance," the driver says. "That's the Highlands, right?

Jackson Park Highlands?"

"Yes," Robbie says.

"I'm South Shore, too. 74th and Paxton."

And Robert sees the eyes in the mirror are clear and unshadowed, nothing like his own or his father's or Peck's or Tom's or Tripp's.

"Me and my girlfriend drive through there sometimes and we pick out the houses we want to live in someday. That's some neighborhood. Jessie lives over there. Ramsey Lewis, too." There is pride in his voice as he adds, "I'm in school at IIT, mechanical engineering."

"My grandfather was a mechanical engineer," Robbie says absently. "He manufactured railroad cars—rolling stock and locomotives."

And there are a man's things again, Robert Muirhead's things this time—the leather-cased tape measures, the inlaid t-squares made from exotic wood, the brass and steel of compass and protractor, the copper tool box built by a man at National Car & Foundry, the scale models of box cars and flat cars, coalers and cabooses and crane cars and locomotives which sit atop the bookcases in Chip's office, and there are the large, strong hands in the photographs of a man Robbie never knew and who Chip remembers only vaguely. And there is that time in high school when he and Chip had broken into one of the abandoned brick barns at Cermack and Paulina where the rolling stock had been built, the vastness of the place extending a city block in length, two stories in height, and the late afternoon light filtering in through soaring windows, the dust rising in vast triangular slants, flickering and alive in a place that seemed, in its hush more suited to choir and ceremony than to the manufacture of rolling stock. And they stood there gazing around in awe, two stalwart boys dwarfed by their grandfather's vast hall. For Robbie reveres accomplishment in any form, does not differentiate abilities, recognizes only degrees of perfection: an accomplished limousine driver who will one day build things; a young man in Philadelphia who is a fine lawyer; a tap dancer in the subway who makes your stomach shiver; and watching Thomas perform an operation early in his career, Robbie smuggled in to stand at a viewing window which he had not left for two hours, though the piss he had to take was a race horse's, and afterwards, Thomas's eyes visionary with the game—with the exertion, demand and concentration of it, his body finally permitted to tremble when it was done. "No," he'd said when Robbie had touched him. And the two of them, young men of light, quick bones, facing each other in that sour-smelling hospital coffee room—Thomas solitary, the garments bloodied, the body contemptuous and distrustful because Thomas's success, his accomplishment, was come by hard, not by entitlement, not by his own luck (or the luck of another man born a hundred and fifty years ago), but from that determination which would, in time, allow him to sacrifice Robert Snow absolutely. "It's too much, Robbie, too much," Thomas had warned often enough. And Robbie feels that young man he had been, sees him quite clearly again slouched on his spine on the town car seat in what has become the morning rush hour. There he is, that young man Robert Snow had been, wearing that tattered suede golf jacket which had been Robert Muirhead's—too big for the kid, but a sand color and golden. And the hair to the shoulders and the long, skinny colt's legs.

"*I don't know what to do,*" the young man Robert Snow had been says. "*I've lost him.*"

"*I had to go on,*" Robert answers his younger self. "*I am alive after all. I can't preserve it for you any longer.*"

"*I don't accept this,*" the kid says. "*I don't buy it, Buddy.*"

"*I know,*" Robbie says quietly. "*I know.*"

And Robert Snow thinks how this ghost-kid has been intruding for months now, dogging him, walking behind him on the street, not accusatory (though he is that now), but at a loss—unable to act, yet desiring action after nearly a decade of inaction. Perhaps I owe him something, Robert Snow thinks.

He glances there at the empty seat beside him and the bright tint of the morning world beyond the car window where traffic moves thickly now. And then comes the young Thomas McCloud, the young man Thomas used to be, his vitality crowding the car, and full of laughter in his white carpenter jeans and Mexican wedding shirt, that fine gauze showing the pink skin beneath it. Thomas's bright smile and perfect white teeth will rouse them both—Robert Snow the younger, and Robert Snow the older—to high jinks and fun. Thomas will make a picnic of this car ride into town. In a moment he will light a joint, take a deep drag, then cup it in his palm, nudge the driver on the shoulder and pass it to him. And the driver will turn on some music, adjust the base, and, Robbie thinks, inside of ten minutes, we will be completely wrecked and Thomas will not care that I have important business today. He will rouse us from lassitude and inaction, not caring that I and the young man I once was, are at the end of things in this town. Thomas roared with laughter that it began with a boxcar crammed with cheap socks which the first Robert Muirhead (of any account, at least) had bought in Philadelphia not three days after the Fire of 1871 and sold from a rail siding to all the sockless of this town and by that bit of timely cleverness grubstaked us all. Yes, Thomas will shake his head at the things he does not understand, but wants. He listened solemnly enough, because he got his golden girl and he got his golden boy, and both of us jumped high for him, and he made himself from nothing.

"Let me get this straight," Thomas said once. "Socks. Like what you wear on your feet?"

"Yes," Robbie answered, "socks. And then a printing company and a little real estate and one of his brothers cornered the wheat market."

"Cornered the wheat market?" Thomas repeated, incredulous.

"Yes," Robbie said, "twice. And built a house of blue enamel and buff brick, trimmed with copper against brown terra-cotta walls with a purple slate roof."

"A purple slate roof!" Thomas gasped the words, rolling with laughter.

Robbie colored, for he was telling stories that you only talk about with your family, but Thomas always wanted to know about these things. It made Robbie very impatient, for he loved Thomas in the moment. "All that's my mother's cousins who are descendants of the wheat-cornering guy. We don't have any of that," Robbie said. "They're the rich ones. They live in New York and don't talk to us. And the house is gone. You can't even look at it because it's gone. It's not even a vacant lot. It's part of a public housing project."

"A purple slate roof!" Thomas choked the words—this poor kid from Newark.

"Yes," Robbie said, and suddenly he saw the absurdity of it all, what he had never seen before—a purple slate roof and a boxcar full of cheap socks sold dear and high-hat cousins full of themselves—and then he was laughing, too, because Thomas had made him see that it had nothing to do with them, for he and Thomas were in the moment on a perfect May morning, and they can do anything they want, go anywhere they want, they are absolutely free. For it is what Thomas did, drew everything and everyone to himself; drew all the sweet mornings and wondrous nights; and that house they shared at college and the music and the people who came to that lighted airship they flew, the gondola gliding on wafts of marijuana-scented air, throwing out raucous music and popping champagne corks and spewing beer cans and laughter— drew us all with his laughing eyes and his grand gestures and grand pronouncements and the quickness of his bones and the power of his body which he made generous; his deep odor, and the profusion of their semen which slicked the webs of Thomas McCloud's fingers when he pushed a warm, firm hand along the contours of Robert Snow's body, spreading the ball-stuff up Robbie's belly and shuddering chest because he could and wanted to and because, beyond everything else, they were generous to each other in those years.

"He is my brother. He is my lover. He is the best of me," declares the

young man Robert Snow had been.

"*I know,*" Robbie says softly. "*I know how deeply you believed that.*"

And then there is only the hum of the wide tires of the town car.

III

"You know," Robert says a few minutes later to the driver, "I was just thinking of this friend of my father's, a lawyer here in Chicago. The guy would work his ass off for months at a time—sixteen, eighteen, twenty hours a day for weeks on end. And then he'd have enough. He'd say, 'Fuck it all anyway,' and he'd grab a cab out to O'Hare and get on the first plane he could find and . . . well, just fly away! Shit, he'd be gone for weeks sometimes and nobody, not even his wife, would know where he was. He'd end up in Detroit or London or Rio de Janeiro, it didn't matter, and then he'd come home and start it all over again. All that crazy work. And then six months later, he'd be out at O'Hare again looking for a plane."

The driver snorts and glances in the mirror. "I know brothers like that. They'll be working a good job and right in the middle of a shift they just up and quit." He pauses, shakes his head. "Shit, man—somethin' funny with that."

"Do you ever feel like you're going to explode?" Robbie asks suddenly. And he asks the question because this young man understood that to see the past in a series of pictures is sometimes an exercise in pain. They idle in traffic now, just before the first of the Loop exits.

"Sometimes I think I'm going to spontaneously combust," Robbie adds with a laugh, for lately he feels less restraint in speaking his mind because he has little to lose and much to gain by speaking from the heart. But the driver is checking the mirrors and easing the car over into an exit lane.

"If you stick to your engineering and keep alert and find the people who'll help you, you'll go far," Robbie says. He pauses, turns with the driver to look at the car which permits the lane switch. The driver gives a quick wave of acknowledgment as Robbie continues. "You know, there's nothing that people like better than a sincere request from someone to learn. People who know things are often willing to teach you if you ask."

Again he pauses, knowing he is speaking not only to the driver, but to himself, and to Thomas and Caroline and Jimmy, and to Tripp, speaking to them all, to his brother Chip and his father and Peck and to all the ghosts of this town.

"Life is extraordinarily rich, extraordinarily satisfying. When you live it at your best, at your largest capacity, it's everything at once."

Again he pauses. "Sometimes you have to go down to hard and painful things. Suffering and disappointment, and a cruel death may be waiting for you, but you have to go down to the ugly things because if you don't, they'll get you."

There was a long silence as the car inches forward.

"I don't mean to frighten you," Robbie said quietly.

"Who taught you?" the driver asks suddenly, meeting Robbie's eyes in the mirror. The car slows, then is stopped by traffic.

"Many people," Robbie answers eagerly. "Many men. A few women. Some were my superiors, some were my peers, some were what the world would call my inferiors, but that's just the world talking. What you feel at a certain age is an obligation to tell what you know, and you don't give a damn whether it's welcome or not, whether anyone wants to hear it or not. It's all very satisfying. And if you're lucky, you'll find a friend or two who is as eager as you are to learn. A cut buddy. Someone you can take things to and ask, 'Is what happened to me what I *think* happened to me?' It's all very rich—I want you to know that." He paused. "It's the richness of things, you understand—the richness."

And the driver nodded. "Cool," he said, as the glut of traffic loosened and the car moved ahead.

But Robbie could see that the kid understood a tenth of this.

"You fear less and feel more accurately because you know why you're feeling," Robbie said at last. "And you accelerate. That's the odd thing, how quickly time slips away. You'll feel that as you approach fifty. It's a rapid burning off of fuel that's terrifying and exhilarating because you're moving toward *something* and you know you can't go back." Robbie laughed again to cover all this nakedness and to bring himself back from a place vast and blue and cool which he had glimpsed in his mind, a place where he could have stayed forever if he'd permitted that to himself—like sitting all of a chilly October afternoon with your back against sun-warmed clapboards thinking nothing, feeling nothing, possessing nothing except the sun, the air, the smell of warm, painted wood.

"Listen. Study hard," Robbie tells the driver. "IIT is an excellent engineering school. You're halfway there. And big houses are pleasant. That's their chief use—to be pleasant. But if you expect anything more from them—look out!"

"Right," the driver says—dryly.

"I don't know what I want," Robbie says thoughtfully.

"Right," the driver says—dryly again. For he knows that if you have a big house, they'll hesitate—the cops and the crackers—because big houses can mean big consequences. They'll hesitate a moment before they drag you out of it—that big house you've earned. He glances in the mirror again, but that guy back there named Snow is gazing out the window. You're a weak man if you don't know what you want, the driver concludes, looking ahead again at the rusted trunk lid of the junker in front of him, because if you don't, you'll never get anything. But he does not entirely dismiss this man named Snow. He is used to the confidences of strangers, and this has been an interesting ride.

"'Like all good jolly fellows, I drink my whisky clear. I'm a ramblin' wreck from Georgia Tech and a hell of an engineer,'" Robbie recites.

"What's that?" the driver asks.

"The end of a song my father used to sing," Robbie says. "Just an old drinking song, older than the two of us put together probably." But he feels a little sick, now that he has come to this place that once belonged to him, but doesn't anymore.

Robert Snow had done this once: had seated himself one morning at the kitchen table and, with pen in hand and close to the dream state before coffee, he had committed to words a thought that had tugged at the edge of his waking. This is what he had written:

"There is a kind of erection you get when the emotions and the senses are in balance and the other person is in the same kind of balance so that there exists a commonality and equality between you. In those moments the mind is alive with deep feeling that pushes the blood from the heart to the flesh and extends it. The excitement is at the base of the belly and in such moments the cock is an offering and received gift of sheathed blood and warmth given in trust. These are astounding erections because you are fully in the senses yet perfectly clear in the mind which is suffused with a pervasive joy."

Robbie had read what he'd written, realizing that it had come from months of remembering the exact nature of the excitement he'd felt with Thomas. And he'd never understood it until he'd written it down—what long ago and everyday had been as natural as breathing and no more thought of than breathing. And he'd thought, not for the first time, how profligate Thomas McCloud is, a great squanderer, who'd thrown away so much of value, and suddenly Robbie thought Tripp who'd stepped up to him when Robbie had been certain no one would again. And it occurred to him that there was a possibility that Tripp might be the last person he would care for deeply, the last of a lifetime. Presently, he got up from the kitchen table and went to shave.

But now, on this most glorious of June mornings, Robbie saw to the east the skyline of the city sharply defined against the morning sky. The number of

new buildings that had sprouted in the eight years of his absence surprised
him, and gazing at them, he knew that it was his own generation that had sent
them glittering to the sky. But that is an old Chicago story, the way each generation leaves its mark on this town, a constant never-ending, ruthless process
of tearing down and building up again. Yet he loves the place, feels displaced
everywhere but here; thinks, too, that for thirty years since he was eighteen,
coming home has always been a very lonely business, and was that first
Thanksgiving vacation of his freshman year at college, when he had stepped
off the plane at O'Hare and had felt an immediate disappointment that there
was no one there at the end of the boarding ramp to meet him—not his brother Chip, not his father, not Peck. And so he had gotten a cab, and it was on this
same expressway headed into town when he had first felt something akin to
what he feels now, though less defined. He had ridden in silence gazing off at
the familiar sky-scape of the Loop, not knowing what he was feeling until the
taxi left the expressway and angled east to South Shore Drive. The cab rolled
along with the lake cold and empty in the rushing November twilight on one
side, and, on the other, the scattered lights in the tall apartment buildings of
Hyde Park showing the warm good cheer of Thanksgiving Eve. Looking up at
those lights is when he had felt for the first time that desolate, lonely feeling
which would come to be associated with all his homecomings. And the feeling gathered force as the taxi took the gentle curves of the old carriage roads
of Jackson Park, moved through the darkened park beneath leafless trees lighted only by occasional street lamps. Soon they were on Constance Street and
as he waited for the cabbie to make change, Robbie looked at the darkened
house with Peck out for the evening, and his father over at the country club at
his bridge game, and Chip with his college buddies in Bermuda.

   "It was so desolate looking at that house," says the young man he'd been,
who turns to face Robbie. *"When I went in I saw that Dad had left a note on
the hall table telling me to come on over to the club for dinner, but I didn't
want that. So I just went from room to room turning on every light in the house,
up in the attic and on all the porches, too. Then I went out and got wood—trip
after trip—and lighted fires in the dining room fireplace and the living room
fireplace and in the study and even upstairs in my mother's room where there
probably hadn't been a fire since before she died. And I curled up in a ball on
the living room couch because I wanted everybody at home having a drink and
a fire going and dinner cooking and the turkey thawing and the phone ringing
with my friends' calls. That's what I wanted."*

   "I know," Robbie tells his younger self. *"You wanted some warmth. I
know all about that. And you got it finally, when you found Thomas, didn't*

you? That September morning in the housing office at college when he called out to the room, 'I've got a house, who wants to share?' you stepped up and it was warm, wasn't it? It was like standing under the sun before a golden being, wasn't it?"

"Yes," says that young man Robert Snow had been.

"There you have it," the grown Robert says. *"But part of him lacked substance, didn't he? Part of him couldn't see things through. You knew that—or at least suspected it—didn't you?"*

"Yes," answers the young man he'd once been. *"I both suspected and knew."*

"When the phone rang that September afternoon and it was Chip calling to say . . . ," the grown Robert begins.

"To say," the younger Robbie continues, *"that our father had dropped dead of a heart attack at the top of the subway stairs at State and Jackson, that's when I knew the limits of Tom's. . . ."*

"Courage?" the older Robert Snow offers.

"Yes, courage," says the young man he'd been. *"When my father died, I knew."*

For Robbie had hung up the phone and said, "Tom, my father's dead." And he had looked around that room Thomas McCloud had just entered, drawn from his school work by the odd tone of Robbie's voice on the phone.

"I've got to go home," Robbie said. And he looked around again. "I can't believe it. I thought for the longest time that Chip was talking about our grandfather who's past ninety. My father's father." He paused. "Tom, I've got to go home. I should pack. I should call the airline. I need a dark suit. I need a white shirt. I need my cuff links."

Abruptly he sat down.

"My father's dead," he repeated, and he looked up at Thomas as though he hadn't seen him until now. "Tom, Daddy's dead. He's so small. He's such a tiny man and he was alone when he died. He's so little, Tom, and he was alone," He looked at Thomas. "I'll need money," Robbie said. And he stood abruptly and strode down the short corridor to the room they shared and he went to his bookshelf and begin pulling out books, fanning the pages over the bed. Bills fluttered out—twenties, fifties, hundreds.

"Jesus," Tom said from where he leaned in the doorway, hands thrust deep in his Levi pockets. He had no idea Robbie kept so much cash in the house. There had to be easily a thousand dollars strewn on the bed.

Robbie looked up, still holding a book. And again it was as if he did not see Thomas. "I need to pack," he said, dropping the book. "No," he said, "I need money."

"Robbie . . ." Thomas began.

"I'll need a dark suit. I'll need a white shirt and a dark tie. Black shoes."
And he looked down at the bed, saw the money scattered there and suddenly
his legs went weak and he sat down abruptly on the mattress and began picking up the bills and methodically arranging them by denomination as though
he was sorting play money for a Monopoly game.

And Thomas stood leaning against the door jamb, then seated himself on
the floor beside the low bed, and settling back against a chest of drawers, drew
up his knees, resting his hands on the bony caps where skin showed from
thread-webbed rips. Thomas sat for a minute or two and watched Robbie
closely, who had left off sorting the bills and sat motionless with fixed eyes.

"What happened, Robbie?" Thomas asked after a moment. "What happened to your father? Tell me, guy. Come on, tell me." And Robbie's eyes
came up to meet Thomas's.

But Thomas was frightened because at twenty-two death had come into a
house where he lives, and he had never seen death before. It frightened him,
how death seems to dim the lamp light and how death palls the soft, study-
music and suspends all life. Robbie frightened him because Thomas had not
realized until that moment that to love this man might require more than he
had ever imagined. And so presently Thomas reached to take the bills out of
Robbie's hand and set them on the dresser top, and without looking at Robbie,
Thomas sat down on the bed, then lay back into the dusty odor of Robbie's pillow.

"Scoot on over here to me, guy," he said and they swiftly adjusted their
bodies so that Thomas held Robbie close, his knees behind Robbie's knees.
They lay quietly like that, ignoring the frantic telephone which seemed to ring
every five minutes, no doubt with urgent business from Chicago. Then gradually it came out of Robbie: at first intermittent shudders (Good, Thomas
thought.) And each time Robbie's body quaked, Thomas's arms would tight-
en around him, then hold, then loosen as the trembling rippled away; then
came a racking intake of breath that indrew and tightened Robbie's stomach
nearly to his spine, and which Thomas felt against the inside of his forearm
and it frightened him, but he waited because he knew he must, knew that if he
did not wait, then this man Robert Snow would be forever and irrevocably
damaged. And then, all at once everything gathered, everything burst, deep
sounds coming from Robbie's racking body, sounds that Thomas McCloud
had never known a human being could make and which he felt against his
chest as he held Robbie Snow close. And those sounds would stop, and

Robbie, as rattled as Thomas at the noise he was making, would try to speak, try to laugh, try to say something light and easy, and up they would come again—those anguished and frightening sounds, and Thomas wondered at their source, thought how deeply love must have been suppressed in that strange household from which Robert Snow derived. And then, after hours it seemed, and to his surprise, Thomas McCloud learned that death can be an aphrodisiac because death sharpens need in all the living, and in young men, warns of mortality, signals it in the tenor of the breath and by a rippling travel of blood and the hot stir of the groin.

"Do you remember," the grown Robert Snow says to that young man he used to be, *"what it felt like to get a hard-on like that—out of grief? Do you remember that it frightened you and Tom?"*

"Yes," the young man says softly.

"And so you felt the urgency of time," Robbie says.

"Yes, I felt it," the younger Robbie confirms. *"Time was in the light that filled our room, and in the way Tom smelled, and in the heat of his body, and in the laughter of a bunch of guys from across the street going out to the bars. We lay together, and it frightened me, but it terrified Thomas."*

"I know," the grown Robert Snow says softly.

And the young Robbie replies, *"You're going to think of that fellow Tripp now, aren't you?"*

"Yes," Robert Snow says to that young man he has not been for a long time.

And almost with relief, he does think of Tripp, of sitting a few days ago late at night on the couch at home in Philadelphia with the darkened apartment thrown open to the warm flow of the night, the square so silent beneath the wide windows of the living room that you could hear the splash of the fountain behind the iron fence of the little park, and Tripp there with him, sprawled full length on the couch, his head in Robbie's lap, and cupping Tripp's skull with one hand, holding it for a long time to feel the peace of the moment and how that continued moment after moment, a sweet chain of moments that became an hour of peace, of rest, of a slow drift to nowhere.

Then Tripp stirred, opened his eyes, looked up at Robbie, whose features were indistinct in the half-light. And Robbie did not know that Tripp was thinking, *I must remember this always because a man I consider remarkable cares for me. Yes, I must remember it because all of this will vanish soon. Even if I do remember it, it will be gone—all he is and all he knows and feels, and all I am and all I know and feel. So I must remember this.*

And Tripp could feel a comfortable moistness at his temples and forehead and at the back of his neck where he rested against Robbie's thigh. And Tripp crossed his arms on his chest and crossed his ankles and thought, *It would be easy to reach up, pull him down to me and kiss him. I don't know what that would be like, or what would happen after that, but it would be an easy thing to do.* And Tripp stirred and sighed. *"Not today,"* Tripp told himself. *"Not tonight. Not now. Not yet, if ever."*

Then Robbie spoke, saying, "You know, I felt every human emotion with Thomas that you can feel, and I felt them over and over again with such intensity that its been enough to last a lifetime. I don't need to feel that keenly again. It's an easy form of human love that I want now. And I want to be able to say, 'I'll fight this fight but not that fight.' I want, and believe, that I've earned the luxury of choice." He laughed, then added, "I'm getting to that stage of life when you say, 'Oh, what the hell, let the grandchildren gather the apples.'"

And Tripp's deep laugh surprised Robert Snow, and then before he knew quite what was happening, Tripp reached up, clasped Robbie's neck, used it as a fulcrum to lift himself up as he pulled Robbie down, and the kiss that Tripp gave was swift—an odd, dry, exuberant, affectionate bumping of lips. Tripp laughed very lightly and Robbie laughed, too. And then Tripp lay back again in Robbie's lap and became very still and quiet. And Robbie, astounded by the swift change of course life often takes, spread his arms along the low back of the couch and looked out at the shadowed room filled with old, storied things, thinking, He just bumped my mouth and he's not even flirting. Then, I've asked myself often enough for almost a year now whether I love him or not, and I know it doesn't matter if I do or not, because it's inevitable that I will.

And suddenly Robbie understood that until Tripp had stepped up to him, he'd had no idea what he'd had with Thomas, because until Tripp arrived, there had been no standard of comparison.

"I feel so stupidly young," Robbie said almost to himself, "so stupidly young and uninformed."

But Tripp had turned his head, fixing his eyes somewhere in the shadows of the room, and so half heard what Robbie said, because Tripp was thinking again.

He has asked for nothing, but shouldn't I offer him something? What can I give him that his dignity will allow him to take? And he considered Robert Snow's body: the lankiness, the hardness of his bones, the spongy muscles, the male smell mingled with tobacco and sometimes bitter breath. And Tripp understood a man's hard body given to the softness of a woman's, and he could imagine easily enough what a man's hard body given to another man's hard body might be (a tangle of hard legs, was as far as his thinking would take him). And then he thought without meaning to, *For him to enter me would be too much. His entering me would be reckless beyond all reason. It would be the last place, the very last I could go with him. Knowing him, he would enter as deeply as he could, right up to the hilt, and he would think he's bringing all the universe with him—stars and planets and suns, air and rain, and you name it—and he would expect nothing less than levitation because he believes with all his being that sex is not worth having unless its transcendent and in that he's more Catholic than the Pope. And so he would be inside of me, a shaggy old roan and a maverick and a desperado; and he would hold himself there and I would hold him there and his hand would have me clasped and then what? Then what? Probably nothing except I'd be in that last place, which would contain all of him, every bit of him that there is and then what would I do? No, I cannot understand buggery, cannot comprehend its purpose under heaven—for the life of me I can't.* And Tripp stopped thinking, turned his head back from looking at the room which is Robert Snow's, and gazed up at the tree shadows on the ceiling, very discouraged because he was at a loss.

"Lately I feel like I can hold only one thing in my mind at a time," Robbie said. "The pivot action in there has gotten a little rusty." And he gave a disparaging snort.

"Cool," Tripp said, because he did not want to think.

But Robert Snow loves to watch them dance, Tripp and his girl Helene— Laney they call her; feels happy watching them dance that modified swing of theirs where the hint of movement from one causes the other to move in counterpoint. Lovers dance like that, Robbie knows, used to each other's bodies, and a man and woman dance like that because they dance when they are alone.

And the heavy town car takes the whirling exit ramp, dives into the city, which rises around him now, the human scale of the sidewalks and streets where people are. And Robbie marvels at himself and Thomas McCloud, how as young men they crossed into a new place but all that remains of that place they made, occupied, and abandoned, is what exists of it in their minds and memories, where transparent ghost-boys perform a ghost-love. Robbie lowers the window to let in the air and noise of life.

"Remember me," the young man he used to be interrupts Robbie's thoughts. *"I've got to go now."*

Oh yes, Robbie thinks, how could I forget *you*?

And suddenly Robert Snow's eyes grow shrewd when he thinks that in a few hours he will sign a labor agreement which will cow a minor plutocrat, a Lawn Mower King, and though that contract rankles and humiliates, it is in the fellow's best interests to sign. Then, with a laugh which the driver hears, Robbie thinks what a pleasure it will be upon the signing of those settlement papers, to crow, to triumph, to perform a crazy victory dance.

"Ha!" Robbie's voice explodes from the backseat.

The driver glances into the mirror, smiles broadly, and laughs. He laughs. Why not?

ERIC MAY

Three chapters from *Necessary Evils*

IN LOVING MEMORY OF FERNANDO SANTIAGO

Chapter One

Let's get one thing straight right off the top: I-love-my-job. So, unlike *some* old scribes I could name, there'll be none of that woe-is-me foolishness about how newspaper reporting drove me to drink and divorce. (Those accomplishments I achieved all on my own, thank you very much.) There'll be no accounts of how news reporting ruined my "creativity" or burned me out. As I've said any number of times, working on a newspaper is a sweet deal; there's no heavy lifting, it's reasonably interesting at least part of the time, and you can do most of it while sitting on your ass. Finally, there'll be absolutely nothing about the so-called *Watergate II Scandal.* I've been interviewed about that story so many times that I'm as sick of it as our ex-president must be as he lives out his last lonely days on that ranch in Idaho. (And just in case you were wondering about the Pulitzer Prize money, and the book deal money, and the movie-rights money that came from all of that; my ex-wife got most of it, along with the house and the dog.)

What I will do is answer a question I've been asked any number of times: How did I get into this line of work in the first place? Here's what happened.

On the night of Tuesday, November 13, 1984, exactly one week after Ronald Reagan rolled to his second presidential victory, Fernando Santiago, age 35, fell asleep while watching television with a beer in one hand and a lighted cigarette in the other.

According to the Chicago Fire Department, the cigarette fell from his hand as he slept, which ignited newspapers scattered on the floor, which set fire to nearby curtains, which then set fire to some of the wallpaper in the small room.

It was the smoke from the fire that killed him. When firefighters smashed in the door to his room at the St. Thomas Hotel (a run-down SRO in the South Loop) they found the short, stocky man sitting on a beanbag chair, his head flopped to one side and the beer bottle, ironically, still upright in his hand.

Mr. Santiago, who was a native of Bello Valle, Mexico, was not married and had no children. His survivors included his parents and a grandmother back in Bello Valle, two brothers living in Milwaukee, a brother in Cleveland, two sisters in California, and numerous aunts, uncles, and cousins.

The reason I found out this and other stuff about him was because I was the person *The Chicago Daily Record* sent to cover the fire. Which is a story in itself because I wasn't even a reporter back then. In fact, I had never been a reporter anywhere before that night. At the time (I was 24) I was working as a copy-aide (i.e. clerk/gofer) on the paper's Metro Desk with no desire whatsoever to be a journalist. On weekends I sang and played guitar in a band and my life plan, such as it was, was to become the next Black giant of rock n' roll—move over Chuck, move over Bo, move over Jimi. (In preparation for this role, I had grown, over the previous four years, a head of thick dreadlocks. This disappointed my parents no end and drew irritated looks from many of the old dry balls in the newsroom, all of which I found most amusing.) Back in '84, I figured I'd work at the CDR for maybe another year before heading off to New York or L.A. and my career as a rock legend. But on November 13, all that changed.

As usual, things were pretty quiet that night in the newsroom, a wide, high ceilinged place that a lot of old timers at the paper still called the city room. The daytime din of hundreds of overlapping conversations had by then, given way to the intermittent talk of the relatively few staffers on duty. These were editors and copy-editors, mostly, who sat at the center of the room, a square of frenzied touch-typing activity surrounded by a vista of vacant desks.

As for me, I did stuff like answer the phones, type in the day's lottery numbers on computer, and retrieve story and photo files from the paper's reference library.

Around nine-thirty I was engaged in one of my favorite work pastimes: scanning the wire services for unusual and/or gross news stories. I had just found this cool UPI feature about a Down-South phenomena called Lying-In-The-Road-Death, when the Metro phone rang.

Still gazing at my computer screen, I picked up: "Daily Record. Metro Desk."

The man on the other end began talking in a rush. I told him to slow down. He paused, then asked me if I knew about the big fire.

"What fire?"

"The fire at the St. Thomas, man."

I wedged the receiver between my ear and shoulder and picked up a pen and note pad. I knew where the St. Thomas was. Back when I was going to college downtown and still living with my folks, I used to pass behind the hotel on my El rides to and from school.

"How big a fire are we talking about?" I said.

"Flames are shooting out the top windows, man. The whole building look like it's gonna go up."

I scribbled down these details and told the guy I was putting him on hold and to not hang up.

All the newsroom chairs were equipped with wheels and I rolled across the narrow aisle to where Bernie McGlaughlin, the Night Metro editor, was examining a story, his eyes transfixed on his screen. Bernie had been at the *Record* longer than I had been alive. His big belly stretched his knit shirts like an advanced pregnancy and he kept his pants up with metal clip suspenders. He wore black horn-rimmed glasses that sat at a pronounced angle on his wide face, which was red-nosed from decades of drinking. His jowls were invariably nicked in a spot or two due to a shaky shaving hand, his full head of white hair always looked as if he had just gotten out of bed, and he talked out of the corner of his mouth like a caricature of a B-movie tough guy. Two years before, on my first day in the city room, Bernie had looked at me askance after catching sight of my dreadlocks and said sarcastically: "What happened? Your barber have a heart attack?" I didn't get defensive or anything, 'cause that's not my style. Taking notice of his white hair going every-which-way and his nicked face, I said matter-of-factly: "Naw, he didn't have a heart attack. He went blind. But from the looks of things, he's still managing to find work." Bernie and I got along just fine after that.

"Yo," I said, tapping Bernie on his shoulder. He swiveled around in his chair. As was usually the case when he was busy, his eyes were bulged and there were touches of spittle at the corners of his mouth.

"What is it!" he said. Such exclamations were normal for him when he was interrupted on deadline. I told him what the man on the phone had told me.

"Aww, fake a shit and fuck me," said Bernie, employing one of his favorite expressions. "I got nobody to send over there, abso-fucking-lutely nobody."

The Metro section's night-side reporting staff consisted of one reporter, who at the moment was on the far Southwest Side covering a triple shooting. (The paper had done away with the rewrite reporter's position in a cost-cutting move.)

"Ask the guy on the phone if anyone's dead," said Bernie.

I rolled back over to the phone. The guy said he didn't know if anyone was dead. "But smoke is coming out a top window, and there's a big-ass crowd of people on the street, and a Channel Seven news truck just pulled up."

I put him on hold again and spoke across the aisle. "Bernie, he says TV's there."

"God-*damnit!*" Bernie snarled. "Another farm-fucking mess. Get the guy's name, and ask him if he lives at the St. Thomas or knows anybody who does."

When I asked the guy his name, he said it was Crazy-Legs. Thinking that maybe I heard him wrong, I asked again.

"You heard right," he said cheerfully. "That's what folks call me, Crazy-Legs. With a capital L. That's the only name I go by."

I didn't believe him but I wasn't going to argue. I asked him if he lived at the St. Thomas and he said he lived down the street at another SRO named the Carnegie. "But I know folks at the St. Thomas, man; I know a whole lot of 'em."

Putting the guy on hold yet again, I turned to give Bernie this new information only to find him leaning over his desk with his back to me. He was writing in one of those narrow, spiral notebooks that reporters use. After half-a-minute he swiveled around and thrust the notebook towards me.

"Here," he said.

I had no idea what he was talking about so I just looked at him with what must have been a dumbfounded expression.

"Take it!" Bernie snarled.

I leaned over and took the notebook from him. I glanced at it and saw that all the way down the top page, in surprisingly neat printing, were a list of questions.

"You want me to ask the guy on the phone all these questions?"

"*No*, I do not want you to ask the guy on the phone all those questions. I want you to get your ass down to the St. Thomas and ask all those questions."

"*Me?*" I said.

"Yeah, you. You haven't done a thing around here all night except take up space, so you might as well make yourself useful. If the fire is a fatal then we ought to have something about it in the paper. I don't want to depend on City News Bureau because with that shooting out south, they might get to the fire or they might not."

"So who am I supposed to talk to once I get there?" I said.

"There'll be a fire department spokesman on the scene, probably a battalion chief. Battalion chiefs wear white helmets. There may be a spokesman from the police department too since the hotel is so close to headquarters. Just take down what they say. You get the caller's name?"

When I told him, Bernie didn't so much as bat an eye.

"Okay," he said, "tell this Crazy-Legs to meet you at the gas station across the street from the St. Thomas. See if he knows anybody at the hotel, a night manager or janitor who might be able to tell you something pertinent."

I got back on the line and told Crazy-Legs to stay by the gas station pay phone and that I would meet him there in fifteen minutes. He said okay.

I stood up and pulled my varsity jacket off the back of my chair. Bernie opened his desk drawer and fished out a card the size of a large index card. It had PRESS printed on one side in big black letters and under it the newspaper's name printed in script.

As I pulled on my jacket, I noticed that the Metro copy editors sitting nearby were snatching these concerned looks at me, and at Bernie, and between each other, like there was a problem. This I found a little puzzling since it was standard night-side procedure at the CDR to send a copy-aide to cover a story on those rare, rare occasions when there was no reporter available. Although I had never been sent out before, I knew a couple of weekend copy-aides that had, so I didn't think my going was that big a deal. (The next day I would find out the reason behind all those concerned looks—boy, would I find out.)

Bernie signed his name on the back of the PRESS card and then slid it inside a clear, plastic cardholder that had a small clip attached. He then handed the protected card to me along with two rolls of quarters.

"Be sure to take a couple of pens. As soon as you get to the hotel, call me on a pay phone. (Although the paper had by then, purchased cell phones, the devices back then were these big, bulky, gray contraptions with receptions that were at times problematic. Old hands at the paper like Bernie considered the things more trouble than they were worth.)

My face must have looked worried because Bernie said: "Don't sweat it. When you get to the St. Thomas just act like you belong there. You can fool lots of people lots of the time if you just look like you know what you're doing."

As a person who had played in more than a few bad bar bands, I knew *that* already. To be perfectly honest though, I wasn't worried at all. The task seemed simple enough to me: go to the scene, ask some questions, write down the answers, then return to the newsroom. More than once I had seen a reporter leaving to cover a story after having spent his or her lunch break at a nearby saloon. I mean really, how hard could reporting be?

"Take a cab," said Bernie. "I'll reimburse you later."

I slid the notebook in the back pocket of my khakis and grabbed two pens.

"Who's gonna answer the phones?" I said.

"Let me worry about that. Just get going."

Outside it was dry and not unpleasant for a night in mid-November. I got a cab right away and took it straight down Michigan Avenue past the Art Institute, and Orchestra Hall, and Columbia College. Right after I passed the

Conrad Hilton, traffic slowed to a crawl. I got out a block north of Roosevelt Road, figuring I could make better time on foot. I was right. By the time I turned the corner, the cab I'd been riding in hadn't moved twenty feet.

The St. Thomas was located one street west of Michigan Avenue at the southwest corner of Wabash and Roosevelt. It was a narrow, twelve-story building with a gothic style façade. Once a grand hotel, it had become home to 200 or so people, most of them subsisting on small pensions and/or meager wages. You could get drugs there, you could get prostitutes there (or so I'd been told), and if you were crazy enough to eat in the first floor storefront hot dog stand where the dust stuck to the greasy walls like fur, you could get ptomaine too.

I didn't see any fire coming from any windows. The sidewalk directly across from the hotel on the eastside of Wabash was crowded three and four deep with people who were looking up at the building as if any second now they expected something exciting to happen. There was also a crowd on the north side of Roosevelt Road, and from the El platform that spanned the street, more people stood watching and waiting. I sniffed for the scent of smoke but didn't smell any.

Two squad cars, blue and white lights flashing, were parked bumper-to-bumper across Wabash just south of Roosevelt. Two officers were in the middle of the intersection directing the southbound Wabash traffic west towards State Street.

There was a fire engine and a fire truck (the trucks are the vehicles with the collapsible ladders on top) parked on the Roosevelt side of the building. Parked on the Wabash side were another truck and engine, along with two ambulances, a big white command van, and a red battalion chief's sedan, all with emergency lights going.

I walked a short ways west and at the alley, angled across the six-lanes of Roosevelt Road through the stalled traffic. At the high wooden fence that bordered the other side of the gas station I saw two pay phones, but no one standing there.

It was then that I realized that I should have asked Crazy-Legs what he looked like and what he was wearing, and told him what I looked like and what I was wearing. In addition to my dreadlocks, I was coconut shell dark and six feet tall. Along with the cuffed khaki slacks I was wearing navy blue sneakers that matched my wool, Parkland High School varsity jacket ("Go Pirates! Go Pirates!") The jacket had maize colored lettering stitched on the back spelling the school's name, a large maize 77 on the right sleeve, and next to the front left hand pocket, a large maize P that I had received for running track my senior year. The gaudy jacket displeased some of my more arty "avant-garde" friends, which I found just as amusing as the negative newsroom reactions to my dreads.

I walked under the station's wide awning, the lights from the fire and police vehicles dancing red, white, and blue flashes all about. When I reached the pay phones I looked around to see if anyone on the crowded sidewalk was looking expectantly in my direction. No one was.

I broke open a roll of quarters and called the Metro Desk. Bernie answered.

"I don't see any fire," I said. "I don't smell any smoke and if you ask me—"

"Assume nothing!" shouted Bernie. "Find the farm-fucking spokesmen, write down what they say, *then* call me back. Understand, lamebrain? Now get it done!"

I heard the phone slam and I stood there staring at the receiver. In my time at the paper I had of course heard lots of stories about the way Bernie gave reporters, especially new reporters, a hard time. On more than one occasion I had seen him red-faced at his desk as he screamed at some reporter over the phone. Hearing stories about his famous rages or watching him go off on other people had always been fun; however, now that *I* was the target of his wrath, my usual calm deserted me and I found myself angry as Hell at him.

I gave up on Crazy-Legs and decided to see if I could find a spokesperson of some sort. I walked back across the gas station to the intersection where the bumper to bumper squad cars were parked. I clipped my press card high on my jacket and carried the reporter's notebook loosely in my hand.

A uniformed officer, a White guy around my age, was standing near the squad car closest to my side of the street, watching the two officers in the middle of the intersection directing traffic. He had his cap low over his eyes and his dark blue jacket was unzipped, revealing his sky blue blouse and dark tie.

"Evening, officer," I said casually, as if I did this every day. "There wouldn't happen to be a spokesman anywhere around, would there?"

His eyes narrowed and I knew he was trying to compute what was obviously for him the incongruous sight of my skin, the dreadlocks, and the casual clothes combined with the press card and the reporter's notebook.

Who knows? A few years back the cop might have asked me all sorts of questions, but Harold Washington had been elected mayor of Chicago the year before and having a Black man running the city did have its effects, I suppose.

With a quick nod toward the other end of the block, the officer said in that nasally, Chicago White Folks twang: "He's down there."

I gave him a lazy nod and said thanks. I stepped into the street and strolled south with the crowd to my left and the parked emergency vehicles to my right. A band of yellow tape, like party bunting, was looped from parking meter to parking meter the length of the block. The crowd stood obediently behind the tape and kept looking up as if they were expecting something. Many had no coats or jackets. A few had wrapped themselves in blankets that they must have hastily grabbed while on the way out of their apartment doors.

As I continued on, I glanced through the space between the front of a fire engine and the rear of one of the ambulances and got a glimpse of the open doorway of the St. Thomas. Inside the bright lobby, I saw several firefighters moving about in their big coats and boots, none of them in much of a hurry.

Midway down the block, in the middle of the street, I saw a dozen people gathered around a man in firefighter's gear wearing a white helmet. Five of the men in this group wore black, athletic-style jackets with colorful TV station logos on the back were toting video cameras with the lights turned off. The rest of the people had on various styles of trench coats and as I got closer I recognized several of the men and women as reporters I'd seen countless times on the tube. A couple of the others I recognized as reporters from the *Sun-Times* and *Tribune* I'd seen drinking at the Billy Goat, a Downtown basement saloon and longtime journalists' hangout that had been parodied on *Saturday Night Live.* ("Cheezebooger! Cheezebooger!")

The man in the firefighter's gear was pale with bushy blond eyebrows, a small, angular nose, and thin lips. His face reminded me of an owl. He was smoking a cigarette and he and the reporters were talking in the familiar manner of people whose professional paths cross frequently.

Not knowing what to do, I stood at the back of the group and said nothing. No one paid me any notice. Then, as if by some silent cue, the men in the athletic-style jackets raised their cameras to their shoulders and hit the lights.

The firefighter, cigarette dangling in his mouth, blinked hard a couple of times in reaction to the sudden brightness. His coat was open and the white shirt underneath gave off a high reflection, like the coat's reflector stripes.

He took a long last drag, flicked the cigarette to the ground, and exhaled a stream of smoke. The smoke hung in front of his face and he waved his hand quickly back and forth in an attempt to clear the cloud away. As he did so one of the cameramen off to my right called out in a teasing voice: "Better clear it away fast, Jimmy, you don't want that cigarette smoke caught on camera." This produced smiles and smirks from everybody, including Jimmy and one of the reporters, I didn't catch which one, said in a mock-serious basso profundo: "Tonight, a Fire Department scandal. Battalion Chief caught smoking on duty. Details at ten."

The reporters and cameramen laughed. Jimmy held his hands palms up in front of his chest and said in a plaintive but still friendly tone, "Hey c'mon guys, no making me laugh; we got a dead guy here." He gave the air in front of his nose one last wave and as his hand dropped to his side, just like that, his bushy eyebrows lowered and the thin lips mashed together in what was almost a grimace.

From somewhere, someone said, "Okay, Jimmy."

As if he had rehearsed it, Jimmy said calmly, "The Fire Department responded to a call, at nine-seventeen p.m., of a fire on the twelfth floor of the St. Thomas Hotel. Firefighters arrived at the hotel at nine-nineteen.

"When firefighters reached the twelfth floor at approximately nine-twenty, they found the hallway full of smoke. They forced entry into the room that was the source of the smoke where they discovered an unconscious man sitting in a chair. He was taken by ambulance to Cook County Hospital. As of yet there is no report on his condition. His name is being withheld until his next of kin can be notified. What I can tell you is, the man is a resident of the hotel.

"The fire was knocked down at nine-twenty four and was confined to the single, twelfth floor room. The cause of the fire is still under investigation; however, it appears the man fell asleep while smoking a cigarette.

"Right now firefighters are checking for any other heat sources in and around the room. We expect that people will be able to return to the hotel within the hour.

"There were no other injuries from the fire, although one resident is being treated here at the scene for a sprained wrist she received when she tripped and fell while exiting the building.

"CTA El service on the Dan Ryan/ninety-fifth Line that runs directly behind the hotel was shut down at approximately nine-twenty. It should be resuming shortly."

The camera lights went off.

"So this guy is going to be D-O-A at Cook County?" said one of the reporters.

"Yeah," said Jimmy. "Like I was saying before, he wasn't breathing and had no pulse by the time we got to him. We should have the official word pretty soon."

"Okay, thanks, Jimmy," the reporters said. I stood and watched as Jimmy the battalion chief reached inside his coat and pulled a pack of cigarettes from his shirt pocket. Tapping out a square, he turned and walked towards the hotel while the reporters and cameramen drifted off in various directions.

It was then that it hit me. I hadn't written anything down. So mesmerized had I been by the lights and all, that I just stood there as Jimmy told his dry, but nonetheless engaging story.

With my thoughts racing, I attempted to recount the details I had just heard. What time did he say the call had come in? When did the firefighters arrive? When had the L service been shut down?

I looked around for Jimmy but, as if by magic, he was gone.

Now what was I going to do?

Chapter Two
Fart in a Fog/The Riot Act

I immediately walked over to one of the firemen standing alongside a truck in front of the hotel. He was a wide-bodied guy with a walrus mustache and a round face. He gave me one of those, "What are you doing here?" looks then caught sight of my press credential and shook his head.

"I don't talk to the press."

I told him that I didn't want to talk to him, that I wanted to talk to the battalion chief who had been talking to reporters earlier. The firemen nodded towards the open doorway of the hotel where other firefighters were still milling about the brightly lit lobby. I gave Mr. Walrus a thank-you and took a step towards the doorway, only to have him say, matter-of-factly: "You can't go in there. You'll have to wait for him out here."

So I did. I waited and waited and waited. Firefighters came in and out, but none of them was my Jimmy, and I knew that back in the City Room, Bernie was wondering, in loud and profane language, why I hadn't called with any information.

I looked at the crowd across the way still standing behind the yellow tape, and at the TV reporters in the middle of the road with their backs to me and the hotel, taking their turns in the bright lights as they gave live feeds to their stations. Great. I thought. It's on television. I could just see all the editors looking up from their machines to the TV set high on the support column. Bernie was probably going ballistic, his face red and the spittle flying.

After nearly twenty minutes, Walrus guy got behind the wheel of the nearby truck and the rest of his crewmates climbed aboard. The flashers above the cab went off and the red behemoth pulled slowly away, going south on Wabash. I stood by a parking meter and watched with increasing dread as firemen returned to the engine parked in front of the hotel and took off. I glanced down at my wristwatch. It was nearly ten-thirty. I knew that battalion chiefs rode in cars and the red Fire Department sedan was still parked a few doors away. So I felt safe that I hadn't missed Jimmy. Finally, around ten-thirty-five,

I saw a white helmeted figure enter the hotel lobby from the stairway. I let out a sigh of relief, a good feeling that lasted only a few seconds because as the guy got closer I saw that although he was a battalion chief, he wasn't the battalion chief I was looking for. This fellow wasn't as tall as Jimmy and he looked a lot older, with white eyebrows and a squinted expression, like he was trying to do an imitation of Clint Eastwood.

He stopped just outside the lobby entrance and turned to his left in the direction of Roosevelt Road. He waved at one of the firemen standing on the corner. The fireman crossed Wabash and using hand gestures, got the waiting residents to return to the hotel by crossing at the corner in an orderly double line.

The squint-eyed battalion chief stepped past me towards the parked red car.

"Excuse me, chief," I said. "I was looking for the other battalion chief who was speaking to reporters. One of the firemen said he was inside. I have to get some info from him for my paper."

The squinted eyes glanced at my credential and looked back at my face. "What are you doing standing around here for? The guy you want was over by the Roosevelt Road exit."

"Was?"

"Yeah. He just left. He was over there for a while talking to a couple of radio reporters and a guy from the Tribune."

"And he's gone now?"

"Yeah. I'm afraid so."

"I muttered another fuck as I watched hotel residents file back inside.

"So tell me," said the battalion chief. "You work for Bernie McLaughlin?"

"You know Bernie?" I said, my sinking mood doing an abrupt about face.

The battalion chief smiled: "Who doesn't know Bernie? I remember him from the days when he was standing on street corners covering fires. How's he doing?"

A big, dumb smile spread across my face. I told him that Bernie was doing fine, just fine. And then, seeing as how this battalion chief and I were now on such friendly terms, I asked: "So, could you give me the information about the fire?"

Still smiling, the battalion chief said, "That's not my job, kid. Besides, I don't have all the media information."

I winced and then shook my head.

The battalion chief was still smiling. "I guess Bernie is going to be pissed, huh?"

"You say you know him," I said flatly. "What do you think?"

The battalion chief chuckled. "Yeah, that old Bernie is something when he gets his Irish blood up."

I looked over at the corner of Roosevelt and Wabash, my attention momentarily taken by the pulling away sounds of the fire engine and truck that had parked on the Roosevelt side of the St. Thomas. I looked back at the battalion chief. He wished me a good night and headed for his parked car, leaving me standing there feeling stupid as the line of residents continued making their way inside.

I felt even stupider a few minutes later when I called Bernie from a pay phone in the lobby. Under the watchful eye of a nearby corpulent desk attendant, I put a finger in one ear to drown out the sound of echoed talk.

In the ensuing conversation I found out that not getting the information the first time was only one of the things that I had, as Bernie so quaintly put it, "fumble fucked like a shit-drunk sailor."

"Let me get this straight," he growled. "You spoke to another battalion chief but you didn't think to ask him for the name of the first battalion chief?"

"Yeah, but—"

"And you didn't get the name of this second battalion chief either?"

"No, but—"

"And even though you were standing around those fire engines and trucks for over half an hour, it never occurred to you to write down the numbers of said engines and trucks, or the helmets of the people you spoke with?"

"I do know the first battalion chief's name is Jimmy. And he looks Irish."

Bernie's voice went suddenly relieved: "Really? Geez, kid, why didn't you say that in the first place? Now all we have to do is find an Irish Chicago fireman named Jimmy. Shouldn't be too hard."

He then paused so that I could recognize the full, humiliating weight of my lame response. And then, just as I expected, Bernie shifted to shouting mode.

"I GIVE YOU AN ASSIGNMENT SO SIMPLE A GRADESCHOOLER COULD DO IT AND YOU FARM FUCK IT TO HELL AND GONE!"

"Bernie, I—"

"SHUT UP! SHUT! UP! JUST GET YOUR ASS BACK HERE."

"But what about the story?"

"OHHH, DON'T YOU WORRY YOUR POINTED LITTLE HEAD ABOUT THAT! *I'LL* MAKE SOME CALLS. *I'LL* GET THE STORY. NOT LIKE I HAVEN'T GOT ANYTHING ELSE TO DO TONIGHT!"

And then he hung up.

I slammed the black receiver down and the rotund desk clerk gazed at me with a furrowed brow, "Hey! You watch it there."

"No!" I said pointing a finger at him. "*You* watch it!" Even as I said it I knew it made no sense. Which did not stop me from marching out of the lobby in righteous indignation, much to the bewilderment of a cluster of people standing nearby.

Chapter Three
Recoup

I was so mad that by the time I reached the corner of Roosevelt and Wabash, the greasy spoon at the corner closed for the night, I had a good mind to go straight home. There was a subway stop just the other side of the el tracks at State Street. I could catch the train there and be at my apartment in Rogers Park in less than an hour. The worst that could happen to me was that I'd get fired. Big fucking deal. Fuck the goddamned Chicago Record. And fuck Bernie McLaughlin. Where the Hell did he get off talking to me that way? Like I was his fucking kid. Like I was one of those newbie, White Boy reporters who were so scared of him. That old fucking, broken down Paddy could kiss my Black ass.

The light changed but I didn't move as a wave of an even more intense anger swept through my thoughts. This anger was directed at myself because I knew I wasn't going straight home. Running out on a job before it's finished isn't my style either. When I was a kid, one of my grandmother's favorite sayings was: "If a job is first begun, never finish 'till it's done. Whether a task is large or small, do it well or not at all."

You laugh. Old Girl used to make me and my sisters memorize that and a whole host of other work-ethic homilies, which we had to repeat whenever we went to her house, which was often. At the time it didn't seem weird to my siblings and me because we were getting the same sort of stuff at home. Our parents had met while serving in the Navy and we, their children, were drilled in the "Navy way" to shower, mop floors, make beds, hang clothes, and so on. For most kids Saturday mornings meant TV cartoons; for me and my sisters it meant weekly, white glove, bedroom inspections. Whenever I've had a notion to just say to Hell with it, I get hit with this Pavlovian-like response and I can see in my mind's eye, my dear, departed grandmother's wide, fat-cheeked face as she says: "No matter your level of talent, you can always do your best. A best effort is the least a person can do."

I muttered a "thanks a lot Grandma," to the traffic, which I immediately felt guilty about since I knew it wasn't all on her. A fire with a fatality was the sort of story that belonged on the front of the Metro section and the *Record* was going to look awfully stupid the next day if it didn't have a story that every other news organization in town had. And like it or not, I had been the person assigned to get the story. If I just walked away, the last memory anyone in the City Room would have of me was that I had fucked something up and then, in an act of rank cowardice, had not even had the balls to show my face. Most of the people in that newsroom I could have cared less about, but there were a few I did respect, the city editor who had gone to the same high school as I had, the city hall reporter who had come out to see me play a number of times.

The light changed again and I stood with my mind racing, trying to see if there was any way I could fix this farm-fucking mess.

I looked down at the list of questions Bernie had written and I reviewed what he had told me before I left. I turned around and went back to the hotel lobby. As soon as the clerk saw me he got this hard look.

"What do you want?" he said.

"I want to talk to you," I said.

"What about?"

I held up my credential card. "About the fire, what else?"

"I already talked to four of you media assholes. The Trib, the Sun-Times, that blonde bitch from Channel Two."

A few people standing nearby voiced similar observations.

"Well," I said, "If you talked to so many assholes already, what's talking to one more gonna hurt?"

The clerk laughed, his mannish breasts jostling beneath his too tight blue shirt.

"Okay," he said: "What do you want to know?"

I asked him when he had first realized a fire had broken out and what he had done, how many folks were in the hotel that night, how many were residents. He only gave me, "ballpark" numbers on that, even after I pressed him. I asked him if I could go to the room where the fire had taken place and he said the Fire Department was closing off the entire floor until sometime the next day.

"The fire inspector is up there now while folks on that floor get some things from their room for overnight."

"There's a fire investigator up there right now?"

The clerk said yeah, but that the fire investigator said only folks living on that floor could come up. I took some comments from a few more people and left. I then went right around the corner to the hotel's Roosevelt exit, my thinking being that I could maybe take a back stairway up to where the fire investigator was. However, about six feet inside the door a man was a sitting in the hallway shadows. I couldn't make out his color or age, but I did see the bat he had lying across his lap. As soon as I reached for the door handle he began rising up, so I stopped and went back to the corner of Roosevelt and Wabash where I could keep an eye on both exits, which I realized was what I should have done earlier. It was another thirty minutes before I saw a short man in a dark blue jacket and pants step out of the Wabash doorway. To my surprise he started walking my way.

He had a baseball cap pushed towards the back of his head and a clipboard under his arm. He had a thick mustache and olive colored skin and I figured him for a Hispanic. When he reached me I stepped towards him as he turned the corner towards State Street.

I raised my credential and he frowned and shook his head.

"I ain't the media guy," he said with a light Spanish accent.

Walking alongside him, I told him that I knew that. Figuring that the truth would be too long (as well as too embarrassing) to explain, I lied. "My idiot boss sent me to cover the fire but he sent me too late and the Fire Department spokesman was gone by the time I got here. Of course, as far as my boss is concerned, its all *my* fault. I just need some bare bones information. Basic stuff. "

He nodded as if he were considering it, then said: "I'm not the media guy."

"Please. If I don't get this information, I am so screwed."

He made a face and said casually, "Then I guess you're screwed."

"I'm begging."

He raised a forefinger skyward and still speaking casual said: "Never beg."

"Okay, I'm beseeching you. I'm imploring you."

He smiled. "I give you A for effort. But the answer is still no."

"Why? It can't mean that much to you and it would mean so much to me."

He laughed.

We were at the Roosevelt exit. The guy in the shadows was still there. The fire investigator stepped into the piss foul alleyway where I now saw that another Fire Department sedan was parked a few feet inside. The El tracks ran the length of the alley overhead for blocks in either direction.

"What do I have to do to convince you to help me?" I said.

He stopped and looked around.

"I dunno," he said with a shrug. "It's a dark alley. Maybe we can step inside and see what develops. "

"C'mon, be serious," I said.

"I am serious," he said.

I threw up my hands.

He pointed a finger at his chest. "You want me to be serious?"

"Yes."

"Then you got to be serious with me."

"How so?"

He shrugged again. "You could start by being honest."

"I'm honest. Ask anybody who knows me. I'm as honest as they come."

"Really? Now I know I'm not going to tell you anything."

He walked toward his car. I stood debating whether to follow him.

"What did I do now?"

He stopped and turned around.

"You say everybody who knows you, knows you're honest?"

"Yeah."

"Which means you're truthful with everybody?"

"Yeah."

"So with ev-rey-body else you're honest. And with me, you lie."

"About what?"

He smiled and shook his head. "You say you got here late and yet earlier, I could have sworn I saw a guy look just like you standing around the battalion chief with the other reporters. Maybe he was your twin? An evil twin, like in the movies?"

I let out an agonized breath of air.

"I saw you earlier from the doorway of the lobby. So you tell me why I should help someone who disrespects me by lying? You lie about this and who knows, maybe you lie about other things. Maybe I tell you something and you go back to your newsroom and write a lie. Reporters have done that before. Why should I take that chance? Answer me that."

I thought about trying to explain that I had lied to save time, but since I knew that wasn't completely true, I doubted he'd buy it.

"I got no answer," I said. I closed my notebook and stuck it in my back pocket.

"You have a good night, man," he said, then he turned and went to his car. I headed toward Wabash, my plan being to walk to the Hilton on Michigan Avenue and catch a cab back to the paper to face the wrath of Hurricane McLaughlin.

I was almost to the Hilton's front entrance when a Fire Department car heading north, made a U-turn and came to a stop at the curb near me. The fire investigator lowered the window on the passenger's side and beckoned me over.

He had his clipboard on the passenger seat and leaned over it in my direction. I squatted down beside the door. He spoke flatly.

"Take out your pen and your little notebook."

While the red coated Hilton doorman watched from under the lighted awning, the fire inspector gave me all the information I needed, plus the name of the dead man and other stuff nobody else had: the beanbag chair, the beer bottle, etc.

When he was done I thanked him profusely and finally he held up a hand and said, "Enough already."

There was one more question I had to ask.

"What changed your mind? What made you decide to come look for me?"

"I didn't change my mind. I followed you down the street. I just decided to let you sweat a little.

"Out here all you have is your word. Remember what I said, folks find out you lie about the little things they figure you'll lie about the big things and once you get a reputation like that, you'll never shake it."

I thanked him again and stood up.

He looked at me like I was crazy.

"How many stories have you covered, man?"

"This is my first one."

"Okay. But don't you think that it might be a good idea to ask me for *my* name? Maybe Bernie might be interested in that little piece of information?"

"You know Bernie, too."

"I know of him."

I had my pen ready. "Okay, what's your name?"

"You promise not to laugh?" he said.

Less then ten minutes later I walked into the City Room with my hands stuffed in my pants pocket and my jacket open.

"Well, well, well," said Bernie from his chair. "Mr. Farm-Fucking-Mess himself has returned." A few of the skeleton crew snatched looks my way, some didn't. I took note of the ones who were smirking.

"We were wondering if you had the guts to come back after the way you fuck fumbled things tonight. Why I was just saying to—"

I pulled the notebook from my back pocket and dropped it on his desk.

"What's this crap?" said Bernie.

I pulled off my jacket and draped it on the back of the chair across from him.

"What's it look like?" I said.

Bernie leafed through the pages, then held the notebook up and wagged it at me.

"Well fake a shit and call me Janet Cooke," he said. "First you fuck up, then you come in here with a bunch of shit that you probably scribbled down in some bar between here and the St. Thomas.

"There's only one thing worse than a fuck-up kid, and that's a lying sack-of-shit-fuck-up who tries to cover up his bungling! Grab your jacket and get out of here! "

I leaned back in the chair and crossed my legs at the ankles.

"I'm not going nowhere, I have a story to write."

Bernie's face went pink. He swiped a swatch of white hair from in front of his lopsided glasses. He threw the notebook at me and it hit me in the chest and landed on the desk beside me.

"You heard me!" he said, sending spittle in various directions. "I said get out! Or I'll call security and have you thrown out!"

Although I kept my eyes on Bernie I knew every skeleton crew eye was watching me. I calmly picked up the notebook and lazily tossed it back to Bernie's desk where it landed among the printout copy he was editing.

"Check out the name of the fire investigator I talked to. I got his name and the number where he can be reached all night. Call him if you think I'm bull-shitting."

"I'll call that bluff," sneered Bernie.

He swiveled around and turned his broad back to me, the suspenders taut across his white shirt. He tapped out the number with a fat forefinger while mashing the receiver to his ear.

"Yeah, this is McLaughlin calling from the Record. I need to speak with the fire investigator on duty. Santiago. Fernando Santiago."

There was a pause. He introduced himself again and asked whom he was speaking to.

"You speak to one of my guys tonight? A smart-ass kid in an athletic jack-et with hair going every which way?" There was another pause. "Uh-huh. Uh-huh. Okay, thanks. Good night."

When Bernie swiveled back around I already had my big dumb smile ready.

He frowned and slapped the notebook a couple of times on his wide thigh.

"Well, well. Talk about pulling the farm-fucking-fat out of the farm-fuck-ing fire."

"So," I said easy as you please, "How do you like your humble pie, Bernie?"

"Humble pie?" he said. "I figured *you'd* want me to eat crow."

I raised my hands palms up. "Pie, crow, makes no difference to me."

"All right, Rasta Man," said Bernie. "you've had your little fun, now roll your chair over here, we got to get this story written like a mad bastard if we're gonna make the next edition."

I positioned my chair next to him and got a strong whiff of his body odor, a combination of sweat, cheap cologne, whiskey, and cigarette smoke. He did all the typing, his fat forefingers with the dirty nails moving quicksilver over the keyboards, tappa-ta-tappa-ta-tap, the aqua green words appearing across the dark screen. The only time Bernie stopped was to flip over a page of my notebook or when he wanted me to clarify some small detail.

We were done in less than fifteen minutes, and after he dotted the last sentence, he scrolled back up to the top.

"So what do you want for your by-line?"

"I dunno," I said. "I never even thought of that."

"Well fake a shit. Think of something. We ain't got all night."

"How about LaQuantas," I said matter-of-factly.

I heard one of the copy editors guffaw.

"Sure, smart-ass, whatever," said Bernie, just as matter-of-factly.

I put a hand on his wrist and I felt him flinch.

"Hey, I was kidding. Just put my name. Felix Johnston."

When he was finished with that he hit a key and the story disappeared and appeared on the screen of copy editor a couple of desks away, and the rest, as they like to say, is history.

ETGAR KERET

Eight Percent of Nothing

TRANSLATED BY MIRIAM SHLESINGER

Benny Brokerage had been waiting for them in the doorway for almost half an hour, and when they arrived he tried to act as if it didn't make him mad. "It's all her fault," the older man sniggered and held out his hand for a firm, no-nonsense shake. "Don't believe Butchie," the peroxide urged him. She looked at least fifteen years younger than her man. "We got here earlier, except we couldn't find any parking." And Benny Brokerage gave her his foxy smile, like he really gave a shit why she and Butchie were late. He showed them the apartment, which was almost completely furnished, with a high ceiling and a kitchen window that almost gave you a view of the sea. He'd barely gotten through half the usual round, when Butchie pulled out his checkbook and said he'd take it, and that he was even okay with paying a year's rent up front, except that he wanted a bit off the top, just to feel he wasn't being taken for a ride. Benny Brokerage explained that the owner was living abroad, so he wasn't at liberty to lower the price. Butchie insisted it was small change. "As far as I'm concerned," he said, you can take it off your commission. "What's your cut?" "Eight," Benny Brokerage said after a moment's pause, preferring not to risk a lie. "So you'll still be left with five," Butchie announced, and finished writing out the check. When he saw that the broker wasn't holding out his hand to take it, he added, "Look at it this way, the market's in the cellar, and five percent of something is a lot more than eight percent of nothing."

Butchie, or Tuvia Minster, which was the name that appeared on the check, said the peroxide would drop by the next morning to pick up an extra key. Benny Brokerage said no problem, except it had to be before eleven, because he had some appointments after that. The next day, she didn't show. It was eleven twenty already, and Benny Brokerage, who was aching to leave but didn't really want to stand her up, pulled the check out of the drawer. It had the office phone numbers, but he preferred to avoid another tedious conversation with Butchie, and went for the home number instead. It wasn't until she answered that he remembered he didn't even know her name, so he opted for "Mrs. Minster". She somehow sounded a little less dumb, on the phone, but she still couldn't remember who he was or that they'd made an appointment for that morning. Benny Brokerage kept his cool, and reminded her slowly, the way you do when you're talking to a child, how he had met with her and her husband the day before, and how they'd signed for the apartment.

There was no response at the other end and when she finally asked him to describe what she looked like, he realized he'd really blown it. "The truth is," he crooned, "that I must have the wrong number. What did you say your husband's name is? That's it then. I was looking for Nissim and Dalia. Those 411 people messed me up again. I'm really sorry. Good-bye," and he slammed the receiver down before she had a chance to answer. The peroxide arrived at the office fifteen minutes later, eyes at half-mast and a face that hadn't been washed yet. "I'm sorry," she yawned. "It took me half an hour to find a cab."

The following morning, when he arrived at the office, there was a woman waiting outside on the sidewalk. She looked about forty, and something about the way she was dressed, about her fragrance, was so not-from-around-here, that when he spoke, he instinctively went for his most genteel pronunciation. Turned out she was looking for a two- or three-room place. She'd prefer to buy, but she didn't rule out a rental, as long as it was available right away. Benny Brokerage said he did happen to have a few nice apartments for sale, and that because the market was in a slump they would be reasonably priced too. He asked her how she'd found him, and she said she'd looked in the Yellow Pages. "Are you Benny?" she asked. He said no – that there hadn't been a Benny for ages, but that he'd kept the name in order not to lose the goodwill. "I'm Michael," he smiled. "The truth is that when I'm on the job, even I forget sometimes." "I'm Leah," the woman smiled back. "Leah Minster. We spoke on the phone yesterday."

"This is a little uncomfortable," Leah Minster said all of a sudden, out of nowhere. The first apartment had been too dark, and they were walking through the second one. Benny-Brokerage tried to play dumb, and started talking about how simple it would be to renovate, and stuff like that, as if she'd been referring to the apartment. "After you phoned me," Leah Minster ignored his reply, "I tried to talk it over with him. At first he lied, but then he got tired of it, and confessed. That's what the apartment is for. I'm leaving him." Benny Brokerage continued showing her around, thinking to himself that it was none of his business, and that there was no reason for him to get uptight. "Is she young?" Leah Minster persisted, and he nodded and said: "She's not nearly as pretty as you. I hate having to say a thing like this about a client, but he's an idiot."

The third apartment had better light, and when he showed her the view of the park from the bedroom window, he felt her moving closer, not touching him exactly, but close enough. And even though she liked the apartment, she wanted him to show her another one. In the car, she kept asking him all sorts of questions about the peroxide, and Benny Brokerage tried to put her down but to stay kind of vague at the same time. He didn't really feel comfortable with it, but he went on, because he saw it was making her happy. Whenever they stopped talking, there was a kind of tension, especially at the stop lights, and somehow he just couldn't think of anything to say, the way he usually could, a little story that would take their minds off being stuck. All he could do was stare at the traffic light and wait for it to change. At one of the intersections, even when the light changed, the car in front of them, a Mercedes, didn't move. Benny Brokerage slammed the horn twice and cursed the driver through the window. And when the guy in the Mercedes didn't seem to give a damn, he stormed out of the car. Turned out there was nobody to pick a fight with though, because the driver, who seemed at first to be dozing, didn't wake up, even when Benny-Brokerage nudged him. Then the ambulance crew arrived and said it was a stroke. They searched the driver's pockets and the car, but they couldn't find any ID. And Benny Brokerage felt kind of rotten for cursing the guy without a name, and he was sorry for the mean things he'd said about the peroxide too, even though that really had nothing to do with it.

Leah Minster sat beside him in the car, looking pale. He drove her back to the office, and made them both some coffee. "The truth is that I didn't tell him anything," she said, and took a sip of the instant. "I was lying actually, just so you'd tell me about her. I'm sorry, but I just had to find out." Benny Brokerage smiled, and told himself and her that there was no harm done really, that all they'd done was see a couple of apartments and some poor guy who'd dropped dead, and that if there was anything to be learned from the whole experience it was that Thank God they were alive, or something along those lines. She finished her coffee, said Sorry again, and left. And Michael, who still had a few sips to go, looked around his office, a two-by-three cubicle with a window, overlooking the main drag. Suddenly the place seemed so small and transparent, like the ant colony he got for his bar mitzvah a million years ago. And all the goodwill that he'd boasted about so solemnly just two hours earlier also sounded like crap. Lately, it had begun bothering him that people called him Benny.

Thanksgiving

Miss Evangeline grabbed me under the armpit like she was snatching a Kleenex out a box. I was just about to eat the baked apple section of my turkey TV dinner. Our class was celebrating the pre-Thanksgiving dinner that all the 6th grade classes put on every year. Miss Evangeline's big old horse butt was inches from touching the rim of my TV dinner, when she bent over to pick up something off the floor. She grunted and rose up like some rusty old street bridge. "Mr. Washington you will not disrupt this gala event just because you're determined to grow up and become some dope fiend derelict. No sir!" She said as she held up a cigarette, an inch from my nose. "That cigarette ain't mine. It was already there," I pleaded slapping my hand atop the desk, the force of it off-centering my TV dinner. My daddy said, to drive home your point, always look a person in the eye. So I searched through the cushions of fat and bifocals to find Miss Evangeline's eyes. This time I was really telling her the truth. I was real pissed when she grabbed me in front of everyone. Some of them had stopped eating to gawk like they were watching Soul Train or something. Marvin Whitehead did the *Miss E. dance,* sticking his butt out and waddling around the floor flatfooted and shaking his finger in folks' faces. While Miss Evangeline was busy tussling with me, I caught a glimpse of my best friend, Kilroy sitting two desks down from me. From the sad look in his eyes, I knew the cigarette must have been his. In a flash, I went from wanting to punch him in the mouth, to wanting to hug him, but dudes don't hug, so I nodded at him, signifying everything was cool.

I was a Pilgrim, until Miss Evangeline started in on me. My black and white construction paper pilgrim hat was now crumbled on the gray and maroon tiled classroom floor with the prints of my sneakers on it. As a form of protest I had snatched the hat from my head and stumped it into the floor. "I don't care bout being no damn pilgrim!"

All thirty-two student desks were arranged to form two long tables that were covered with orange crepe paper tablecloths. The Pilgrims were on one side and Indians on the other. Big baskets filled with pumpkins and ornamental corn stood in each corner of the room and at the back of the room, was a huge barrel filled with canned goods that the class had brought for the needy. I was positive most of those cans of yams, spinach, and sauerkraut would litter the school grounds, dented and smattered with 6th grade blood, artillery in our annual unauthorized food fight. And I would have to miss it all.

I was putting up a pretty good scuffle with Miss Evangeline. She being a big old mountain of flesh made her slow and clumsy. Whenever she'd get after any of us she was bound to knock someone's desk out of line with those big old horse hips of hers. The only way she'd get you was by surprise, like she got me at the turkey dinner. When she got her hands on you that old lady perfume she wore would make you dizzy. It smelt liked dead roses pressed in a Bible. She wasn't like Mrs. Brandon in 5A, who was young and dressed like they did in the magazines, smelt soft and sweet like those little flecks of purple gum she was always chewing. But Miss Brandon had strange hands, big man hands; veins roped all through them, stubby blood red fingernails, clown hands, Frankenstein hands. They were all the scarier cuz you didn't expect a lady like her to have hands like that. Once she got a hold of you there was no getting away. Stevie Moss thought that Miss Brandon might be half man half woman. He swore he'd seen pictures of one in one of the magazines his father kept in an old fishing tackle box hid in the basement. "I swear she had titties like a woman and a thang like a man," Stevie said cupping a hand under his chest and grabbing at his crotch with his other.

Most times I could wiggle loose from Miss Evangeline. She wasn't any match for any eleven year old. But one time, to get away, I had to bite her on that big wobbly piece of fat that hung from her arm. "Mr. Washington you can't do right to save your life." She'd always call you Mr. or Miss when she thought you'd done something wrong. There were other kids in the class much worse than myself. Marvin Whitehead peed in Miss Evangeline's purse, while she was in the hall talking with Stevie Moss's mother. Someone's mother was always coming up to school for something he or she had allegedly done. Stevie had brought a magazine with naked people in it to class. He said that there was a city where people lived naked, Sun City. Nobody believed him until he brought the magazine to class. It was full of sunburned naked white people, women, men, children, and old white people too; swimming, barbequing and playing baseball like they weren't buck-naked, living it up. That night I dreamed Ernie Banks was naked, getting ready to bat. All the Cubs were naked and they got into a dust flying fight on the field with the also naked Atlanta Braves.

As I said I wasn't the worst kid but I was a close second. Miss E. would sometimes make a troublesome kid sit under her desk for punishment while she continued with the lesson. After awhile she must have forgotten I was under there and sat down at her desk. "She ain't wearing no panties!" I loudly announced to my classmates. It was a lie but it was fun to say. That was the last time she made any kid sit under her desk.

"You don't never believe no one when they telling the truth," I said with indignation, trying to well up some crocodile tears. It was raining hard outside. Everything was gray at two o'clock in the afternoon. The wind had pasted wet brown and yellow leaves up against the windows. All I wanted to do was eat the baked apples in my TV dinner. I had agreed to trade my turkey and dressing with Fat Frank for his baked apples. I had made the best pilgrim hat in the class, a tall Stovepipe with a black and white braid and buckle around the base. I had even made a few for the kids who couldn't get the hang of it.

Beethoven's Pastoral was playing on the record player stamped all over in big black letters *Property of the Board of Education* as Miss. E was wilding my ass.

"You children are culturally deprived." She was always saying things like that. Miss E. never passed up a chance to give her *you should be thankful* speech; and there was no better time than during the class's annual Thanksgiving Dinner. Just before she came over to where I had been sitting, she had stapled a black and white UNICEF poster of a little potbellied African boy to the bulletin board. His eyes were so big, he looked like he smoked crack. He was eating something mushy with his fingers out of a wooden bowl. I thought it was cool how he got away eating with his fingers. Mama or grandmamma would yell at me, "Anthony, boy, don't lick your fingers!"

Miss E. started in with her you-should-be-thankful speech. "You children should be thankful that you're able to get an education, thankful that you have enough to eat and clothes to wear, thankful that you have freedom. You should be thankful that you're Americans." Miss E. said this last part as she eyeballed Alicia Shabazz. Alicia didn't have to say the pledge of allegiance, after her father came up to school and had a talked with Miss Evangeline and Principal Connors.

While I was trying to yank free from Miss E., I accidentally bumped Millicent Robertson against the blackboard. She had spent the last ten minutes writing in red, gold and green pastel colored chalk, the words *10th Annual Stephen Douglas Elementary School Thanksgiving Dinner.* Millicent had the best handwriting of all the 6th grade classes, maybe even the whole school. I really felt bad that because of me, her masterpiece of penmanship was now ruined, plus she had gotten colored chalk over the front of her white blouse. But she just giggled. Now I wanted to entertain her, because she had the prettiest eyes I had ever seen. So I let my body fall to the floor while Miss Evangeline continued dragging me. "You filthy little fool,"

"Who you callin filthy?" That really hurt my feelings. The class went wild, whooping and beating the desk, tearing the crepe paper tablecloth, laughing at me. Stevie was holding his big nose with two fingers and waving his hand back and forth. To a 6th grader's lexicon, filthy was too close to funky. Everyone knew funky meant that you stunk and I certainly didn't stink. My shirttail might occasionally been half in half out of my pants, my laces untied, my face shiny, even dirt under my nails, unkempt, but certainly not funky. Ronny Pruitt was the funky one. He smelled like the coppery-colored smoked fishes with the heads on that funked up our entire house, whenever my grandmother, a clean woman, would eat them at the kitchen table, right off the newspaper they were wrapped in. Ronny Pruitt was forever digging boogers out his nose, smearing them across his desktop, or scratching in his ass, and to top it off he was snaggletooth.

Miss E. continued, "You haven't the sense God gave a gnat. All this buffoonery won't get you on Saturday Night Live or anywhere else in life!" I couldn't stop from laughing because of that word buffoonery. I had no idea about the meaning, but it sure sounded funny. As she was jerking me out the door I caught a glimpse of Fat Frank who had been sitting at the Indian table, stuffing turkey and mashed potatoes from my TV dinner into his mouth.

Miss E. always got real proper when she was around whites or high yellow black folk. She must have felt bad 'bout being dark skin. Some of the kids call her Nightshade. I don't, cause I'm blacker than her. Mama says the blacker the berry the sweeter the juice. When daddy was home he'd always say, "Marry you a dark skin gal, cuz them yellow gals crumble like paper when they get old; not like yah mama, smooth as silk." Then daddy would slap her on the butt and mama would slap him up side the head. Sometimes they'd wind up in the bedroom. Other times they'd keep on slapping until the police came.

You had to go see Miss Bentley, the assistant principal's office, before you could see Principal Connors. Miss Bentley could pass for white, just plain white though. There was no pretty on her. She could pass, until she opened her mouth, then you knew she was one of you. You might as well be invisible because she never looked at or said a word to you—nothing—just went to the file cabinet and pulled a folder with your name typed on it. She'd just whine one or two words through her nose, like disruptive, truant, foul language. Miss Evangeline always went into a long rigmarole as to why you were there, followed by that little baby teeth *house nigger* grin of hers. That would kind of make me feel sorry for her, until I remembered what we were there for, and that most likely my mama would have to come up to the school.

My mama would be pissed if she'd have to miss another seventy-five dollars and cab fare. She had just built up her fortune-telling slash housekeeping to five days a week, two days with Mrs. Brumstein and three with Mrs. Phipps. Mama said, "Boney white women with too much money and time, willing to believe in anything but God." They were couch anthropologists, who were fascinated when they discovered that mama was Haitian. They started askin' her questions about Voodoo and Sainte Maria. Mama ain't been back to Porte Prince since she left in the seventies, some twenty years ago. All the sudden she's talking with an accent, wrapping her head with miles of scarves and carrying around a dried chicken foot in her purse. She tells me in her new-found accent, "Fool boy, the money's good."

Mama don't much care for Miss Evangeline. She'd say, "That heifer go catch me wrong one day. Thee lesbian cow will get the evil eye from me. Make her have the pink eye if she don't watch it." I think my mama starting to really believe she's some Voodoo priestess. She don't like Miss Evangeline, cuz she has a way of talking to you, using big words and asking you *do you understand,* like you were from China or somewhere.

Inside Principal Connors' office Miss E stands in back of me with her hands resting on my shoulders like she really cared about me. Principal Connors was sitting behind his desk, fingers forming a pyramid, looking at me like he was straining to pass a turd. He has liver spots all over his shiny big bald head with tufts of pissy gray hair at the sides and elephant bags under squinty green eyes. "Anthony Washington, it seems as if you're in this office more than me. How are you going to devote the proper time to your studies, go to high school, maybe even college, become a productive member of society . . ." I don't say anything. I stand there in front of his desk with my head down, digging my nails in the palms of my hands, trying not to laugh and trying not to inhale his breath, which smelled like feet. I spot a ten-dollar bill resting on Connors' oatmeal colored carpeted floor and bend down to swipe it; when suddenly behind me, I hear Miss Evangeline's flabby arms flopping down to her sides. I knew she wouldn't see me picking the money up, 'cuz she couldn't see. Miss. E was always squinting around in those swimming goggles she wore. I've taken pencils, paper clips, and the teacher's edition with the answers in the back from her desk.

"Anthony, what do you have to say for yourself? And stand up when you are being addressed by Principal Connors!" Miss E. says. I just know she's grinning like a pig in mud in front of Connors.

"Can't you see I'm trying to tie my shoe?" I stood up with the ten crumbled in my fist. Principal Connors sitting behind his desk hadn't saw me pick up the money. If he had he would have let loose with a *Thou shalt not steal* in his thunderous rendition of Charlton Heston's Moses. Old Blister Head had a pretty loud mouth that made up for that puny body of his. The biggest thing on him was his head. Every nickname we had for him included the word head: Blister Head, Headquarters, The Giant Head, Head of state. . . . That loud mouth might have been intimidating coming out anyone else. But like I said, he was nothing but head.

"This child is endangering the health of others along with himself," Miss E. said, bending forward and triumphantly placing the cigarette in the middle of Connors' leather desk mat. I felt her spongy breasts heavy against my back, as she bent over me resting her hand on my shoulder. Connors screwed his face up as he pushed the cigarette with the tip of his pen, examining it as if it were a used condom, and then looked up at me.

When I got out of old Blister Head's office it was 4:00; the schoolyard was deserted, except for Kilroy, waiting at a side door with an umbrella big enough for half our class to stand under. Neither of us said a word as we walked under the umbrella. That afternoon raced through my mind, Miss E. holding the cigarette up to my face, and the look in Kilroy's eyes. I was glad he was there; he was always there as a sounding board or a jester. Moments earlier walking down the hall to the only unlocked door, which opened onto the school playground, I had imagined myself getting soaked in the rain, reading the letter over and over informing my mother that I would be suspended from school, until she came up at her nearest convenience. It was never convenient for my mama to miss a day's pay.

It was November and those extra hours of daylight we had enjoyed during the summer had morphed into gray sky; this along with the rain had turned day into cool night. Streetlights were on. The rain intensified the smell coming from the lunchroom, peanut butter cookies the cook made every Monday. I heard the cooing of pigeons; looking up I saw a row of them huddled under the eaves of the school building. I hated pigeons. Mama said they were no more than filthy flying rats.

Kilroy broke the silence, "You think yo mama gonna be mad?"

"What do you think, monkey face? Hell yah, if she has to come up to school again, and for nothing. Think of all the real stuff I got away with. Now she got to come for some shit that ain't mine." I stressed the last three words, turning my head and looking at him. He didn't look at me. "Anthony, know what?"

"What?"

"What if we killed Miss Evangeline?"

"Don't be silly, then we'd have to kill Blister Head Connors and what about Assistant Principal Miss Bentley?" Kilroy turned his lips down pondering what I had said.

"What if we did all three?"

"Kilroy, don't be crazy; everyone in *class* saw Miss E and me get into it. Guess we'd have to kill the *class*, then that would really make us look suspicious, us being the only ones alive. Yah, the police would come straight to us." Kilroy shook his head, looked at me and snorted, "Anthony, man, all we'd have to do is blow up the school but we'd get out before it blew, we'd be the only survivors."

"Man, I ain't got time to be dealing with no police and lawyers, know what I'm saying?" For moments nothing but cool exasperated breath was exchanged between us. "Forget you then, hotdog lips, all I was trying to do is help yo' ass." After that he kept his eyes glued to the pavement as we walked. Him calling me hotdog lips never fazed me. Mama said that I had lips like Dr. Martin Luther King, and if I worked hard in school and tried not to get killed, I was sure to be the next somebody or anybody. Kilroy was mad at me because I refused to play the game as usual, until one of us had run into an impenetrable brick wall of logic, like when we played, what if you found a million dollars? How would you spend it without letting anyone know? I didn't want to think about it anymore. Besides, he had no reason to be mad at me. Nevertheless, I felt sorry for him 'cuz of his mean mama.

My mama didn't beat my ass; she'd just light in on me with words, rants for hours. It felt like you were getting 28 rabies shots to the navel. She'd tell you how hard she was working, that she was the only one taking care of you now, how she could have left me for three hots and a cot like my dad living it up in the penitentiary. And then there were the times she'd finish off with singing Amazing Grace. Her voice was so bad I'd wish she just beat my ass and get it over with, like Mrs. Jones, Kilroy's mother. Well, not exactly like Kilroy's mother. She was brutal with her kids, stomping them in the chest, whipping them with ironing cords. I remember once I went to the launderette with Kilroy and we were playing around and must have left a pillowcase in the washer or dryer, cuz while Mrs. Jones was refolding sheets we had folded, stacking them on the dining room table and cussing 'bout how Kilroy couldn't do shit right, all of a sudden he's on the floor with his arms folded over his head and she's kicking him in his back and ass. "Mrs. Jones, stop it! What's wrong with you?"

"Boy, you better take yo 'lil black ass home." I did and told my mama what had happened. She said it was terrible but it wasn't any of our business and the next day when I mentioned it to Kilroy, he told me the same.

Remembering what a crazy bitch his mother was, I gave in and played the game. "I guess we could dynamite the teacher's lunchroom and Blister Head's office. That way, nobody who didn't deserve it would get hurt." I said bumping my shoulder against Kilroy's. He looked up at me and said, "Man, I'm sorry, I didn't mean . . ." I cut him off 'cuz I know how tough it is for a dude to say those words. It would have made me uncomfortable to hear them. "Man, thanks for waiting for me. I sure don't want to get my suede jacket wet." My father had sent me a brown suede jacket with Indian fringe on it for my birthday. I don't know how he managed that from prison. It was my favorite; the one my mother told me not to wear to school. Now that my mother was working five days a week, she didn't get a chance to monitor what I wore to school. I gave the preppy corduroy one to Kilroy, since he was lacking in the wardrobe department.

Rain fell lightly against the umbrella, as a strong wind pushed us down newly paved asphalt streets that shined like black patent leather shoes, on past vacant lots and rundown apartment buildings toward home. "Let's go to Sam's store and get some pop and chips. I've got ten dollars." I said.

"Give me half."

"Half my ass, you get three."

"Anthony, man, lets walk to 63rd Street, get some chicken wings."

" I don't want no wings; my mama fried chicken yesterday, still got some."

" Anthony, you know yo' mama's fried chicken taste like fried owl."

"I can't tell since your funky feet always under our table."

Kilroy and I run into Fat Frank and Ronny standing on 63rd and Cottage Grove underneath the Green Line el tracks. "Waz up?"

"Waz up?"

"Waz up?"

"Waz up?"

"Man, Ant, I hope you ain't bitched out 'bout me eating yo turkey and stuff, cuz I was 99% sure you wasn't coming back and anyway it was already cold. So we cool?"

I reached out and pounded fist with Fat Frank. "Yah, we cool. I didn't have much of an appetite after knuckling with Miss E."

Ronny smiled his infamous snaggletooth smile, his breath smelling like a fish market. "Anthony, my man, you the man for not punkin' out on yo' boy, Kilroy."

"Man, Ant, you thug to the bone." Fat Franks joined in with a mouth full of BQ potato chips. This was the compliment of compliments any eleven-year-old boy from the hood could receive from his peers. You gotta be hard or give the *appearance* of being so, if not, then evens girls will be kicking yo' ass.

Kilroy was quiet all the while Ronny was yammering on. He doesn't much like Ronny; most of us don't, 'cuz he's always keeping up shit. "Nigger, you lucky Anthony had yo' back 'cuz if it was me, I would have been singing on yo' ass like a canary. You always losing something." Ronny said, snatching half a Snickers out of Fat Frank's hand before he could push it in his mouth.

In the dark, 63rd Street was lit up with neon lights from R&B Records, Zebra Lounge, and Roy's Barbeque Palace. The four of us walked over to an old red velvet couch in front of the old Trianon movie theater. A soaking wet boney gray cat that had been lying on the couch saw us coming, jumped down and ran up a ledge into one of the Trianon's broken windows.

The Trianon was an old spider-web movie palace with tarnished gold leaf, faded burgundy velvet drapes, clouds of gray crystal chandeliers hanging from the ceiling and threadbare carpeted long stairways leading to balconies everyone was scared to go up to. It was the place we hung out whenever we cut school. I straddled one of the arms of the couch, Kilroy sat on its shoulder above me, and Ronny sat on the other arm with his feet on the seat. The couch was soaking wet, but that didn't keep Fat Frank from plopping down in the middle, sitting there like he was watching TV. Orange sparks shooting from a passing el train above us flickered and fizzled into the night.

The train drowned out whatever Fat Frank was saying. Whatever it was, I knew it was a lie, 'cuz he'd always get to lying whenever he was eating a couple of candy bars. And it was all about sex, how he was put out of Catholic school, 'cuz Mother somebody caught him fucking Sister so and so in the convent's chapel. Or how he had a threesome with Millicent Robertson and Alicia Shabazz. He must have been getting turned on; he was sweating like a pig in the cool night air. I let him go on, basting in one lie after the other. Eventually he ripped open a bag of Sugar Babies with his teeth, scarfing most of them down before anyone could ask him for any. He was smacking and talking through a web of caramel. "Yo, Kilroy, yo' mama would've come up to school and whopped that ass like she done last time, if it wasn't for my man, Ant." Once Kilroy's mother had to come up to the school, 'cuz she got a call telling her he wasn't doing well in Language Arts. She's one mean biscuit. She stormed in while the class was saying the pledge of allegiance, grabbed him by the collar, starts slapping him across the face and over the head. She yelling and spitting, "Boy, I ain't got no time to be missing work, coming up here, 'cuz you ain't getting yo' lesson!" Everybody knows Mrs. Jones don't work, unless you call selling weed out your bedroom window work.

"Shut up, ass pig," I said to Fat Frank. I swung my legs from over the arm of the couch toward Fat Frank and sent a hard kick to the side of his thigh.

"Nigger, what's wrong with you!" He yelled with Sugar Baby juice drooling down the side of his mouth.

"Shut the fuck up," I said with the killer cool voice I've perfected, that signifies I mean business. Ronny knitted his eyebrows, looking at me, accessing whether he should say something.

"Anthony, Kilroy must be yo' bitch or something."

Kilroy looked over at Ronnie, "Yo' mama's the bitch, snaggletooth bitch." Ronny jumped off the arm of the couch. He don't like nobody talking about his mother, 'cuz she's got multiple sclerosis. I jumped in front of him before he can touch Kilroy.

"Nigger, what you go do? You better step off!" I say. We're chest to chest staring each other in the eye as if we 'bout to fuck or fight. I heard Fat Frank opening another bag of something.

"Come on Kilroy, let's get out of here," I say, as I usher Kilroy forward. He snatched the bag of M&M out of Fat Frank's hand, most of them falling into the creases of the couch.

"Nigger, what's wrong with you!" Fat Frank tried to rescue the few left on the wet seat. Kilroy and I left under Ronny's hateful eye.

The block we lived on was made up of two and three story graystone flats. The hallways of the buildings we passed were black as ink, unlike the streetlights that automatically came on when it was dark. For landlords six o'clock meant six o'clock, no matter how dark the halls were.

Kilroy lived two buildings down from me with his mother, three brothers and a sister. As we entered the chain-link fence gate, we saw Mrs. Jones standing on the front porch at the top of the stairs, with a can of beer in one hand and a lit cigarette in the other. From the gate I could see into Kilroy's living room window. It was Mrs. Jones' regular party crowd; snapping fingers and swaying to BB King's, *The Thrill Is Gone*, opened cans of Budweiser on the table next to arms and elbows, plates of fried catfish, playing cards fanned close to the breast and laid out in books of Whist. It was party time, since Mrs. Jones had sold her monthly cache of marijuana. And she must have been celebrating all day with her loyal customers.

She was standing there in beat down old flip-flops and a man's tweed coat over her housedress. "Boy, why is it that whenever I need you to do something for me, it always take you so long to get home from school? Get yo' ass up here!" Kilroy was trying to say something but his words got all garbled up with fear. He needed help, so I inched ahead of him to plead his case.

"Mrs. Jones, Kilroy and I were . . ."

"Boy, shut up, ain't nobody talking to you. Kilroy get yo' ass up these stairs and I mean now!" He slowly walked past me and up onto the porch. "Boy, look at me!" She thumped the half smoked cigarette to the wet ground, slapped him across the face so hard, I thought she might have taken it off. I moved closer, hoping to convince her that it was my fault. Standing at the base of the stairs, I could see tears welling up in his eyes. She slapped him again, this time with the back of her hand, knocking him to the ground. Standing over him, she reached in her coat pocket and pulled out a thin brown extension cord. She doubled the cord, wrapping enough of it around her knuckles until she had the length she wanted. Each time she struck him upon his head and shoulders, the cord made a whooshing sound. I don't know if he grabbed the cord or his hand got tangled up in it but this only infuriated her more and she began kicking him in his side as she yanked the cord free.

I must have charged into her because the next thing I knew she was on her ass, glaring up at me and calling me all kinds of black so and sos. Out the blue, Kilroy jumped on my back, pounding me over the head and face, crying, "Leave my mama alone!" I bent over and tried to shake him off. Instead he leapfrogged over me and was facing me. He sucker-punched me on the bridge of the nose, at least I'd like to think it was a sucker punch. The blow stunned me. I saw stars. I never believed it whenever someone said he saw stars. Well, it's true. All I could see were sparkling little fists plowing in and out my face.

The mailman and Smiley, the apartment building super, who had been watching from the living room window, came out on the porch with beers in their hand. Instead of pulling Kilroy off me, Smiley flashed a gold tooth smile and egged him on to keep fighting. But Kilroy just stopped all a sudden. He looked at me, his face all crumbled up and crying and he started to look around all wild-eyed, looking around the porch until he saw the extension cord next to Mrs. Jones, whose butt was still glued to the porch pavement. Kilroy grabbed the cord and started beating the air. Smiley moved backward into the doorway, almost falling over Mrs. Jones, who ain't budged and was taking a swig from the can of beer that she's managed to hold on to. Kilroy started screaming; his face looked as if it were tearing apart. He turned to his mama and began to lash her, across the face and over the head with the cord.

If it had been summer, flies would have flew into Mrs. Jones' and everyone else's mouth on the porch that night. The mailman stepped out the doorway and locked his arms around Kilroy from behind. Kilroy thrashed wildly, knocking the mailman's cap to the ground. "Smiley, give me some help with this boy; get his feet."

"Hell naw, nigger is you crazy too; that little nigger done gone crazy!" Smiley didn't move. Mrs. Jones, who was now thoroughly marinated in beer, grabbed the hem of my suede jacket leaving wet fingerprints on it. She pulled herself to her feet; standing with one shoe on, she started to pound the mailman over the shoulders. "Get you damn hands off my baby. Don't you hurt my baby, let him go!" She yelled at the mailman, who had Kilroy all straight-jacketed up. "Don't you ever touch my boy. I'll kill you!"

"The whole goddamn family is nuts! The whole damn family" The mailman let him loose and pushed Kilroy toward her. He threw up his arms and waved his hands at her. Mrs. Jones now had the side of Kilroy's face nestled to her breast.

As I backed away from the stairs, Kilroy turned his face toward me and mouthed the words "Anthony, man, thanks." I turn and nodded to him. "See you tomorrow."

GARY POPLAWSKI

On Top of the Butte
from *The Hard Road Home*

Old Charley Singing Buffalo sat cross-legged in front of his clay lodge high on the one flat acre at the very top of Aztec Butte, deep in the unmapped wilderness range at the eastern border of New Mexico. The jet bowl of the night sky was pierced by a million times a million cold white stars, smeared from horizon to horizon by the liberal hands of the gods. His back was warmed by the fire he'd just lit inside the lodge, and the yellow glow from the low doorway fanned out around him in two diagonal washes across the red dirt on either side.

Little Dog in Two Lands lay curled in his lap, as she did every night while he sat there watching the desert, slowly chewing his peyote buttons. A small, feral girl, not more than nine summers old, Little Dog ran wild on Aztec Butte with Charley Singing Buffalo, wearing only paint and wet clay on her quick, brown body.

"What are you waiting for, Grandfather?" she asked, as she always did. The firelight just barely licked the crown of her head and the tips of her bare toes as she lay there, looking up at the wrinkled cliff of Charley's face. Under the watching stars, her black eyes glittered sharp through the tangled mass of her waist-length hair.

He stroked her head, pinching a flea and cracking it between the nails of his index finger and thumb. The visions were strong tonight, the stars swam like ghostdancers across the heaven, swirling the great shapes of the stony mesas in mile-long shadows across the desert floor. Tonight might be the night.

"I don't know yet, Little Dog," he replied. "Wait and watch."

She squirmed deeper into the old blanket covering his knees, tucking in her arms against her chest. Her fingers toyed with the beaded tribal choker around her neck.

"I'm tired of waiting," Little Dog in Two Lands yelped. Mischievously, she nipped at his kneecap with her strong white teeth.

"Then look," Charley said. She felt his body stiffen, his legs shift as his back straightened. "Look out there." Charley's right hand was extended out over the edge of the butte, one dry brown finger pointing at a tiny point of light crawling towards them over the moonlit expanses of red rock far below. A strange, uneven sound, like a buzzing gnat, drifted up to them from across the miles of empty space.

Little Dog sat upright, sniffing the air.

"What is it, Grandfather?"

"It's a car, or something bigger. They're coming here. At last."

Charley Singing Buffalo rose slowly to his feet, his old joints popping and cracking. Little Dog hopped off his lap and stood watching him expectantly.

"We must get ready, Little Dog. Go inside and prepare food."

As the girl scampered inside the lodge, Charley walked to the tall pyramid of coarse, knotted rope, coiled up at the very edge of the cliff. His wiry muscles tightened as he hefted the stone weight tied to the end of the rope, and flung it far over the edge with unusual strength. The line arced out into space, wriggling like a huge snake under the starlight, then, its horizontal movement exhausted, fell downwards to the desert below, uncoiling itself with a deep, fluttering hum.

Charley squinted out at the desert. The approaching speck had resolved itself into two bobbing headlights, attached to a large, blocky vehicle as big as a school bus. It rocked and foundered across the roadless stone plains like a boat weathering rough seas, almost toppling over several times, now and then gouging its front or rear bumper into abrupt slopes of earth. Without a doubt, it was headed directly for Aztec Butte, holding as straight a course as if it was guided by a plumbline. Sam Wildbear had given his directions well.

"This has got to be it." Spanky peered at the scrawled directions on the napkin under the map light. He glanced quick eyes right and left through the windshield. "That big round hill over there is Whale Ridge, and the limestone needles to the north got to be The Daggers." He tapped the paper with a skinny finger. "So there it is, straight ahead."

Junior grunted, his big shoulders hunching as he fought the steering wheel, which pulled side to side as if by invisible hands, wrenched by the suspension pounding over the unpaved terrain.

"It better be," Junior said, "This old boat's gonna fall apart in a few more miles of this. Shoulda never left the road."

"And walk all this way across the desert?" chimed in Darlene from the kitchen. "With coyotes and wolves out there, and who knows what else? Not likely."

The bottom of the frame walloped a large rock as the Winnebago lurched into a shallow depression. Their heads snapped back as though they'd been rear-ended by a minivan. With a curse, Junior shifted into extra-low towing gear, coaxing the ten-ton RV slowly back onto level surface. They sat idling on the cracked red dirt plain, an infinity of stars laughing at them, wheeling through the empty dome of night overhead. The dark bulk of Aztec Butte loomed dead ahead, blotting out a full square mile of stars, featureless and black except for what looked like a faint yellow flicker of light at the very top.

Junior frowned at a persistent clattering sound that had started up somewhere in the motor compartment for the past few miles. Most of the gauges on the dash didn't work any more, so it was useless to look there for either reassurance or warning.

"I'll see if I can get a little closer," he said, putting the RV in drive. The machine jerked forward ponderously, her nose rising as the earth sloped up around the butte. "You all start getting ready."

"I'll get some food together," said Darlene, bracing her tall figure against the cabinets.

"We might need extra clothes, and blankets," added Irma, weaving down the hallway to the bedroom. The old woman steadied herself with one hand against the wall, keeping a small towel ready in her free hand to blot away the blood that speckled her lips whenever her coughing spasms grew vicious. In order to keep breathing at all, Irma had increased her cigarette intake to over four packs a day.

"Don't you cough on the dry goods," Darlene called after her. "We don't need any more blood on the linens."

"I'll get the shotgun," said Earl. He slid stiffly from behind the kitchen table, calling after his wife, "Dammit Irma, you take it easy on those smokes." With one liverspotted hand, he rubbed the bristles of his high-and-tight silver crewcut in exasperation.

Spanky tucked Sam Wildbear's map into his back pocket. He glanced at Junior. "This is it, buddy. We either find your land or it's a big dead-end. A big fucking nothing."

"Spanks, you got to be the most pessimistic person I ever met." Junior's head bobbed as the left front tire bumped over a low outcropping of shale.

"You guys see that light way up on top there?" Little Howie was leaning over the back of Spanky's seat with his torso stuck out the window, both hands braced on the door. He'd cocked his head way back so he could see up the steep slope looming closer and closer. "I bet it's that old Indian. Jeez, there's no way we can get up there."

"Get back inside boy, you're going to fall."

"Okay, okay."

"The boy's got a point," mused Spanky. "Look at that cliff, Junior. I sure don't see any roads. Shit, there's not even a path."

The ancient stone face of Aztec Butte rose up before them in the bouncing glow of the headlights, a sheer wall of reddish-brown rock soaring straight upwards for five hundred feet. They could see a few scraggy mesquite bushes clinging to narrow fissures in the rock, looking like black tufts of hair in the distance. Dark transverse lines of cracks and ledges crisscrossed the butte face, hardly enough to wedge a handhold or toehold into. As they watched open-mouthed through the dusty windshield, a pack of ragged clouds crossed the moon, rushed along by unfelt winds that never reached the desert floor, sending dark shadows racing over the vertical cliff face as if mocking their earthbound limitations.

The Winnebago jolted to a halt with a decisive shudder, her dented bumper plowed firmly into the twenty-degree slope of rising earth.

"Well, this is the end of the line," said Junior. "We're not getting any farther on wheels." He shut off the ignition and climbed out of the driver's chair, shrugging his leather jacket on over his overalls. "Let's take a little hike."

Darlene quickly packed an ice chest of beer and sandwiches, and they all prepared to leave. Junior hefted the cooler up on one shoulder, propping it against his meaty neck. "Time to have us a look around. I got a feeling about this place."

The door to the utility room thudded open, a thick brown arm groped out of the darkness within.

"I got a feeling too. A powerful feeling like I never felt before." Big Moms squeezed herself majestically into the kitchen, balancing her unstable girth between her wolf's head canes. She had grown even larger in the last few days, as though the unborn baby within her was building up pressure for some explosive and triumphant emission. The features of her face were all but hidden in swellings of flesh, her chin vanished into pillows of fat where a neck would have been; her limbs were seemingly absorbed to elbow and knee by the vast, ever-growing globe of her fecund torso. Well over four hundred pounds now, Big Moms could scarcely move unaided. Her normally rich brown color had taken on the hue of old leather, and her blind, chalkwhite eyes bugged in hysterical circles within their nests of fat. She licked her lips in fear, waving one cane before her like a wand.

"There's something up there will bring a great circle to a close. Something that needs to be finished and started up again."

"What are you afraid of, Big Moms?" asked Junior, frozen in the door.

She turned to the sound of his voice. "Big Moms isn't afraid of nothing, least not in the same way most folk are. I see too much of things to be afraid of 'em, and being afraid is just being blind. But changes, big changes, always disturbs me."

"Enough of this, already. We're wasting good moonlight." Spanky creaked open the passenger door and hopped out onto the ground. He thumbed on a flashlight, and played the circle of light over the slope leading up to the butte.

"I want to see what's up there, that's what we come to do, isn't it?" His narrow back disappeared into the night, silhouetted by the flashlight beam dancing before it.

"Wait up, Spanks!" Junior shifted the cooler on his shoulder. "Earl? Got the shotgun?"

"Yep," came the reply, "Come on Irma, the night air'll do you good."

Irma staggered out the door after Earl, a bundle of clothes under one arm. The glowing cigarette tip in her free hand flailed about her head like a red, malevolent firefly. Darlene followed, steadying the old woman from behind.

"Howie, you take Big Moms' hand and lead her along," Darlene commanded over her shoulder.

"Thank you, child." Big Moms let herself be guided to the door by Howie. "Nothing could make me stay behind tonight, not Death and the Devil hand-in-hand."

"Jeez Big Ma, look how high that place is."

"Child, I never felt a place so high before in my life."

Stumbling along the stony path by the light of the moon, balancing the sweating cooler on his shoulder, Junior bent his neck back until he could see the dark summit of Aztec Butte far above him, a black knife edge cutting across half the sky. He had come up to the very foot of the looming cliff, his boots slipping on loose shale, small lizards and nocturnal desert creatures scuttling away from his path. He rubbed his neck and studied the rock face. No way up there. Would they have to search around the whole butte for a path? That could take days, and with Big Moms and Irma in the shape they were...

"You won't need that."

Junior started at the sound of a high-pitched voice almost in his ear. He spun around. Nothing.

"Over here, mister." There was a rattling of loose gravel.

He looked in the direction of the sound and saw a small brown girl squatting naked on top of a great rock not six paces to his left. She looked to be about nine years old, with huge, luminous eyes he could see twinkle even in the uncertain moonlight. Paint daubs of amber, white and green streaked her skinny limbs and torso, and a leather choker crusted with patterns of beads circled her slender neck.

She pointed at the cooler and repeated, "That. You won't need that."

Junior just looked at her stupidly. "The cooler?"

She grinned, a flash of white teeth in the darkness. "Not up there.

Charley's got plenty for everybody. Leave everything down here."

Junior set the cooler in the dirt. "Charley? Charley Singing Buffalo? You know him?"

"I know him. He's been waiting for you." She jumped lightly to her bare feet and stood on the rock looking down on Junior. With one hand, she pushed away from her face a thick, tangled mass of black hair that hung almost to her hips. "Come on. Follow me." She turned away and crouched as if to spring off the rock.

"Wait!" Junior yelled, "Let my people catch up. Just a second. Who are you?"

She glanced back at him, her hair touching her ankles.

"My name is Little Dog. I'll take you to Charley. Hurry up now." And with that, there was a dry skitter of sand across stone, and she was gone. Junior felt a strange tingle in his head, somewhere between fear and happiness, he wasn't sure. But he knew he believed the little girl, knew it with more certainty than he had ever felt anything.

The flashlight beam wobbled up the path, splashing over the rocks.

"What were you yelling?" Spanky trudged up behind Junior. "See anything?"

"I sure did. There's some little Indian girl knows where Charley is."

Spanky played the beam around. "Oh yeah? I think you been driving too long. There's nobody here."

"I told you…"

"What the dickens you two yammering about?" Earl's nasal drawl cut through the night as he and Irma came struggling up, the red speck of her cigarette bobbing through the darkness.

"Think I found something, Earl." Farther down the slope, Junior could just make out Darlene trudging along with Howie, hanging onto his hand with all her might. The boy tugged desperately, trying to pull away and explore the dark, rocky landscape.

"Maaaa," he whined, "Lemme go, I just wanna see what's over there. It looks like a path or something." His pudgy legs bowed as he strained to free himself.

"You just stay right here," Darlene snapped, "It's bad enough your father has gone and lost his mind wandering around this Godforsaken wasteland."

"Up here, Dar," called Junior. "We're almost there."

"Will you boys slow down already? This is crazy walking around in the middle of the desert at night. My shoes are all full of sand, and Big Moms can't move too good."

Darlene had tied a string around her waist, and the other end was knotted around Big Mom's wrist. The huge old woman drifted along some dozen paces behind Darlene, colliding every now and then with a rock or cactus, stumbling into a hole, but always righting herself and continuing in the general direction of her tow line, her canes piercing deep into the earth at each step.

"Dogs in the moonlight," Big Moms was moaning, half to herself, half to the world at large, "Great changes gifted to all God's animals running in the high places tonight. Lord, move me in the right direction tonight! Darlene honey, where are you?"

In a few moments, they'd all gathered around Junior under the shadow of Aztec Butte. The little knot of travelers huddled beside the soaring wall of stone and looked about apprehensively.

"Where to now?" asked Spanky, spitting in the dirt.

"I tell you, there was a girl…"

"Shit, you got girl on the brain."

"Oh Lord, just let me sit a while. My bad leg is all swole and I can't even stand up no more. There's movements going on inside me."

"Junior, Big Moms shouldn't be outside now. She's…"

Darlene's voice was cut off by a tiny scuffle of dirt. They all looked, and Little Dog stood there beside them, half of her naked body cloaked in the shadow of the butte, and half bathed in the silver moonlight. She studied them with serious eyes glittering from a nest of hair.

"I told you," hissed Junior.

Little Dog crooked her finger and trotted off around the curve of the butte wall. When she was about fifty feet away, she stopped to wait until they began to follow.

"Leave the blankets, Dar," said Junior. "Irma, put down the extra clothes. And Earl, leave the shotgun too, I still got the .45. We can pick it all up on the way back. She says we got to travel light. Come on now, we're almost there. I can just about taste it."

Irma opened her arms to drop the bundle of sweaters, jackets, and extra socks. Her ragged breath came out with the sound of a coarse saw on damp wood.

"That's a relief," she gasped, pushing the unchanging curls of her wig far back on her sweating forehead as though it were a stocking cap.

"Are you all right, honey?" asked Darlene.

Earl put his arm around his wife's shoulders and studied her face closely.

"She's fine," rapped out Junior. "We'll rest soon enough. Let's keep moving."

Placing the roll of blankets on top of Junior's abandoned cooler, Darlene shook her head woefully. A woman's place was to stand by her man, whatever might happen to the place or the man. These were words she'd been raised to live by, and words she would not forsake, God help her and help them all. Readjusting her grip on Howie's hand, and tugging lightly on Big Mom's string, she started after Junior.

"Come on now, you heard him."

After ten minutes of scrambling over dark rocks and climbing through crevasses and winding arroyos, they came to a halt before the silent form of Little Dog, who waited motionless on a flat boulder as big as an automobile. As they watched in dismay, panting from their exertions, Little Dog pointed straight up the face of the Butte. A very long rope, thick and bristly with home-woven fibers, hung all the way down the cliff face from the summit, dangling about three feet off from the rock surface. Unseen air currents swayed the heavy line in gentle undulations.

"Charley," said Little Dog. She nodded her head at the rope. "Up there."

Winded from the hike, Junior stood bent over with his hands on his knees.

"You, you," he gasped, "Expect us to climb all the way up there?"

She made two fists, one over the other, and shook them at the rope. "Just hold on." When no one moved, Little Dog pulled Junior to the rock wall, and placed his hands on the rope. He curled his fingers into a tight grip, and looked up. The heavy cable, thicker than Howie's wrist, disappeared upwards into the sky, shrinking to a cord, a string, a human hair, before it vanished to an invisible point far overhead.

Junior glanced over his shoulder at Spanky, "I don't..." The words started out of his mouth, then were cut short in a grunt as the rope tugged powerfully upwards. His hands locked down hard as Junior felt his feet leave the ground.

"Junior!" Darlene shrieked.

He looked down, and already the heads of his companions were at foot level. The rope was moving quickly upwards in two-foot jerks, as though someone were pulling it up, hand over hand.

"Don't worry," he called down, "I'll be okay!" But as he rose higher and higher, Junior didn't feel much confidence in his well being. Every now and then he kicked with his feet to keep himself away from the rock. He was moving upwards so fast that his boots only touched the wall every ten feet or so. After rising a couple hundred feet, Junior glanced up to see the thick branch of a gnarled tree sticking out over the edge of the cliff. The rope was feeding out through a fork on the very end.

Suspended there two hundred feet above the desert floor, Junior felt the cool wind against his cheeks, felt his weightless boots dancing off the vertical wall, felt the inexorable pull of the line raising him towards an invisible goal, and he felt a great peace. He opened his mouth wide and laughed at the stars, laughed like a child again, laughed like he had finally figured out something huge and important and timeless, and it didn't mean anything very complicated at all.

With a final yank, Junior's head and shoulders wedged into the fork of the tree. He hauled himself up onto the wood, and crawled along the branch until he saw solid earth under him. Swinging his legs gratefully onto the dirt, Junior found himself staring back at a short, lean old Indian wearing nothing but a blanket wound around his waist. Obsidian eyes glittered at him, overflowing with humor.

"You laugh on the way up?" the old man said. "Good."

Junior pressed his burning hands against the thighs of his overalls. "I don't know, things just struck me funny all of a sudden. You Charley Singing Buffalo?"

"I am," replied the old man. He bent to gather up the huge coil of rope that had gathered at his feet. Bent low under his burden, he walked to the tree on skinny, bowed legs that planted themselves firm and steady on the earth with each step. Like each and every footstep was a major decision, thought Junior, made to last a lifetime.

"Are you the one who pulled me all the way up here?" Junior asked incredulously. "Pretty damn strong for a stringy little piece of Injun. Do you know Sam Wildbear?"

Somehow the old man smiled, although his face didn't change at all. "There will be enough time for talk. Now, we must get your family up here."

Charley Singing Buffalo tossed the rope out through the fork, and the line sung humming over the wood as it plummeted below. Charley handed the free end to Junior. "You get behind me. We will pull together." Junior looked sadly at his blistered palms and peered over the edge. He could barely see the yellow pinprick of Spanky's flashlight. A few hundred yards to the south, where they started their hike under the guidance of Little Dog, he could make out the canted bulk of the Winnebago, standing out from the surrounding rock formations by its rectangular outline, a too-regular shape which had no place in nature. Occasionally, by a trick of the wind, he caught faint scraps of words from below: ". . . lost . . . never . . . dickens . . . die . . . faith . . ."

One by one, all the members of Junior's road family were hauled up the cliff. Little Dog encouraged each of them, looping the rope securely around their waists, then bending their reluctant fingers around the line, pressing their hands tight with her own until they clamped down with instinctive deathgrips on the first surge upwards. The hauling grew easier and easier, as each person who was pulled up added their efforts to the work. First Darlene and Howie came together, the boy clutching the rope with one hand and wrapping his other arm around his mother. Darlene wailed and sobbed most of the way up, but grew quiet when, like Junior, she experienced a sudden calmness, dangling halfway between earth and the butte summit.

Next, Earl and Irma came up in a similar double load, their sticklike limbs all tangled together. Although they were a bit heavier, the task was not much harder, since Darlene and even Howie were working at the rope. Then Spanky scampered up, almost flying up the rock wall, adding his own hand-over-hand climbing to the rope's motion. When his tousled head popped into the crook of the tree branch, his face was alive with exhilaration, cheeks flushed, and grinning with joy. He jumped onto the summit, baggy pants flapping, and proclaimed, "Well shit, that was the best thing I've done in a good long while."

Then at last, it was Big Moms' turn. They all took their places, Charley standing closest to the tree. The old Indian's white hair straggled over the protruding vertebrae on his back as he tensed for the effort. "Now when I sing out, we heave," called Junior, "All together. Got it?"

"Got it," they replied as one, strung out on the rope like beads, ready to pull, with all their hands clamped before them on the common line, a necklace of fists: big as blocks, or brown and hard, raw and white, young and tender, old and liver-spotted, trembling, steady or hesitant, tireless, or slipping with unforgiving weakness. All, all prepared to pull together at the terrific, earthbound resistance that was Big Moms Lafitte.

"Okay then, heave!" Junior shouted.

The company groaned in unison and the rope growled up two grudging feet through the tree fork. Big Moms had asked Little Dog to tie the line under her armpits, explaining, "Little pup, my baby's been through enough without being lynched before it's born." With the first jerk, Big Moms was lifted to her very tiptoes, her shoulders raised up to her ears, her arms pushed out forty-five degrees by the fierce tug of the rope.

"Lord, here I go again," she exclaimed, "Always down below, being raised up to Heaven. Thank you Lord, for blessing me with . . ." Her words were cut off as she jumped up another yard, her worn-out shoes falling from her swollen feet to thump into the dirt.

"Ohhhhh," Big Moms moaned in dismay. Feeling the coolness on her toes, she turned down towards Little Dog, saying, "Child, take my shoes, will you? They're the only ones that fit me now." But the little girl did not reply, although Big Moms called several times. That's curious, thought Big Moms, I suppose she has her own affairs to attend to.

Each time they heaved backwards at the top of the butte, the rope slithered through the crotch of the tree with a dry, zipping sound. A fine haze of fiber particles and sawdust drifted up in the air. The million stars of the cold desert sky and the huge orange moon on the jagged horizon illuminated the toiling row of haulers as if by daylight. Charley Singing Buffalo braced his toes against the wood of the old tree, the tendons standing out on his brown forearms like roots. Softly, but loud enough so they could all hear, he began chanting rhythmic words none of them understood, but which somehow gave them all strength and spirit to continue. Junior groaned like an animal at the end of the line, gasping, "Pull! Pull!" at three-second intervals, while Spanky and Earl ground their teeth, sliding their shoes in the dirt as they leaned their weight back against the rope. Irma wasn't much help, as she kept collapsing in wet coughs every time she gave the line a good heave. With desperate, guilty eyes, she sat in the dirt, wiping her reddened mouth. Darlene tugged doggedly near the front of the line, although she frequently released the rope to blow on her chafed hands. Whenever she really dug in to pull, Junior could not help but notice, even in the extremity of his efforts, how snugly her Capri pants fit over her straining rear end. Howie stood behind Junior, snorting loudly as he pulled on his Daddy's overalls to add his own eighty odd pounds to the struggle.

Far down the rock face, Big Moms swung back and forth in wide arcs, her feet bouncing her body off into space like an immense weightless balloon. Backlit by the moon, she cast bulbous shadows almost up to the very rim, her great, bloated girth looking as shapeless and yielding as the sac of a giant spider. As she grew steadily nearer, old Charley could peer over the cliff edge to see the white saucers of her dead eyes rolling in the moonlight, searching the empty air around her with senses denied those granted common sight. Yes, the old woman had the vision, he knew. It was no coincidence, her coming to this place, coming to him, with these people. There were no coincidences at all, only the motions of spirit.

"One, two, pull!" grunted Junior at the back of the line. "One, two, pull!" At each "Pull!" Big Moms jerked upwards another few painstaking feet, their hands burned like the rope was a hot iron rod, and unseen goblins of pain danced on their shoulders and backs.

And then, square in the middle of one of those eternal instants that seem to hang frozen in the center of time, the thing they'd all waited for and dreaded and puzzled over for so long came to pass. The resonant baritone of Big Mom's voice had been echoing up to the laborers as she neared the summit, mingling in an oddly harmonious counterpoint with Charley's pagan chants. She sang from somewhere deep in her chest and stomach and vast guts, hearty and stoic hymns of voodoo Christianity, subtropical heresies involving black saints and humid miracles boiling in the murky depths of bayou swamps. Suddenly the powerful voice stopped, and they heard bellow up to the skies, rebounding from the moonlit mesas and cracked plains for miles around, "Great God in Heaven above!" There was a great gushing as if a waterfall had blossomed in the arid desolation of the desert, and a putrid, fishy stink climbed to the top of the butte.

Darlene wrinkled her nose, and ran to the edge of the cliff. Looking down with wide eyes, she shouted, "Her water's broke! Hurry! Get her up here!" A long, silvery, flood of amniotic fluid was flowing down the rocks below Big Moms, who looked up apologetically at the sound of Darlene's voice.

"I'm sorry, child," she called through cupped hands. "It's all the walking and lifting and bouncing about. It wants to come out."

Irma crawled to Darlene's side, too weak from her last coughing spell to stand, and poked her nose over the edge. "I've never seen that much before!" she cried. "It's, it's not even human! There's got to be gallons of the stuff!"

The men redoubled their efforts at the rope, finding reserves of strength where they had thought there was none left. In a few seconds, Big Moms' dreadlocks appeared in the fork of the tree branch, which creaked ominously under her weight. Charley tied down the rope, and they all rushed to help the old woman to solid ground. She lay helplessly in the dirt, her dress soaked from the waist down, clinging to her barrel thighs and boulder hips.

"Bring her to the hut," commanded Charley, "Over by the fire."

Junior and Spanky grabbed Big Moms' ankles and shoulders and dragged her sideways towards the low clay lodge, Earl pushing as best he could at her midsection. Breathing hard, they pulled her close to the small fire burning by the lodge entrance. Junior rested his hands on his hips and looked down.

"How you feeling, Big Moms?" he asked.

"It's coming," she moaned, "Sweet Lord, it's coming."

Darlene knelt alongside the big woman and took her hand. "Oh dear, oh dear, there's not a doctor in a hundred miles."

"Doctor?" smiled Big Moms, "I don't need doctoring for this. Done birthed children more times than I can remember. Don't worry child, it's a natural thing." She shook Darlene's hand gently.

"Well, let's get a blanket under her at least," said Irma, "The cold earth can't be a good place for this to happen."

Charley disappeared into his lodge, stooping low to get through the doorway. "I will get," he said.

Junior surveyed the top of the Butte anxiously. Nothing but a few square acres of rock and scrub, dropping off on all sides to the empty desert far below. Why anyone would want to live up here, or be able to live up here, was beyond him. He had hoped to find Charley, get the deed and the directions to Dancing Bob's land, and be gone long before daybreak. But now this. Big Moms was forever changing the direction of things. A baby delivery, for Christ's sake, in the middle of the wilderness. At best, there'd be another member of the family to care for. At worse, well, Big Moms was way too old to be making babies anymore, she knew that when she went and got herself pregnant.

Charley emerged from the lodge with a blanket folded over his left arm, and an earthenware bowl in his right hand. He lay the blanket down beside Big Moms, indicating with a nod of his head that they should roll her onto it.

"Now we wait," he said calmly, sitting cross-legged by the fire. He swept his spindly arm in a circle, inviting them all to sit with him. "You, big man, beside me here." Meeting Junior's gaze, he patted the earth next to him. They settled down in a rough semicircle, with Charley at the head, his hut behind him, and Big Moms stretched out by the fire in the very center.

"Good," pronounced Charley. He whistled three times, and a small brown dog with a beaded leather collar pattered into the firelight, and lay down with its head resting on his leg. Spanky frowned, looking away from the alert, intelligent eyes of the animal.

"Little Dog in Two Lands," said Charley by way of explanation, stroking the dog's head. "She watches for me."

"That was the girl's name," said Junior, "The girl who brought us here. She's still down there…"

"Oh, that's all right," smiled Charley. "She runs where she wants. Maybe come up here later, maybe not." He held out the bowl. It was filled with a thick, lumpy paste the color of dark earth. With one finger, Charley scooped out a dollop of the paste and sucked it into his mouth. As he rolled it around his tongue, he passed the bowl to Junior, saying, "Mash from cactus buttons. Very good for you, good for the thinking. Take some now while we wait for the birth to come."

Junior took the bowl. After hesitating a moment, he dipped out a big sticky lump of the stuff, and smeared it onto his tongue. It tasted of dirt and old wood and blood, and he felt it slide all the way down his throat to dissolve in his stomach.

"Not bad," Junior pronounced, smacking his lips as he handed the bowl to Spanky. "Give it a try, Spanks."

Spanky took a fingerful, and nodded slowly, passing the bowl on. "Tastes like dirt," he commented. "But you're right, somehow, it's not bad." Soon the bowl had made the circuit around the fire, and they all were chewing reflectively, watching Big Moms writhe on the blanket before them. She had begun to sing again, in a strange French patois no one could understand — low, rumbling words that were almost a hum. Her song climbed up into the black sky like an invisible column rising higher and higher, above the flames, above Charley Singing Buffalo's lodge, above the highest butte, above maybe even the wheeling stars themselves.

Junior shook his head and wiped a hand across his sweating forehead. He had been staring upwards, as if he could follow the sounds in the air. The firelight danced in his dilating pupils. "So Charley," he struggled to focus his wandering thoughts. "Charley. Sam Wildbear told me I'd find you up here."

"He was right. I know Sam."

"I'm Junior Johnson. Boyd Johnson's brother. He had some land out this way that he sold to Dancing Bob Two Feathers."

"Yes. I know Dancing Bob. He was my cousin."

Big Moms grunted, curling her legs so that the blanket bunched up under her wet thighs. Very, very slowly, Darlene crawled forward and readjusted the blanket. She said something, but Junior couldn't quite make out what.

"He gave you that land when he died?"

Charley leaned towards Junior. In the moving fire, his black eyes looked huge, like the two openings onto long tunnels that led far, far backwards. "Land is the land. It was here before us. You can't take it or give it. It's not ours to begin with. It gives us, it takes us." He handed Junior the bowl again. "Here, have more." It seemed just as full as before. Junior took another dollop of the mash, giving the bowl to Spanky's hand, which appeared floating before him before he could even close his mouth. This time Charley gave him a gourd of water too; very clear, very cold water that stung the mouth when swallowed. This too, Junior drank and passed on, wondering: why are the stars moving?

Because the millennia-slow crawl of the constellations overhead seemed to have accelerated, so that the stars began to sweep in slow, majestic arcs, wheeling around the pole like a great Ferris wheel. Junior felt his face burning, and a knot of nausea cramping his stomach. He was getting sick, probably a fever from those gunshot wounds. Damn dizzy spells like a little girl, making the heavens move. Had to get hold of himself. This was no time for sickness, no time at all. He squeezed his eyes shut, but quickly opened them again, alarmed by the vertigo that seized him in the darkness behind his closed lids.

"All that may be so," Junior said between lips suddenly parched dry. "But did Dancing Bob give you any papers about the land? White man's deed? A survey?" He needed to think, stay rational, remember why he came here.

Charley nodded, stroking Little Dog's head. "Oh yes. I have all that. In the hut. When they die, my family, they give me these things and I keep it and the land goes on."

"Good. Now we're getting somewhere," said Junior. He forced his eyes to focus. "Do you..." His words were cut short as Spanky suddenly yelped in surprise.

"What the hell's the matter with you?" he asked Spanky with annoyance.

For several minutes, Spanky had been staring at the cloud formations — high, thin, ragged white shapes racing across the stars and immense orange moon. They were moving faster than any clouds had a right to move without wind, casting mile-long shadows galloping over the desert floor below, up the side of Aztec Butte and off to the distant horizon like a soundless herd of gigantic bison. When he turned to bring the clouds to Junior's attention, he was startled to see a trick of the light had made Junior look like a medium-sized brown bear, hulking in a beat-up leather jacket. When the bear opened its jaws to growl "What the hell's..." it changed back to Junior, so Spanky just replied, "Nothing, just thought of something funny is all."

Junior tried to return to his conversation with Charley, but found himself fascinated by Big Moms' squirming bulk before him, the pasty cactus buttons disintegrating in his mouth. Darlene was kneeling between Big Mom's knees now, stooped over to peer into the dark, moist crevasse between those shuddering thighs. Darlene met his glance with eyes as large and penetrating as housecat's, and wailed, "Oh Jesus, it's coming! It's coming!"

Irma flicked away her cigarette in a spattering orange arc, and hissed at Charley, "Get us some water, you damned Indian! Can you see she's broaching!" Earl grabbed his wife's elbow, but recoiled at the dry feel of her skin, hard and scaly. He hopped back with a screech as her nicotine-stained tongue flicked out at him.

"Will you two stop it!" Junior yelled. Through his blurry eyes, he could barely make out Earl squatting beside his wife waving his arms in the air, the old woman crouched flat on the ground. "This is no time to start fighting!"

Spanky jumped up, shoulders hunched, and pointed a long finger at

Charley. Angry inkdot eyes glittered between his large, narrow nose and sloping forehead as he squealed at the Indian. "Water! And another blanket! Now, old man, or so help me…"

"Ease up Spanks," growled Junior, casually swatting the man-sized rodent to the ground. "We're guests here, remember?"

Charley Singing Buffalo just smiled as the peyote mash simmered in his brain. With great satisfaction, he gazed about the circle of firelight at the bear, rat, monkey, lizard and housecat all arguing among themselves under the laughing moon. The little piglet nuzzled desperately at the housecat's side, its fat legs digging at the earth.

"I'll get the water, Grandfather," said Little Dog in Two Lands, rising and walking into the hut. The soft rope of her hair swayed about her lean hips as she moved.

"Where's your dog going?" asked Spanky.

"Getting the water."

"Dogs can't fetch water."

"This one can."

Suddenly Spanky didn't feel like arguing any more. He noted with a sort of detached interest that only Charley Singing Buffalo and Big Moms still had human forms. He flipped his hand over beneath his eyes, taking comfort in the familiar hairless knuckles, fingers, and opposable thumb. Looked like he was alright too.

Big Moms emitted a tremendous bellow of pain and arched her back. Darlene gripped both knees, prying the legs wide apart. "I see something – I think it's a head!"

"What do you mean, you think?" said Junior.

"I, I, don't know. You come here."

"That's woman's work in there."

"Here, let me," offered Irma, crawling up beside Darlene. With one hand, she lifted up the edge of Big Mom's dress and squinted at the straining vagina. "Sweet Merciful Lord!" she cried, "It's a monstrosity!"

A double-domed and irregular cranium was forcing its way between the withered vulva flaps, a great, staring, pupilless eye visible near the top of the skull.

"Hold the dress," commanded Darlene. Scrunching up her face with revulsion, she gripped both sides of the protruding head and pulled. A shoulder appeared, along with a scrawny arm ending in a C-shaped claw. "It won't come," she wailed, "It's too big. Help me, Junior!"

"Jesus, do I have to do everything?" Junior left his spot beside Charley, and stepped between Big Moms' legs. Squatting down beside Darlene, he grimaced at the bloody, waggling globe in her paws. "Move aside Dar, let me give it a try." Gently, he pushed aside the trembling, supple feline, noticing how its fur was matted thickly with Big Moms' fluids. "Dar's gonna have a Devil of a time licking herself clean," he found himself thinking. "And why am I the only normal one besides Big Moms and Charley?"

Junior's fingers were quickly coated in bloody slime. The uncertain firelight and wheeling stars made it difficult to make out exactly what he was gripping, much less where was the best spot to grab hold, so Junior worked on feeling alone. Big Moms yowled as he worked his hands in deeper and deeper around the slithery shoulders of what he assumed was a baby. He felt his probing hands dilate her birth channel wider and wider, as his knuckles disappeared, then his wrists. Still he could not grasp the wriggling creature that now dangled a good foot and a half out into the night air. With a determined shove, Junior thrust both his arms in all the way to the elbows, and Big Moms took them with a enormous groan that rumbled across the butte summit like summer thunder.

"I think I got a grip," Junior grunted, his face pressed sideways into Big Moms' belly. A wet tangle of small limbs, twisted and many-jointed, blossomed out against his chest. The bulbous head was free at last – wet hairs plastered thinly to its purple skin, one eye black, expressionless, reptilian, the other golden and slit-irised, dilating wildly in the open light. Its heavy jaw jutted muzzle-like from a veinous, limp, serpentine neck far too thin to support any weight at all. Junior's fingers locked onto a bony lump, moving loose somewhere in Big Moms' cavernous interior, and he heaved backwards with all his might, hearing all around him:

"That's the way, Junior!"

"What the dickens is that damn thing?"

"Gently darling, gently!"

"Is it my baby brother, Dad, huh? Is it?"

"It'd be a mercy to let it die."

The sickness locked hold of his stomach as he felt the whole world reeling under him, all of Aztec Butte rocking under the crazy, speeding stars like a million-ton buoy anchored down in heavy seas. He was drenched in sweat, his knees slipping in the stinking black blood that soaked the rumpled blanket beneath him. The wounds in his leg and side throbbed, pulling his memory back to the Compound, and back to Delilah, back to that big goddamn giant she was fucking while he was gone. No sense returning to that. Nothing there but regret. Got to move to the future, got to yank it out squalling into the present.

Flicking his head to shake the stinging sweat from his eyes, Junior heaved again. His arms slipped out of Big Moms' vagina with a wet, sucking sound, both hands locked around the crooked haunches of a malformed abomination the size of a large watermelon. He sat down with a sigh, the thing squirming weakly on his lap, some of its stubby limbs pawing at the wet denim of his overalls, its snout puckering as though already searching for the teat. The racing shadow of a cloud passed over the top of the butte and was gone. As if from a great distance, he heard Earl and Irma cry out in unison. Howie's footsteps ran pattering around to the back of Charley's hut as the boy sobbed in fear.

"Oh, the poor thing!" whimpered Darlene.

Spanky leaned over, teeth clenched, and snipped through the umbilical cord with his pocketknife. The pool of blood and fluid spread slowly in the moonlight, soaking into Junior's clothes, but still Junior didn't move, his limp arms tucked under the thing in his lap. Big Moms bent her head back, into the dirt, her empty eyes glaring up into the sky.

"Lord, I guess my child bearing days is over," she said.

Darlene touched Junior's shoulder. "Honey? Honey? Come on, why don't you move aside now. Let me get the placenta."

Junior looked up at Darlene with a blissful smile. He saw the stars turning in great circles behind her, swinging in and out of the fringes of her disheveled hair as she bent down over him. Like sparks, or bees, or like those million and one angels that could dance on the head of a pin if you thought about it hard enough.

"I love you Dar," Junior said, "You're like the whole world. You're everything."

On any other day, Darlene would not have expected such words from Junior. She'd simply dismiss them, disbelieving on one level, saving their improbable sincerity as a remote fantasy to be savored in private. But today, with the hallucinogenic peyote mash electrifying her sluggish synapses until they clattered in concert like a thousand celestial teletype machines, today, Darlene believed every word he said, and fully understood the deepest feelings that prompted them.

"Junior, I know it," she replied. Squatting on her heels beside him, she lay one arm around his shoulders, and with the other, stroked the wet, twisted creature in his lap. A miraculous hybrid of animal forms, the child bore the mismatched limbs of a rat and monkey curled to its scaled torso, while a rudimentary hoof on one foot dangled beside the beginnings of a broad, clawed pad on the other. It responded to Darlene's touch, turning its lumpy half-face towards her hand, reflexively sucking in its black lips, blinking its mammalian eye with the slow deliberation of an aged grandfather, narrow iris glittering under the cloudy membrane of afterbirth.

Junior lifted the newborn up to his chest, cradling it in his arms, and looked into Darlene's eyes, as huge and staring and intense as his own. Together, they bent over the child, feeling as though they at last formed a complete circle, a reproductive wholeness that had come full cycle to sustain itself. Darlene didn't even feel it when one of the scrabbling claws of the thing flicked up to scratch her cheek with a gash of red. She almost felt her breasts filling, swelling, surging towards the searching, discolored muzzle that suckled blindly at the hard lump made by the .45 in Junior's overalls. A familiar tingling began deep in her belly – the same tingling she'd been feeling since Junior had made love to her in the bushes at Cap'n Bo's Campground.

"My baby!" Big Moms called out weakly for her child. She had been almost forgotten, even though they sat cradled in the V of her thighs. "Where's my baby?" Her arms fumbled in the air.

"You did good, Junior." Spanky wiped the umbilical goo off the blade of his pocketknife, and then clicked the knife shut. "Real good. Now let it go."

"Let me take that now," Irma appeared, coughed once, then bent to lift the thing from Junior's lap. The sticky flesh clung to his overalls, pulling the cloth up with gummy tendrils of mucous.

Earl looked over his wife's shoulder at the baby in her claws. "Sure is a big strapping fella."

"Ugliest baby I ever seen in my life," Irma pronounced. "Can't even tell if it's a boy or girl. Or a human being at all." She handed the creature into Big Moms' arms.

The prostrate woman groaned, her nimble, seeing fingers dancing over the creature. "Oh Lord, how many is this? How many have you given me?" she moaned in a sad, husky sing-song. "What sign is this?"

Junior staggered to his feet, feeling the blood rush to his face. He swayed, keeping one hand on Darlene's shoulder. From somewhere, he heard high-pitched crying, a child's crying, Howie. He looked about for the boy, but only saw Charley Singing Buffalo sitting cross-legged at the head of the fire, watching Junior with an inward-turned face, still and hard as if it had been chopped from oak wood with a hatchet. But the old man's eyes, Junior could have sworn, all black bottomless iris, glittered at him with a secret humor, as if enjoying some ancient joke to which he, Junior Johnson, was the eternal punch line.

"Hey Indian!" cried Junior, "Where's my land?" He held out his hands, palms up. "Where's my home now?" Junior knew that he'd find his home, knew it with a calm and terrible certainty. And now, as he stared into the void laughing behind Charley's eyes, Junior saw he would never really choose what that home would be, or shape the completion it might bring him. He took an uncertain step out from between Big Moms' legs, but his toe caught on her shin and he fell sprawling, his chin thudding onto the earth. Junior raised his head with difficulty, tasting blood in his mouth. The entire top of the butte was spinning about him now, crowned by the surging starfields overhead. He thought he heard Darlene's voice saying something, thought he felt hands or paws pluck at his clothes, whether to help or hinder him he could not say for sure.

Junior tried to open his mouth to speak, but found that he couldn't. Rolling heavily onto his back, he decided it was much better to let sleep, or unconsciousness, or even death wash over him for the time being. And dream dreams of rosy fat children running through the sunny rooms of their house as he aged into a happy old man sunning himself on the porch, patriarch of all he could see, his proud woman at his side 'til death itself couldn't even part them, but rather bring just a pause, a hiccup, a bare stutter in their love until it was resumed in some higher, hidden eternal place reserved for the strong and true and grounded, those fertile and giving and blessed in the endless chain of generations. He closed his eyes, smiling ear-to-ear at the wonders dancing behind the lowered lids.

JEFF JACOBSON

from *Foodchain*

Frank figured this was where circuses went to die.

The long black car pulled up to the sagging barbed wire gate and stopped. Overhead, the neon sign read, "WORLD'S MOST DANGEROUS ANI-MALS—ALIVE! ALIVE! ALIVE!" and flickered bad enough to make an epileptic chew off his tongue. Corrugated tin walls stretched off into the twilight; garish paintings had been splashed haphazardly across the rippled metal. Bright slashes of blood dripped off oversize teeth and claws, massive snakes curled around buxom, silently screaming women, alligators ripped and tore at pith helmeted white explorers, and all kinds of other horrors were promised.

Beyond the gate, Frank heard strange cries and howls.

Inside the car, nobody said anything. Actually, the two quiet gentlemen in the front seat hadn't said anything all day. They were big; big enough that the black suits had to have been tailor made. They didn't even have necks, not really, just muscle; the bottom of their ears damn near brushed their cream collars.

And the quiet gentlemen took their jobs very, very seriously. Frank didn't think these guys would change their expressions even if he set their black hair on fire. No anger. No impatience. No joy, either. No nothing. It was as if all their emotions had been sucked out by an especially enthusiastic abortionist who had jammed his hollow knife into the back of their skulls and vacuumed out all feeling.

The guy next to him in the back, a skinny guy with thinning red hair and a billion freckles, sniffled a bit now and again, but that was all. Frank figured he'd better keep his mouth shut too. There was still a chance he might make it through the night in one piece.

Both Frank and Red's wrists were bound with those plastic cuffs, the kind that cops use in riots. Lucio, the quiet gentleman in the passenger seat, had snicked the cuffs tight enough that Frank's hands were starting to turn a faint purple. He'd lost feeling in his fingers hours ago. But at least Lucio had cuffed their hands in front of them, instead of behind their backs.

While they sat and waited, Frank tried to twist around a little, just enough to see out the back window. There wasn't much to see. Just the empty highway, and the seemingly endless high mountain desert wastelands of northern

Nevada. To the west, jagged peaks shaved off the final slivers of the sun.

A swinging light appeared in the darkness beyond the gate and Frank got a good look at the guy. He was short, and nearly as wide as he was tall. Folds of pale, hairy flesh spilled out from around the leather apron and erupted around his chin. Loose rubber boots rose almost to his knees. A metal tube dangled from his belt. He carried the flashlight in his right hand and a large plastic bucket in his left.

Dario, the driver, nodded at the fat man and eased the long black car through the narrow space. The car slowly purred along through rows of dead carnival rides. Frank recognized a few rides from his childhood. The Whizzer. The Tilt-A-Whirl. The Mangler. He glanced back and saw the fat man relocking the gate.

Red started sniffling harder, breathing in hushed, staccato hisses.

Frank got the feeling Red had been here before.

Frank exhaled slowly, squeezing his eyes shut. He hadn't meant to kill the horse. No, that wasn't exactly true, he reminded himself; that's not exactly being honest. He'd meant to kill the horse all right, just not then, not that way. Around the racetrack, the grooms called him, "*El Caballo Susurrero.*" The Horse Whisperer. Frank was the guy you'd go to when you needed a horse dead, quickly and quietly. At least, Frank told himself told himself at night, he killed the horses humanely, not like that sonofabitch who'd slide lubricated wires into the horse's asshole and then connect the wires to a car battery.

Two weeks ago, he'd gotten a call from Mr. Enzo Castellari. Ten minutes before the Breeder's Cup at the Arlington Racetrack, Frank injected the Castellari's horse with fifteen ccs of his own special cocktail. As the drug slipped though the horse's circulatory system, it was supposed to gradually stimulate the animal into a frenzy of strength and speed. And then, after the horse won the race, the insurance would be raised significantly, just before the horse slipped into a coma and died within five days.

But a group of animal rights activists had stormed the track, delaying the race for an hour. Once the race finally got started, Castellari's horse burst out of the pack early and seemed a sure bet, until blood burst from its nostrils and it collapsed in the soft dirt in a tangle of long, impossibly thin legs, flicking the tiny rider away.

Frank was jerked out of his memories when Lucio pulled a tiny cell phone from the inside of his jacket and opened it so carefully you'd think he was preparing to juggle a rotten egg. He extended one stubby finger the size of a plump hot dog and hit a button. Frank wondered how he managed to hit just one button, considering the size of that finger.

"We're here," he said, in a clear, polite voice, his first words all day. He nodded, and Frank guessed that he didn't use cell phones that much. Or any phones, for that matter. Lucio nodded again, then held the phone out to Frank.

That's when Frank realized that he was a dead man. This was a goodbye call. He gingerly took the phone with the heavy realization that no matter what kind of salvation was promised, every word was a lie.

"Yeah," Frank said flatly.

"Hello Frank." The voice slithered into Frank's right eardrum, curling itself up and making itself at home. "I imagine right now you're a little… worried. That's understandable."

Frank didn't answer right away, just waited until it became apparent that Castellari wasn't going to say anything until he acknowledged the question. Or was it a statement? Frank wasn't sure. So he just said, "Yeah."

"Take a good look at the man sitting next to you. Take a good look."

Frank shifted the phone slightly, tilting it away from his ear, and hit the volume button with his pinkie. The voice continued, getting just loud enough to catch the skinny guy's attention. Red stopped sniffling, his eyes meeting Frank's and getting bigger by the second.

Castellari said, "There's a man who can make numbers dance and sing, make no mistake. No matter how foul my excrement smelled, this man could sift those numbers through that magnificent devious brain of his and it would always come up smelling like roses. Always." A plastic sigh, full of resignation.

Frank made sure Red was getting it. And boy oh boy was he getting it, all right. He'd frozen altogether, staring at Frank, at Frank's right hand, at the phone.

"Now, this man was warned. Make no mistake about this. But some men simply do not listen, no matter how loudly you speak, no matter what lengths you have to go to in order to . . . impress upon them the significance of the matter. This man has been in your shoes. He's been here before. He knows what awaits him." Castellari took a deep, patient breath. He was enjoying this. "This man has seen God. He's seen God, up close and personal. Unfortunately, this man was not . . . impressed with God." Castellari paused. "Few men need to see God twice."

Air hissed out of Red's nose like it was escaping a tiny hole in a balloon.

"So. Now you're in the position of trying to understand the significance of this matter. You watch and try to learn something. Are you listening, Frank?"

Frank didn't say anything. Let the sonofabitch wait *this* one out. But Castellari didn't wait long. "Okay, Frank. Okay." The phone went dead.

Mucus bubbles swelled in Red's nostrils, popped, and the soft shrapnel got sucked back inside. "Hey," he croaked. "Hey. You fellas listening? I can make you rich. Rich. Oh Jesus, I've got so much money stashed away, you have no idea. Please. Just listen to me. Please."

The car stopped in the middle of a large, open circle. Four streetlights rose into the gathering darkness, dribbling a pale yellow light onto the gravel. Empty cages and bare concrete slabs surrounded the car. It looked as if the place had been abandoned halfway through construction.

Red seized on his chance, thinking that the quiet gentlemen were actually listening to him. "Yeah, yeah, just listen to me, okay? I got enough for everybody in this car to walk... well—hell, you two to walk away with more than enough to set you up for the rest of your life. I'm talking cash here." The pleading broke down into sobs, tears, and all that mucus dripping onto his stomach and the plastic cuffs.

If nothing else, Frank was glad he hadn't broken down and begged. He'd never begged anybody for anything in his life.

The swinging light reached the car once again, splashing through the back window. The two quiet gentlemen opened the back doors and gestured at the dusty gravel. Frank nodded up at Dario and stood, a tall, bony man with long black hair. His knees were a little shaky, but not bad. Darkness had finally leeched the light out of the sky. Night had fallen quick.

The fat man leaned on the trunk and stood wheezing for a while, sucking air through the gaps in his teeth in a whistling symphony. Tiny dull eyes gazed out from between snarled eyebrows and blackheads.

Red didn't want to get out of the car. He kept bleating, "Please, please, PLEASE," until Lucio finally just grabbed hold of the thinning red hair and dragged him out into the gravel.

They walked. The fat man led the way, picking his way through rows of cages, flicking his flashlight back and forth in the dusty air. Animals started to appear; animals too old, too tired, too unpredictable. This was where they ended up, refugees from dying traveling circuses, unprepared private owners, and cancelled casino shows. But it didn't strike Frank as so much of a zoo, it seemed more like a waiting room for the damned, as if hell was simply too full at the moment, and so the animals would have to wait awhile, grimly holding onto survival, even if death was a better alternative.

The owner waddled on ahead, swinging the light back and forth, checking the cages. Frank could hear the chittering of something close, monkeys maybe. The light kept finding cage locks and doors, cringing animals, and the black shadows under the flatbeds.

Something cold squeezed its way up Frank's throat. "This is a hell of place you got here mister," he said to the fat owner. "These animals are goddamn lucky they got you lookin' after 'em."

The man stopped, swung his flashlight back into Frank's face. He looked at Frank like he'd just scraped a plump white bug out from under his toenail with a pocketknife. The fat man snorted, coughed up a thick ball of phlegm and stuck it in his bottom lip, saving it for later. He grinned. "Scared, ain't ya?" He slid the phlegm out with his tongue and swallowed it. "'Sides. What the fuck do you care, anyway. You from the SPCA? One of them PETA fucks? Looks to me like you got more pressin' problems right now." The light dropped to Frank's cuffed hands.

Dario gently tapped Frank's shoulder. Frank glanced back, saw Dario put one of his hot dog fingers up to his lips. "Shhhh."

Frank nodded.

The owner flicked a cigarette into the corner of his mouth, coughed for a second, then got enough of a breath to draw in, and fired up. "Everybody's always brave, always, 'till they see what's in the tank." The light came back into Frank's eyes. The fat man spoke slower now. "Well, you'll see. You're gonna see all right."

Frank didn't say anything. In the light that spilled over when the fat man had pointed the light at Frank's hands, Frank had seen what was in the bucket. Bones. Plenty of gristle. Chunks of meat, some covered in gray fur, swimming in blood. Lots and lots of blood.

A tiger paced incessantly along the thin bars, rumbling low in his throat. Several lionesses lay in separate corners of one large cage, tails flicking at sluggish flies. At the sight of the fat man and the bucket, they pulled themselves to their feet and snarled. It sounded like old muscle car engines, old 454 V-8s, the kind of sound that would vibrate your teeth and shake your fillings loose.

The entire zoo erupted in more snarls, howls, screeches. It was feeding time and everybody was hungry; although Frank figured this went beyond simple hunger. These animals were slowly starving to death. He could count ribs on nearly every animal.

The fat man strolled from cage to cage, reaching into the bucket and tossing scraps of bloody meat through the bars. Frank recognized leg muscles, paws, and other pieces of dogs from the meat in the bucket. The cats pounced instantly, growling, snarling, snatching the chunks, ripping the morsels away from each other. If they were human, they would have been strapped into straightjackets, locked away in small white rooms.

They reached the last cage in the row. It held a huge male lion, nearly ten feet long. He jammed his massive snout against the cage door, straining the thin bailing wire that had been twisted around the bars, securing the door. A very deep, very drawn sigh hushed out from his chest. He tilted his head and roared, shaking the matted mane and exposing teeth bigger than the quiet gentlemen's fingers. The sound reminded Frank of a jet taking off. The roar held enough authority to quiet the rest of the zoo, at least for a few seconds. Then everybody started back in, desperate, urgent.

Frank noticed the fat man didn't get too close while tossing the meat into the cages. No, he stayed well back; he may have been fat and lazy, but he wasn't stupid. Frank took a long, hard look at the bailing wire holding the door shut. It looked like it had been there for a long time; most of the wire had rusted together.

The fat man pulled a greyhound's head out of the bucket, holding onto the slim ear. He caught Frank watching and said, "I run a rescue service for retired racing dogs—see, that way I get all the fresh meat I need for free." He tossed the skull into the lion cage.

The lion seized and cracked the greyhound's skull between those giant teeth. It sounded like small branches being snapped for kindling.

Red started crying again, really sobbing. His nose dribbled more mucus, then suddenly erupted with blood. The thick crimson liquid bubbled out of his nostrils, sheeting his upper lip in blood and snot, and kept rolling down, across his bottom lip and down to his chin. Frank wondered if the accountant had discovered the wonderful world of cocaine; if so, that might explain Castellari's financial concerns. Frank almost felt sorry for the guy. Almost.

The lion crunched the greyhound skull into tiny pieces in about three or four bites, swallowed it, and glared out at the five men, tail flicking back and forth. The fat man backed away from the cage, keeping the flashlight trained on the growling lion.

Acting like they were on the move again, Frank took two steps forward and collided with the fat man. The fat man flinched, jerked away. The bucket hit the ground and toppled over. Blood and meat spilled out into the dust.

Frank stepped back and mumbled, "Sorry," aware of the blood seeping into the dirt, watching the lion's nostrils expand and contract as its eyes locked on the spilled blood.

The fat man shoved him, holding the flashlight against Frank's throat. The metal tube came out of his belt and made a crackling sound as he held it up to Frank's face. "What the fuck is your problem?" he spit. "I'll fry your brain like goddamn scrambled eggs, unnerstand?"

The lion roared again and slammed into the bars, eyes narrowing into slits, nostrils flaring.

Frank said, "Yeah."

The fat man ginned. Laughed. "You're gonna see. You'll see. You betcha. You, I can't wait to hear you scream and beg. You fucks always beg. Always."

That was Red's cue. "I got cash," he rasped. "Please." He coughed, then bent over and vomited. Thin, foamy, it splashed into the dust.

The fat man snickered again and pulled away from Frank. He reholstered the cattle prod, retrieved his bucket, and they started moving again. Red was having problems with his legs. Lucio helped out by grabbing hold of the red hair again and damn near carried Red along. The fat man led the way, around a corner, moving down a stretch of silent flatbeds and empty cages.

A lone flatbed blocked the path. It looked like some kind of tank, at least thirty feet long and ten feet high. Narrow metal stairs had been secured onto the side, rising from the ground and clinging to the side of the tank for about twenty feet before descending back to the ground.

The fat man stomped up the stairs; the rusty metal shuddered and groaned. He sidled along the catwalk, flinging the remaining blood in the bucket into the air over the tank. After dropping the bucket next to him, he turned and looked down at the prisoners and the two quiet gentlemen, dark and somber in their black suits. "Awright then," he said. "Make 'em strip. I ain't fetching any more clothes out this time. It ain't good for 'em, fucks 'em up but good." He shook his chins. "They puke out that shit for days."

Red dropped to his knees, keening, "Please, please, please," over and over and over. Blood seeped down from his nose, down his chin, down his shirt. Lucio produced a knife. One moment his hands were empty, the next, he held a wicked looking six-inch blade. It was like a magic trick. Frank found his mind drifting again, wondering if Lucio had learned it from one of the magicians in the casino shows.

Lucio brought the knife down and effortlessly split Red's shirt in half, from the back of the collar down to the small of his back. Red suddenly found his feet and herked and jerked his way up the stairs. It didn't look like he even knew what his legs were doing.

Lucio reached out and caught the back of Red's khakis. The knife came down again, splitting the fabric covering Red's bony ass. Red fell forward, grunting and spitting blood, and crawled out of his wounded pants.

Up on the catwalk, the fat man said, "Take off them socks."

"Oh God, please. Just listen to me a minute. Just for a—"

The fat man jerked out his cattleprod and cracked it across Red's forehead.

"I said, take off them fuckin' socks." Lucio started up the stairs and Frank hoped the catwalk wouldn't support their weight. The metal moaned a little, but held. Red curled into a ball, drawing his bony knees up to his pale, hairless chest and covering his head with his thin, freckled arms.

"Jesus humpin' Christ. You pussy." The fat man thumbed the switch and the cattleprod crackled like bitter laughter. Without hesitation, he jabbed Red just under the armpit. Red flopped and wriggled for several seconds, making "Uhhhh uhhhh uhhhh" sounds. A dark stain spread across the front of his white underwear and urine ran across his hip, his thigh. Lucio, apparently familiar with the effects of the cattle prod, held off on grabbing Red until the fat man withdrew the prod. He caught hold of Red's toothpick calf and the six-inch blade snickered through Red's green sock.

But Red wasn't giving up easy. He kicked out with other leg and caught Lucio square in the balls. Lucio exhaled harshly, took half a step backward, then leaned back in and slammed the blade into Red's thigh, driving it deep, all the way to the hilt.

Red's scream even shocked the monkeys into silence.

Then Frank heard what he'd been waiting for—a distant, twanging, metallic snap. Frank shot a quick glance up the stairs, but it didn't look like the fat man hadn't heard it. In front of Frank, Dario allowed a flicker of impatience to flash across his emotionless features. He fixed his dead gaze on Frank and pulled out his own knife. Frank didn't want to get stuck like Red so he quickly yanked his shirt off, tearing the buttons over the plastic cuffs. He kicked off his shoes.

Up on the catwalk, Red wouldn't stop his high-pitched screaming. Lucio plucked the knife out of Red's thigh and grabbed hold of Red's bleeding nose with his other hand, pinching the nostrils shut with his huge thumb and forefinger. He held Red's head very still and wiped the blade clean in the red hair. Then he sliced Red's underwear in half at the hip.

Frank kicked off his jeans, pulled off each sock with his other foot. Dario nodded at the boxers. Frank took a deep breath, slid his boxers down to his ankles, and kept watching the darkness under the cages.

Red managed one more "-*please*-" before the fat man and Lucio lifted his naked, bleeding body and dropped him into the tank. He landed with a dull splash.

Above and behind him, Frank heard quick, savage movements. A gurgled shriek. Brittle leather scraped over wet iron. Water, thick with algae, splashed over the rim, slid down the outside of the tank, and dripped onto the top of his head, trickling down the back of his neck. It felt warm, like a used bath.

The fat man and Lucio turned to stare down at Frank, and his stomach plummeted into a bottomless pit. He tried to breath slow, easy, and found that he couldn't even take a breath. His exposed balls felt cold and shriveled in the night air. His lungs still wouldn't work right. He curled his toes, felt the sand and grit underneath. It was time to make his move. He'd stalled long enough. He had to try something, anything. Trouble was, nothing was coming to him. Nothing was left inside. Nothing except the urge to simply bolt, to spring naked between the cages, to flee shrieking into the night.

But the quiet gentlemen would catch him. And they'd make his death last for days. So he started up the stairs, legs feeling weak, like overcooked spaghetti, head down, hands cupped over his dick and balls. Dario followed him up the stairs, snicking the knife away.

The surface of the water seethed and boiled as if it was alive. Frank caught a flash of white, a belly maybe. Whatever it was, it wasn't Red. A flat, tapered tail slapped the surface with eagerness. Something dark rolled several times and disappeared in the roiling water. Bubbles, silver in the yellow light, popped and fizzed. The fat man bent over and banged the cattle prod several times against the side of the tank.

Instantly, shadows rose to the surface. They were large, maybe seven, eight feet long and nearly two feet across.

Frank finally realized that the tank was full of alligators.

Freezing terror scrabbled up his spine and sunk its fangs into the bottom of his brain. His knees quivered, threatened to collapse completely. He should have known. Should have known that the tank would be full of some kind of goddamn squirming nightmare.

Frank didn't trust anything that didn't generate its own body heat.

A single word, "PLEASE" erupted in his throat like the silver bubbles in the tank and nearly popped in his mouth. But he choked it down. He'd be damned if he started begging now.

"Go ahead. Shoot me. Get it over with," he said.

The rubbery folds in the fat man's face split into a smile. "Fine. Shoot him then."

Lucio shook his head. "We can't. Mr. Castellari gave specific instructions."

"Just shoot me. C'mon, you spineless fucks. You fucking wop *motherfucking cocksucking*—Frank's voice got high and tight, like an overstrung violin, and he screamed, "Shoot you greasy motherfucking—"

But instead Lucio and Dario curled their thick fingers around the muscles just above Frank's elbows, and the sudden sense of being powerless, of being *forced*, slithered into his mind and squatted above the gleaming fangs of terror, enveloping his consciousness in a white, blurry haze of shock.

And just as the two quiet gentlemen started to tilt Frank forward, forcing him to topple facefirst into the alligator tank, just as all the strength left his knees and he felt his own warm, humiliating piss run down the inside of his left leg, just as the fat man played his flashlight over the rolling black water, catching the awful flat, black, eyes of the alligators, the lion leapt.

Frank could only guess that the lion had been driven into a frenzy by the smell of the blood and raw greyhound meat in the dust, maddeningly just out of reach, and had somehow forced its cage door open just enough to slip out, obeying the oldest instinct of all, older than fear. Hunger.

Frank sensed, rather than heard the roar behind him, felt the impact of the lion hit the catwalk like a five hundred pound wrecking ball. The lion came down hard on Lucio, claws slicing through the tasteful suit like a plow breaking through the last frost of the winter. Lucio's eyes popped open as shock ratcheted into his soul.

Frank grabbed Dario's left wrist with both hands as he fell forward and pulled the larger man down. They toppled into the tank together and Frank rolled on top of Dario, right hand fumbling for the car keys in the quiet gentleman's front pocket. Frank's bare feet hit the slimy bottom and he instantly kicked out, driving his heels into Dario's chest, pushing himself back towards the catwalk. He heard nothing but a rush of bubbles and the thin, staccato beat of his own heart.

The lion's back feet, claws outstretched like lethal grappling hooks, caught the bottom rung of the railing. As the front legs bounced off the catwalk, those ungodly massive shoulders rolled with the impact and the back legs tensed, pulling the giant cat backwards.

The fat man stumbled away, fumbling with the cattleprod, and fell backwards down the stairs.

Lucio turned and managed to get his .38 clear of the holster just as the lion's front left paw swung through the air like a scythe and sent the quiet gentleman's arm, fingers clenched around the taped handle, sailing out over Frank and the alligator tank. The arm spun, spitting a fine mist of blood into a rainbow above the black water and yellow light. The hand muscles twitched and the gun flinched, firing a round into the night sky.

Lucio took one solid, confident step forward. The lion rolled his back hips over the railing with a fluidity that matched the surface of the water and stalked forward, inch-long splintered claws slipping into the gaps in the steel mesh.

In his mind, Lucio raised the .38 and squeezed off three quick shots.

The lion struck faster than a rattlesnake, clapping his paws on Lucio's shoulders and crunching the man's skull between his jaws like a hammer under a walnut. The cat shook his head once, twice, and raggedly ripped Lucio's head from his broad shoulders.

Frank gathered his legs under his chest and shoved down as hard as he could manage, throwing himself onto the catwalk, just under the flicking tail.

Lucio's headless, one-armed body sank to its knees, as if he had finally given up completely, and toppled backwards, bounced down the stairs and landed heavily on top of the fat man, who was desperately scrabbling away when the limp sack of bones and flesh slammed him into the dirt.

Frank rolled under the bottom rung of the railing as two quick explosions shattered the water's surface. Frank didn't know if Dario was shooting at him, the lion, or the alligators; he didn't care. His bare feet hit the dust and he broke into a flat-out run, ignoring the sharp bits of gravel, car keys clutched in a tight fist, cuffed hands swinging, elbows flailing in the cool night air.

The lion shivered, shaking his head, crunching those giant teeth together. Blood dribbled over the black lips and tawny fur of his bottom jaw. Elegant crimson drops clung to the long, thick whiskers like heavy dew on a spider web. The tufted tail flicked happily back and forth. The taste of blood had jump-started his other senses; smells suddenly gained new dimensions of texture. Every sound became crisp, clear. Even the quick snick-snick of the .38 being cocked.

Frank ran. Behind, gunfire popped in the night. The lion roared.

The shooting lasted for a long time and as the thunderous, almost numbing sound of gunfire continued to ring in Dario and the fat man's ears, neither heard the engine of the long black car start as Frank stomped on the gas, rocketed past the dead carnival rides, plowed through the front gate, bounced out onto the dark highway, and shot into the night.

A Fine Madness

Emma stood there staring at Ezy's closet of clothes. Some fresh from the cleaners covered in plastic. A pair of work shoes, one toppled on its side, stuffed with socks like he'd just stepped out of them. How was it possible that he was dead and buried now if his own shoes looked as if they expected his return? Maybe it was all a dream. Perhaps he would come back, and she could sit with him and say, "I'm sorry for not giving you a chance that day in the hospital, but I'm willing to listen now. Go 'head, tell me what you couldn't say in front of that girl . . .that you loved me . . . you *always* loved *me,* even when we were just kids, I knew. That's why I hit that boy, that boy in the school lunchroom a long time ago. That boy who hit you in the head first and then I ran and I hit him for you . . . and I knew you loved me, too. That's why I found you that day, after you left that bear on my porch, and I cried when you asked me to marry you, because I knew you always loved me. And, oh, Ezy, if you just speak to me one more time, I promise, I'll forgive you because I don't know how to do nothing else but love you back."

But they had already lowered his casket in the ground. And there were people with bowed heads that had watched, too. And that girl—that *Freida*—had done all that shrieking at the lip of the open grave. And even the final hymn had been sung:

Beyond the sunset,
O glad reunion,
With our dear loved ones who've gone before,
In that fair homeland we'll know no parting,
Beyond the sunset forever more!

Still though, Emma had not been able to completely believe. She had seen the sun breaking through the trees and glinting off the chrome of the gray casket. It was a sign. Ezy couldn't be gone. And when she went home and opened Ezy's closet, this evidence of his being seemed more powerful than even the most final pronouncement: ashes to ashes, dust to dust.

The ticking of the clock took Emma's attention. She went into the kitchen and stood, looking up at the wall clock: a pink ceramic cat with bulging eyes and pupils swishing opposite the pendulum-swing of its tail. It sat above the stove where the pork chops should've been thawing. The time on the clock's belly was 7:30. The kids would be home shortly from the movie that she made them go and see. The pork chops were still in the freezer, and she hadn't even had time enough yet to finish getting things straight in her head. But there was little chance for that now, because soon Peace and Kiwi would come through the door, and then she'd have to wait until late in the night to be alone again. That's all she could handle—not thawing meat, or breaking up the fights between her kids. She needed to find some place to be. Just for a little while longer. The bedroom? No. The bathroom? Too bright.

She returned to his closet. She hugged Ezy's work shirt as she tucked herself beneath the hanging clothes. The smell of him filled her head, her chest: tobacco and spearmint, coffee and liniment. She closed her eyes and waited. Waited to feel something other than the vacant space Ezy had left behind. But there was only the shifting of the leaves outside, the tick-tick of the bug-eyed cat just down the hall. She fingered the frayed strings of his work shoes, drawing her knees close to her chest with the shirt pressed in the space in between. Emma waited, remembering the sight of Ezy's young wife screaming his name insistently at his grave, her head shaking violently and legs growing limp as sympathetic arms wrapped around her. In the warm darkness of his closet, Emma contemplated the importance of rage for the loss of Ezy. She imagined herself with his young wife Frieda's outpour: head flung back with a mouth stretched wide and a throat gurgling with utterances for the mercies of heaven. Her body writhing with the pain of grief, feet stomping to curse the very earth that had taken Ezy. But sitting among those things that had caressed him, she still felt only numbness. And then there was the thought, *would it come?* It didn't. Not right then, at least. So she pushed herself on out of that dark place, with her mind still fastened on the question.

She rose early the next morning, brushed her teeth, went to work, came home, cooked dinner, washed dishes, scolded her kids for fighting—all the time waiting without the awareness of it.

Time announced itself by killing things: grass, flowers, the muddy earth hardened by wind. And finally, the snow burial. It was then, perhaps, that Emma first understood what Ezy's death meant. The sharpness of her thought stopped her cold, one late afternoon, right in the school parking lot as she bent to slip her key into her car door: now her home, her bed were really empty. She fixed on a reflection of her dark grimacing face in the window. Her mind pin wheeled backwards over the years and entangled every important memory of her life with the presence of Ezy. So that it seemed no other time existed when he wasn't a part of her. In her thinking, he had defined her very existence, and she'd not known it so profoundly until his absence: his ugliness made her beautiful, his weakness made her strong; his tarnished love reverenced her to importance. Snow fell quietly, lit and melted on the corner of her lax mouth. *Oh, Lord.* There would be no one now to look at this face. Not the way Ezy had, with sly boyish affection. No one to flirt with and feel secure in his want, his desire and the power of her thighs that she knew he could never forget. She recalled old women she had known—the talking dead—who had laid themselves to rest back with the memory of their husbands, never to take up with another man again. It made sense to her now. Too much of their former selves were ribboned behind them along that great stretch of road from altar to grave; what remained of these women now could've only been adored by their own men's eyes, and his hands alone could only yearn to knead the flesh, thickened and marred from childbearing. So there was no need to even wonder *what now?* Emma believed she could not afford to wonder. At thirty-five she counted herself among the old, her worth buried in Ezy's grave. Therefore she could not afford to let her mind, her eye roam and notice the razor-edged evenness of hair at the nape of another man's neck, to notice the moonlight fringing his broad back, or the way black strong trees stretch their limbs in praise of his greatness. Because Ezy was gone, and her sureness of acceptance was gone.

Not that evening, but the very next, she got in her car and drove to the cemetery. Holding the neck of her tweed coat, she tromped and stumbled along the rock hard ground, slick in spots from ice patches. The wind moved over the open terrain of graves, traveled up her coat and caused her to shiver. She searched from one snow-capped headstone to the next. But where was he? Then she saw the big tree and remembered; his spot was angled a few yards to the right of it.

Emma stopped there, huffing, chin quivering as if she'd lose the fight against tears any moment. So she didn't speak right away. Just stared at the headstone. White and cold, with brown rotted leaves blown against the etched words:

Ezekiel Hawkins
1947-1983
Beloved

She began softly, "You son-of-a-bitch." And then louder, "You cowardly son-of-a-bitch!" She kicked at the headstone and had to catch her balance. "Why couldn't you fight, huh?! *I* fought!" She beat her chest. "*I* FOUGHT! I didn't leave *YOU!* I didn't leave *you!"* She fell to her knees with a soft whimper. The wind stirred. There was the smell of something old, rotted that wrapped around her. She sat down on the ground, feeling it, finally, the rumblings of her very own howl. Steadily rocking, back and forth, back and forth, shaking her head; her arms began groping along the surface of Ezy's grave, painfully aching to hold him just one more time.

The hardest part was having too much empty time on her hands. Her kids, Peace and Kiwi, thirteen and twelve now, had already discovered the horizon beyond their mother's face, and were anxious to explore it. She wished them to be little again, those times when they would complain of nightmares and ask that she sleep with them. Then she would have something to distract her, at least for a little while.

Her friend Hannah would call, asking at the close of the conversation which Emma kept brief, "You remember to take your medication?" (The doctors had given her something for depression.) Hannah also suggested that she "see somebody" she could talk to, since Emma apparently had chosen to shut herself away from family and friends. A shrink, Emma supposed, but she didn't want to deal with that again. She didn't want *anybody* picking apart her loss. After she'd listened to Hannah and finally packed up and gave away the last of Ezy's belongings, Emma took to locking herself away in the quiet sanctuary of her small bathroom. There, she would sit on the edge of the tub, turn on the water and just listen to it run. If she concentrated hard enough, her mind could transform the uneven spurts into a white lush waterfall. Sometimes she stayed in there for hours, changing her position, maybe, from tub-side to crouching by the small space near the sink, or twisting herself into a curve on the dirty white tile, marred by the last of Ezy's footprints that Emma still couldn't bring herself to mop away. *If I could just stay here in this little room,* she'd think, *and feel the cool floor against my head and listen to the water hushing me to peace, I'd be happy.*

And for that reason, she stole as much time there as she could, especially at night when she couldn't sleep. On occasion, she'd take a little scotch to help her sleep. And on weekends, when scotch alone didn't seem to do it, she'd slip off—just for a spell—to the bar a block away. Most times she didn't stay long enough to even take off her coat, or trouble herself with finding a seat. She simply stood watching from near the door. The loud music, the buzz of laughter and the tinkling sounds of liquor bottles tipping over empty glasses carried her mind back to a good place: Bean and the parties. In the hazy, smoky images, she could even *see* Bean in her tight red skirt, wriggling and pressing herself against that man near the wall, and hear the boom and her long-ago friend, G-Man's laugh. And for the first time in the longest time, Emma would feel a smile coming on. But then she would have to leave, knowing her kids were alone.

Quickly, though, her running off became a habit; she was willing to gamble that her children would not awaken. But then, in time, she began exploring other bars in the neighborhood, sometimes talking to and dancing with old men who'd buy her drinks in exchange for her company. And then there were a few spots near downtown she'd taken a liking to—the more upscale places with live piano music and younger men. There was no preoccupation with whether her children would wake during the night and finding that she was gone, because often times she would leave before they were in bed, and she would return only when her appetite had been satisfied.

On one such night when she was leaving a bar, somebody swept out of the crowd behind her and grabbed her arm. She jerked around, startled. At first sight, she said without thinking, "G-Man?" And then the half-smile slipped from her face when she realized how ridiculous that was. But the tall caramel boy who was grinning at her didn't seem to have heard. "I watch you all the time come into this place," he said, "and you always leave too quick."

"Look," she said, "I just—"

"Sit wit me," the young man said. He still had hold of her arm, not firmly, but with a strong enough grip to indicate he wanted his way. She hesitated, looking down at his hand attached to the bend of her coat sleeve, and then eyeing his grin. "This place is too crowded," she said. "There's nowhere to sit."

"Come wit me," he said. He took her hand and led her through the thicket of people, squeezing passed them, bumping them and saying excuse me, until they made it to a dim far corner booth that seemed to be fully loaded with people drinking and talking in each other's faces. But the young man said, "Hey, ya'll make some room," and they did.

He sat down first and Emma edged on to the very end of the booth next to him. "Told you I'd find us a spot," the young man said. He had the satisfied look of a kid, moving his eyebrows up over black pupils that twinkled from shots of liquor. He breathed the scent of rum out of wide nostrils that overpowered his narrow face. It was his spectacular smile alone that saved him— a broad spread of generous pink lips that showed neat white teeth.

"How old are you?" Emma asked.

The young man laughed out loud. "Fully grown all over," he said.

"Well, you look a little young to be hanging out here."

"Naw I ain't. Axe my uncle. He own the place." He gave a nod in the direction of the bar. Through the space between the people walking and milling around, Emma saw a heavy-set man bobbing to the music and pouring drinks.

"What's your name?" the young man asked.

"Emma," she said, studying his face again, trying to reason to herself why she was even talking to this boy.

"Well, my name's Toffee."

"Toffee? Like the candy?"

"Yeah." The grin got wider as the tip of his pink tongue flicked out to the corner of his mouth. "You wanna drink, Emma?" he asked. "I can get you whatever you need. Won't cost you hardly nothing."

"Now when is the last time I heard that?"

Toffee pointed to his ear. "What you say?"

"Nothing. Yeah. Yeah, okay. I'll have a scotch."

He got up and disappeared into the crowd near his bartending uncle, and then reappeared moments later, carrying a bottle in one hand and two glasses in the other. He sure did remind her of G-man. That same sort of tall and wiry skinny. Except Toffee (or maybe his people) had money, judging by the way he dressed. She took the sheen of his plum shirt to be silk, and the pleated waist and razor creases of his olive pants to indicate a finer quality of fabric. She got up so he could claim his spot again.

"A whole bottle?" she asked, watching him pour.

"Well," he said, sliding his eyes evenly over to her, "we don't have to finish it here."

The delicious thought of being desired was enough to arouse her. She held her thighs together to suppress it. She took the scotch he gave her. "How old did you say you are?" she asked him.

He spoke with the glass raised to his mouth. "Does it matter?" he asked.

"Yeah," she said, "if it means I'm cradle robbing."

"I ain't *that* young," he said.

She shook her head, laughing a little. "I don't believe this."

"Believe what? That I'm interested or that you like it?"

She stopped laughing. She felt hot. She slipped out of her coat, twisting herself toward him to stuff the thing down behind her. She was aware of his eyes moving along her pugnacious breasts, straining against the fabric of her black turtleneck; she fiddled with the coat a little longer.

"You got a man or something?" Toffee asked.

"I don't have a man," she said, "*or* something."

"Good," he said. She looked at him. He continued, "I'd hate for some dude to jump outta your bedroom closet swingin' a ax at me."

She laughed. It felt good to laugh so she didn't even bother putting him in his place about the bedroom reference. Besides, she liked the way his face lit up because she enjoyed his joke.

"You real pretty when you smile," he said. "Not that you wasn't pretty scowling by the door."

"How long have you been watching me?"

"Since you been coming here. 'Bout a month or better. At first I thought you was looking for somebody. Then I knew you was just looking."

She knew then he had figured out her secret, her scorching lonely secret.

"What's the matter?" he asked.

"Nothing."

"Was it something I said?"

"Nothing. Nothing. I should be getting on home now."

He grabbed her wrist when she stood. "Emma," he said looking up at her. But that was all he said; his eyes locked with hers, his hot hand firmly holding her wrist, even though she was not trying to get away.

It wasn't until she closed her bedroom door, and in the dark, felt Toffee breathing and tasting the back of her neck, that she felt afraid. Of what, she didn't know exactly. Bits of reasoning tried to break through in her head as his hands slid under her armpits from behind and then moved to massage her ribs, around to that point where her breasts rested. Shuddering, she closed her eyes. *I don't know this man. Man? Boy.* His hand moved down, down along her belly and then grazed the zipper of her jeans. She could feel him, hot and hard pressing against her behind. Water began collecting in her mouth. He eased closer to her ear. "Turn on the light," he said, "I wanna watch."

"No," she said softly. It sounded more like a plea.

He persisted. "I wanna watch you on top. I wanna look up at this beautiful body, your face." His hands stroked and gently squeezed her breasts. "I wanna see you glow."

The lights were turned on, and as he undressed her, he didn't seem to notice at all her stretch marks, the flabby fold of her stomach, or the sagging sway of her breasts as she mounted him on her bed, towering over him, rocking with the grace of a willow on its knees; he looked up at her whispering obscenities, sometimes opening his mouth wide with small sounds caught in the hollow of his throat. She peered down, taking in the caramel boy with the slippery smile. Letting her thoughts revel in his look of sleepy-eyed pleasure, sometimes surprise, all while they were drifting, rising and rolling along wet shores.

I feel him melt with me, feel him moving up, up through me, until I can taste his hot sweetness on the back of my tongue. It is a candy sweetness that lingers there like a faint memory. Teasingly.

Her strong, thick thighs gripped his lean body, a grip so firm she felt his blood course beneath his skin. His eyes closed slowly as if he was being rocked to sleep.

And I know if I don't wait for the memory to come clear, if I touch his caramel skin with the tip of my tongue, I will recognize this taste. And it will flood my mouth and my head, strike my nostrils with a fragrance so strong I will become intoxicated.

She arched her back, then swayed. His hands moved up along her waist and steadied her.

Then I will only want more of him. I will want to melt him down until he runs liquefied like creamed coffee. And I will drink him, savor him slowly, and feel his sweetness coat the inside of me—my breasts, my arms, my legs.

Tiny sparks began moving through her, a sensation that started at a small point between the thighs, but then grew, and with it came a violent, steady quaking. She grabbed his shoulders to keep the room from vibrating.

And with his sweetness inside of me, I will feel beautiful. And I will never forget the flavor again. When it retreats to the back of my throat, this time I will conjure it up with a simple flick of my tongue. But for how long? How long will the taste remain in my mouth? How long will my power last?

He pulled her down flat on top of him and swallowed her mouth; she laid there listening to the erratic drum in his chest, listening to the unsteady rise and fall of their breathing. And trying to remember, with sleep coming quickly, if she did, in fact, lock the door.

She felt the neighbors' gossip, every time Toffee came and went from her place: *She ought to be shame, old as she is wit that boy. Actin' all loose in front of her kids. Some peoples jess ain't got no morals.* But that didn't stop Emma from seeing him as long and as often as she could. It even became common for Peace to walk into the bathroom and see Toffee soaking in their tub, with his brown knees sitting like caps atop the gray water. She didn't like him. Emma put a Band-Aid on the problem by sending the kids to Hannah's place for frequent weekend visits.

It didn't take long for Hannah to figure out the routine, watching Emma step inside her door just far enough to kiss her kids and wave good-bye, then rush off to the car horn honking out front. One time, Hannah sent the kids into the family room, and stopped Emma's quick exit so they could talk privately.

"Listen," Hannah said, "you know I love Peace and Kiwi, but I think you need to spend more time with them."

"Hannah, I'm with my kids everyday. What are you talking about? You tired of me bringing them here?"

"No. You know that's not it."

"Oh, I see. I see. This is about Toffee, isn't it?"

"Well, yes. Having a strange man practically *living* in her home makes Peace uncomfortable."

"She misses her daddy, that's all," Emma told her, conscious of Toffee waiting with the car running. "But I can't bring Ezy back. And I can't pretend that *I'm* the one who died. She'll get used to the change. We all have to." And then Emma was out the door.

Truth was, Emma not only had gotten used to being without Ezy, she relished what she'd found in place of him. In her eyes, Toffee was beautiful; and equally so, he was reckless, wildly fitting for a lonely middle-aged woman. His youth, his lust, fortified her worth. His gentle whacks on her behind, as they passed the neighbor's gate, announced their claim on one another. She loved the attention they drew—ripping through the neighborhood streets in her frayed cut-offs on summer nights, her wild black arms flailing while weaving and dodging between parked cars, zigzagging around trees, Toffee, bare chested, barefoot, his water balloon upright and aimed, both in a fit of hyena giggles, and then splitting passed a neighbor's house, Emma yelping at the cold splash against the backs of her thighs, aware of dark windows lighting up, and discreet peeks through the slats of window blinds, and eyes hidden by porch shadows; she'd collapse against the light post so they could see her well in the pale pink glow, her head tossed back and chest heaving, and Toffee falling against her, grinding himself there for a moment, before pulling her by the hand on to more mischief.

And then there was one late night—right there, outside, on her first floor back porch—when he unbuttoned her blouse, and slipped his hand inside while burying his face in the curve of her neck. She didn't stop him. Just closed her eyes and enjoyed the heat of his breathing against her ear, and the feel of his soft hands on her flesh. It didn't even matter when she heard old Phoebe Wilson's next door bedroom window rattling open. She let Toffee keep at it, because she knew he wanted her to, wanted a woman who was free enough to give into pleasure.

She was not sure if this was love, but what she did know was that she never wanted to feel any differently, and she was willing to do for Toffee whatever it took. So she didn't care if folks said her tight lycra pants were down right nasty on a woman as old as her. Didn't care that they called her "wicked" for flaunting herself in them, draped on Toffee's arm. And certainly, if it took meanness to protect what she'd found, then so be it; word got around quick when she shattered a bottle over a man's head for threatening Toffee. That put an end to any open ridicule about her; most folks were too afraid of her now to even raise a question. So when they heard that she and the boy were planning to marry, everybody swore the devil had curled his tail. Her momma, Mrs. Powell, even took it upon herself to come by Emma's apartment, just to tell her what a fool she was, and how beat she looked from all that late night rambling. The two of them started yelling so loud, the people upstairs called the cops.

Shortly after, Toffee moved into Emma's place. And to her pleasure he seemed to really be making an effort with her kids. He'd pick Peace up from chearleading practice so Emma could stay behind and help Kiwi with his math homework. He'd make sure to get food for the kids if she had to work late.

That's why, many months later, when Hannah pulled her into the kitchen by her wrist and hissed in her face, "He molested Peace," Emma couldn't make sense of the words. She tore her wrist away from Hannah and backed into the sink. *He?* Who? She shook her head. "What are you talking about?"

"Emma, listen to me. Peace just told me, out in the car." Hannah was pointing toward the hallway and Emma was looking there, wondering why Peace hadn't followed Hannah into the apartment after being away all weekend. "That man, that *Toffee*, molested her."

Molested? That couldn't be right. Emma was wearing his baggy sweat suit—a thing lovers do—and had been working the pink rollers out of her head for her night out with him, so how could this be if Toffee was a child molester? Then it became clear. Peace *had* to have been coaxed. Emma pushed herself away from the sink by the elbows and came a step closer. "I never would've . . . You bitch," she whispered.

Hannah's mouth fell open. Stunned and horrified, she said, "What is the matter with you?"

"There's nothing wrong with *me*," Emma told her. "The problem is you and everybody else trying to tear me down."

"Tear you . . . *Listen* to yourself, Emma. Don't you even care about what I'm telling you?!"

"Not when it's lies, Hannah. I expected better from you. At least *you*. I never thought you'd be petty enough to lie on anybody, even if you didn't like him!"

"I'm not lying! If you just—"

"What is it? You mad because I'm not hanging on to you all helpless any more? Is that it? Are you the only one who's supposed to have a man to come home to, Hannah?"

"This is crazy, Emma. Just talk to your daughter."

"Get out of my house, Hannah! Get out now!"

"God help you, Emma Hawkins. Because I'm done trying!"

When Hannah turned to leave, they both noticed Peace standing in the hallway, just before the kitchen. Her mushroom of hair almost hid her swollen wet eyes; she looked like a little girl just then, trying to be all grown up in her belly top. Emma knew then it was true. She grabbed Peace and squeezed her to her chest. How could she even begin to say she was sorry? "Momma didn't know. I didn't—" She tried to remember losing herself to the point of going blind. And for what? She flashed on Toffee's slick grin. There was a car driving up out front. She quickly pulled Peace away and ran to the living room window. No. It wasn't him. Then she decided not to wait. She rushed back into the kitchen passed Hannah, who stood watching with her arm around Peace. Emma began yanking open cabinet silverware drawers. "What are you doing?" Hannah asked. It wasn't in the drawers. The sink. Emma used the knife earlier to cut onions. She tore through the dirty dishes, sending off shattering noises. Peace pressed herself closer to Hannah who held on to her tighter. "Emma? Emma? What are you doing? What are you looking for?" And then Emma came up with the wet knife. She held it face-level just long enough to contemplate how sharp the blade was. "Please, Emma. Don't do anything foolish. Come on, let's just take Peace to the doctor, okay?" But heading for the door, she marched by Hannah with no thought for the shrilly calls of her name she left behind.

She stormed into his uncle's bar, wild eyed and breathing heavy, the knife in her hand and the sleeve of her baggy sweatshirt shoved up to the elbow, legs gaped, ready to charge at him, looking from one empty round table against the wall to the next. And then a giggle from the back booth. A man leaning into a woman's long neck, her head thrown back. Emma turned to the clinking of bottles being shelved behind the bar; the man bending into the crate was slim and gray haired. Emma didn't recognize him, but asked any way, "You seen Toffee?"

He didn't look at her as he raised himself and slid the next bottle onto the mirrored shelf. "Naw," he said, with a smoker's phlegmy rattle. Coughing, bending. "But I think he 'spose to come through here."

So Emma took the barstool parallel to the door, tapping her gymshoe heel on the stool's rung, the knife held tight in her lap and her eyes turned on that man back there in the booth seat, licking the woman's fingers now. *Mothah fuckahs.* She thought of every last one she'd known—every hurt, every bruise they'd caused. Years of trying to forget them, but bearing the scars they left behind. And now Toffee had done this filthy thing: sullying her baby and slicing out Emma's heart all at the same time. *He'd* pay. All she wanted was for him to step far enough inside that door so he couldn't back up and run. Just far enough for her to swing out and slit him open from his nuts up to his lying throat. Her grip on the knife handle was slick with the anxious sweat; Emma asked the old man behind the bar again, "You sure he's gonna drop in?"

"That's what he said," was the answer, and so Emma kept on waiting. Then it got late and folks started streaming in, some women—alone and in pairs—but mostly men, talking loud and looking around to make sure somebody noticed, eyeing the women and sliding up along side them, at tables, at the bar. One of them came up behind Emma, sniffing her hair and giving out his own funk of sweat and liquor. She spun around on the stool to look up at him. He was a big man. Swaying. Sweating. "Big Percy," he called himself, grinning with large yellow teeth, but the cheek teeth were missing. "You taste as sweet as you smell?" he asked, leaning in, breathing on her.

Her stomach churned. "Get the hell away from me!" she said, pressing her back against the bar and angling her face for air.

The bartender told them to cut it out. The men with him laughed. "Now tha's *one* taste you ain't gon' git, Percy!"

His grin slid away; his face took on the look of a pitbull who tried to kill her once. "A *fine* bitch is one thing," he said, his hot liquor breath burning her forehead, "but a ugly one ain't got no—"

The knife jabbed so swiftly into his gut, he couldn't finish. His eyes and mouth popped open with no sound at all. It was the bartender who dropped the liquor bottle with a holler, and the man and woman seated beside her who screamed and shuffled away. But it wasn't until Emma felt the hot blood on her hand and yanked the knife back and watched Big Percy buckle to the floor at her stool, that she realized what she had done. She stood up. Looked at the knife. Looked down where Big Percy folded himself with teeth bared. He was bleeding from the belly something awful. The commotion was swelling—crying from women, men hollering, "Git a ambulance!"

Big Percy was growling, dying and growling at her feet. And she couldn't even enjoy it because it wasn't Toffee's face she was staring down on. She heard somebody call her a crazy bitch. They didn't understand that this was meant for Toffee. Dying was meant for Toffee. If only this horny nigger would've just left her alone. So she hollered at him, "I TOLD YOU TO BACK OFF!" swinging the bloody knife and putting her shaking fist to her head.

Big Percy looked up at her and said, "You better hope I die, 'cause if I don't, I'm coming back to kill yo' ass!"

This time he deserved it. She swooped the knife down across his face. He screamed like an animal and grabbed his cheek with the gush of blood running through his fingers. "More will be waiting for you, if you try," she said. She looked at every face in the room, staring back at her in fearful fascination. She stepped over Big Percy and walked out. Nobody stopped her.

She went home. So what if the cops would find her there. She tracked Big Percy's blood all the way to her bathroom. She didn't call out for Peace or Kiwi, because she knew Hannah had taken them. She stood at the sink and turned on the cold water. Still gripping the knife, she stuck her hand under the rushing faucet. She watched the blood slide from her dark skin and swirl down the drain. She kept watching, holding her hand there until her skin began aching and then went numb from the cold. She remembered hearing, one time, this is how you prep yourself for slitting your wrist. That way the freezing cold won't let you feel the pain. She looked at herself in the mirror, pink rollers and portions of her hair sticking up, her face dark and drained. The wear of wild misery was on her. This was the bottom she'd dropped to. She wanted relief. A final disconnection from the pain of it. But could she really bring herself to end this with a bloody mess for her kids to find? No. What then? How? She opened the medicine cabinet. The Thorazine. She had enough of it left to do the job. She flung her head back and emptied the bottle down her throat. She doubled herself over the sink, choking and fighting to swallow, while scooping handfuls of running water into her mouth. And then she sank down to the floor. For only a brief moment, she thought of that man, Big Percy, bleeding at the bar, and was sorry that she hadn't left a message for Toffee: "This was meant for you." Her whole life, it seemed she screwed up time and again. "I can't even kill the right nigger," she said. At least she had known Hannah, and her kids would be taken care of. Her toes; she couldn't feel them. Emma looked down at her bloody gymshoes and tried to wriggle them, but the tile floor was undulating, so she wasn't sure if her toes were moving or if the floor was making them move. She leaned her head back against the cool tub rim to relieve her weak neck, then closed her eyes because now the ceiling was rolling in loose waves, too, and it was making her dizzy. She became aware then of the tingling in her fingers that began creeping up her arms. *This is too slow,* she thought, listening to the water still running. *Oh well, I guess they'll have a mess to clean up after all.*

DEVON POLDERMAN

The Hotel Kalamazoo
from *Famous Kalamazoo Bullshit Stories*

Phil At 29

June 18, 1989. Phil's first stop the morning of Big Daddy's bachelor party was a liquor store outside the Kalamazoo airport. He needed to snake a pint of Old Crow, to see if he could still steal. He could.

The way he'd figured it flying in was, as long as he didn't get *too* deep into anything Bobby Bug-related, he could pretty well handle himself clear of trouble. His whole life had kind of been like that—you had a lot of times where you could have died when you were best friends with Bobby Bug—but since he'd made New York his safe home for sticking to the pledge, ducking Bobby was more of a game than a responsible lifestyle, so Phil relaxed and sipped as he cruised past long fields that had been replaced with strip mall larvae, mattress shops, outlet stores, or various incarnations of fast food. It made him think of a play-city. The whiskey took him south, where the old places were, and soon he was surrounded by light forests loosely strung with neighborhoods, the houses and yards growing gradually larger as he drew upon Liar's Lake. He followed the shore drive east, away from his family's home, until he saw ahead the little park where men gathered to drink to Big Daddy. He swung his rented Honda into the lot alongside a bright row of pick-up trucks and muscle cars.

A thin path from the parking lot vanished over a small hill that hid the park proper, and with his window open he could hear their deep throaty laughs booming from the far side. He wondered whose they were. He hadn't confirmed with anyone that he was coming. Another swig of whiskey and he unfolded himself from the car, tucking the pint into his pocket as he rose. His head began to hum as he stood, and that felt good and familiar. His shadow cut sharply against the morning sun as he made for the drunken voices.

Atop the hill sits a squat, brown utility building; to the right of the path, a tight pine grove beside a playground with swings, teeter-totters, and a pyramid of bolted tires. Beyond all this, in the wide, grassy main between the utility building and a small crab apple orchard that closed the far end of the park from the forest, stood Big Daddy and his entourage, a dozen and a half guys and a pair of smoking grills. The scent of meat, lots of meat, flapped Phil's way. He didn't make five steps before Benny caught sight of him and began jumping and waving his arms, bellowing "Holy Shit! Phil! Over here, man! Over here!" As though Phil wouldn't have figured them for his people otherwise.

One by one the heads in the pack gandered his way, and with each man Phil saw an old face pop with surprise as he turned to recognize him. It made him vaguely uncomfortable and he jammed his hands in his pockets. He hadn't seen most of these guys more than once or twice in the ten years since he'd moved off, if at all, and seeing them now was disconcerting, kind of like looking at aliens. Even from a distance, he found himself scrutinizing faces to confirm they belonged to people he'd once known.

"C'mon, you fucker!" Benny cheered, and the group laughed their support. There would be a lot of laughing. "Get yer ass on over here!"

Phil concentrated on his buzz, then jogged over to their circle.

"Fuck me blue. Phil Lockwood!"

"Hey, Mr. City Shit comes home!"

"What's up, Cunt?"

There's an old Indian curse that says if you're born in Kalamazoo, you will come back here to die. An elephant graveyard. Phil had always thought of it more like an old country inn. The Hotel Kalamazoo. Go, do what you do, your room will keep. Through the cusses and the back slaps, Phil wondered if that's why coming back always felt like such a goddam chore: Because it always felt like he was supposed to. As the group clambered about him, Phil finally pressed out his arms to clear some space, shot out both middle fingers, and shouted "Where's the groom?"

Phil didn't need to ask. Even in a town like Kalamazoo, where everyone is a giant, Big Daddy stood out. Phil stood six foot seven, and working as a personal trainer kept him a solid two sixty-five. Most of the guys at the party weren't far behind. But Big Daddy loomed over them all like a monolith, an inch and a half over Phil's head and almost twice as broad. Bricklayers, the whole family, for a couple generations. Big Daddy and his daddy, his uncles and grandpa were as recognizable in this part of town as the bright red pick-up trucks they tooled around in, the words "Millions Laid" stenciled on the cab doors beneath the family name. He and Phil were connected the same as most of these guys—through their fathers. Big Daddy's daddy had laid a pathway through Phil's father's greenhouses years ago, after a customer had clumsied over Mr. Lockwood's scattering of secondhand patio squares and turned an ankle; Mr. Lockwood had done the wedding flowers for Big Daddy's two older sisters. Now Big Daddy was getting married. He was staked out amid the food, two grills squared tight with sausages, bacon, brats, skirt steaks, runny eggs in small iron skillets, tinfoil packets of home fries. Beside the grills was a picnic table loaded with cheeses, thick, black-striped toast, potato salad (because if there is a grill, there must be potato salad), and beer. Lots of beer. Coolers of it. Phil waded through the bodies and eats toward Daddy, pumping the groom's hand and reaching to rub the bald crown in his dark baby-thin hair.

"How you doin'?"

"Alright." Big Daddy clapped his hands together and rubbed them. "Ask me tomorrow at the funeral—I mean the wedding," he added with a wink, "and see what I say then."

Everyone laughed loudly. Kalamazoo is nothing if not rehearsed. That's how you can tell the Zoo, no matter how long you're gone. They still pack their cigarettes hard and angry, teaching the damn things a lesson as certainly as you'd teach your kid to quit pissing the bed; they still flick their car keys from their pockets fast and sure, no doubt it's time to go. They're coarse and friendly and familiar and wary. They know what's coming next and they make sure they do it right the way everybody wants, and they know that at some point someone's going to fuck something up and then no one will know for sure what's to follow, or if it's going to happen again so that they can expect it next time, or whether or not any of this should make a hell of a lot of difference.

The grills were largely clear of meat and a steady pile of empties had collected beneath and around the picnic table when Big Daddy hauled himself from a huddle of big guys, took two giant steps forward, and slugged Phil in the middle of his chest with a closed hand. Thud. The blow rocked Phil, beer slopping from his can, and Benny, Ike, and the couple others Phil'd been talking with hopped clear. Big Daddy stood in the center, towering over his buddies and glaring at Phil.

"Fucker," he spat. "Think yer big shit? Fucker."

Phil steadied himself and stood tall beside the table, a few feet from the bigger man but abandoned by everybody else. The sun was directly above them now, hot enough to pinken the skin of the guys without shirts. Phil's eyes, small and icy and the color of granite, locked with Big Daddy's, who was absent-mindedly flexing half-moon indentations into his beer can. Phil kept cool, leaning into the cooler and digging a fresh beer from the ice without ever breaking eye contact.

"You're lucky I got a beer in my hand, ya lump," he said, flicking ice from his hand as he popped the tab. "Otherwise I'd have to beat your hick ass for that."

Tilting his own beer above his head, Big Daddy drained it and flattened it at the same time, then took another giant step forward and slapped Phil's full one from his hand. It splashed and flew damn near twenty yards.

"Now ya don't."

Phil shrugged. There was nothing more to say. He slipped the pint from his back pocket and placed it beside the beer cooler while he hooked his shirt off with the other hand. Big Daddy skinned his own shirt and they squared, squatting and fanning their big mutton arms as the rest of the party tightened around them in an excited knot. In fine Zoo tradition, the bachelor party wrestling matches began.

It's not the sharpest wrestling you'll ever see, but beer does that. Still, if you like sumos, you'd enjoy this. They circled the ring once, twice, small grins chewing the corners of their mouths, squinting, and on the third turn they rushed one another and clapped together like bulls in heat, heads lowered, shoulders tight. Locked together they wrestled on their feet, pawing for heads and necks and arms and backs and staggering and re-staggering their feet to keep balance. Like watching linebackers try to fuck each other. The crowd jeered closer and closer, then exploded back as Phil managed to duck a swipe of Big Daddy's forearm, cinch his arms about Daddy's waist and haul him into the air before driving him into the ground back-first. Soufflé. Big Daddy jack-knifed his legs, but before he could right himself Phil torqued a shoulder into his back and dug in with his own legs, pinning the groom on his belly. Big Daddy stared out at the thin grass in front of his face, then Phil slammed his head flat to the turf as he wedged himself against Big Daddy's ear.

"You know," Phil huffed, "you're really a bit of a puss for a guy your size."

Big Daddy's friends roared, and his face and neck boiled red as a three hundred pound lobster. The groom's not supposed to lose, especially when he's Big Daddy's size. He began spasming his body until he could reach behind with his free arm and catch Phil's head and neck in a circle of biceps. "I'm gonna knock your dick in the dirt, Lockwood," he growled, then squeezed and flipped them both over.

Phil scrambled, crabbing one way and then the other, trying to roll them both again, until Big Daddy unleashed a torrent of vicious cross-faces, big bricklayer blows. As the two tumbled across and over one another, grass cling-ing to their sweaty backs, crowd kicking them back to the center when they toppled too close to the grills, Phil began questioning why in the hell he'd boarded his plane this morning. It would prove to be the least serious question he'd asked himself this trip. He'd come to wrestle. For every way New York was better than Kalamazoo, there was nobody there for him to wrestle.

In the end, Big Daddy was just too damn big. With his leg bent somewhere up behind the small of his back and his head nearly up his own ass, Phil finally cried "Give." The crowd simultaneously groaned and cheered, Big Daddy grinned tiredly. Loosening his grip, he pushed himself up and yanked Phil to his feet. They stood beside one another, bent over, elbows on their knees and heaving.

"Good to see ya back, hot shot," Big Daddy gasped, smacking Phil on the back so hard that he almost knocked him to the ground again.

"Big fucker," Phil replied.

Somebody handed them both a fresh beer, and they drank hungrily as the unmarked swarmed in to assess the damage. Phil's puffy eye was the worst of it, otherwise just standard scratches, scrapes, and bruises. Like being a kid. That's the best way to experience Kalamazoo, because for a kid, it's got everything—woods, lakes, beer, wrestling. Phil decided he wanted it to stay that way for the rest of his trip, so as he and the groom sat on the creaky picnic table and shared whiskey, he jabbed Daddy in his bare ribs and asked, "You're not done, are ya, Mr. Husband?"

Big Daddy turned his head slowly, eyebrows arched. The simplest challenges are the best. Staggering to his great big feet, he roared at the park and the rest of the Zoo and the world "Who wants some?!"

Everybody did, of course.

And so in the middle of that gentle field, wind shushing through the crab apples and gently bobbing the teeter-totters, twenty or so large hairy drunken men gathered in a roaring circle to see who could pin who to the earth. They cheered like Romans around mouthfuls of meat and beer as Big Daddy purged the line of challengers. There went Little Barnes through the air, then through a Styrofoam beer cooler (an empty sliced him wicked above his eye, and he war-painted his face with the blood). Ike leapt and was caught mid-flight, snapped into a bundle of arms and legs. Big Barnes sprinted at him, and Big Daddy extended his leg out straight to floor him with the flat of his foot. And the next, and the next. Perched on the end of his picnic table, Phil applied a cold can of beer to his swollen eye and caught up with each of the guys as the groom dispatched them.

After about an hour or so of this, the Bug brothers, Bobby and Mattie, came loping over the hill, hands stuffed in their pockets.

Bobby strode up, Mattie trailing a couple steps behind, the same way they'd traveled when they lived in the house across from Phil's family, and when Bobby stopped a couple steps from the grill, his brother stopped the appropriate distance behind him. No one noticed them, or else no one cared.

Big Daddy poured beer over himself to rinse off the dirt and grass. Phil hunted up the mustard for a fresh brat. Bobby hovered there on the edge like a
specter, waiting, stoned, bleary gaze ranging over the group and his own
bloodshot world. Finally, after dropping his brat and heading for the grill to
pluck a fresh one, Phil did see Bobby, and was a hundred times more discon-
certed than he had been seeing the whole group earlier.

Bobby Bug. In the flesh. The most feral animal in the Zoo. The only one
who might have given him a run was his old buddy Richie Starr, but Richie
had died young. Bobby hadn't changed at all: steel-toe work boots, jeans older
than Jesus and a Sabbath T-shirt, Caterpillar hat yellow and backwards with an
oily pony-tail drooping from the bill. Except, Phil thought, his face. Still narrow and sharp and unctuous, like a greasy knife. But thinner. Withered. Even
stoned and slack that face was evil with evil, still young and at the same time
just this edge of old, his entire life threatening to catch up with him at once.
Phil imagined wrinkles as articulate as the ash on a cigarette burned into that
young face. Mattie was a younger, blonder, simpler version of the same. If it
hadn't been for the promise of free beer and strippers later on, they wouldn't
have crawled out from under their respective rocks. Phil wondered what he
and Bobby would speak of.

Before he had a chance to find out, though, Bobby, without once remov-
ing his hands from his pockets, shouted "If you faggots are done grab-assin',
we got a tee-time in thirty minutes at Old Mill." And then he turned without
another word and started back for the cars. He gave no indication of having
seen Phil. Or anyone else, for that matter.

A few whoops burst from the crowd. One carload of guys tore out after
fresh beer; another snuffed the coals on the grills and packed up the remaining food and the cooler. The rest, Phil included, moseyed at a fine lazy pace
toward the vehicles. Phil hopped in the back of someone's pick-up to ride to
the links, laughing with the rest of them as the gaunt, unsmiling image Bobby
Bug burned in his head.

Golf courses can spot a bachelor party a mile away, a couple pick-up
trucks splashing drunks over the sides plus the go-get-more-beer car, a
Mustang jammed full of screaming jokers. They trail crumpled empties from
the parking lot to the clubhouse, where they mill and curse as the least-drunk
guy talks turkey with Fred Golf Course (who always has a mustache, or at
least looks like he should). Half the party shadows the store, quietly flipping
balls at one another or loudly discussing pussy. Big Daddy's got a driver
cocked over his shoulder, pretending he's about to club Bobby Bug's stoned

head in, Ike's plunged his fist into a fishbowl of colored tees, coolly filling his pockets. The rest, Phil included, remain outside tossing back beers and yelling at the guys inside to hurry the fuck up and generally scaring the funny hats off of every dink who's there to just golf. After they haggle a group rate for eighteen holes, you can count on at least six violent cart collisions before they reach the first tee; there, the group takes turns whistling shots at the 18th, the road, and the parking lot before pounding the fairway into a herd of divots. Other golfers, birds, squirrels, and snakes flee before them as they advance from hole to hole. The tell-tale broken flag is their mark. The clubhouse manager counts their money, slips it in his pocket, and sighs on an elbow. He'll boot them by the 6th, and then the party is on to Benny's to kill the rest of the afternoon until the strippers arrive.

A dirty red pick-up truck slashed across the open field behind Benny's barn, lurched sharply up on two wheels, and snapped like elastic back in the direction it had come. Over the forest on the far end of the tall grass the afternoon sun burned dark, sooty orange. The truck swiped across the field in wide, abrupt diagonals, and every time it zagged a new direction the boys in back steadied themselves against the flatbed's sides just long enough to let roar another round of rifle shot into the air. The screaming engine swallowed their cheers.

"Fuckers are gonna kill each other with those damn guns."

"Fuck it," Bobby replied.

Phil snorted back. The two of them leaned against the side of a weathered gray-brown barn midway between the field and the house. About a dozen guys had gone shootin', and another dozen were in the cool of the barn throwing darts and watching porno. All of them were drinking.

Bobby Bug and Phil had remained outdoors to watch the gunmen blast at the clouds. The heat, as it had all day, hung over all like a net, tightening around the pair and drawing them closer with each afternoon hour—Bobby'd ridden to the course with Mattie; on the links, he'd wound up in a foursome two ahead of Phil, getting high and driving the cart but not golfing, always in sight and shouting distance of one another but only that close. Then Bobby had hitched with Little Barnes over to Benny's and Phil was in the back of Big Barnes' truck, separated from Bobby by vehicle and yellow line and a hail of whizzing empties as the two pick-ups raced the country drag side-by-side. Now that they were here, now that they were drunk, now that they were just goddam tired of the goddam heat, Phil Lockwood and Bobby Bug finally resigned themselves to being caught together again.

"Fuckin' hot," Bobby said.

"You bet." On cue, they both ran a beer bottle across their foreheads. It didn't do either much good. Bobby skinned off his shirt.

"Jesus Christ, Bobby. The hell happened to you?"

"What?"

Bobby stared blankly at Phil, sweat gleaming off his sides. There was nothing wrong with him; if anything, he looked more fit than Phil remembered. Throwing sheet steel will pack muscle on your bones as sure as a health club. But the arcing blue lines that peeked around the edges of Bobby's ribs and neck made Phil stop and squint.

"Oh, this," Bobby said calmly, jerking a thumb over his shoulder. He grinned and spun.

Phil had had a million and one predictions for Bobby once he'd seen him at the park that morning, with no real chance yet to confirm or deny any of them, but this was unexpected. Bobby had transformed his back into a menagerie of random, staring eyeballs. Tattoos. Big ones the size of eight-balls and tiny ones clustered like grapes; bulging, furious eyes and flat tired ones; eyes that wandered dreamily off and dedicated, pagan eyes that watched the world. The ink appeared well-settled, not faded but deep, a few years old. Cost a fortune, Phil guessed, and then felt disturbed at how plainly he'd ratified Kalamazoo bohemianism. In New York he struggled through days where he wanted to wring the neck of every Village new jack hippie he saw, their beads and their scarves and their flannel and their Rasta caps and of course their goddam tattoos. Safe little Hell's Angels, right. The Midwest-in-you must die harder as you age, Phil decided. And now the same bullshit in the Zoo, Bobby Bug painted up in fad. But Phil had had too long a day already to really care the way he felt he should. Plus, it was Bobby.

Another shotgun blast shook him back to life. Bobby craned his neck round, still grinning. "Pretty cool, huh?"

"Jesus, Bobby. You're not even thirty. You might have to live with that shit another forty years."

"Fuck it." Thumbing a smoke from his jeans pocket, he turned to settle his eyeballs against the corner of the barn and face Phil again. Phil slumped beside him, the nylon of his gym pullover rasping against the rough wood, and they stood there in silence until the wall bucked from the inside. More wrestling. Shaking their heads in rehearsed unison, they both stepped away. Phil whisked a couple lawn chairs out of the sun into the shade of the barn, and they both sat carefully (there is not a big guy alive who hasn't crushed a lawn chair). After mildly watching the truck for a couple puffs, Bobby pointed at Phil and asked, "What about you, 'Roid Head? Wanna get inked? I gotta pal . . ."

"Don't touch the shit," Phil replied, thumping his chest and wondering just how much pot Bobby had smoked on the links. "Hell, I even quit drinking. Five years now."

Bobby nodded at the beer in Phil's hand. "Yup."

But he understood, even more than he knew. Bobby Bug was the kind of guy, especially at twenty-nine, having already given up on his life (and he understood this, too), that just feels when they understand something, rather than the type that does or even can articulate exactly what it is he understands. And Phil understood this because he usually relied upon his New York friend Benjamin to help him articulate things (a rare thing—articulation was another citified parlor game to Phil). What they both understood at that moment was that they each still knew the other better than either would care to admit—honesty is too close to vulnerability—and part of that understanding meant accepting things they wouldn't believe of the other. Like Bobby's tattoos. Like Phil's sobriety. Just simple factoids to jam into the mental file of the person you knew so well, no examination needed.

They swilled off the top of their cans, another shotgun blast tore the air. They glanced again at the field, in time to see the truck whip around for another pass, Ike pounding its horn the whole way. Phil thought the field looked more and more like a tic-tac-toe board for a retard. The wind shifted, muting their happy noise and carrying a rich farm scent, and Phil sneered at the smell. He and Bobby sat in silence until Bobby finally broke the protective disinterest.

"So," he began.

"So."

"See that last Tyson fight?"

"Nope."

"Sucked."

"Yeah?"

"One round. Some white guy. Gorilla beat the hell outta him."

"Yup."

They danced, watched the field and talked to the air, little questions and smaller answers. Occasionally one or the other would shift in his chair (carefully), and the other would shoot the mover a rude look until he settled again. Finally Bobby, drunk and understanding that it had been enough, picked up his chair and spun it to face Phil. Phil straightened, expecting Bobby to explode into light or something equally tremendous.

"Seriously though, man," Bobby began, narrowing his brow and lowering his voice to let Phil know this was the part to take seriously.

Phil marveled. Not just that Bobby had taken the first step past understood waters—Bobby and the abstract were at total odds with one another (mostly because Bobby couldn't get high or get off on the abstract, even accidentally)—but also that he had the gall to do it seriously. This piece of shit, Phil grimaced. Takes his life as seriously as a comic book ever since he learned to catch a buzz off a whip cream can, but he pulls that low voice shit on me so now I gotta take him seriously. 'Cause he says so.

Phil'd gotten at least a moment of the low voice from almost everyone today. Hell, at the golf course it was low voices from the third hole on. And with "Seriously though, man," the Phil Lockwood justification of New York City begins.

Friend: "So, things are good, huh?"

You: "They're all right. I like it."

Friend, with the low voice: "Seriously though, man." Like you're lying.

So you tell them about your job at the gym and the celebrity girls that come with it. That always impresses them, especially if they're married. You talk about the bars, not because you go anymore, but because they are an option; the fact that you can turn them down means more than any ribald story about the blow job you got in the bathroom buying coke from a four foot punk rock girl with six safety pins in her eyebrow and dirigible tits. And the friend presses with the goddam questions. Yes, it's big. Yes, it's expensive. No, I ain't been mugged. Yes, lotta blacks. And Chinese. And Cubans, Puerto Ricans, Arabs, Indians, anyone you can think of that we didn't grow up with. No, there's not a hooker on every corner, but there is a bum. Yes, no, yes, no, until you just want to grind your friend's bones to meal. And as they hear you grow weary of their unending fucking questions their voice finally drops so goddam low only a whale could hear them ask "So things are good, huh? Seriously?" insinuating that things just might not be, or else hoping so, and you want to detonate because it's the same fucking question they started with.

Bobby was staring at Phil.

How serious should I be? Phil wondered. I don't drink, and I'm drunk. A couple hundred yards from me's a group of guys in the back of a truck firing guns at the sky. A couple more hours and there'll be strippers in the barn. And Bobby's back is covered in eyeballs. How serious could I be? But Bobby's staring at Phil with that bottomless look on his face, dark and sad because he's smart enough to know he's missing something but not quite smart enough to know what. Bobby could never be this insightful with someone he didn't know so well. It certainly wasn't planned. Real friends never plan to be insightful on you. They just are.

"I just told you."

"No, but. I mean . . ." He struggled, chewing his lip. Phil understood right then that Bobby wanted to somehow ask if he had grown up. It was a brave question, because if Phil had, Bobby was fucked. He understood that. "I mean . . ." Bobby was vulnerable right now, which forced Phil to meet him there, at that vulnerable spot. If Bobby revealed that he cared for Phil and his emotional well-being, Phil, whether he wanted to or not, would have to reveal it back if he really answered. And if he didn't really answer, that would be revealing, too. "I mean . . ." Bobby kept stubbing his tongue, each trip a step closer to revelation, and they both could feel the few short feet between them growing thicker than any heat had all day.

"I mean . . . is it what you want?"

The guns in the field blared again, but this time neither of them looked up. They held each other eye to eye, the same way they had back when they would reckon that another fifth was a good idea. Phil swallowed and Bobby, understanding he was on the verge of over-extending himself, waited.

"Yeah."

They both relaxed, slouching again, comfortable in the guilt that Phil's cop out afforded. He hadn't had to answer if he'd grown up, wouldn't have known the answer had Bobby used those words, and Bobby hadn't had to deal with any answer. Comfort, that's all guilt is. This non-conversation, this obligated friendship had just coalesced reams and reams of psycho-babble into the simple comfort of guilt. It is a thin, thin line that separates guilt and nostalgia, whichever you need to get over your decisions. These are useless things, just like talking.

A burst of honking from the pickup interrupted them from anything more comforting. There were shouts from inside the barn, and the door crashed open to see what all the noise was about. Barnes had tumbled over the truck's tailgate, and every time his brother tried to haul him back in, Ike would punch the accelerator and leave him lurching. Bobby's face hardened again as he watched.

"Barnes is gonna get killed," Phil commented.

"Fuck it," Bobby said. "'Nother beer?"

"Whiskey inside?"

"Yup."

"Yup."

* * *

Things were blurry by the time the girls arrived. Since the sun had dipped beneath the far end of the shooting field, the new blood that had been trickling into the party all day had surged—Mike Garret and Binkoe, Roger and Hip, a Treimstra, a Baker, Vanderpold, VanKrapp (his real name, sadly). All the brothers—the Kramers, the Veldes, the Stouts, the Breyers, a couple less significant sets. Phil, at peace with Bobby and everybody else in the Zoo, peacefully drunk, tottered through the forest of big bodies, pausing long enough to grasp a sweaty hand and moving on before the grins could devolve into more low voices. A fresh grill flared with fresh meat when Big Daddy's daddy and granddaddy rumbled up in a brick truck, and the party continued to welcome anyone who knew anybody. Ungerly, Frick, Billy Smack. Trace, Lane, Keilwalter. Fatback, Newt and Ute. Before long there was no telling who was who in the light of the bonfire that blazed in the pit beside the barn. When there were finally too many faces with too many names, the day and his out-of-shape liver hit Phil like an anchor and he dragged himself up to the barn's loft to steal a nap on a stack of burlap bags. He slept for an hour until a rumble of applause woke him.

Still drunk and rubbing his eyes, Phil peered over the edge of the loft. The lights were on, orange-yellow wall mounts that left Phil in shadows as they illuminated the floor and its raving throng. Tall thin Ike was snapping excitedly across the dirt, kicking up dust and stopping at every cluster of guys he crossed to jaw wildly, arms cupped in front of his chest. Somebody threw open the barn doors, and through them Phil saw the idling red pickup. The driver hit the high beams, flooding the center of the barn floor in real light, and then the walls began to shake with the rhythm of seventy clapping callused hands. Benny wove amongst them to the center of the room with a boom box, extension cord trailing behind him. Phil wearily saw it was time to come down and get back to work.

As he descended, half-awake and half-drunk, the rhythmic clapping took on the steady throb of a pulse, and the beat suddenly began to invigorate Phil. Half-drunk and half-awake, it seemed more and more to him with each rung of the ladder that the cheers were for him. He could see it: He was a hero… for being home, for being alive, for bearing all the goddam low voices. Maybe just for remembering all of their names. That seemed enough to Phil—he'd remembered them, smiled at every damn one of them after all these years. That's heroic isn't it?

Then the girls sauntered into the middle of the ring, the roars trebled, and Phil's heroic imagination wilted. They cheers weren't for him. He touched down on the barn floor and found a spot in the shadows outside of the headlights where he could still see.

The girls didn't impress him, just your garden variety strippers in denim skirts, shiny bras, and wobbly heels. The blonde had ribs like a xylophone, and as they strut out of their skirts, Phil saw tiny pocks of cellulite dimpling the brunette's ass and thighs. They need a visit to the gym, he decided. But he couldn't take his eyes off them, either. Here they come, naked and hanging and smiling like Easter into this sweaty zoo. Sure, they've got an escort in the car, but every man, woman, and child in the G-K area knew this mob would happily chew him to pulp if it came to that. Yet these girls, not a whit of concern; they tame lions with feathers, all teeth and tits and twat, and the lions lay down to roar. Phil's notions of heroism faded further.

So with the girls flanking the boom box in the center of the barn floor and waving stupidly to the drooling guys, Ike finally hauled Big Daddy out of the crowd and into the light, lurching along on his toes as he kept one arm hooked about the groom's collar. The other hand held his beer. The girls rushed with short steps to help, each taking an arm and pulling until the three of them had herded the giant man into the center. They held onto the groom, manacles of flesh, as Ike flapped his arms to quiet the howling crowd.

"All right now!" he shouted. "Everybody shut the fuck up or ya'll ain't gonna see no titties! Ya hear?"

The blonde popped a boob from her bra, and the animals pressed closer, desperate to break their invisible cage and get at the girls. Ike scolded her, she flipped him the bird, the crowd roared some more. Ike finally calmed everyone to an agitated murmur (he was holding the girls' money, after all), then smiled broadly and grabbed Big Daddy again, who just looked embarrassed.

"I tell you what, you big motherfucker," Ike began, still shouting. His voice was hoarse with drinking, and his ears glowed in the high beams. "I'm the Best Man here, and long as I known your ugly ass, I can't believe anyone's dumb enough to marry you."

The expected preamble drew the expected laughs, except from Big Daddy's daddy, who didn't allow the slightest curl of a smile to besmirch his lips. Old school. He sidled up beside his own father and each rubbed their beards, graying and gray. They folded their arms across their chests and simmered like wise old dragons.

"But because you did . . ." Ike went on, staggering as he spoke. He took a sip of his beer. "Because you did . . . fuck, what the fuck was I gonna say?" The boos poured over him, straw was thrown, Big Daddy frowned. "Fuck it," he finally cried. "Let's see some naked girls!"

More cheers, blaring music, wiggling girls, pint bottles passing hand to mouth to hand, the keg taking an absolute beating. All was right in the Zoo.

Phil hung on the fringe, smiling with the rest of the crowd, nodding when he was slapped on the back, peeking between the large bodies to observe. All he could see of the girls was the tops of their heads as they wrestled Big Daddy's jeans to his ankles. In bright white boxers the size of a movie screen the groom now stood proud as a mountain, hands on his hips and cracking jokes. Phil watched and forced beer down his throat until he felt his brain slowly refill with electricity.

He saw Bobby across the circle, beyond the girls and Big Daddy. Like Phil, he was grinning and bobbing his head to the bump and grind, and also like Phil he stood back in the shadows. His eyes were so red they glowed across the barn. Compared to the rest of the caterwauling, Bobby was calm. Like Phil.

Fourteen years ago, shortly after Phil and Bobby had begun driving, Big Barnes turned twenty-one, and mean as that Barnes was he got a job bouncing the Mermaid Lounge, the Zoo's preeminent titty bar. Years before that, Gil Lockwood had played poker with Bart Barnes, which meant Big Barnes had seen Phil every Monday night when Gil dragged his kid to the game because his wife was out with the Ladies of the Church. The end result was that Big Barnes actually liked Phil. And even though he thought the Bug kid was a worthless little shit, Barnes had let Phil and Bobby visit the club as long as they didn't come too often. By the time the pair turned eighteen, even that rule had been relaxed—Phil and Bobby drank themselves stupid for free five nights a week (and also dropped a hundred bucks between them, one bill at a time). They would even lie about getting married just to get the bachelor special that Big Daddy was about to get. So this bacchanalia in Benny's barn was hard for either of them to go ape over.

Images of Bobby and a random cross-section of strippers had taken Phil's mind elsewhere, anyway.

His last summer in town, when he and Bobby had lived with Sandy, the boys always had to jump in the lake before coming home from the titty flop so she wouldn't smell the baby powder and four dollar perfume on them; even Bobby had to bathe it off, because Sandy was smart, and if she smelled it on Bobby, she'd know his evil twin had been there, too. She didn't mind so much that they went, she was as much fun as either of them, she just didn't want to smell it on Phil all night in her bed.

Through the undulation of hairy cheering men Phil saw one of the strippers gagging Big Daddy with her bikini bottom while the other knelt and shook her brunette mane over his crotch in a mock blow job.

Damn, he thought. Why do I think of her now? That stuff was years done and gone, as dead as her folks. He hadn't seen or thought of her since he didn't know when. Not since he quit drinking, he was sure. And when he did drink, he'd find someone to help him not think of her, a drinking buddy or a fuck buddy. He certainly had enough drinking buddies tonight. And why, of all things, do I remember she only cared about the shit that I threw in her face, which was mostly the stuff I did without her, anyway?

Now the strippers poured beer down Big Daddy's chest and licked it off. Now they had him crouch so they could lick it from each other's tongues an inch from his face.

He saw her image, Sandy's, in the doorway to the tool room across the profane circle, blue eyes cross and tapping her foot. She began to blitz him from all over the barn, peering from the loft, squirming between every third reveler, sitting on Ike's shoulders. Sandy Sandy everywhere, three apples tall and a swirl of red hair, or cactus orange, or blonde when she let it grow without dying it, gazing at the stars over the lake from beneath him and climbing trees in the woods behind her house and shooting across the Michigan country side in her lime Nova, all those Sandys plus a thousand more looking at or looking for Phil.

He suddenly felt like Bobby Bug: Watched, a thousand eyeballs at his back. He shook his head, faded another step into the shadows. Oh fuck, Bobby, he moaned to himself, gulping beer and slicing his gaze through the barn. Don't ask me if I've grown up right now, 'cause neither of us is gonna like what the answer does to us.

"Phil, you big old New York fuck!"

The slap was hard enough to make him sputter on his beer. Phil turned to find Benny on the other end of it. Benny'd grown into their group because he was the only one with weed as regular as Bobby. Phil tried to smile at him, but it didn't work.

"Whoa ho," Benny exclaimed, all teeth and glassy red eyes. "You're blasted, dude!" Phil sneered—Benny wasn't who he needed to see right now—but then Benny shoved a fresh bottle of Jack into his hand and broadened his grin. "Drink up!" Phil glanced at the bottle, felt its weight, then looked back to the center of the ring. Someone had hauled out a stool for Big Daddy and the girls had assumed the see-saw position, sitting face-to-face on his shoulders, a crotch across the back of his neck, the other's cunt firmly in his face, so that when they straightened their legs they could see-saw on his head. Phil turned back to Benny, who was still beaming at him. Strippers, Benny; Sandy, bottle. Phil finally shrugged for Benny's benefit, tipped a belt, and felt his neck unknot.

"Aaall right, man!" Benny laughed, nodding, already fading back into the crowd but leaving the bottle in Phil's hand. "All right."

The deeper Phil got into the bottle, the less he was able to shake the idea that the blonde stripper was somehow singling him out of the crowd. The girls had finished with Big Daddy and were writhing now for anyone who waved a dollar bill, but Phil felt the blonde searching the stew of wild eyes for the quiet stranger in the back, and the feeling made him scowl. The Lockwood scowl is cosmic. Spence has it, Phil, Gil and all the Lockwoods back in the old country have it, scowling as they plant their tulips and raise their dykes in the merry old Netherlands. Phil kept sipping, whiskey hot in his mouth and the lines in his forehead sharpening. Why didn't anyone ask me about Sandy today, he wondered, confused. What's that mean? He drained the bottle, spun, and hurled it into the dark corner where it vaporized into wet shards. A dozen heads spun from the light, but when they saw Phil they cheered against his scowl. And what do they mean by all that cheering? Through the raft of faces he saw the xylophone girl. He suddenly felt like he was at the gym, the mirrors reflecting dozens of silent, foreign eyes straining to catch a glimpse of the Big Guy. The blonde's eyes were predatory, more menacing than the seductive glances of the leotard-clad gym-girls. In response he stalked out the open barn doors and swung them shut behind. The high beams screamed against the dull gray wood.

It was quieter out here by the fire. Its heat washed over Phil's hips and bare knees as he tried to relax by gazing up at the stars. In New York, stars are a novelty; the Zoo has all the fuckin' stars you'll ever want, the night sky is corrugated with them. Phil counted them until he felt himself enough to forget his injury and remember he was drunk, and as he calmed he saw he wasn't alone. A smattering of guys stood around the rim of the fire, their conversations drifting across the flames like whispers. Before they could notice him staring and have an excuse to stare back, Phil concentrated on the field behind them. Eager with fireflies, it wasn't so different than the sky.

From out of that twinkling space on the far side of the fire pit a tall, thin shade emerged. Phil squinted as it shambled free of the fluttering shadows and around the fire. It continued without a word until it stood grimly beside him.

It was Spence.

"Hey," Phil said, lightly startled, and gripped his brother's hand loosely. "When'd you get over, man?"

"Left the shop around 7:30," Spence answered, and as he released his brother's hand, Phil sized him up. They still saw eye to eye, and Spence was still thick. Only now did it register with Phil that Spence had limped as he approached. Football. With his back to the flames, his brother's face was dark and hollow, and his mouth barely moved as he spoke, his voice cadaverous. "Got here a little after eight. You?"

"This morning. For the party."

They nodded at one another, then turned side by side and shoulder to shoulder toward the fire as someone pitched an untapped beer can into it. The aluminum quickly began to buckle and bulge, its colors blacken, the silver dull. The tab burst and beer sizzled and danced over the embers.

"Get in all right?"

"Yeah. Drank on the plane."

"Hmmph," Spence grunted, and for a moment the dismal sound cleared Phil's bleary head. Spence had had a sobering effect on people he met even before following his big brother's cue and forswearing the bottle. The football injury had done most of it, and what little smile had remained disappeared the day he sobered. Now, unless you were his brother (or perpetually drunk like Bobby), he's downright chilling. But Phil understood. Spence hadn't escaped the Zoo. He hasn't been for several years (Phil wondered if he'd come again), but Spence drinks when he visits New York like Phil drinks here, and for the same reason.

"Busy?" Phil asked. It was summer, when he knew the flower shop was slow, but he asked out of courtesy.

"Eh," he shrugged. "Load of flats today. Greenhouse-full."

"Yeah?"

"Yeah."

They hate this, both of them. There's no place for small talk in the world of big guys. It's just too small. Bad as a low voice, especially with Phil drunk and Spence still wishing he was. And though the miles and the troubles and their obligations to being big had caused the brothers to forget how to talk, it had also long ago taught them both to tolerate the things they hated. They both searched for something more meaningful to say, something they wanted to say, until their silence was gratefully interrupted by the sudden arch and drop of the music from the barn. They turned to see a tall, lanky silhouette legging it toward the fire, a tipsy hitch in his stride. Picking around the edges of the fire, the figure circled until he recognized Phil and stepped beside him and Spence.

"Hey, man," Bobby nodded, and before Phil could reply, he'd plucked a spliff from the breast pocket of his T-shirt with one hand and a Zippo from his jeans with the other. He toked a nice red run off the joint and extended it to

Phil, who was too drunk to care, then peeked around the bigger man and saw Spence. "Hey, man," Bobby wheezed. "You're here too. Hey."

Spence nodded back.

Only half-understanding their silence, Bobby shifted for a moment before jerking a thumb over his shoulder toward the barn. "Coupla skanks, huh?"

Phil shrugged and inhaled sharply, thinking they looked the same as any other Zoo strippers he'd ever seen. Spence added that he hadn't seen them, but Phil's shrug had killed Bobby's interest; he squatted to rub something that only he could see from the toe of his boot. Phil grimaced down at him. Bobby had always treated Spence like shit. Sure, they'd included Spence in a fair share of adventures, let him hang out the summer Phil and Bobby shacked up with Sandy, Bobby had even gotten howlingly drunk with him without Phil. But all that was just drinking. When shit came to shout, Phil'd never shaken the impression that Bobby saw Spence as some unwieldy tumor growing off his friend. He couldn't imagine the relationship had improved with him gone and Spence dry.

(Sandy, on the other hand, Phil's brain whispered . . . she'd treated Spence like royalty. Like he'd earned an extra helping of respect for bearing both his older brother and his older brother's incorrigible best friend. Phil made a mental note, that he would forget, to ask Spence if he'd kept up with her at all, then proffered his brother the joint.)

Spence took it tentatively, either because it was Bobby's, Phil guessed, or because he'd dropped that habit, too, but then his brow arched in a "Why not?" and he drew until his chest swelled like a thundercloud. As he passed it back to Bobby he glanced at Phil just long enough so that the brothers could match shrugs the same way they'd once matched smiles. The three stood in a small silent triangle passing the joint until Bobby popped the smoldering roach into his mouth and gulped.

"Hey," Bobby suddenly hiccupped, nudging Phil. "You wanna blow this place?" Spence might as well have been a ghost. "I got some weed at my place," he added, trying to sweeten the pot.

"I just got stoned, Bobby."

"Fuck it, we can just kick back and drink a few."

"And for someone who doesn't drink, I'm really goddam drunk."

Spence snickered lightly at that.

Bobby shifted again, planted his hands in his pockets, puzzled or agitated or both. He glanced across the fire quickly, suddenly wary of being watched, it seemed, and when he saw everyone on the other side still doing their own thing he turned back to Phil. "You sure, man?"

His voice was almost pleading, a tone Phil had heard from him a thousand times. It meant Bobby wanted to take it up a notch. Code Red. Out of sheer muscle memory Phil felt himself flinch at the bait, but caught himself.

"Think I'm fine, man. Maybe after the wedding tomorrow."

Bobby squinted, trying to understand, then gave up and spat. "Yeah, maybe. Fuck it."

The three stood not talking, letting the empty space fill with laughter from the other side of the fire and the muted beat from the barn. The Lockwood brothers turned again in unison to watch the fire, deliberately, like they'd made a telepathic decision; Bobby scuffed his feet at the charred bits in between the confused squints Phil kept ignoring. Within ten minutes, Phil and Spence had brothered Bobby out.

"I'm gonna hit it, man," he said, still digging his toe around.

"Already?"

Bobby looked back up at Phil, eyes semi-hard, like it was a challenge. "Yup. Headin' out to Cap's." Cap's was a rough bar on the far far outskirts of the Zoo. Like everywhere else, Phil and Bobby had history there. Phil felt the twinge again, till he recognized it as another ploy.

"Alright. See ya tomorrow."

"Yup."

Phil offered his hand, but Bobby'd already turned. When Spence yelled a half-teasing "Bye," Bobby waved without a look back and staggered for the cars, nearly falling when he began to dig through his pockets for his keys. And then he was gone.

Once he had vanished, Phil and Spence turned to the bonfire again, their safe spot, and watched the red and yellow and orange and pink weave in and out of one another, the brothers side by side and silent as Stonehenge. Silence, such silence you could hear mice padding across the floor of the field, worms wriggling away from the hot earth under the fire. Libraries and cathedrals yearn for this kind of quiet. Somewhere on the moon something ticked.

"Sure is quiet," Spence finally said.

That popped it—the dope took hold and they busted with laughter like it was the newest thing going. Like they hadn't since they were kids, or since they had both drank. They both fought to stifle themselves to a snicker, but when they turned to face one another a fresh batch of giggles bloomed. Now it was good to see Spence. Phil threw an arm around his brother.

"Come a long way, hasn't he?" Phil asked.

"Shit," Spence snorted. "I was running a load of flowers over to Wickes' a couple weeks ago." Wickes' is a funeral home. When someone is married, when someone is born, when someone dies in Kalamazoo, there's a Lockwood there with something bright in his hands. "I'm running a load of flowers to Wickes'," Spence repeated, mouth working wider and wider as he found his way around all the words, "and I'm at the flower door in back. About a half-dozen sprays and this giant white and red rose casket dress I gotta cart in. The Boldersma funeral."

"Not Miss Boldersma?" Phil repeated. She'd been their Sunday school teacher a million years ago.

"Yup."

"Shit. I didn't know she died."

Spence cocked his head, a lazy shrug. "Just ran out of juice. Can't keep living just 'cause you're gone." Phil straightened too subtly for his brother too see in the flickering dark. Spence kept grinning as he continued to tell. "Anyway, who do you think comes through the door?"

"Get out? What was he doing there? He didn't know Miss B. He can't even spell church."

"Naw. He came to see Benny. Benny works there now," Spence chortled. Phil had a quick sight of Bobby and Benny lounging on a casket in oily T-shirts, sweeping the hair from their eyes and grinning a crooked 'He-ey' at the mourners. He laughed with his brother. "So, while he's helping me unload the flowers," Spence continued, his voice starting to rise, "he tells me sometimes he makes a few bucks helping Benny load in the new caskets. But get this. They gave Benny a key."

"Ah shit," Phil laughed.

"Yup. And so Bobby starts telling me how him and Benny hang out after hours in the basement. In the draining room."

"Draining room?"

Spence's voice went up another notch. "Where they prep the bodies. He took me down and showed me. Must have been high, being so friendly. Anyway, it's this big white room, air-conditioned as hell. Just freezing cold. Fulla long metal tables, and at the head of every one there's a giant sink with tubes and shit they hook into your body to suck out the blood and pump you full of embalming fluid."

Other people around the fire began looking over at them as they giggled.

"So these two jokers, what they do is hang out down there after everyone goes home and blaze up with the corpses. They make bongs out of the replacement tubing in the closet. Christ, he pulled a joint while I was down there with him. Like, one, I'm gonna get stoned with him; two, I'm gonna get stoned when there's a chance of them bringing some dead guy down; and three, I'm gonna go back to the shop—and Dad—high. Jesus.

"And then," Spence choked, trying unsuccessfully to hold his voice steady for the topper, "and then, he asked if we had any extra work at the shop. Could he be a delivery boy."

They both split. Bobby working for their dad is just about the most ridiculous thing ever. Gil Lockwood would be making Bobby's casket dress before the end of his first day.

They were laughing hard now, rocking on their heels and lightly catching each other for balance. Both brothers felt good, elevated beyond the brambles they'd let grow amongst them and the bars each had built around himself. Howling. Phil forget he was so damn drunk and stoned and slapped his arm around his brother Spence, ready to go higher until a small voice interrupted.

"Are you the guy who lives in New York?"

It was the xylophone blonde. Except for an army coat that engulfed her, she was naked, which explained why they hadn't heard her sidle up; naked people are the quietest people. Phil and Spence, choking on their laughter, were too startled to respond. But she knew she'd found her man.

"Hi," she said, stepping between them but looking square into Phil's eyes. "I'm Missy." Xylophone smiled coquettishly, and then like a peace offering she added, "They told me inside where you lived."

"They did."

"Yeah," she smiled.

Phil took her in. Straw blonde hair pushed behind either ear, and when she smiled the fire exposed a gap in her front teeth wide as a whistle. She let the coat slide down to her elbows, and he saw that her tits were small and loose; the temperature change from the barn had puckered her nipples (which helped him quit staring at that gap before he got caught). The rest of her was skinny meat, and a small sober part of his mind began plotting a workout regimen to firm her up in all the ways that he liked—tone the arms, little pec work to bolster that sag, some light lunges to tighten the glutes and hammies so you can bounce a quarter off 'em. They never knew it, but every routine he threw at his female clients he designed around his dick. Xylophone had a young body fashioned out of cheap beer, a bigger project than most of his New York clientele.

And, clearly nervous that he hadn't said anything to her yet, she spoke again.

"Do you know Robert DeNiro?"

The Lockwoods roared with laughter. Phil wondered what exercise he could conjure up to fix the hole in her head. Xylophone started to laugh along with them before asking, "What's so funny?"

Between them, Spence and Phil managed to choke out that nothing was funny, which made them laugh all the harder. She shrugged, satisfied, and asked if she could stand closer to the fire. Before either could answer, she stepped forward and turned her rear to the flames so that she faced Phil.

Like Bobby, she understood what to do. In this case, admire Phil, especially for no reason. She busted a gut at everything the brothers said, even when their jokes were so inside she couldn't have had the slightest clue what they were talking about. The army coat eventually slid to her ankles as she casually ran her nails across his gym top, letting the synthetic hiss fill his ears. She gabbed on and on about her vision of New York, never been and never would, and for a moment Phil feared she'd spring the low voice on him. But in her ultimate wisdom she never did, and soon she had what she wanted—his attention. Adulation is just another way to get drunk. Phil began to ogle her. The fire at her back ringed her in gold, and now that she had kicked her coat away, Phil leered at the thin down covering her arms, her legs, every curve the soft glare illuminated. In a junior high biology class he had watched a film on single-cell organisms. One of them was the paramecium, a little blob awash in tiny hairs called cilia. The cilia flagellate to propel the blob. Phil suddenly thought of the girl as a paramecium; the gentle backlight made each individual hair on her body stand out separate and vibrant from the others.

"Hey. Hey, cutie." It was Xylophone. Thoroughly intoxicated, Phil shook his head and flinched when he focused and saw her smiling back. "Yoo hoo. You awake?'

"Uh, yeah, yeah, sure," Phil mumbled. He looked around. Spence had vanished. "Where'd my brother go?"

"I dunno," she said, stepping closer. "He said 'That's that,' and left." She reached to touch his arm, took another step, near enough to breathe on. "But I'm still here." Now she clasped both his arms. Music still throbbed from the barn, but there was no one on the other side of the fire. Phil stood stone-still.

"Why are you so shy?" she asked, sounding doubtful for the first time. She grinned weakly. "You don't have cooties, do you?"

Abandoned, he answered on auto pilot. "Nope."

"Good," she replied, happy again. "'Cause I just got rid of them."

"Alright."

He was drunk as fuck, completely at her mercy, and he knew it. She laughed again, her breasts jiggled. "I guess you must like me now, huh?" he added dryly. She took it as another joke. They always did. She started to say more, but Phil couldn't handle another word, so to shut her up and clear his mind he walked her into the field and fucked her under the stars, fireflies, and everything else.

The Hotel Kalamazoo. Fuck it. Who wants some?

Putting Mama in Big Spring
from *Grassfires,* memoir as novel

When Mama looked down from our front porch upon the ruined face and figure of Daddy as he stumbled out of Uncle Arthur's car, she was stricken into unmoving silence. His familiar corpulence had been reduced to a thin bent reed. Even with the new cane, something we'd never seen him use before, he was having difficulty with the running board and his first several steps. He was nearly sightless.

Six months ago when he'd left us to go to the hospital in San Antonio he'd worn a black eye-patch, staunchly mounting the top step of the dun-colored Pullman car at the train station. There he turned with a frowning wave against the low October sun. From below, teary-eyed, we watched the black eye-patch as it disappeared into the belly of the Pullman. Now his black eye-patch was replaced with a walling glass eye, mucous rimmed from the long trip home. My Daddy returned to us after months and months of War Bonds, and Fire Side Chats, and A Slip of the Lip Can Sink a Ship, and gold stars in windows and death lists in the papers, and kamikazes could blow up your house, and U-Boats lurking off the coast, and Buy a Bond for Freedom, Today!

After unsuccessful eye treatments in a strange hospital four hundred miles away in San Antonio, where neither Mama nor I had ever been, they'd served him up to us with only a little vision left in one eye. No long distance phone calls then—war time. No hearing Daddy's warm, gentle voice breasting the worst of it, bucking *us* up, not even at Christmas. Driving to San Antonio was unthinkable during gas rationing; just imagining herself steering our blue Plymouth over that whole map-web of highways, Mama got a worse case of "heebie-jeebies" than she could "afford to put up with." The cost of round-trip Pullman tickets and one night in a hotel was out of the question.

From him we got envelopes fat with ruled tablet paper. Sometimes we'd find two or three lines, a whole page, or most of a whole letter completely blackened with pencil lead. He couldn't tell if he was scrawling those big, looping words, with his familiar fat l's and t's, right on top of each other over and over. All in the same space. Nearly every week we expected to hear he would be coming home. The doctor would send us a letter! The hospital maybe? We both wrote letters to Daddy at the same time by agreement.

Then one late fall afternoon, sitting on the porch steps in cool sunshine try-ing to decipher the letter the postman had just handed us, Mama finally real-

ized she couldn't make sense out of one single word in Daddy's letter, six flapping pages of it. They slipped from her fingers, I let go of mine, too. Caught
in the perverse little wind picking up from the east, they started moving away
. . . until I gathered them from the Bermuda grass. Those cheap tablet pages,
some shining with solid lead marking on both sides, had the power to with-
hold Daddy's voice. We cried together on the steps by the ivy-covered red
brick chimney and the open front door.

Later he told us he could barely distinguish light during that period, that it
was like living in a pit except for the voices. Gradually over the months that
dragged by in the hospital, he knew light from dark, recognized people and
objects if they were up close.

"Ellen! Ellen! The spitting image of Abe Lincoln!" his brother Arthur said
a dozen times as he delivered Daddy home to us from his own brown Chevy.
He helped Daddy crawl out of the car. I ran out for my first fumbling hug,
while Mama still stared at what was left of her husband. His body was thin
beyond recognition, but his arm was urgent around my waist as he tried to lean
back at a good angle to see me. I squeezed his poor wasted body again, afraid
I'd hurt him, feeling his arms, ribs, and shoulder bones with no padding of
flesh. I ran back to Mama thinking she would surely fly off the porch and join
us, then abandoned her when I saw she wouldn't, and raced back to take
Daddy's other arm. Uncle Arthur, who still had the height, weight, and carriage that Daddy had lost, was looking up toward the porch where Mama
silently waited just at the head of the steps.

"Ellen! Abe Lincoln—You'll see!" he called out to her in his big speech-
maker's voice. He was well known and just as well liked around the state.
Mama said bitterly that Daddy put him through college and a master's degree.
At Daddy's funeral Uncle Arthur confided to me that in his opinion, Mama
had always held Daddy back, only married him anyway for his school
teacher's pittance because she was terrified she'd die of T.B., and that she saw
Daddy as her ticket to the sanatarium and getting well. The "san," she called
it fondly. To hear Uncle Arthur tell it, she was the sole cause of Daddy not
being a "famous educator" in his own time. Not that Daddy wasn't plenty
famous in West Texas, we all knew that. Arthur, until recently, had been
Rehabilitation Director at Huntsville, the most feared of all the penitentiaries
in the Texas Prison System. Daddy said what did Arthur know about rehabilitation, he was liable to get his head shot off. That job, he said more kindly,
nearly busted his brother's heart. "'They don't want rehabilitating,'" he loved
to quote the miserable Arthur, "'they just want out!'"

* * *

The three of us were toiling across the supernally thick turf of Mama's Bermuda grass which was preparing to turn green, Daddy trying to hold onto his grey felt hat with the familiar wide black grosgrain band as he searched for his wife through the windy brilliance of a March spring in Texas. She was still waiting on the porch at the top of the steps, and smelling his death, no doubt.

On the sidewalk below Mama, I hugged Daddy one more time. "You're grown now, grown woman," he said to me solemnly. We were standing below the porch in front of the canna lily and castor bean bed that Mama had blasted out of pure rock with a long crowbar till she exhausted herself. Then, while he still had muscle, Daddy took the crowbar in his hands. I admired the swinging heave of his plump arms and shoulders as he repeatedly assaulted the unforgiving bed of stone till it rang with each stroke, chipping away so the sparks flew, prizing up whole sections of rock.

Near blindness could not rob him of the lightning changes in my body. The gray and red plaid dress with close fitting bodice set off comely breasts and svelte waist, exposed the new long curving line of my body before it fell into soft pleats over my woman's hips; it bespoke approval and achievement! I would wear that dress to school everyday if I could, and I chose the way I wanted to look for Daddy. In this booming three o'clock light off the prairie, he was not so blind as to miss the sharp flash of green from my eyes that looked very much like his. Dub's eyes (one of his affectionate names for Mama) came to mind; *her* eyes were a sort of light warm brown, darker than caramel and always dramatic to him under the black brows.

Up there on the porch, from what he could see of her, she was standing behind a curtain of shade which drew a formidable line between them. Her arms were folded across her chest, waiting inexorably like some terrible justice ready to fall on him. His good maroon sweater was buttoned over her thin print dress. The only movement was the wind rippling her skirts; she'd not budge an inch, he'd wager, till he beached his weary body up there, too. It wrung his heart, but no mind, Dub had a rough time of it and not over yet, not by a long sight, and he could think no more about their unending troubles, but gave himself over to the reunion, whatever it might bring.

"You're sick," Mama said while he was still pulling himself up the steps half led by child and brother, neither me nor Uncle Arthur wanting to seem to lead him. After their awkward hug, Daddy and Mama drew back from each other. "You'll *never* be well." She sounded betrayed.

It was the beginning of an accusation of failure, spoken in a voice which carried also the crumpling of her imminent collapse and retreat from health

and life, a voice which in its weakness was impregnable. It ignored our questions and advice and clumsy efforts to comfort with words. We felt concern. I
said, "Why don't you go lie down? It's your nap-time. We can get supper on
the table; you cooked everything ahead. Let me do the rest!" And Daddy said,
"Sure, Pet, you do just that! Our young lady here can get things on," and
Daddy tried to put a hand on each of our backs at the same time. She managed
to dodge just inside the screen door, her shoulders pinched up like we'd tried
to whip her.

"That's the ticket, Ellen!" Uncle Arthur said. "You'll be like new when
you come to the table." His bushy eyebrows almost met in a worry frown
while he smiled at Mama. He sounded like he was talking to a crowd.

She went to bed. I failed to recognize the enormity of Mama going to bed.

We warmed up the supper she had cooked for us, pork roast, sweet potatoes, and greens. Daddy poked his head into the front bedroom to tell her
everything was on the table. When he came back looking more drawn than
ever, trying to cover it up with a smile, I fixed her a plate of food and brought
it with a fork to her bedside. She was under a pile of covers, more than the
temperature of the house warranted in March. "Not hungry," she whined. Her
nose was red, which meant she'd been crying, and I even ignored that. I was
in one big hurry to get back to the table and the grown-up talk, and refused to
see why she shouldn't want to be there, too.

I put the plate on a straight-backed chair and drew it up to the mattress at
what I guessed was the right point. "There! You can have it when you want
it." She fixed me for a moment with her sick eyes, a kind of piteous look, like
a dog mutely begging not to be shot.

"Why don't you come on in?" I asked. "It's Daddy's first night and I want
to hear what they're saying."

"You go ahead," she said huskily.

I dipped my head Yes, turned on my heel and left, closing the door all the
way with a hard little click, just as I had found it, but without considering the
right way to leave her. My interests had already honed in on the talk rising in
the dining room, the fabulous interplay of rich male voices, Daddy's much
softer than Arthur's. I think I'd dreamed so long of this being a good time, a
happy night—how could it *not* be when Daddy had truly come home?—that I
shut my eyes and ears to every possible signal Mama could resort to.
Something in me said, *This must be good!* So while Mama cried in bed, and
refused her husband and her supper and the company that would go with it, I
took every pleasure I could find in Daddy's being home. I simply craved a
moratorium on loneliness and heavy emotion.

Uncle Arthur stayed the night so we had to make a bed for him on the sofa, Daddy fumbling to help us. Uncle Arthur talked and talked and talked with me and Daddy in his ebullient way. He was then running for the state legislature, and full of political hopes.

Late morning the next day, Daddy and I said our goodbyes to Uncle Arthur as he backed his brown Ford out of the driveway. Mama stayed in her room. At the last minute he said, a little uncomfortably, "Tell Ellen goodbye."

"She needs her sleep," Daddy said, by way of apologizing to Arthur. We hadn't heard a peep out of her.

Toward noon, Daddy was fumbling and groping around in the kitchen, re-acclimating himself to the space and routines he used to know. He was sort of elated and sort of frustrated. I led him around showing him where things were, then he thanked me, and asked me to leave so he could putter around and practice his moves without the embarrassment of someone watching.

Alone, sitting down at the piano in the living room, I needed to inject something *speedier* into this pokey old place where nothing good ever happened for long. I started playing Rachmaninoff's "Prelude in C-sharp-minor," right against the wall that was also the wall of Mama's bedroom on the other side. I played that old dirge, my favorite, soft, but as fast as I could manage those big chords, because when you play it fast, it becomes something else! Mama was still asleep and I was afraid to wake her up and afraid of what she'd be like if I did. Yet, though I played it soft, I must have known that for every key my fingers struck, our common wall became a sounding board to her.

"Go tell Daddy I want to see him!" she hoarsely yelled. I raised up from the piano bench, scattering treble notes in mid-measure. *Me*, call Daddy? When she could just as easy call him herself or get up and go where he *was?* I wanted to see if she looked like she might be getting up, it was almost noon.

I swung open the door with such an excess of force that it *cracked!* against her high chest of drawers, and then came the familiar sound of my framed baby picture plopping face-down onto an embroidered scarf-runner. The shades were drawn, the room dim and cold. In her cave of quilts, Mama was struggling to prop herself up on one elbow, her dark, silver-streaked hair mussed and working out of its knot. Those covers were mostly "breeches quilts" she'd made out of Daddy's old wool pants; they were heavy as bricks, in my opinion. She looked aggrieved, somewhat flushed, and deadly serious.

Since she took to her bed, she'd had almost no conversation with either of us, and certainly not a word for Arthur. Everything and everyone in the house bore the constraint generated by her silence. I routed Daddy out of the kitchen; he followed me, moving carefully with his hands along the walls down a cen-

tral passageway. I threw open the second door to Mama 's bedroom, the nearest door. "Come over here," I heard her say across the room to Daddy in her
high, unreliable voice that meant she was verging on tears. "Shut the door,"
she admonished me. I was as taken off guard as Daddy. I heard him approaching her bed with something like, "You wanted—"

Closing the door when I knew I had to, I whipped back around through the
dining room into the living room, taking my place on the piano bench, my
knees drawn up, poised and ready to eavesdrop. The door to Mama's room
was still slightly ajar. I expected I'd got myself a fine listening post. "Shut that
door, too," Mama whimpered, but very determined. "Okay," I promised, leaving the tiniest crack, hoping she'd pay it no mind.

Suddenly Daddy said, "Oh, don't feel that way, Pet, I don't mind"—She
wailed, a long thin wail, her smaller voice rising in pitch, Daddy's stronger
voice insisting,

"I can do without—"

"Yes you *do!*" she rose over him," I *know* you have, all these years! You're
a man, and men . . ."

"No, no, really Pet, it makes no difference to *me* wheth—" Someone
jerked the doorknob from the other side. I was shut out.

That's the last I ever learned about that conversation from that day to this.
How I've wrestled with it! Was she apologizing for ruling out sex? Like many
of my friends whose parents slept in separate rooms, and who even occupied
the same double beds as their fathers, as I had, until the onset of puberty, I
wondered how they ever had *me*. Was *I* the end of sex? Or the exception to *no*
sex. During the depression, the practice of separate rooms was invoked as a
crude method of contraception; people couldn't afford large families, and the
drop in the national birth rate was seen to reflect that. But for all the muffled
words I missed, Mama's voice still sounded guilty. And why the confession
now? Was she planning. . . to *die?*

She stayed in bed the next day and the next day and the next. Afterwards,
she could not get at any part of the stronger self that had seen us through
Daddy's six month absence.

Then one night a few difficult months later, I was in the bathroom in front
of the medicine cabinet mirror, brushing my teeth for bed—I slept in the dining room now—and admiring my new breasts which were pleasantly expanding my pink knit nightgown. Suddenly Daddy appeared over by the toilet
against the outside wall, speaking some strange, choppy language to me to get
my attention, though he was stooped and cowering back as if he'd been flung
into this space. He looked as if he couldn't imagine how he'd landed there at

the enclosed end of the bathroom, unsure of his balance, or how to extricate his feet which appeared wedged in a narrow crack between toilet and wall.

"Daddy?" I said stupidly, as if I'd never seen him before. I couldn't for the life of me think how he'd managed to come in from the hall and pass behind me without my seeing him in the mirror. Then turning, foaming toothbrush in hand, the Pepsodent white runny spittle creeping toward my elbow, I made myself look him right in his one eye, which was calming down and wanting to calm me. Thoroughly ashamed of myself for fearing him, for whatever reason, my voice, too, was unserviceable:

"Da—Daddy!" What a pair we are, I thought, smiling. Neither of us able to talk right. "What's wrong?" I saw no blood or bruises on him.

"'Aw—ite, aw-ite", he tried to be understood with all of his now returning powers. With index finger he pointed several times to his open mouth, jerking his hand up and down for emphasis and clarity.

"Your *teeth?*" I fairly squawked, at my wits' end about the mystery, but encouraged to see his old head-strongness back.

"Unhhh!" he swung his head back and forth, a smile beginning through his exasperation. He was hanging onto his patience, though energetic and eager to clear this up. He moved easily out of his trapped position against the wall, seemingly without even thinking, so anxious was he to get his meaning across. He came up quite close to my face, and I put my hand cheerfully on his shoulder in the old way, speaking normally to him. Almost. Catch in my breath.

"Okay, Daddy, what *is* it? Tell me again."

I cocked my head. I was determined to listen better, which seemed silly. But why not? I had no other remedies up my sleeve.

"Ud . . . *sulk* . . . ny!" he thumped it out distinctly, his meticulousness beginning to make me feel dumb, like I was the problem.

"One more time!" I begged like the child I'd just about lost. "I'll try harder!" He smiled, nodding. I would be rewarded, that's what he meant!

"Um ok-a!" he beamed, confidently, as if something had just relaxed in his brain. "Um okay, I'm okay! I jus . . . 'alk . . . fum, fumy. I jus' talk funny!"

"Oh, Daddy," I breathed softly, for fear the good thing would all go away. He sighed deeply, grinned, and stuck his hands in his pants pockets with a great show of confidence. He was not through trying to take care of me. I hugged his arm in return; there was never enough of him to hold, he just kept losing and losing.

"There!" he said, trying to hide exhaustion, "I'm all right! I didn't mean to scare you!" I shook my head, tears of relief rising, which he saw, as he hugged me to him against the sink, and going on quite naturally to cover for me. "I was pretty sure the whole time it was just temporary; everything else was normal, the words just wouldn't come out right. I think that's called 'aphasia.' Happens to lots of people, all ages. But not *you!*" He poked a finger against my chest, "Not you, little girl!"

I giggled, but it was lighter than I felt. Though we both went on doing all the things you do at bedtime, I asked him every once in a while, "Are you okay? Are you sure?" And he said he was okay. The next time I went into the back bedroom, I spied him by the up-turned seat of his pants, stooped way over straightening the papers that stuck out of his yellow leather briefcase, "book satchel" he called it. Red and black typed file cards and their small wooden boxes had spilled from his roll-top desk onto the floor. Yes, he'd had quite a scuffle with himself and these suddenly uncontrollable familiar objects.

That was Daddy's first in his "series of little strokes." And by any measure the most benign. He was behind his lectern at the college teaching the next morning. I told Mama what happened when she woke up to go to the bathroom. "He's all right," I said. She seemed oddly undisturbed but listened intently. "Are you sure?" she asked me twice, fixing me with one of her old sharp, businesslike looks that meant it was important to her to get a good swift, accurate accounting.

The next and the next and the next "little strokes" were progressively damaging though not paralyzing. A second aphasia incident while he was eating *worsened* until, jerking violently, he passed out, slid grotesquely from his chair to the linoleum, bleeding from his ear and the knuckles of his hand crushed under his own weight. Heavy, prolonged after effects—sporadic loss of memory, dizziness, poor balance, increased debilitation, a building fear he'd be taken any time, any place. "Pass out teaching!, or on the street!—and never see it coming!" he said. Then on a grey Saturday at the end of a long week of teaching, an exacerbating wind howling off the prairies, Mama kept developing her ranting and her fears, until by mid-afternoon she'd suckered us into arguing with her in the most frantic way, until we were no better than her. We took our arguments and shouts and accusations and counter recriminations inside again, to the living room, and Daddy, uncharacteristically agitated, pacing round and round faster than I thought he was able, suddenly took a lightning pause to rest his elbow on the corner of the piano, and commenced to blubber and shake all over and before we knew it, he'd crashed to the floor with a good sized deep gash at his temple where he'd cracked his head on the corner of the mahogany piano. There was blood all over the floor, and at first we didn't recognize where it was coming from. "The corner of the piano!"

Mama shrieked, thoroughly beside herself, pointing to Daddy's blood on the top and sides of the piano. I had missed the blood because I had run to the black wall phone in the hall to dial numbers I knew by heart, the doctor and the ambulance. The ambulance came fast, but when I came back from phoning, Daddy was of course still lying by the piano in his own blood, jerking and blubbering a little less spasmodically now. That's all I remember until the two men with the ambulance brought the metal gurney in and lifted Daddy onto it, strapped him in and carried him right out the front door of our house. He was lying still and spent.

He survived that one, too, but his steely will had taken a good shaking, which he tried not to show if he could help it. Mama actually came out of herself enough to urge him to go to church with me on Sundays.

"Why don't you *go* with her?" she'd point at me. "I know you *want* to." We both believed this. But he'd look over at her just seething with disgust and sarcasm, mainly for himself, a glimpse of his formidable loathing for his situation.

"Go to church and *keel over* in front of everybody? *All those people?* Is that what you want me to do? Just *keel over* in the pew? What's the good of that?"

One afternoon my friend Joyce and I were playing, sitting talking, really, on a rise of ground between my house and the Concho River. The air was mild, the day sunny. We could look north to winding groves of shaggy pecan trees that followed along the banks of the Concho. Joyce lived three blocks east of us, the other side of the calichie pit. Her family had become glamorous and exciting to me. The mother a fiery, vivacious woman who ran the sewing room at the hospital, worked at a job which paid money, which made their whole world different—from the way they talked to what they ate. Their father was a calm man, good with his hands, and I got to help them put on a new roof. It was a stabilizing force to know their family was keeping an eye on mine. They helped us climb out of some of our abrupt medical emergencies as Daddy went on having his "series of little strokes" (a phrase I came to despise) and Mama deteriorated grandly.

We'd read two chapters of *Wuthering Heights* back and forth to each other. It lay open between us, face down on a clump of broomweed we'd bent down to ground level to keep our book out of the dirt. We were talking about my family situation. Joyce surprised me.

"It doesn't look like your mother and daddy are ever going to get well."

"No," I shrugged, "I don't think they are." Something I'd been keeping down inside myself stirred, horrifying and yet sweetly exciting.

"Well, what's going to happen to you?"

I'd never heard her so pointed before. The stirring down deep in me kept going. "I don't know," I answered as if it mattered not a whit. "I don't know."

. . . Knowing yet not quite knowing, I was trying to keep myself from knowing what it meant whenever I came home from high school, out of the strong light of Texas afternoons into the drawn shade murk of the front bedroom to find Mama in her perpetual nightgown, crawling under the bed and out, under and out, retrieving her unloosed stockpile of pills, her voice gargly and slurred, counting her yellow nembutals and red seconals like gold. It was her weird brand of security and by now the only thing she seemed to care about. Those pills embodied her available powers of choice: suspend her misery at will, temporarily—or spend big and try to rub herself out completely. I could never get used to that sprawled out, drugged voice, harrowingly out of control, yet utterly controlling.

Mama's splintery voice did not at all resemble the voice of the precise, demanding woman she used to be, witty or complaining by turn, and capable of open affection, though she reserved it for rare and surprising moments. Not the voice of the woman who loved to sing at the kitchen sink, or at the piano with the sheet music spread, and the chords, so rich with longing, flowing from her fingertips into the shades of twilight. Not the sturdy, if worried, voice of the woman whose courage and will and, yes, even beauty blossomed under the burden that fell upon her shoulders with her husband's illness and absence, then snapped like frayed thread, as if all had been error, this wrestling with World War II ration coupons for everything, sugar and gas and butter and tires and shoes, this poring over the odd wording of fine print in our house mortgage and Daddy's insurance papers which he had to borrow heavily against to pay off hospital debts, even though the college, Thank the Lord, kept his salary coming . . . Then I'd find Mama crawling around under her bed chasing little pills so bright they looked as if they could speak and predict the future, solve everyone's predicament.—"tweny-one, twen-twooo". . .

It meant that once more, if Daddy were hospitalized with one of his "little strokes," I, the child in the house, not my mother, would call the doctor and the ambulance.

. . . Mama tried a little bit of everything to make us fear for her life. Long, secret walks in the middle of the night in her kimono without waking me or Daddy. We never knew whether to believe her or not when she told us in the morning, "Wore out these poor weak legs tramping all over the earth!" She'd rub her thighs over her kimono and fix us with a rueful expression that seemed like bragging and blaming at once, but trying to tell us . . . *what?* While I was at the high school on one side of busy Oak Street and Daddy was trying to teach at the college on the other side, she was left alone for hours.

Naturally I did all the driving, and always got Daddy up the long wide flight of steps leading to the college, then steered him between two enormous fake Greek columns and well inside the heavy doors, left him to the hub-bub of students, and then went across the street to the high school. In his class-room, teaching psychology, sociology, education, C.C. Minatra held his open text book horizontally right below his one "good" eye; he did this with his plate at the table, too; it was the only way he could see what he was eating. At lunch, in my new job as family manager, I darted back across Oak Street and pored his thermos of coffee for him, and set up his baloney sandwiches and ate mine with him in his cramped second story office shared by two other men who, thank God, he genuinely liked and respected. "Minatra could teach with his hands tied behind his back," they said.

In moving about the college, he insisted he could feel his way along the wall past his roomy old Dean's office, with the broad counter where I used to sit in the afternoons and eat glazed doughnuts from McClure's Bakery and drink RC Cola till I popped. Daddy, as Dean, leaned imposingly on his elbows across the counter and tried to help students, and find, or pretend to find, *any* point of agreement with faculty. (Oh he'd been a fabulously busy man, and powerful.) At three-thirty when my last class let out, Algebra, I crossed Oak Street again and picked him up in the small office where he'd been waiting all afternoon at an empty green-topped desk. He always had his overcoat on, his felt hat on his head, and his cane drawn up beside him.

On the way home we shopped for groceries. We had not a clue what Mama had been doing all this time. She was exceedingly close-mouthed about that, but ranting to-beat-the-band about everything else under the sun that was wrong with our lives, moving from bed to couch to daybed, coughing as she did so. Overnight she broke into a terrible rheumy sounding cough and swore she had her T.B. back. In the middle of a rant—"What can I *do?* What can—" she fell into uncontrollable fits of coughing, her face a muddy red color, until she couldn't draw breath. And for a few moments her constant stream of speech subsided into gasping. Then she started up again at fever pitch—"It's my T.B., I've got my T.B. back!" She never ceased declaring she would perish of it.

Doctor Mac eventually cut off all her sedatives at every drugstore in town. She could no longer go to the phone and order them. This left her with more frantic, wakeful hours to work herself into a perfect frenzy by the time we got home. Dr. Mac examined her and said the cough was just that, a cough, which infuriated her. She screamed that all the doctors "in the kingdom" would let her die! "What am I going to do, what am I going to do, what have we come to?" repeated faster and faster. She used it like a whip against our raw nerves. We took her to different doctors, who put her through different hospitals, thumping her, testing her, moving the stethoscope over her chest, listening to her breathe and cough, and determined each time that she did not have T.B. Daddy made expensive, complicated arrangements for the personnel at the vaunted John Sealy Hospital in Galveston—famous in Texas for its medical, surgical, and psychiatric services—to meet the train we somehow got her on, and carry her bodily into their elite institution for her most thorough examination yet. This included screening for both medical and psychiatric symptoms.

"Nothing physical" . . . "Nothing physically wrong," they said in a letter. Daddy felt they were hedging, blaming himself for not being able to "go down there with Pet and squeeze the truth out of those bandits! Why in blazes can't they say what they mean? What we need is plain answers!" He'd drop his head in his hands, then look up at me from under his eyebrows and swear his oath— "I'd have booted it out of 'em! Oh, Pet—oh, Pet—where do we go from here?"

Steadfastly and stealthily, while she was asleep or in another room, we sneaked scissors from medicine cabinets and drawers, hid razors and blades. Foolishly aware that knives ran rife in the kitchen, that broken glass would do the job, that a thousand things. . .

Three different taxi drivers, all strangers, brought her into the police station in back of the Civic Auditorium three different times, when they let her out of their cabs and saw her climbing with one foot up on the railing of the Beauregard Street Bridge. The story was always the same. Just when they got to the crest of the bridge, she tells the driver to stop, and gets out in her slippers, gown, and kimono. Why would they pick up a sick looking woman dressed in bedroom slippers, gown, and kimono without asking some questions in the first place? But when they saw her in that get-up, apparently trying to boost herself into position where she could leap into that green, sluggish water, they got out and did whatever was needed to peel her down off that concrete railing . . . They brought her into City Hall where Daddy's name as Dean of the college was known; no one wanted to embarrass Professor Minatra, neither the Magistrate nor the Women's Matron, who was a former student of Daddy's. So they *don't* notify us until the third time she climbed, or attempted to climb, the bridge railing. They just took her home in an unmarked car, and she went right into our house; no one locked their doors.

Out of the several bridges that crossed the three branches of the ambling North Concho, Mama picked the same bridge our family routinely took in order to get from the westernmost side of Angelo where we lived, to downtown where all the banks and department stores and churches were clumped together. I see Mama balancing at ease up on that warm concrete railing, looking down the river, like a circus lady in pink ballet slippers resting from her exertions on the trapeze. Breathtakingly she absorbs into herself the lovely winding terraces laid out park-style in the near distances below, with stands of bamboo shivering in the morning light, hugging the banks of the lazy waters of the Concho spangled with sunbeams moving gently up and down as the breeze ruffles the surface . . . tantalizing Mama. If she'd tried to kill herself on the other side of the bridge, she would have looked down and probably remembered the really neat sunken garden with great tilting slabs of granite I scrambled up and down, and a slip of a stream I could jump across, back and forth, over and over. . . even a slender wooden bridge with twisted vines for a handrail where I could rest my elbows, cup my face in my hands, and dream away at the lily pond choked with exotic color.

When I was much younger, Daddy and I went to the sunken garden nearly every nice Sunday after church (Mama didn't go to church very often, though she loved to sing) and then we stopped by the drugstore to get a Mounds Bar and the funny papers from the huge *San Antonio Light*. The Concho River Park, adjacent to the bridge, was where we had Easter Egg hunts every spring and fireworks displays on the Fourth of July when we would all three sit or lie on a blanket, surrounded by other families on blankets in the sunken garden, and stare up at the heavenly drama. Darkness thickened about us, mosquitoes grew bolder, the citronella bottle came out. We rubbed the pungent stuff on arms, neck, face, legs. Colored flower-bursts of silken sparks gliding down the dark channels of the sky, lit up the bridge underneath as well as both sides of the top (cars passing in either direction) as white as daylight!

Her ranting, shrieking, raving jags—"What are we going to *do*, What are we going to *do?*"—would not stop for hours. We were gripped with sheer wondering whether she would be alive when we came home each day.

We had no money.

Miserably, reassuring each other, Daddy and I talked it over. "Nothing physical" stuck in our heads. Did that mean we had to go on the way we were, just getting worse? What could worse be like? Would she really kill herself?

We fell silent. We couldn't even contemplate "worse," it was so bad now, and had been for so long. Finally, Daddy said, trying for my sake not to let the quaver into his voice and not doing a very good job of it, "We've got just one more choice; we could send her to Big Spring." To Daddy's ears those words fell like a death sentence. Big Spring was the dread state institution closest in our area; Mama was his beloved *Pet*. Oddly he jerked out one dry, raw laugh, supporting his forehead with his palms, elbows on knees. I knew what he meant. Daddy straightened up.

"While you're at school," he said, more firmly.

"No! I want to be here," I said and I meant it. I wouldn't leave all the dirty work to him; I didn't need all that extra guilt. But he was adamant. We argued, but in the end he prevailed. I was not to talk with her about it before the chosen day when he would tell her himself after I'd driven away as usual to school. This seemed even more cruel of me, Daddy guessed from the choked face I was showing.

"You may feel bad about it now—of course you do!—but when you're older, you'll see that's the only way this can work, and a strange kindness to your mother in the end." I looked at him gratefully, incredulously, but I couldn't speak. I was still going back and forth on the subject of my getting out of all the hardest part. He fumblingly managed to hug me, and receive my hot quaking gasp against his boney neck. He probably guessed at my pent-up tears because he urged me, "Go ahead and cry," but I squeezed it all down back inside me, afraid of waking Mama up in the front bedroom while we sat whispering on the edge of Daddy's bed just one hall's width away.

I think that was when I first became proficient at holding back emotion. For so long, the only way we could get through the roughest spots was to "grit our teeth and bear it." Daddy used to say that as an ironic joke, an exaggeration, "Guess we'll just have to grit our teeth and bear it!," when nothing bad was happening at all, and Mama and I would laugh and pull dour faces in pleased agreement because he'd turned a chore into some degree of humor—like everybody having to take themselves out front in the still hot five-o'clock afternoon and dig up the horrible grassburrs threatening to eclipse Mama's thick Bermuda lawn.

I heard Mama coughing up phlegm and fled into the kitchen to start supper. That evening I went on batting things back and forth in my mind about what would happen to Mama and how we should do it. I slept unexpectedly well. By the time I woke up the next morning, the miasma had lifted. I felt clear-headed. Our decision inflated me with relief and a numbing kind of horror.

I accorded myself a little hope.

* * *

On the day Daddy made the arrangements for, I thought Mama knew nothing, but she was uncharacteristically quiet. Oddly, she had not gone into one of her raving rants yet, though these tended to be more frequent, even non-stop as the day advanced. With my school books stacked atop my zipper notebook of stiff rough leather and the whole affair wrapped in my arms, I bent down and kissed Mama goodbye on her dry hot cheek where she lay on the day-bed we set up for her in the dining room.

"Where're you going?"

Mama's fretful eyes, her sharp, perfect nose reddening at the tip as if she'd already been crying, the slight tremble of her chapped lower lip and chin—all accused me of abandoning her, as if she'd known all along I would, as if she were sensing something about to reach critical mass, something unthinkable which she must stop but was too weak to stop, something indelibly final that could not be undone, not ever. I managed to straighten out my voice as each word passed between my lips like a knife aimed at her heart.

"*You* know," I said, nodding to emphasize the normality of my point and also my power in the matter, "I'm off to school."

My voice echoed in my own ears, sounding weak, easy for Mama's binding logic to penetrate. She continued to search my eyes in her cloudy yet probing way. I repositioned my books to hold them with one arm. My favorite red fountain pen slipped from the treacherous zipper notebook, rattling against the oak floor. I leaned forward to take momentary hold of Mama's wrist. Her hand lay quiet across her chest, as if it were listening.

"It's Monday now; I have to go."

I gave her thin wrist a little shake, I can't say whether it was gentle or not. Slowly she blinked her large brown eyes, and I thought she dipped her chin a bit lower in acknowledgement; I released her wrist. Mama may have wondered why I was going and Daddy was staying, not going to the college, but I didn't give her much of a chance to ask. I stood up with my books, ready to go. A split second later Mama took her brown eyes off me, and twisted her neck around, showing me the back-side of her loose dark bun still unraveling from her night. She would have me believe her main interest lay in the branches of our mesquite tree scraping restlessly back and forth across the brace of three tall window panes on the other side of her narrow iron day-bed. Out there only the most fitful sun played on and off, and the raw November wind chased it. Quickly I picked up my fountain pen and crossed the room on the way to the kitchen, the back door, the car waiting in the drive.

Balancing my heavy books on one hip the way I carried them, I couldn't

keep myself from turning and taking my very last look at Mama. She lay with
the hand and wrist I had shaken draped across her forehead palm up, fingers
uncurled, her eyes wide open staring at the dining room-kitchen wall. There
was not even a picture on that wall, only sunburned wallpaper with chains of
nasturtiums criss-crossing in a diamond pattern that got harder to make out
every year. Her kimono, a washed-out blue with wide, rose-colored border,
had fallen uncharacteristically open to the floor exposing through her semi-
transparent nightgown her flattened chest and bare legs; Mama had lost so
much weight her body took on girlish angles. The fact of her thinness she
adroitly wove into her rants, never missing a chance to show me in the bathroom, holding her kimono out at each side, offering her slender figure—"See
these hips?, see my thighs?"—as proof that she was dying. It was actually a
becoming weight for her, but loss of weight to a T.B. patient signaled the
downward path to death. Most of the time she was driven by a high state of
mental and physical agitation.

Watching her on the iron cot, because I knew I might not ever see her
again, I was compelled to go on tracing the gentle curve of hip-bone and her
arm nearest me spilling languidly over the side of the bed. It was as if Mama's
blood under the skin, the veins clothed in her flesh, had never known a warm
pulse. It was shocking to see her so still for so long.

"Goodbye, Mama," I barely murmured, far back in my nearly paralyzed,
aching throat—terrified I might trip the wire that would start her ranting and
raving non-stop, pulling me in, pulling me in . . . and the whole plan would
come undone right there—but I couldn't help myself, seeing her lying there
disinterested like that; I had to tell Mama goodbye. She didn't move a muscle.
I waited maybe thirty seconds and left, almost knocking into Daddy in the
kitchen.

He'd been messing around in the breakfast-nook making coffee in his big
steel coffee urn on the little porcelain table. He was carefully lugging over to
the sink two of the gallon bottles he treasured for storing coffee in the icebox;
his worried eye told me he'd heard the whole thing between me and Mama but
been courteous enough to give me this time with Mama alone, time I would
never have again. He put his finger to his lips, then pointed to the little service
hall and the back door. I couldn't waste time, his determined look said. And I
well knew my limits had been tested.

The last image I had of Daddy that chilly fall morning, the image I drew
forward and held up beside Mama's in classes all day till the final bell clam-
ored through the halls, was that begging beseeching command he shot levelly
at me under his raised brows. That one eye, though nearly blinded, stayed

paired with the empty socket of the amputated eye, raw and red and gaping, and *thundered* his message at me. *Go!* Beseeching me to trust him one more time, helpless though he knew he looked. But already he was dressed, early for a day when I was not driving him to school to teach his two classes. His dark pin-striped pants were unmercifully belted-up, but hung off his hips too low, spilling over the tops of his old brogans. He'd hunted up a passably clean white shirt to wear but his matching pin-striped vest kept sliding off his shoulders, which were rail-thin; the dark lining of the armholes made them appear disproportionately huge and generally of a mind to swallow him whole. But the gold watch on the silver chain that crossed his breast, and the watch-fobs threaded through the buttonholes of his vest, ah, that showed he could still somehow cope with tedious detail and achieve a desired effect. Had all that tipped off Mama? If he wasn't going to teach, who was he dressing for? In spite of her driving, downward spiraling into the cold depths of her own shrinking world, I was sure Mama's sharp eye remained intact, that same talent she'd always picked away at us with. He must be going to tell her right after I left; and that meant the ambulance would come soon on the heels of his announcement. At that moment it splashed over me like ice-water: Mama knew everything!

Daddy's tremorous silent thunder held.

Sideways, I threaded myself through the back door that he had left half open. It moaned and squealed since Mama didn't oil it anymore. I struggled with the pretense that I was a shadow merging into freedom. Outside the house, my body was a boxy cargo awkward to handle, graceless, with no sign of moral fortitude, bleak abandonment my crime. At last I jumped clean over the middle concrete step, stumbling off the bottom step onto the red-brick path Mama'd laid diagonally across our back yard to get to the car and the garage. Right now it was overrun with two summers' crops of crackly dried grass-burrs.

I struck out for the '38 second-hand blue Plymouth I'd parked yesterday afternoon halfway between the corner of Daddy's back bedroom and our white garage. The useless garage door had been stuck on the concrete apron ever since Daddy went to the hospital in San Antonio to the doctors we'd hoped would cure his second eye.

I could not lift my head against pressure hammering up from the base of my skull. Fire and ice crawled along my skin from the nape of my neck up, up, up then seemed to drizzle back down my torso and limbs. I tried to slow myself down, but only dropped my prized red fountain pen again. I didn't even know I still had it in my hand. I rescued it from grassburrs without conscious thought. Shocked my feet were still under me, I jerked open the driver's door slamming books, notebook, and pen onto the passenger seat of the Plymouth. Afraid but horribly tempted to glance back at the house to see if Mama—or Daddy—had made it to the door, our high back stoop, and were closely watching my escape.

I concentrated on my crazily creeping scalp which roared at me to be clever and wise and turn the key in the ignition (no one we knew locked their cars) and stomp on the clutch and put her in reverse and *wham* out of there. I backed erratically around our leaky septic tank, like Mama always insisted, so one of us wouldn't "fall in one day," past the huge mint plant there against the foundation of the house....past the *front* door, the *porch* where Mama might be peering down inches away from the roof of the car with Daddy dragging her back—I didn't look! I didn't look!—ahhh, I'm driving too fast down Webster already to the corner where Daddy'd busted a few axles on the big embedded rocks, before they paved our street. He took teasing from Mama just about every day. "I know you're almost home when you hit that rock!—Ga-whoomp! There goes another axle!" Not funny, not now. I churned slightly uphill to turn left onto North Street, my scalp relaxing gradually like maybe it belonged on my head. After I got past the cheery white house where Joyce Graf and her family lived, deserted except for their dog Hobo lunging, barking as if he would choke himself struggling sideways at the end of his tether, a leash chain attached to his collar at one end, to a clothesline at the other, allowing him to move up and down a few feet between their back steps and their garage. That sudden, vicious, fever pitch of barking always made me jump inside, and feel relieved to get by him without incident.

In every class I attended that day, I saw Mama, all stretched out, cut off and miserable, yet powerfully paying me no mind. What did she want? I had done it all wrong! But she had been stronger than me. She had let me win and I knew it.

I was monstrous!

Books on my hip, I came draggingly through the back door. Daddy wasn't in the kitchen puttering around trying to solve any kind of food problem, seeing with his one weak eye. He wasn't even at the sink fumbling with a dish he wanted to wash so I wouldn't have to.

Then I spotted him in the living room on the couch, alone, bolt-upright. I let my books slide quiet as dust to the dining room table.

"Come in!" he said, staring straight ahead. Of course alone, what was the matter with me? Mama was. . . gone! I dropped down beside him on the old grey plush sofa but twisted around so my knees under the red and black pleats of my beloved skirt touched his emaciated leg.

"Did she resist?" I asked.

"No, not much," he said staring at our fake fireplace, flanked by glassed-in bookshelves tight with all the books he couldn't read now.

"What did you say?" I asked. "How'd you get started?"

From the depths of the grey couch where he'd been imprisoned for what seemed like days, he now addressed the row of books nearest him. They were old friends. A brown cloth-bound set of twelve volumes of commentary on Lincoln stared back at him. "Book poor!" Mama complained. Then he swung his heavy-feeling head around toward the business at hand, and with a focus that seemed to come from far back in his mind, he gave artful answers to all my questions.

"She was actually sitting right over there in the big chair with her back to the windows, and I was here. She knew something was up. I hadn't seen her sit up in a chair in the living room since Arthur brought me home. 'I've got something to say, Pet,' and she met my eyes for the longest, or at least I flattered myself she did..." He trailed off, smiling, embarrassed he couldn't guarantee, in his condition, exactly where anybody was looking. He barked a clipped laugh I hadn't heard before.

"That's alright, go on," I said, afraid I'd never get the story, and afraid I *would*.

"Well, it just seemed to me she tilted her sweet head back and looked me straight in the eye after all these months!"

"She could do that!"

"I said, 'Pet?' she didn't stir a hair, 'I've got something to say to you. It's come to this, my old, my only love—'" His mouth twisted. He took himself sternly in hand and began to summarize so he could be a little less personal, and the formality might get him through. It was enough that he had to say it to Pet this morning. But he knew I needed not to feel closed out. He knew that, in a way, I'd made a sacrifice not staying home and being a part of this whole incredible lifetime blunder. "I simply told her I'd made arrangements for an ambulance to pick her up and drive her in comfort"—inspecting the ceiling fiercely, he slapped the bony knee of the leg that was touching me. I jumped. ". . . in *comfort!*," he repeated. Then he got a grip and smiled at me, and I felt the warmth of his spirit and was prepared to go along with just about anything he said.

"And what did *she* say?"

"Well, once I'd told her, she acted like she'd known all along." He said this admiringly, and for a moment, I seriously admired Mama, too. "'I thought you'd have to do that,' she said, and looked away from me down at the rug." I think Daddy understood that we *both* needed to have cause to admire Mama at that moment.

Remembering her words seemed to hurt Daddy's throat; he touched two fingers to his weak looking Adam's apple and drew them down the length of his windpipe, pressing hard all the way to the collar bone, like there was something embedded in there. He cleared his throat.

"She said to me right off, 'I don't see what else you can do; send me to Big Spring. All you can do,'" he said. This gave me a turn, too, hearing him repeat it like that. I wondered if he was deep in remembering times *before* this morning when she'd told him he'd have to do something.

"Did she get in the ambulance without a fuss, too?" I had to know, I couldn't believe our luck! Mama could have run out the back door and across the prairie and Daddy could never have got her, or picked up one of the razor blades that kept popping up in spite of us and slashed at her veins, or run across the street in front of a car gunning itself up the hill.

"Yes, yes, she did everything she knew she had to!" He jerked his head up with a wrench of finality. It was the worst hour of his life, worse than six months of solitary blindness in a strange city, he *would* tell his only child what she had to know! "She calmed down pretty fast." He sat up straighter. "Brave!" he said. Then a long, dense pause. "She wouldn't look at me when they pulled away. Lord God, it was hard!" He rubbed his forehead slowly and let his hand drop. I looked out the empty front windows where it happened. I could not keep myself from yearning for a life that would be as simple and bright as Joyce Graf's seemed to me, even if their dog did scare the living daylights out of me. I was through with my questions.

Daddy drew himself up, still as the perfectly scalloped Comanche arrowhead fragments we used to find, half-buried in the hard grey dirt on our afternoon walks across the vacant lots while Mama napped. We'd tramp out past all the telephone wires where only rocks and algerita grew, and barren prickly-pear and tiny brittle white lichen in miniature rose-like patterns joined flat to the ground or on rock. When Mama woke up we huddled at her bed, Daddy and me, showing off our new candidates for her arrowhead collection box, which she kept in an old tea tin in her top bureau drawer with the family photos. She would decide whether any nearly whole ones were worth keeping or not, turning them around and around in her fingers, inspecting each one from every angle. We considered her the expert and she actually kept a few for her box. I can't for the life of me remember any of us ever finding a perfect whole one—but largish fragments were greatly celebrated, especially if the chipping was neat and even. It never occurred to me to imagine the hands, forearms, full figure of the Comanches chipping out and shaping these triangular arrowheads.

Through our tall triple windows at the front of the living room, Daddy looked past our lawn of Bermuda that never turned completely brown and across Webster Street to that brushy expanse of November prairie cast in the dull gleam of winter afternoon—but seeing Mama . . . Mama calmly lying on the ambulance gurney in her blue and rose kimono. It had been her constant companion on her night tramps around the neighborhood, taxi rides to the bridge, and any other time when she was ranting away at home, flinging herself from bed to cot to couch, or just still as ice, profoundly ignoring me the way she did this morning.

The two genial men in white shirts and black pants and cowboy boots the state has sent Daddy to get her, wrap her slight frame snug in a pale blue blanket of hospital issue and strap her in as securely as she could want. They lift her into the open back doors of the ambulance, black as a hearse. The omnipresent West Texas wind lifts the loose hairs around her face and neck, the same hairs I had seen that morning in my cowardly rout from our home. And Mama does not turn her head once to look at Daddy waiting there at the curb, very close. These two muscular fellows rock and jiggle her, and at the last moment induce the mechanism to carry her gliding into the hungry ambulance.

So there is Mama not turning her head to look at Daddy as her head itself disappears into the shadowy recesses at the back of the ambulance. Nothing of Mama is showing except two glints of steel that indicate the gurney's last two wheels. The younger, blond, gum-chewing man, hops inside, squeezing himself between Mama and the wall. The thick-waisted older man brings the doors together, and wiggles both handles back and forth to see that they're locked. There's not one single sign of Mama left, and nothing to hear except the wiggling of the door handles.

The older man dusts his hands together, turning to Daddy. Inside, Mama stares upward toward the roof of the ambulance with those big brown eyes devoid of sparkle. She is concentrating in a strange way, trying to penetrate, or *not* penetrate, what is left for her in this life. Was she punishing him, not looking at him? He *was* being punished.

I believed Daddy when he said that she gave no resistance, and I believe him now; I believe he did not tell it that way only to relieve me of guilt and worry; I believe she went to Big Spring, the very large state hospital many miles away, as an admission of her own failure to manage her life, and as a present *for us*. The notion of turning herself over to a pre-ordained regimen in a vast institution, like her well-ordered life in the sanitarium, may have contained allure for her: doctors and nurses to tell you what to do at any hour of the day or night—she would never again have to figure out what to do with herself. Would she release all connection with us?

She spoke of "the san" in Colorado with a certain unabashed affection, sometimes even vivacity. At the "san" they all had little brown paper bags safety-pinned to the edge of their mattress to "expectorate" (or spit) in, to deposit all tissues containing their sputum, to control germs and stop contagion. At the "san" they all had to brush their teeth with powdered charcoal, rubbed on with the finely sliced and softened end of a green twig used as a toothbrush. It was thrown away at the end of the day and resupplied after breakfast, another way to keep down contagion. It always sounded to me like they were having a strict good time. She did a lot of charcoal drawings at the sanitarium, but when I begged her to let me see them, she said I couldn't because they all had to be burned when she left, to avoid her recontacting germs.

At the "san," the wind blew a certain delicious way through the big pines at a particular hour of the afternoon. Years later, rummaging through the basement, a black and white snapshot fell out of a box. It showed Mama sitting on the lap of an ecstatic Daddy, good looking, laughing, alive with pride; her arms adoringly around his neck, and him hugging her tight in his abundant love. Her patient-friends, all laughing young women Mama's age, were gathered 'round. Mama's face under a pretty ruffled night cap, set on her dark curls, was turned to the camera, smiling like a movie star with love for Daddy, and twice as beautiful! She had made good choices; she got *well* in that place!

I didn't know, then, Big Spring would never permit us to see her. Even Daddy, who taught the psychology courses required for the degree in nursing, may have known little, I don't know how much, about the horrors of electric shock therapy routinely scheduled for all inmates of large state institutions like Big Spring. No one ever came back to tell about it.

"You'll take good care of her?" Daddy half asks the older man, half demands, aware of the futility of his game.

"Nothing to worry about, I'll see to it." Experienced, he eyes Daddy not unkindly.

"Thank you," Daddy says on a brief hand-shake.

"Don't mention it," says the other, with a casual off-handedness that's hard to take. He seems to melt toward the front door of the behemoth, climbing behind the steering wheel before Daddy can gather himself for these last moments. The ignition turns over with an oily, well-tuned efficiency. In his near blindness, Daddy takes a few steps back, skirting the bumper (he hopes) and stops. The driver cannot resist sedately revving up the powerful motor one time. It scares Daddy, and he stumbles a step or two back. The nameless older driver puts the ambulance in gear and takes off in such a definite, official way, taking Mama away up the hill without a cough or strain of the motor. And this is war-time, and most of our cars were not in good shape.

It was not at all difficult for me to see Mama's farewell, the physical details of it; by then I had called the ambulance for Daddy, for his series of small strokes, at least a half dozen times and watched him get strapped onto a gurney or a stretcher by two strong men, almost always too old to be fighting in Europe or the South Pacific. In the shadowy nave of the ambulance, I saw the younger man and Mama crammed together all the way to Big Spring. Do they talk? Does he try to rile her, is he mean? Does she break her silence for any reason, ask him questions about the state-run hospital? I can imagine him riling her; I can imagine her riling him. I can imagine just about anything. It's hard for me not to think of Mama as adversarial; then something snaps—I see her in a lonely, terrified situation, badly handled by a sadistic aide. . .

So now the older guy, the one behind the wheel, shifts his gears up the hill on Webster, and keeps the speed down from what he'll be allowed to use on the highway, 35 miles an hour under war-time gas rationing. Mama and the two men move nice and smooth up old Webster Street. Roosevelt's WPA crews have come and gone, taking with them the mountains of torturous rocks, leaving us the pure gift of neat curbs and fresh laid pavement.

But this ambulance, for all its shine and slow pace and silenced sirens (which only makes it more sinister), this fiery chariot is too big to miss, fierce-looking, a potent symbol that some violence, some havoc is being wreaked. With its double back doors, the big, long, hearse-like car purrs and throbs its way past the vacant lots that protected my mother's privacy and let her take naps so she wouldn't get her T.B. back, but brought her loneliness, too—and runs the gauntlet of red-brick houses up the hill above ours.

Neighbors of thirteen years who've seen ambulances in plenty lately at the Minatras' house, draw together on the sidewalks in respectful little knots of worry and curiosity, intent on puzzling out the mystery, as the monster powerfully mounts their hill. Murmurs rise like sparks from the clots of people watching the progress of the ambulance—No-no-no—It's *not* him! See?, they point downhill with their backs to the sun, He's still down there! And sure enough, Daddy's emaciated figure sags at the curb, his face tilted upward as if he had two good eyes fastened on the rear bumper of the ambulance. Not him *this* time, it's *her!* Big Spring? The chrome-struck license plates do not lie. Big Spring...they're putting her in Big Spring! As the ambulance throbs by, the driver nods. They press their small children closer until the great coiled length has safely passed.

On that day of huge betrayal for our family, after school has belched me up and back to home where my thoughts have centered all day long, and Daddy has done what he was sent into this world to do, reassure me, he collapses into himself, contemplating his deceit without externally moving a muscle. He sits beside me rigid on our velvety grey sofa—purchased in great excitement with Mama, her brown eyes alive, her cheeks flushed in the thrill of auction bidding in the thirties at depression "fire-sales" where they gave you "funny money" or coupons, anything to move the merchandise—bought the same way as every other stick of furniture we owned.

Pet, my girl, Daddy thinks, we had some good times then! How the devil did we come to *this?* What could bring you back? He was now more anguished than relieved. He looks out through the long triple windows of the living room, and seems to scan the windy prairie with the one working eye that can't really see that far. Then I notice that the old reliable indicator, the green glass eye, has grown strangely becalmed, betraying earnest thought. But here was something new and strange. He looked so poised, I concentrated to see, to hear if he was breathing. Faint and uneven, like knotted silk drawn through a wedding ring, I heard the presence, more than sound, of air entering Daddy's lungs, then being expelled, oddly relaxed.

How little I knew of death.

To C.C. Minatra, the first Dean of San Angelo Jr. College, Texas, in the year nineteen hundred and forty three, on this most fateful of days in his life, it seemed centuries since he'd crawled out of bed in the pre-dawn light. All night it had been coyotes yelping and howling from the mesquite prairies shared by prickly pear at the north edge of town—thwarting any attempts at ragged sleep until the roosters took over, crowing way up the hill west, where the poor whites squatted on land they didn't own. He had gone to bed merely to keep from raising Pet's suspicions with his lumbering about, slamming into things as usual. Or perhaps to fortify himself. He longed to read to pass this singular night away, but ruled it out of the question, not being the comforting distraction it used to be, but a mockery and sore disappointment. Pet would see his light and start up with something. His veins were full of dread like an expanding poison. *It must be done!*, he told himself, *must be done, must be done!*

What C.C. Minatra knew was every single detail that had transpired that day, from fumbling around in the perfectly blind dark for his socks so he wouldn't alert his family and send Pet into one of her regular blitzkriegs of trilling, chilling ranting—"What're we gonna do?, Oh, what're we gonna *doooooo?*"—to the still unthinkable mess of having to tell Pet what was going to happen to her in two heart-piercing hours of waiting (the cruel ambulance arrived right on time, by God!), to watching her leave without a single glance for him, and didn't he deserve that slap in the face? Yes, oh Lordy, he'd forgotten *nothing*, up to this very moment on the couch here beside his little girl turned young woman on him. But now trying to sort out the nightmare after the fact, ahhhh, that was a different matter, like lifting beds and sofas and huge stacks of toppling books.

After his great getting-ready this morning, this vast ordeal of giving his wife like a bride to the state, entrusting Pet to a pair of perfectly strange men, perfectly decent fellows—and then what and then what? Oh, Pet!

And again seeing Mama not turn her head, Daddy forgets about me for a time.

Randall Albers chairs the Fiction Writing Department at Columbia College Chicago, home of the Story Workshop® approach to the teaching of writing and of one of the largest graduate and undergraduate creative writing programs in the country. His fiction and nonfiction have appeared *in Prairie Schooner, Chicago Review, Northfield Magazine, Mendocino Review, f Magazine, Writing From Start to Finish*, and elsewhere. A chapter from his novel-in-progress, *All the World Before Them*, appearing in the Summer 2001 issue of *f Magazine*, was nominated for a Pushcart prize. He is the founding producer of the Story Week Festival of Writers; co-writer and co-producer of Story Workshop® creative writing videotapes, *The Living Voice Moves* and *Story From First Impulse to Final Draft*; and has presented at AWP as well as other national and international conferences on writing and the teaching of writing. A Certified Story Workshop Master Teacher, he is a former recipient of the Columbia College Chicago Teaching Excellence Award.

Andrew Allegretti's fiction has appeared in a number of magazines including *TriQuarterly*, *Private Arts*, and F Magazine's novels-in-progress issues. He is the recipient of numerous Illinois Arts Council Artists Fellowships for excerpts from his novel *Winter House*, and IAC Literary Awards for his short fiction. "Heat Lightning," the prologue to *Winter House*, was a semifinalist for the James Fellowship for Novels in Progress, sponsored by the Heekin Foundation.

William Burck helps design and facilitate problem-solving business events and owns a publishing company that creates books about Traditional Chinese Medicine. *The Elbows* is his first novel. He is currently seeking an agent and publisher.

Brian Costello's stories and essays have appeared in *Bridge Magazine*, *the2ndhand*, *Hair Trigger*, *Sleepwalk*, *The Banana King*, *Inkstains*, and *The New England Journal of My Ass*, and he will be a book reviewer for *Time Out Chicago* starting in March 2005. He is a monthly columnist for terminal-boredom.com.

Frank Crist is a writer and a teacher living in Chicago. He has won the Weisman Award from Columbia College Chicago for his self-published anthology of authors, My Angels and My Demons at War, has an upcoming publication in Hair Trigger, and wrote the interactive, non-linear script to the virtual reality art installation, Special Treatment.

Kevin Freese is currently working on his second novel, *Gig*. An excerpt from his first novel, *Greatness at the Gate* appears in *Hair Trigger 26*.

Philip Hartigan is an English artist living in Chicago. Selected honors include: public commissions from the UK government; private commissions in London and the USA; fifteen group and solo shows in Spain, the UK, and the USA; curator's choice in print exhibitions. His work can be viewed online at www.philiphartigan.com.

Jeff Jacobson lives with his family and a whole bunch of animals in a northwestern suburb of Chicago. He teaches at Columbia College Chicago and The Illinois Institute of Art in Schaumburg. His fiction has appeared in *Hair Trigger*, *Spec-Lit*, and *F Magazine*. "Foodchain" is the first chapter of his second novel.

Etgar Keret is one of the leading voices in Israeli literature and cinema. In the last ten years he published four books of short stories and novellas, three graphic novels and two feature screenplays. His books were published in 16 different languages and gained both critical acclaim and success with the public (his latest, "the busdriver who wanted to be God", was published in the USA in January 2004 by Toby Press). In Israel all of his books were at the top of the best seller list. As of 1998, his stories are a part of the literature curriculum for Israeli high school students. His book "Missing Kissinger" was named one of the 50 most important books written in Hebrew by "Yediot-Acharonot" - an influential Israeli newspaper.

Stephanie Kuehnert is a student in Columbia College Chicago's Creative Writing MFA program. She got her start writing zines. Her third zine, *Hospital Gown,* was featured in *Zine Scene* by Hillary Carlip and Francesca Lia Block. An interview that she did with author John McNally appeared as the web exclusive on *Virginia Quarterly Review*'s website and will be reprinted in *Glimmer Train*'s "Writers Ask." Her essay "Ten Years Gone" will be appearing on www.fresh-yarn.com in April 2005. Stephanie's short stories have appeared in *Hair Trigger* 26 and on www.inkstains.org. "Fairytale," the second story from her novel-in-stories, *The Black Notebooks,* will appear in *Pigeon* magazine.

John Lowery is an M.F.A. candidate in Creative Writing at Columbia College Chicago. Lowery received The Columbia University Scholastic Press Association Award for his creative nonfiction essay, "Fault line". His stories have appeared in *Hair Trigger 24,26*, and his story, "Blood Oranges" will appear in the up coming *Hair Trigger 27*. He won the 2003 John Schultz and Betty Shiflett Story Workshop Scholarship. He is currently working on a collection of short stories.

Eric Charles May is a native of Chicago's South Side and a full-time instructor in the Fiction Writing Department at Columbia College Chicago. A former reporter for the *Washington Post*, his prose writing has appeared in *Angels In My Oven*, *Fish Stories: Collective One*, and *Sport Literate*. He is a summer instructor at the Stonecoast Writers' Conference in Maine and a past Board of Judges member of the Columbia (University) Scholastic Press Association in New York.

Joe Meno is the winner of the Nelson Algren Literary Award and author of three novels: *Tender as Hellfire* (St. Martin's 1999), *How the Hula Girl Sings* (HarperCollins 2001), and *Hairstyles of the Damned* (Akashic 2004.) His online serial, *The Secret Hand*, runs through *Playboy* magazine at *playboy.com*. His short fiction has been published in *TriQuarterly, Mid-American Review, Alaska Quarterly Review, Washington Square, Other Voices, Gulf Coast*, and broadcast on NPR. He is also an editor and columnist at *Punk Planet* magazine.

Lila S. Nagarajan's work has appeared in *Hair Trigger, Kavithalaya, Bandit-lit.com* and NPR's WBEZ, among other places. She has won a number of awards for her writing including an artist's grant at Ragdale Foundation. Lila is currently working on her second novel, *Red Hibiscus* and a collection of short stories, *The Color of Grief*. She teaches Fiction Writing and has acted as Assistant Artistic Director of Columbia College Chicago Fiction Writing Department's Story Week Festival of Writers.

Devon Polderman has been a football player and a florist, thrown engine blocks, built dune retaining walls, harvested Christmas trees, shot commercials, and survived an earthquake, a nor'easter, a tropical storm, Michigan, and a flash flood. He is eleven feet tall. He has published in *f Magazine, Hair Trigger*, and others. He lives in Chicago with 11 plants and 14 fish.

Gary Poplawski is a long-standing MFA candidate at Columbia College Chicago. He has written stories in one form or another since he could first hold a #2 pencil in the second grade. His work has appeared in *Hair Trigger*, *Lynx Eye*, *The Storyteller*, *My Angels & My Demons at War*, *Hindsight*, *Slugfest International*, *SoRaw*, and *Ball State Forum*. Gary currently resides in the Chicago suburbs with a mutated jade plant, an ever-growing collection of single malt scotch, and far too many firearms, in preparation for the collapse of civilization as we know it.

Dr. Alexis J Pride, fiction writer and playwright, is a full-time professor at Columbia College and Artistic Director of The A J Ensemble Theater Company. Her most recent credits include excerpts from her novel in-progress, Stirred With Fire, published in F5 and Ink Stains Literary Magazine (spring, 2005). She is a contributing writer to InnerView Chicago Magazine, served as editor for the internationally circulated literary anthology, PragueMalion, and is presently working toward the completion of her second play, The Trouble with Adam's Rib.

Chris Maul Rice's fiction and essays have appeared in *BanditLit.com, Pigeon, Emergence II, MetroTimes, Hair Trigger 16 and 17, Chrysallis and The Beacon.* Her feature stories have appeared in *Chicago Tribune's Health and Family*

Section, Columbia College Chicago's *Gravity* magazine *and Detroit's MetroTimes and MetroParent* newspapers. Chris graduated from Valparaiso University and has a M.F.A. in Creative Writing from Columbia College Chicago. She has been an adjunct professor in the Fiction Writing Department since 1992, has chaired the Young Authors writing contest since 2000, and has been the faculty editor for *Hair Trigger 23* through *Hair Trigger 28.*

Betty Shiflett—Illinois Arts Council Artists Fellowship Award. Stories, articles, novel and play excerpts in *Life, Evergreen Review, Fiction and Poetry by Texas Women, The Story Workshop Reader, College English, Writing from Start to Finish* by John Schultz, *f5,* and other literary journals. *We Dream of Tours* (play) and *Phantom Rider* (music drama.) Finalist in American Fiction for "The Country Barber," recently translated into Mandarin by novelist Yan Geling for *Sichuan Literature Monthly.* Novel-in-progress, *Grass Fires,* about a literarily atypical West Texas girlhood and family tragedy. Principal Story Workshop Master Teacher, featured in creative writing videotape, *Story from First Impulse to Final Draft,* co-produced by John Schultz and Randall Albers. Professor Emerita in the Graduate Program in Creative Writing, Columbia College Chicago.

Shawn Shiflett is a professor in the fiction writing department at Columbia College Chicago. His debut novel *Hidden Place* was included in *Library Journal*'s "Summer Highs, Fall Firsts," a 2004 list of "most successful debuts." He is working on a second novel, *Hey, Liberal,* about a white boy in a predominately African-American high school one year after the assassination of Martin Luther King Jr. Shiflett was born and raised in Chicago, and currently lives in La Grange, Illinois with his wife and two children.

Jantae Spencer won the 2000 John Schultz and Betty Shiflett Story Workshop Scholarship. She was accepted to the 2003 VONA (Voices of Our Nation) Writing Workshop in San Francisco with Junot Diaz. Her short story, "The Bloody Mess" was published in *Cobblestone* Magazine. She is currently at work on her non-fiction novel, *The Curse.*

Felicia Swanson's fiction has recently appeared in *Mars Hill Review, Lit 9,* and *Big Muddy: Journal of the Mississippi River Valley.* She is a staff writer for Chicago's west-side newspaper *The Gazette,* and has published other nonfiction in *Vision Magazine.*

Doug Whippo is an MFA candidate in creative writing at Columbia College. Excerpts from his novel in progress can be found in *Hair Trigger 22* and *Hair Trigger 23.* He lives in Chicago and teaches ESL in Rogers Park.